"*First Light* is a wonderful story. Even more, it is a wonderful window onto the sweeping events that formed this country and gave it its distinctive character. Once reading I *had* to keep reading, and now I wait impatiently for the next book in this series OF SAINTS AND SINNERS."

Richard J. Foster, Author of *Celebration of Discipline*

"In *First Light* Harold Fickett does it all so well—details the grit and gleam that broaden into the sweep of life in the New World, draws the profile of the boy who broadens into a man. This skilled fusing of story and history is a tour de force, a compelling overview of some of God's ways of shaping destiny through human experience."

Luci Shaw, Author of *God in the Dark*

"Harold Fickett has done it! I'm amazed at the care invested in every minute part of this big, sprawling novel. A spirited romance told by a master of the craft."

Philip Yancey, Author of *Disappointment with God*

"How much we need storytellers like Harold Fickett, writers who can give us access to the centuries-deep spiritual heritage that feeds into our present lives. In an amnesic culture where we can scarcely remember what was in yesterday's newspaper, he trains us in remembering and appreciating the depth of spirit beneath everything we are and do, giving texture to our lives. This is storytelling of epic proportions, large enough for God and belief and our lives to become larger in the reading."

Eugene H. Peterson, *The Message*

OF **SAINTS** & **SINNERS**

HAROLD FICKETT

FIRST LIGHT

BETHANY HOUSE PUBLISHERS

MINNEAPOLIS, MINNESOTA 55438

Fic

Published in association with the literary agency of Alive
Communications, P.O. Box 49068, Colorado Springs, CO 80949.

Cover by Dan Thornberg,
Bethany House Publishers staff artist.

Published by Bethany House Publishers
A Ministry of Bethany Fellowship, Inc.
11300 Hampshire Avenue South
Minneapolis, Minnesota 55438

Printed in the United States of America

Library of Congress Cataloging-in-Publication Data

Fickett, Harold.
    First light / Harold Fickett.
        p.   cm. — (Of saints and sinners ; 1)

    1. United States—History—Colonial period, ca. 1600-1775—Fiction.
2. Shipbuilding industry—United States History—18th century—Fiction.
3. Ship captains—United States—Fiction.
4. Marriage—United States—Fiction. I. Title.
II. Series: Fickett, Harold. Of saints and sinners ; 1.
PS3556.I325F57   1993
813'.54—dc20   93-37744
ISBN 1-55661-179-X (hardcover)   CIP
ISBN 1-55661-175-7 (trade paper edition)

To Hal—

most dear son

As long as we are on earth, the love that unites us will bring us suffering by our very contact with one another, because this love is the resetting of a body of broken bones. Even saints cannot live with saints on this earth without some anguish.

—THOMAS MERTON

CONTENTS

HAROLD FICKETT is the Executive Director of the Milton Center at Kansas Newman College. He is the author of three books and has written for a host of publications including *The New Oxford Review*, *Publisher's Weekly*, and *Christianity Today*. Coming from a family that has been at the heart of the evangelical Protestant experience for generations, Fickett's life has been shaped by countless saints and sinners. In this series, OF SAINTS AND SINNERS, he has embarked on a historical tribute to the spiritual heritage of American culture.

FIRST
LIGHT

*T*his is the story, as I know it, of our family, the Whites, a clan of men and women whose souls, like mine, distilled Calvinist rectitude from Highlander savagery. A story of saints and sinners, the two so inbred that only the Lord, who looks on the heart, truly knows who's who. But I have written this account for myself and my children, so that we will not forget the redemptive power of memory or the magnificent gesture of the past toward what lies beyond us all.

PART I

—

Lifted Up

CHAPTER 1

Clean Away

Ten generations back, in the summer of 1729, the White family lived in a thatch-roofed cottage in the village Glenwhirry, County Antrim, Northern Ireland. Our chronicle begins there, on June 29, in the anxious hours before dawn.

At first light, the darkness liquefied behind the flaring morning star at the eastern horizon. A continent of clouds slid off to the north, uncovering the silverpoint landscape to the transforming heavens. Surrounded by dewy, quilted meadows, the humble home drowsed on its hillside. Only a few crickets, hidden by the barn, disturbed the quiet.

Inside the cottage, Abram White awoke beside his two little brothers, Noah and Zack, in their rough-hewn bed. The moment he opened his eyes Abram thought of what he had planned. He had secretly packed a satchel with his fishing gear, and his clothes were at the ready in the clothing trunk he shared with his brothers. He lay still in the warm bed for another moment, letting his eyes adjust to the darkness. The smell of the dead peat fire threaded through the chilly air above him. Where would he be tonight? Tomorrow night?

As his thoughts swelled, he felt the bed spin and tip, and his own dizziness spilled him onto his feet and started him moving.

He pulled on his wool trousers and the fine cream-colored linen blouse his mother had made and then his two rougher serge shirts—all three on top of each other. He added on the threadbare satin waistcoat handed down from his father, a rubyish remnant of better days, then his own tweed jacket and his long blue wool coat. His arms hung out a little from his sides when he finished.

He took a quick last look at the three beds lining the outside wall. Noah and Zack slept on, unaware of his desertion. Dorsey's covers were a mass of rumples. His parents were lying face-to-face, his father's long, bumpy nose nearly touching his mother's softly triangular one. How could they sleep that way, breathing on each other?

Remembering his business, he reached down for his satchel and took half a dozen quick steps into the main room.

There, the slatted china cabinet, its treasures, and the decision he thought he had made confronted him. A huge pewter salver rested on the top shelf, his mother's initials engraved in the center; it had petaled edges and a dimpled glint like clear running water over stones. *Maman* had held on to it, even as the family slowly starved. She had served the trout he had poached on that salver, and kept the family at the table to enjoy it after his father protested and left the house.

With a wobbling hand he took it down, along with a copper tea-kettle his mother rarely used.

Then, looking under her beaded spinning wheel, a machine as tall as he was, he found the two bolts of linen she had recently finished, and he took one of these as well. The tray, the kettle, and the linen slid easily into his satchel; they were the only things in it besides his fishing gear and spare undergarments.

Abram turned to the door and saw that it must already have been opened that morning; the latch had been thrown, and the door itself was not flush with the jamb, but only resting against it.

Who was up? He tried to think of the sleepers in their beds. He had a clear memory of his parents' noses pointing at each other, and of his brothers lying beside him. Dorsey. He had noticed only her rumpled bedclothes.

He walked around the corner of the cottage and back toward the privy. Knocking on the door, he called Dorsey's name, but she did not answer. He made use of the shed himself, then went up the rise to the vegetable garden. He should have been running in the opposite direction, he knew, but he wanted to tell someone not to worry, and he trusted Dorsey. Even if she discovered his thefts, she would not rouse his parents. Not until he was far away. But why should she be out this morning?

He found his fourteen-year-old sister seated on the stone outcropping at the base of the garden. She looked as calm and resolved as a statue, surrounded by the ghostly light before dawn. He felt as if they were meeting in a dream.

"Dorsey," he said.

She looked up. He saw her notice his satchel.

"You're off then," she said casually.

"Why are you out here? You should be sleeping."

"I came out to pray," she said. "I suppose I came out to pray for you on your journey."

He looked at her dumbfounded.

"Something will be happening with a people like us," she said. "I did not know what you would do, but I saw the trouble coming."

"You haven't spoken with Mother," he said, half-questioning.

She shook her thick dark hair as if shaking off a distracting fly. She put her hands out to each side on her rocky perch, steadying herself. "The hunger wakes me," she said. "That's the only time I feel it. The rest of the day I've lost my appetite. So when I come out of a morning, I stay out and pray—if it's not too cold. We have nothing else to do but pray—women."

"You could—" he began, but did not know how to finish.

"I'd climb in your satchel if I could."

She stood up and came over to him and hugged him. He felt the embrace through all the layers he had on. His lip started to quiver and he swallowed down hard. "I'll start to earn my wages and send them back," he said.

"You will, sure," she said.

"I'll come back for you. For you and *Maman*. The whole family. We'll all be sailing someday."

She half-smiled, indulgently, pain tightening her eyes—he didn't have to say this, her look said.

"It's a promise. *Maman* and Papa, they're not to worry."

"They're too dead to worry much," she said.

He held her as long as he could, as long as he dared. Then, the choking still in his throat, he turned, and colder than he had ever felt in his life, he started walking away.

Abram went over the surrounding hills toward Larne, passing along the high, alder-lined lanes, the often muddy, narrow passes deeply rutted by their traffic of carts and hay wagons. The cold stayed with him. He usually woke hungry, as he was still strong enough to feel the emptiness clawing at him; but for once the thought of eating sickened him, and that was well enough since berries would have to do until he reached Ballymena.

Dawn came, and the clouds that gathered again on the horizon stayed just long enough for their washboard pattern to glow pink, turn lemony, and then disperse as the sun rose. Where the alders dropped away, juniper shrubs lined the small roads, their limbs grown out so long that they switched at his legs. Every time he went by a farm the sweetly sick smell of dung hit him. Wild roses grew in clusters up against the hilly banks.

Not many other travelers passed by him, only a few leathery-faced farmers in their caps. Close by a farm, a little flaxen-haired girl ran by, playing, it seemed, at running away. The sound of her mother's calls to come back drifted after her.

The lane he had taken to the main road toward Ballymena followed a seasonal stream. It was not much more than an irrigating trickle, but he found one of the underground springs feeding it and took a long drink, the water so cold it made his cupped hands ache.

At mid-morning, when the sun sent perspiration streaming down both sides of his face, he came to the main road down to Ballymena, past Ahogill. He stopped and took off the last three top layers of extra clothing, the ruby waistcoat, and the two serge shirts. His perspiration had soaked through all three, enlarging even the armholes of the waistcoat with dark circles and chafings of salt.

Abram looked up and down the wider, chalky road. There was no reason for his father to find him at this particular point—the side lanes joined the road at a dozen intersections. But if his father came after him in a cart, he could catch him on this stretch. He would have to be on the lookout, ready to dive into the fields and hide himself.

Not a cart passed, though. Not one through the long afternoon. From a last switchback on the Malin hills, on a bend that looked down upon Ballymena, he paused, and caught sight of St. Gregory's and the buildings that sat around it like children listening to a teacher's story.

He started passing others on the road now, too many to hide at each approach. They were upon him before he could distinguish whether it was his father or the man whose cart he would have borrowed—probably their neighbor Mr. O'Shaughnessy.

Abram made his way into Ballymena, and the looks of the strangers he passed told him they were thinking only about the trouble he might cause them, if they chose to notice him at all. They were townspeople in finished long coats and shiny apron-adorned dresses only worn in shops or homes with separate kitchens. Abram peered at these passersby, but he never saw his father. He had gotten clean off. His father was probably glad enough, Abram thought, to see both the salver and his son out and gone.

Close to the center of town, a watering trough sat on a curbed island in the middle of a crossroads, a stone statue of the Virgin opening her hands to the trough's mercies. He pumped out some water. It tasted of ceramic pipe—a heavy, dead taste. He remembered the clear draught of the cold spring on the mountainside, and trout fishing.

———

The trouble in the White family had started the year before, when the Reverend Innis announced his intention to immigrate to the New World and take as many of his congregation as cared to come with him.

About a month after the announcement, on a Sunday afternoon, Abram had stolen away from the family farm, crossed over the rolling hills to the east, and up into the high meadows and stands of aspen on Mount Obra to the lush vein in the mountainside where the Battenkill first emerged out of the bare rocks above the treeline. This high up, the trout that kept their noses in the step-falls from pool to pool ran small—only five or six inches, at most. Even so, Abram's fishing had its dangers.

In that day a ten-year-old boy with a fishing rod, trespassing on another's land, did not present a picture of innocent deception. If Abram had been caught, there would have been, at the very least, a crippling fine for his family. Five- and six-inch trout meant chowders to people who were starving, but now that Mr. Garrity owned the land, after his marriage to the other large landholder in the county, the widow Tunston, he was ruthlessly enforcing his rights against such poachers. Only the month before, Garrity's steward had winged David O'Callaghan, who was still in partial hiding so as not to be wounded again in the courts.

Abram kept his fishing rod, a ten-foot hickory limb that he had planed down to a swishy fineness, in the dark hollow of a burned-out oak on the edge of the aspen stands. He took it close by the stream and bent down amid the ferns and skunk cabbages and tied on his line of heavy black thread.

He owned three metal fishing hooks—or he supposed he owned them; it had been two years since he had stolen them from Mc-Donough's village store. Taking the middle-sized hook in thumb and forefinger and threading it with his left hand, he tied it on so that any fish would come off before the hook would, which was how he had kept the three hooks so long.

Although still early in the season, he had kicked up a few whirring grasshoppers on his walk, and he went back toward the meadow and worked the sandy lane beside it until he caught enough to fill the earthen jar he carried in his pocket.

Then he went back to the stream and hooked one of the grasshoppers under the plate directly behind its head. This way the hopper would sit up on the water. With the extraordinarily long, supple hickory rod he could perform an underhand cast and let the hopper float down onto the surface of the water—a French way of fishing recommended by his mother. If a trout came fast enough, he would see its head and a glimpse of the blood-red spots along its bottle-green side as it took the bait.

Standing back in the high grass beside his favorite pool, with the lower limbs of the aspens nearly scratching his back, he tried to read where the fish would be lying. A boulder stood at the head of the pool, separating the current, which fell in two glistening hand's-breadth falls. The current caressed each side, and then braided together again at the pool's waist.

He swung the hopper out where the current knit back together. A six-inch trout came so fast it leapt out of the water as it took the bait, its fine body twisting. Abram struck and pulled the struggling fish smoothly toward the land. With the fish close in, he gave a jerk to the rod and whipped the small fish into the ferns on the bank.

The boy did not immediately retrieve his catch, however, for as the fish popped from the water, the darker shadow of a larger fish had risen underneath it. Abram watched the shadow circle the pool, stalking what it must have read as wounded prey. A one-pound shadow, at least. One of the larger fish, big enough to turn cannibal, must have come up from the pools below to do its own poaching.

Abram went back into the ferns and retrieved the small fish, then sat down on the sandy soil and waited for the pool to settle. The early evening air felt fresh against his sweaty neck. He watched the two bright falls, the scalloped current, and the bleary reflections of the white aspens overhead at the pool's flat tail. Abram knew the cannibal wanted his trout.

He took out his knife, wood-handled, the blade too thin for the fishing and hunting uses to which he put it, but sharpened with a boy's love of knives that made it serve. He cut off the middle-sized hook and tied on his big one; then he reset the barb again with his knife, separating it out to increase its bite. Taking up the six-inch trout, he whacked the back of its head on a rock to bloody the gills, slit its belly with the knife, and pulled its entrails halfway out, massaging the blood on his fingertips into the mucus-coated sides. He trimmed the milky flesh along the underbelly and pared down the tail so the cannibal could take it down more easily. Threading the hook through the mouth, and then, by way of the slit in its stomach, past its gills, he hooked his cannibal-bait right through the backbone underneath the main dorsal fin.

This kind of meat fishing called for a change in strategy. He worked his way upstream, well away from the stream itself, and rounded back down to the boulder above the cannibal's pool. He waded to the boulder and lay down on its top. The lighter underside of the aspen leaves, shaking in the wind, rained down brilliance, and the world took a long, cool breath.

Abram dabbed the trout into the upstream pool and let the current take the bait over the falls and plunge into what he hoped was the cannibal's lair. The black-thread line straightened as the current beat the fish down and under the stair-step fall.

Then he felt a rapid jerk, as if someone had tried to knock the rod out of his hands with a sweeping, sideways blow—the cannibal's head slash as it took the bait.

Abram did not strike immediately. He waited. Tempted to pull and feel the weight of the cannibal against his rod, Abram resisted and left his short line slack. The line did not move much, just enough to show that the cannibal was making its meal.

When he was convinced that the bait must be halfway to the cannibal's belly, Abram lifted the tip of the rod. The fish shot out toward the foot of the pool, raising a wake as it tried to escape.

Abram heaved up and out toward the left-hand bank. The line snapped with a report like a pistol. But the boy saw the fish land in the sandy soil toward the far end of the pool.

He leapt off the rock and splashed through the water. He threw himself down on all fours, putting his body between the cannibal and the water. The huge fish flapped in front of him, so big and awe-inspiring he was afraid to touch it. It flapped and threw itself up against his chest, and the fish's own punch provoked him to act.

With both hands he shoveled it farther up the bank, but it flapped away, slithering to the side, toward the pool. He shoveled it up the bank again, farther this time, until he satisfied himself that it could not wriggle back into the water. He noticed that it measured longer than his calf.

Grabbing its tail, he lifted the trout and swung it like an axe against a boulder, and a paralyzing shiver went through the head and backbone into his hands. A nineteen-inch, two-and-a-half-pound monster.

When his heart stopped beating so hard that the pounding in his ears subsided, he thought he heard someone approaching, and before the Garritys' steward could shoot him, he grabbed up the fish and ran home.

———

Usually when the pink flesh of trout appeared in their chowders, his father's depressed spirits grew darker—he felt demeaned by his son's poaching and his wife's collusion in it. But when Abram's mother, Camille, chose to serve the cannibal whole, laid out on her treasured pewter salver on a bed of fresh cabbage with boiled potatoes and onions around it, sprigs of parsley at its head, and its sterling sides flecked with tarragon, his father Zebulun's looks blackened like a thunderhead.

No one spoke of the main course—even Noah and Zack understood that much about what was happening. His brothers ate ravenously, with his French Huguenot mother's hand striking quickly when they quarreled over who had received the larger portion. Dorsey ate slowly, closing her eyes between bites, almost counting up to a set number, it seemed, before she would allow herself another forkful.

The silence stole a bit of Abram's thunder, and he resented this. So he thought he would use the occasion to campaign for his cause.

He turned to his little brother Zack, a thick-boned, curly-headed six-year-old, and said, "When we are in the New World, we will have as many trout as we like. And a sweet with every meal. Fruit pies. Strawberries and cream."

Zack looked at him as if Abram had dared him to jump off the peat shed roof into the feeding hay.

Unexpectedly, his mother followed his lead. "My sister, Louise, is treated like a dauphin in Pennsylvania. She is *tres content*, so happy. Her letters say that women are . . . more dear in that place."

Abram looked at his father. He was staring down at the trout and potatoes on his plate, clenching his knife and fork in his sausage-fingered fists, holding on to the utensils as if they were surprisingly heavy and eating itself an enormous effort.

Baby Lorraine, who was tied into a chair with tea towels, started crying, but Abram's mother did not move to pick her up.

His father put his knife and fork down, bitterness crimping his colorless lips. "The New World will have its Garritys. My father thought Ireland would be free of them, but every land suckles its own wolves. Those that leave are only looking for a place to play the part."

Zebulun White rose from the table without finishing his meal. "It's the Garritys' monster, and you're acting as if we were Lord Dunbar 'isself," he said. Then he walked out into the night, banging the door behind him.

Noah and Zack scrambled to go after their father. But Dorsey sat them back down and shushed them.

Camille reached across the table and took her eldest son's hand. She said nothing, but her eyes filled with a determined admiration. Her pewter salver had already voiced her sentiments.

Abram's hand, clenching his mother's, became cold and uneasy above the picked-over bones on the salver.

———

Something happened over the next year that young Abram hardly understood; something that grew into his thoughts and feelings and directed them with the same force that caused him to beanpole up three inches. The serving of the cannibal established a bond, an agreement, almost a conspiracy among Dorsey, Abram, and his mother.

They wanted to go to the New World, and when the ship sailed without them, taking the Reverend Innis and two thirds of Glenwhirry with it, their wishes turned to bitterness and depression.

Camille's depression became acute when baby Lorraine died of consumption the next January. Her little one gone, Abram's mother did nothing but sit by her spinning wheel. She stopped taking their chipped plates down from the slat-guarded shelves of the wooden buffet, and she stopped heating up the heavy copper iron and pressing the tablecloths, serviettes, and even the sheets, as she had once done—their linen being her pride as well as their livelihood. Dorsey took over the running of the household.

Camille only sat and worked the flax, and yet she produced far less than she ever had. The flax crop had been poor. Ordinarily she would have been through their stores of it by this time in the winter, but most of the flax still remained in the storage shed. The prices were down, anyway, so there was little incentive to prepare for the spring market.

Abram kept pleading with his father to take the family to the New World in the spring. Working together, shoveling the peat, mucking out the barn, feeding the goats, Abram made use of hearsay from the letters of the immigrants, drawing the unfavorable comparisons his father did not want to hear.

One day in late winter the boy and his father were in the shop end of their low, shedlike barn, hay at their feet soaking up the wet of the dirt floor. His father was trying to mend the harness for the plow horse with leather strips he had cut out of his old field boots. The belly strap needed to be sewn together again and the mounts for the tracings reconstructed, since the old ones had worn through.

Abram remembered their horse, a white-faced chestnut mare with bushy fetlocks that had worn the harness in better times. They had not been able to replace her when she died of brain fever two years before.

His father's sacrifice of his boots would only mean something if they had the money to rent the McWilliams's horse, or they could barter. There was that donkey with the one limp ear that O'Shaughnessy owned, but O'Shaughnessy was a Catholic and his donkey cost Protestants nearly as much as a horse, causing villagers to nickname the beast "The Pope's Arse."

His father looked sideways across his long, bumpy nose at the leather, and his expression said that he expected it to resist him, like everything else, but that he deeply resented the difficulty all the same.

"We'd be letting the McWilliams's dray?" Abram asked.

His father said nothing. His father lived in silence these days, and the quality of this silence, as it had grown upon him through the winter, had become disturbing. The family saw flashes of terror and panic paralyzing his expression, yet never heard the thunder, and the growing interval between the lightning of his fear and its reverberations had become ominous.

Indeed, his father's silences so muffled Abram's own voice that he heard what followed as if it came from the bottom of a well instead of his own throat. "Or The Pope's Arse?"

"Sharpening your tongue on the devil's whetstone won't make a man of you, boyo."

"But do we have the packet?" Abram asked, eager now that his father had opened his mouth.

"The Lord will supply our needs," his father said.

"Only if we are doing his will," Abram said.

He could see his father's grip on the leather tighten and then release. "You ought to be off now, boyo. There must be something your mother wants doing."

"The Lord has called us to the New World."

"So you think."

"Mother thinks so, too. And Dorsey."

His father put down his work. He stood up to his full height and glared at his son. "I am the spiritual head of this family, and I will not go to school to you."

"You disobeyed the Reverend Innis. Now they are in the New World, and their letters say—"

"I know very well what the letters say." His father's voice was as puncturing as the sharp-pointed awl with which he positioned the leather.

Abram went to the low door of the shed, but did not go through it. He hung there, watching. The oil lamp his father worked by made his face look devilish, creasing it with black shadows and turning his cheeks crimson. Abram knew how angry he must be. Unlike most Irish, even Ulstermen, his father almost never exchanged words with anyone—not unless he felt himself physically threatened.

But the boy felt a rising anger in himself that was taking him beyond the childish fear that a year before would have pushed him out of the dark shed. There was something about the witchery of his own anger that he enjoyed. He had never felt like this before. He spoke before he thought.

"Baby Lorraine would be alive had we gone."

"What did you say, boyo?" his father asked, and his voice already had punishment in it. Abram's reply would determine its severity.

"Baby Lorraine would still be alive."

His father stepped out from behind the worktable and came over to him and looked down into his face. His father's expression reminded Abram of a village bully, and he felt his respect for his father deserting him at the very moment he most needed it.

"Am I a murderer then?" his father asked.

Abram had not seen the full implication of his remark—he had not meant it that way, he thought. He tried to reply, to apologize, but the words fell apart in his mouth and he was left stammering.

"Am I a murderer? You think your father is a murderer? I would murder the children I slave to feed and keep? As I have slaved to feed and keep you?"

Now Abram could say nothing from sudden terror.

"*I would murder them?*" Zebulun White took hold of his son's shoulders and shook the boy so hard that he could barely stiffen his neck enough to sustain it.

"You haven't got a decent answer for me? I've raised you up to cross me and not answer?" He picked Abram up and held him in the air. "Have you got an answer then? No?" Suddenly his rage exploded, and Zebulun threw his son back against the stone wall.

Abram's head whipped against the sharp stones, and he felt himself sinking down into a deep hole, down where he would wait, holding himself outside the current, his hooked underlip set.

———

When he swam back to the surface, he ascended toward a light above him that became his mother's oval face.

"You have been so ill, my dearest."

"You've been out for three days, Abram," someone else said. Dorsey?

He became conscious of his own weight against the stuffed mattress. His vision did not clear immediately, and the dark place kept pulling him down again, and the bed underneath him and the room around him would start to liquefy, and he would begin moving away once more.

His mother's voice brought him back. He wanted to see her clearly. She was not wearing her usual white cap with its tucks

- 28 -

around the encircling drawstring. Her long, light auburn hair was tied into a knot at the back, and it had come undone enough to sway forward as she bent over him. Her loosening tresses, flowing to each side from the perfect curve of her high, round hairline, circled her face like a diadem. The skin around her deeply set eyes had its own natural shadowing, a deep and dusky rose. Her brown eyes were the kindest he had ever known. Her cheeks were always cool to the touch and had a golden patina.

"*Mon petit*," she said, "*mon petit.*" She stroked his forehead. Seeing his eyes clear, she smiled, showing the tips of her front teeth.

Somehow, over the weeks of his convalescence, his mother found extra provisions for him. (Later, he noticed one of her favorite brooches, a family heirloom, had disappeared.) She made him sweets with molasses. She cooked a whole chicken just for him. She brought him fresh whole milk, without thinning it with water, as she did for the rest of the family. She served him his dinner—as he sat in his father's rocker with his feet up—before she served the family at the table. His portions, everyone could see, were huge in comparison with theirs. They were the portions his father used to command.

No one spoke of this. If they had, they knew, she would have struck with an open hand as swift as an avenging angel's. The vengeance she took could be even sharper than their father's.

Abram watched her serve the rest of the family, and if his father looked his way at all, the look was so desperate and dumb and helpless that it made Abram pity him, and he hated pitying his father.

Nearly well, with the dizziness he felt when he stood almost gone, Abram was alone with his mother in the cottage one Sunday, the rest of the family having gone to church, when Camille brought her son yet another extravagant meal, with cheese, bread, roasted potatoes, pig's feet, and fresh milk.

"*Maman*," he said, "*Ça suffit.* Enough."

"You are not hungry?" she asked, her eyes concentrating with concern. She put the tray down on the dining table.

"I'm well now," he said. "I should eat like the others."

"You eat what your *maman* brings to you."

"No more," he said. "Please."

She got down on her knees and looked straight into his face. Hers grew still and composed, and then a blurred look came into her kind eyes as the tears welled up and ran down her cheeks.

"I want *one* of my children to be safe and well," she said suddenly, and she leaned forward and put her white-capped head in his lap. He felt the quiver and clutch in her throat against his leg. "What am I to do?" she cried. "I don't know what to do. We are dying. My children are dying. This is such sorrow. I did not think I could know such sorrow."

His mother's appeal made him feel strangely far away. The person who had always cared for him, who had nursed him back to health in these last weeks, the person who had given him life, she was asking him what to do. He felt embarrassed and awkward. He wanted to answer her question, but the answer would have to travel from this new and distant place to which her cries carried him. She had turned to him for help. But how could he help? What could he, a lad of eleven years, do?

His mother raised her head from his lap. Her eyes were red and her face haggard with the aging that hunger brought with it. He held her head in his hands and wiped her tears away with his thumbs. She said nothing else. She did not smile or make light of the moment. Her eyes searched his, and he knew that in her own way she was as violently desperate for an answer as his father.

He bent forward and kissed her cheek, and then he stood up and raised her with his hands under her elbows. He was still not quite as tall as she, but in lifting her up he felt himself growing into her answer.

In the next weeks, he resolved that he would be her champion. He would save her the only way he knew how—by leaving.

CHAPTER 2

"Hey, Diddle, Diddle . . ."

*I*n Ballymena, late in the afternoon, Abram walked through the narrow city streets, some stone-paved, others just dirt, slush, and horse droppings, trying to keep his attention on the storefronts, but conscious of the faces that rose into the open second-story windows. He had business to transact, and he needed to keep his wits about him.

One store window's gilt-edged black letters spelled out "Dorgan & Sons," and a hand-lettered sign pressed up against the glass advised that the shop purchased "homestuffs, apparel, plate, and gewgaws."

Abram continued walking down the street, but when his heart stopped beating so hard, he turned around and went back to Dorgan & Sons.

A young man stood behind a high counter at the back of the shop, which was decorated with the articles referred to by the hand-lettered sign. Shelves filled with crockery and plate lined the walls; coats, trousers, and dresses dangled from wires running just underneath the ceiling, and gewgaws, including fancy-dress dolls, sat on nesting tables. As Abram went toward the back, he felt as if he were wandering through the huge closet of the wealthy, land-owning Garritys.

The clerk spread his hands wide on the counter and looked down at Abram. His dark hair was slicked straight back to where its blunt tips began to curl under. He had pasty white skin and a sparse black mustache that he licked at like a cat. Up close, he appeared to be only two or three years older than Abram himself, perhaps thirteen or fourteen.

"Who would you be, then?" he asked in a voice with a nasal edge to it.

Abram did not answer. He stared at the young clerk, who looked to one side and back again several times. His attentions almost had a pulse.

"This is a place of business," the clerk said, impatiently. He stood taller and let his hand drift to the lapel of his frock coat.

Abram thought how much the youth seemed to like standing there in that frock coat with his hand at the lapel. He guessed the fellow would have new boots on—he was standing up tall, his shoulders arching backward.

"I have something to sell," Abram said finally.

"Do you?" the youth asked.

Abram put his satchel down close to the base of the high counter and quickly fetched out the bolt of linen. He put it up on the counter.

The clerk's hand came down on the cloth as if he were already claiming it for the shop. Picking it up, he stared at its texture, licked at his mustache, and made disapproving noises in the back of his throat.

"This is not much in our line," he said. "We trade in finished goods." He gestured upward toward the clothes hanging from the ceiling.

"If you'd rather not have it, then . . ." Abram said, and reached for the bolt, but the youth pulled it back toward his scanning eyes.

"We can't give you much for what's not in our line," he said. "Eight shillings, maybe ten."

Abram stepped over to the side wall and its rows of crockery and plate. "These must come dear," he said.

"Would you be selling this for your mother, then?" the youth asked.

Abram felt himself flush, and then he heard himself say, as if from a great distance, "My mother is dead." The shop became so silent Abram could hear the steps of a party in the street and their not-quite distinguishable conversation.

"What a pity," the youth said. "We haven't introduced ourselves." He waved Abram closer with his offered hand. "Joseph Dorgan."

Abram came back from the side wall and shook the clerk's hand. "It must take buckets of money to buy things like these."

"That kettle by you will take down a sovereign. The salvers and settings command five."

The young shopkeeper, Abram could tell, was proud of his wares and his knowledge of their value.

"If you were grand," Abram asked, "Lord Dunbar or the Clavens, would you want copper or pewter serving dishes?"

"Lords and ladies have both," Dorgan said. "But for different services. Copper to cook in and pewter for what isn't silver." He finally stepped out from behind the counter and started toward Abram, but then settled at the near corner of the counter, resting his back against it and crossing his ankles. He did have on new boots, his trousers tucked down in them as if for riding.

Dorgan pointed to a copper kettle much like the one Abram was carrying. "That goes for one, six."

With some prompting, Dorgan speculated on a silver serving tray that resembled Abram's pewter treasure. "That's the most expensive thing in the shop. Sterling silver—like sovereigns that's been melted and shaped. Ten pounds, that is."

Abram said nothing in reply. He was thinking that even in a good year his family had never made more than ten pounds.

The shopkeeper became suspicious. "You thinking of doing my job, then?"

Still Abram said nothing.

"I think eight shillings might be going some," Dorgan said, reflectively. "I think if I was to ask . . . I think I'd better give you four."

Abram marched back over in front of the counter with such purpose that the youth stepped behind it again. Once more Abram put the satchel down at the base of the counter and this time pulled both the copper kettle and the pewter serving tray from it.

"Eight for the linen, a sovereign for the copper, and three for the tray," he said.

"You didn't say you had these. You must have stolen them."

Abram looked straight up into Dorgan's eyes, and he used the strain of his lying to make up in intensity what he lacked in earnestness. "My mother is dead and this is what she left me. I mean to ship for the New World. I need the money for my passage."

"We have to have our margin."

"You don't know your prices, then?" Abram asked, and his piercing blue eyes looked right through the youth.

Dorgan grabbed his lapels with both hands and licked at his mustache. He looked about him, as if already arguing with his parents.

"The price is fair," Abram said. "You will sell at a profit."

Dorgan closed his eyes and grimaced.

"There's shops that have the money," Abram said.

"We have it," Dorgan said quickly.

"Then pay me," Abram said.

Dorgan took a step to the left and pulled out a drawer from the counter. Both his hands were half-closed, as if his fingertips wanted to hide away from the sight of the shop's money.

"Four, eight," Abram said.

Dorgan counted out the coins on the counter and swept them up into his hand. He seemed to have conceded the payment, and Abram relaxed just long enough for the conversation to swing around again.

"You're off to the New World?" Dorgan asked. "From Larne?"

"That's where I'm to be found," Abram said.

"Then you'll need a place to stay tonight, and transportation."

Abram waited for him to explain his thoughts.

"My uncle owns an inn," Dorgan said. He put his hands back down on the counter, the money still hidden in his right fist. Then he spread his arms once again, as he had when Abram first approached. "He'll keep you tonight and send you on in the carriage tomorrow. You'll be there by morrow's eve. You'd be two days on your way by foot, and villains would probably fall on you before you got halfway. There's many an intriguer on the way to Larne."

Once again, Abram kept silent.

The youth held out his stuffed fist as if about to let the coins fall into Abram's hands. "Take your two pounds then, and the rest will cover my family's expenses."

"I'll come to terms with your uncle myself," Abram said.

"You'll stay there then?"

"The full four pounds, eight shillings, and I'll be guided by the suggestion."

"You will?"

Abram's hand went to the youth's and opened his fingers and took the money out.

Dorgan closed his eyes again as this was happening, as if to deny that it could be. As soon as he had lost the money, he came out from behind the counter, put his hand on Abram's shoulder, and started them toward the door.

"You've been on the road a while already, haven't you," he said. "You'll want a wash when we get to the inn—that's another tick."

————

The uncle proved a decent sort, serving Abram a bowl of chowder, along with bread and butter, at a small table as far away from the rough men drinking in the tavern as possible. He was a big man with round shoulders and a drooping chest and gut, his hair springing up from his low forehead, its fat brown shafts tipped yellow like a skunk's quills. He stood over Abram for a moment, wiping his hands on his apron. He had such dull, close-set eyes that the obvious questions never surfaced in them. He kept switching a pocket of air from one cheek to another—a nervous habit.

"That going to fill your breach?" he asked.

When Abram expressed his thanks for the meal, the uncle turned away. Busying himself with his other customers for the rest of the night, he gave Abram only hints of his concern: that one moment standing over him, and the small attentions of the sheltered table and an equally segregated bed in the inn's gabled attic. He seemed a man who had decided that the world would have its way.

Alone that night in the attic, in a bed he had all to himself, Abram felt the chill that had stayed with him since he had left his home that morning. He had not eaten much at dinner, despite its being his only meal of the day. A queer lightness in his stomach rapidly diminished his appetite after two or three spoonfuls of the chowder.

He thought of saying his nightly prayers as he always did and felt a horrible freedom as he realized that his mother would no longer be there to insist on this observance. He thought of Dorsey, Noah, and Zack praying at home that night. What were they saying to God about him?

Being from a French Huguenot family, Camille White, a liberal and understanding mother in other respects, had felt it her duty to prove her loyalty to her husband's brand of Calvinism by drilling her children in The Shorter Form of the Westminster Catechism until they knew it better than its authors. The Shorter Form included one hundred and seven questions and answers, plus the Ten Commandments, the Lord's Prayer, and the Apostles' Creed, running to some five thousand words. No child could possibly have thought of it as short.

When Abram's turn came, at six years of age, to learn the Catechism, Camille worked with him every night after dinner by her spinning wheel.

"What is the chief end of man?" she would ask. "What is God?"

One night she kept running through the questions again and again, determined to hear a letter-perfect recitation. Abram had an excellent memory, and he actually knew the entirety of The Shorter Form. But he hated feeling captive to the looping logic of the Catechism's one hundred and seven questions, and something in him made him stumble over a phrase or two here and there. His frustration grew. He felt trussed up and interrogated.

The fifth time his mother asked, "What is God?" he stood up and put his face so close to hers that his curly dark bangs almost touched the lace trimming of her cap. A forking vein pulsed in his forehead.

She tried maintaining her authority. "What . . . *mon petit* . . . is . . . God?" she asked, her voice rising with doubt.

"I DON'T *KNOW!*" he wailed, and hit his own thighs with his fists.

His father, awakened from a catnap, jumped to his feet and looked around him as if someone had yelled, "Fire!"

As Abram knelt in the attic above the inn, he felt the weight of these memories on his mind, and the salver, the kettle, the linen, and the money he now had from them on his conscience. He hesitated in his prayers, looking out the gable's window over Larne's jumble of smoke-stacked rooftops.

He began by reciting the Lord's Prayer, the twenty-third psalm, and the one-hundredth. The familiar words started to drive away the chill of loneliness and guilt. This encouraged him, and he went on to recite The Shorter Form. But he knew that his running away, his leaving, had better provide a more fitting answer to the question: "What is God?"—or more precisely, "Who is God?"

He thought God was a Father who truly loved him; a Father who was providing, through immigration to the New World, a means of escaping starvation. He thought God was the one who had called him to save his family and himself from death.

At the end of Abram's prayers, he asked to be forgiven for the thefts, and then modified that request: "If you would not be thinking of them as clips, Lord, but only a loan or investment. I won't bury the talents in the ground. I'll send *Maman* tenfold and be your servant and hers, I do most earnestly promise."

He climbed into his bed, the chill gone now entirely, and he started to feel so hungry that he wondered whether he could sleep.

————

When the frock-coated Dorgan showed up in the morning, he explained to his uncle that he had arranged for Abram to go with his friend Billy in his caravan. Billy was a tinker and traveled the road, plying his trade. The regular carriage would not come for another two days, and this was supposed to save Abram time and money.

Abram stood between the nephew and the uncle in the tavern, and he tried to look through the dull eyes of the big man to his true thoughts.

"You go along," the uncle said, "Billy's a good enough lad." Then the man turned back to his early-morning washing-up behind the bar, and Abram was left in Dorgan's hovering company.

He was led outside, where this Billy already waited on the bench of his caravan.

"What a package, you are," Billy said. "Come up here, then."

Abram did not move, but stared cautiously at the tinker.

Bareheaded, Billy wore a leather vest and had his sleeves rolled up, which revealed his tanned, muscular forearms. He had a mop of sooty-black hair. He looked three or four years older than Dorgan, maybe eighteen, and, to Abram's surprise and relief, a much more likeable kind of fellow. His big, scooped-out smile gave a foolish cast to his face.

His caravan—a long cart cradling a red, barrel-shaped enclosure with a shingled roof bric-a-bracing its head—served as his tinker's shop and home. Painted wildflowers and Gaelic sayings festooned it, and a black stovepipe, uncapped, poked its way through the roof. Abram could not read Gaelic, but he recognized the imprint of one common motto that could be loosely translated, "Crows never go hungry."

Billy struck the place beside him on the seat. "Look about you, lad. Stop your staring." He leaned over and offered his hand. His hoist up pulled Abram heavily against the side of the caravan and then banged his chest against the edge of the seat as he scrambled over it.

"You're a dickey-looking lad," Billy the Tinker said. Then, "Go on!" he called, shaking the reins in his fists. The swaybacked mare lowered her head, the caravan lurched, and they were off.

When they reached the sloping hills outside Ballymena, Abram saw a young woman emerge from a farmhouse nearly hidden among pines and birch trees. She half-ran through the grass-covered fields with one hand on top of her wide-brimmed straw hat. The other hand held the handle of a small case. Reaching the stone wall of the field closest to the road, she looked back at the house, then climbed over the wall, jumping down from its top, and ran all the faster toward them.

She had long blond hair, was slightly built, and as she came closer, she looked taller and taller. Billy stopped the caravan at the point where her path would intersect theirs. He was watching the girl, his expression expectant and tense.

She hardly looked at them, even as she reached the road and came round the back of the cart. Billy shoved Abram to the farthest edge of the bench and gave the girl a hand up.

"Go on! Go on!" he urged the horse in a strangled yell. "Get your carcass over that rise. Go on!" The old horse actually broke into a loose-ankled trot.

The girl had put her arms around Billy's waist. When he had the horse moving, he put the reins in one hand and clasped the girl closer with his free arm. He kissed her—long kisses that fascinated and embarrassed Abram. He turned his head and looked off, as far away as he could.

He heard a kind of pleasurable murmuring, then a pained shout from Billy.

The young woman jostled into Abram, and he turned to look. Billy was grimacing, and the young woman was laughing.

He growled something at her that Abram couldn't decipher, and she whispered in his ear, laughed a high, piercing, wild laugh, and then threw herself back at the tinker, grabbing him around the neck. She cupped his two cheeks in her hands, stroked them, kissed them lightly, and then kissed his lips again with as much passion as before.

Billy picked up the reins, with her still hanging on him, and gave the horse's back a slap, sending them more directly on their way.

The young woman turned around to Abram then. "Is this Lord Dunbar his own self?" she said. "With his pockets bulging? A kiss for staking us to the holiday." She pinched Abram's ear and kissed his cheek. She smelled like something sweet and something savory, bread and chocolate.

Her long hair was too light to fall in one piece and parted at each shoulder. She had blue eyes. Heavy freckles matted her straight nose and cheeks, and a few chloral veins ran by her ears and down into her neck underneath her creamy skin. The way her veins showed through gave her rubyish lips blue undertones. She was wearing a cheap gray dress, and the only form to it came from the slight curves of her breasts and hips. She was pretty, and she would almost have been beautiful if she hadn't been so slight. Even her face was too thin and long. It was as if someone had taken the fairest colleen and stretched her.

"You may well stare at her, boyo," said Billy. "This is Gillian, and there's not a banshee in these counties that can harrow your soul and toss your bones like she can."

Abram just kept looking at them. She really might be a banshee, he decided. What did that make Billy?

"Oooh, come here," Gillian said. Putting her hands under his arms, she lifted Abram onto her lap. She ran her fingers through his hair, her long fingernails scratching his scalp, producing a strange sensation that he reluctantly recognized as pleasure. She gave him another kiss at the base of his neck.

Billy gave him a shove to get him off her lap. "That stuff's all for me, boyo." He grabbed her and gave her a hungry kiss, chewing her lips in a way that made Abram question what joy they were getting out of it.

The caravan ran over a tree limb lying in the road, and the jolt sat them back. Gillian pulled the brim of her hat down again and looked at Billy. "I think we've gotten clean off," she said. He nodded and grinned.

Turning to Abram, she said, "We'll have our holiday, then, and we'll get you to the ships. I'd ask why you'd be wanting to go to the New World, but who wouldn't want to ship off this green scum rock in the sea. If it weren't for Billy and our shenanigans, I'd go with you, I would." She turned back to Billy. "Perhaps we ought to go, bonnie. Heave ourselves into the fo'c'sle with the dickey lad and pound over the waves all the way to the New World." She grabbed Billy and kissed him again.

He cleared her back from him with a slow but forceful forearm. "The caravan is all we need. I've got my capital in my wares."

"Your capital," she said, and rolled her eyes at Abram. "Why would we be needing Lord Dunbar if you had capital?" she asked.

Billy drove on with his chin lifted.

Nudging Billy with a sly wink, Gillian said, "Let's talk about your capital," and gave a wily, wicked laugh.

"She can be daft," Billy said.

Abram thought they were both daft. He did not like their references to him and his money, either. What would be the price of the trip?

In the afternoon they stopped by a stream. Birch trees lined its banks, but the slope down from the road was not steep and the horse could be watered. There was one old chestnut tree underneath which they could eat.

When they climbed down from the caravan, Billy said to Gillian, "Put your toes in the stream and I'll be along." Before she took two steps, he said, "Here," and motioned her to come back. "Lead the horse down." Billy unfastened the harness, and Gillian took the beast by the strap along its muzzle and led her away.

Billy walked over to Abram, grabbed his shoulder with his powerful hand, and led him underneath the shading canopy of the chestnut tree.

"Where have you got Dorgan's money?" he asked.

Abram did not answer immediately.

"You have to pay us for the journey," Billy said. "You can't expect me to navigate you through County Antrim without a fee. Lads that run away can get those who are kind to them in trouble. I'm taking my chances with you."

"How much do you want?" Abram asked.

"Just the money Dorgan gave you."

"All of it?" Abram asked.

"That's the price. As long as you end up on a ship bound to the New World, what's the difference? The money isn't good there."

"Yes, it is. It's all pounds there, too."

"I won't be cheated," Billy said.

Abram turned and started to walk away. He had not asked for the ride.

He felt Billy's hand on his shoulder before he cleared shade. "I'll be explaining the situation to you, then," Billy said. He turned the boy around and bent over into his face. "You won't be cheating me. I will have my fee."

He pushed Abram back, his two hands glancing off the boy's shoulders. Before Abram recovered his balance, Billy delivered a glancing blow to his ear. "That's not a leprechaun kissing you," Billy shouted.

Before Abram could reply, Billy hit him twice more in the ear, this time flush and with such power that his ear exploded with pain.

"That's not a wee person whispering his name," Billy said. He grasped Abram's shoulders. "That's not the bishop's blessing." He put his nose right up to Abram's. "Listen to me now. I'll kill you if you don't give me the money!"

Abram was taking big gulping breaths and feeling as if he were about to wet his trousers. To escape embarrassment as well as the beating, he ran to the caravan, found his satchel, and took the coins out of the lining. He threw them at Billy's feet, and then went to the backside of the chestnut tree. He was crying hard now, and he was more frightened than he had ever been before. He wondered what Billy the Tinker and Gillian the Banshee would do with him.

When Billy came back from sharing the sight of the money with Gillian, he was smiling that big, scooped-out, silly smile. He curled his wrist around Abram's neck and rubbed his cheek, petting him. "That's over, then, dickey lad. You've paid the fee."

Billy lifted Abram up on the seat, and Gillian and Billy climbed in from the other side, rather carefully, and sat down slowly, taking care not to jostle the boy.

"You'll get to your ship, dickey," Gillian said.

"To be sure, you will," Billy said. "We came to our bargain. You diddled Dorgan with your wit. Those of us as haven't got your invention must even the field as best we can." Billy picked up the reins from his feet. "Go on!" he called, and the mare lurched forward once more.

They traveled steadily through the long afternoon, with Billy and Gillian trying to kid each other out of the subdued mood into which they had fallen. The horse's hoofs pounded down in silence.

Abram burned at being blamed for diddling Dorgan. He had found a way to extract a fair price, nothing more.

That night the three of them slept in a stone-fenced field, in one corner that protected them from the wind. Billy and Gillian wrapped themselves up in one blanket; they could have stayed in the caravan, but they wanted to stay close to their passenger.

Abram had only his coat for warmth. For much of the night he watched a silvery moon—nearly full, but with a piece torn out of its side—sail over the smokey-edged clouds. He did not sleep, but kept thinking over his original plan. Which included dealing with people much more dangerous than these two.

He knew that besides the "drums" who recruited immigrants in a legitimate way, there were also "crimps" who snared young lads, got them drunk, and shipped them off as indentured servants.

Abram had been counting on having a bit of money with which to bargain or sweeten the crimps' deal. If he could not steal the money back from Billy, the crimps might not be interested enough to shanghai him.

He said his prayers again that night, but they brought him little comfort.

The next day, not much past noon, in the last of the hills above Larne, they stopped by a broadening stream. Pine and spruce trees bordered the waters, backed by larger oaks. There were grazing fields on either side, dotted by black-faced sheep. The wooded hills cradled this flattening valley as if they were God's own hand, with the stream his lifeline. Abram looked at the long pools of the stream, and, by force of habit, read where the fish might be lying. He had another purpose in mind, though.

They watered the horse and ate Billy's bread, cheese, and some bitter blueberries they had stopped to pick earlier. Abram watched Gillian as she sat on the sandy ground, eating. She never ate more than a few mouthfuls at a time, and he was eager to catch the first sign that she was satisfied. Billy, despite his carefree show, liked to be off when they had finished a meal as if he were a nervous military man with troop-moving orders.

Soon, Abram saw Gillian stretch her legs out, lean back, and rest her weight on the backward-turned palms of her hands. He gave her another moment to stretch. Then he moved beside her and caught her hand as she raised up to see what he wanted.

"Let's have a bath," he said. He pulled her up and toward the water where there was a flat place, with pink, flesh-colored sand. She put her feet into the water and gasped from the cold.

"Gillian!" Billy shouted. "Hold on." He was standing higher up on the bank, his knife in his hand—a hunter's knife with a square-toothed blade. He turned the knife so that the sun glinted off it and put it away in his pocket.

He started talking as he walked down to them. "I know this lad. I know him. He doesn't want a bath. He wants to dunk us and steal off with our clothes and money."

"I want a bath before I go to sea," Abram said.

Billy came closer to where the two stood on the bank. "You're not one to give up, boyo. Not without cause. We've turned gentle, and you've gathered the wool I knocked out of your ears yesterday."

Billy struck both the boy's shoulders with the butt of his hands, jolting Abram back. "If you do any swimming after the money, I will gut you like a mullet." He took out the knife and pulled it across the strop of his trouser leg. He held the point under Abram's nose. "We mean to enjoy ourselves."

Abram said, "I mean to try the stream. I've been traveling these three days."

Gillian stepped to Abram's side and put her arms around his shoulders, but he did not feel comfort or protection from her—her hands felt wet and cold. He stood there on the bank, lost in the midst of the countryside and trapped in their possession.

"I'll try the stream," he said, insisting, feeling the tears come but still thinking how he could best use them to his advantage.

"He's wetting his cheeks," Billy said, "and soon he'll wet these as well." Billy grabbed the two sides of Abram's britches and hitched them up uncomfortably. "You can bet he will."

Gillian was still clinging to Abram, and she took her hand and pushed Billy's face away.

Billy, looking flushed, said, "He wants his bath and he'll have it." He pushed Gillian to one side of Abram and, while she was rocking back on her heels, stripped Abram's trousers off. The boy only had time to register the look on Gillian's face before Billy heaved him into the air and sent him soaring out over the stream. The water's surface was so cold the plunge felt as if he were breaking through glass.

The cold took away the strength from his legs, and he stumbled dazedly toward the bank. When he looked up, he saw Billy leading Gillian away. He heard her whooping laughter, and his spirit shrank into a tight, frozen knot.

When he had retrieved his clothing and recovered his own thoughts, he went to the top of the rising bank and saw the two sprawled together close by a pair of sheep and their kid. Not even the lamb skipping close to their heads distracted the lovers.

He thought he knew where the money was—the tinker would have an iron-bracketed lockbox somewhere inside the caravan. But even if he found it, he hardly knew the right way to go anymore, even this close to Larne.

He walked quickly back to the caravan and rummaged feverishly in the cab, finding the tinker's box so quickly that he decided to act. The box was locked. He gave it a shake and heard coins clinking together.

Scrambling down from the caravan, he hid the box among the trees at the base of a rock outcropping, digging a hole and covering the box with dirt and stones. His heart was beating hard, and the shriveled skin of his hands and feet, still numb and cold from the water, felt as if it were catching fire.

Remembering the tinker's knife, his terror lifted him far above his circumstances, into a silence and a clarity.

The tall oak trees had large canopies—broad, round domes stretching up over one hundred feet. The trunks were high, though. Spotting the tree with the lowest limbs, he ran straight at it. He did not jump. He ran straight at the tree and right up the trunk, his momentum providing enough force for his feet to get a purchase on the flat bark as the angle of his body arched back toward the ground. One last spring off the side of the tree put him into the air, nearly horizontal, within arm's reach of the lowest branch. He caught hold. His feet failed to wrap themselves around the branch, though, and he swung down, holding on with every bit of strength his terror could supply. The branch felt as if it would tear his arms out of their sockets, but he managed to keep his hold. He swung his legs up and climbed down the limb—as if it were a horizontal rope—toward the trunk, where he could more easily right himself.

Standing on the crook of the limb, Abram noticed the sweat pouring from his armpits and running down his sides. Yet he felt cold.

Hugging the trunk, he took his first ascending handholds on the dusty, slightly furrowed bark with vengeance in his fingertips. Without ever looking down, he climbed to the place where the trunk itself forked into two last branches, and only then let himself realize what he had done.

From his position he could not see much of the ground through the branches and leaves below him, just a patch or two of wet, leafmulched soil. Billy and Gillian would have to lie flat on the ground to see him. But could he be seen through the fat-fingered leaves from farther away? He might climb down a little when he heard them go. If they did find him, he decided, he would shout down to them where the money lay. He doubted whether there was enough industry in Billy the Tinker to climb up and bring him down just to beat him for sheer pleasure. If the amorous pair had been truly criminal, Abram knew, they would have taken the money and abandoned him the first day out. On the other hand, Billy had struck him cruelly, without warning.

Before too long he heard the pair calling him and saw flashes of Gillian's blond head moving beneath him. Their curses as they searched dizzied him. He clung to the tree and hardly dared open his eyes.

He knew they were at the caravan when he heard the horse give a shrill whinny as if Billy had done some violence to it. In less time than he would have imagined, the two had the caravan moving up the lane along the stream to the main road. Gillian screamed at the horse with a true banshee's voice, a wild and wicked shrieking.

Abram watched them go. The pair never looked back. They disappeared over the hill, headed toward Larne. If he kept the caravan's tracks before him until the first houses around the city, he would be safe.

CHAPTER 3

Before the Wind

Abram sat amidst the forking branches of the oak, enjoying his airy perch. Warm drafts of wind curled into the canopy's shaded interior through the dotted mesh of leaves, brushing against his sweaty cheeks. He noticed that his hands felt swollen. The climb had scratched them and his forearms like a frenzied cat.

For the first time he felt sure he would make it to the New World. Then, with a drop of his heart, he realized that he would not have anyone to tell his adventures to; not for a long time, and maybe never again.

Abram climbed down and retrieved Billy's lockbox. Smashing it open with a rock, he found his money and another thirty shillings, plus a gold-plated locket, a set of keys, an old silver coin whose value he did not know, and a woman's gold band.

He thought about posting Billy's valuables back to Dorgan, but knowing he could expect little honor from that thief, he resolved on keeping the valuables as compensation for the beating.

He thought he would move off right away, but his legs still felt wobbly. He stood up, made his way out from under the trees, and willed himself toward Larne. His legs were as loose as a wooden puppet's, with no one at the drawstrings. The chill he had been feeling for the last two days crept back into his hands, and they grew wet and shaky.

He stopped in the middle of the road. Could he go back? He turned around and looked back toward Ballymena and Glenwhirry. Just then, a small whirlwind stirred up the road and flung its chalky dust into his eyes. The grit instantly worked itself up under his eyelids. He sat down in the road to let his tears wash out the dirt.

The wind started rattling the tree limbs and whipping their leaves. He thought again about which way to go. The wind was blowing straight from Ballymena up toward Larne. He remembered running with the wind at his back the Sunday of the Reverend Innis's miracle—the wind that had carried him here.

———

On that Sunday over a year ago, sitting with his family in their pew, surrounded by nearly the entire village of Glenwhirry, Abram had listened to Reverend Innis introduce a thin, tall man with a square face wreathed in an auburn beard. He wore a navy blue uniform with gold epaulets and buttons. Captain Lier had a wild-eyed look, as if he suspected the congregation of some mutiny as he climbed the curling stairs into the high pulpit. His eyebrows were long and flared, the tufts like horns, and this gave him an ancient but irascible authority, like Moses. He shifted from one foot to the other as he stood before them. He put his snail-shaped hat on the lectern at first, but then took it up again.

"As the Reverend Innis says, I am Captain Lier. I will be commanding the good ship *Evangel*, a twenty-ton, three-masted brig . . . trustworthy . . . appointed well in all particulars, for an Atlantic crossing. We are to sail for New England this next month. The port of New York."

He gestured with the hat, his arm flying out so suddenly that his hand seemed to catch it out of the air. This was unnerving to his listeners, and it seemed to unnerve him, too. His eyes opened wider and his wild-eyed look grew panicked.

He gazed around him as if assessing the damage his ship might have sustained in a sudden squall. But then his eye caught on Abram's: a boy with a fierce and ready look of his own.

Captain Lier stared at Abram for a long moment, as if he wanted to say that this boy at least understood him; this boy could see what needed to be done. As he steadied his gaze on the lad, the captain's look grew more restful and determined. He settled on his feet, put his hat down again on the lectern, and leaned forward comfortably on the pulpit's rail. When he continued, it was as if he were addressing passengers after a crisis had been taken well in hand.

"The way will not be long," he said, "compared with the endless abundance of riches to be found. That land's nothing but a sugar teat for you to be sucking on.

"A' ship, your provisions will be ample. Five pounds of salted beef for every family per week. That's better than a penny pickle, isn't it? Or your fagged scallions and juniper. No one wants to diddle you. The *Evangel* was hammered together for pilgrims such as yourselves—the fo'c'sle is over five and a half between decks!"

Abram felt that the captain was finding his way through his speech because of their mysterious connection. The boy even tested this by nodding and seeing the captain's head bob to his. He was shocked. The world worked this way only in his dreams.

"You can be sure of your safety—the Lord goes with the immigrant ships," Captain Lier said. "How many of your kin have already made this journey? You have their scribbles. What do they say? How many purchased oats and flax this spring from the gifts of their lockbox? You don't want to live on charity, now, do you? Why not join them and reach into that horn o' plenty for yourselves and your wee babes?"

Abram believed what the captain was saying, although he did not understand, as yet, why he did or why it should matter. What could this voyage have to do with him?

"Your pastor asked me to speak because he cares for you. He's a good man, isn't he now? I may be a wormy box, but that's a man of God you've got there. The Lord himself strike me down, what I have said is the truth. A new land, a new life, is waiting. And that's what I came here to say."

The Reverend Innis stood up from the big elder's chair, with its crimson upholstered armrests, and hobbled over to the base of the pulpit—the minister had a dragging limp from an accident in the fields. The whole congregation saw the grimacing look that he gave Captain Lier as the seaman descended the curling stairs. Who was in league with whom might have remained their business, and the captain's language, well, it might have been more restrained.

So as he took his place in the pulpit, the Reverend Innis had to begin his sermon with the cat out of the bag and roaming suspiciously.

"My good people," he began, as if reminding them of their place and duty, "my good people.

"Let me read to you from the Exodus: 'And the Lord said, I have surely seen the affliction of my people which are in Egypt, and have heard their cry by reason of their taskmasters; for I know their sorrows; and I am come down to deliver them out of the hand of the Egyptians, and to bring them up out of that land . . . unto a land flowing with milk and honey.' "

Even as young as he was, Abram knew enough to feel the surge of excitement that flowed through the congregation at these words. It was going to happen here, too, in Glenwhirry! The immigration fever was breaking out!

He looked over at the landholders, the former widow Tunston and her portly new husband, Mr. Garrity. Beneath her silk bonnet, the new Mrs. Garrity had graying hair done up in what must be the severest possible knot. She had a nose that just kept getting bigger, liver spots on her cheeks, and the scrawny neck of an underfed chicken. Mr. Garrity was round-faced, mustachioed and mutton-chopped, and black-tipped protuberances, the shape of bullet-heads, spiked his forehead, cheeks, and neck. He tried to cover his balding pate with long, reddish strands that he combed over from a part just above his ear. Both were sitting upright now, very still, as explosively still as the moment the fuse is lit.

"How many times have I looked upon you, brethren, from this pulpit. It's been fifteen years now. We know each other well enough, I suppose. And in these fifteen years what have I seen? I've seen your children born and some of the elderly folk among our number join the chorus in the heavenlies. I've seen the good years come and the bad. The drought these past two. The typhoid that took away our children, my little David and Elizabeth among them.

"But for some time now, when I've tried to go to sleep, don't you know, I've seen very little but your faces. They rise up to meet me instead of my dreams. They are my dreams. Or I can dream of nothing but you.

"Nothing but your faces growing thinner. Your eyes stark and feverish with hunger. I know how many of you are hungry this morning. Or have eaten the oats you should be planting."

Abram thought of his morning's stirabout and realized with a start that the oat sacks in the shed were disappearing and no planting had been done yet.

He glanced at his father. Zebulun White's bumpy-nosed profile was as set as the figurehead on a coin. But he did not look angry like the Garritys; he looked stunned, his thoughts paralyzed.

"Since the rack-renting began ten years ago, at the end of the first leases," the Reverend Innis said, "many in Ulster have gone to the New World."

That sealed the man's fate—or he had chosen without recourse. Lord Dunbar, who lived in England, owned the lands of the Glenwhirry villagers, and when the original fifty-year Ulster plantation leases started to expire ten years ago, his agents had raised the rents. But more importantly, in those fifty years the Widow Tunston's late husband, and her new one, Mr. Garrity, had managed to position themselves as Lord Dunbar's primary tenants and made everyone else their sub-tenants, or the sub-tenants of their sub-tenants. And they had let the rents float upward to the fair market price of the years when the linen trade prospered. But the linen market zigzagged, and the periodic droughts like this last year's diminished the flax crop that supplied the fabric. Linen meant cash, but sometimes it also meant catastrophe.

There had been no mention of the rack-renting before from the Glenwhirry pulpit, because for years the only cash the Reverend Innis saw came from the Tunstons and the Garritys. The other members of the congregation helped him fill his peat shed, helped him raise his own flax, and brought over joints of meat on those rare occasions when they slaughtered. But the cash came from the newly named rack-renters, the people whose rates were seen as an instrument of torture.

"The rack-renting is but one of your burdens, that's certain," the Reverend Innis said. "Over these years so many have compared our situation to those of the Israelites in bondage that I have joked about this.

"But the Lord came to me and turned those jests into bitter herbs on my tongue. A reproof to me and a sign of the bitterness of our community's experience. He chastened me. He taught me to prefer the wisdom of others.

"Are you not indeed like those people, the Israelites, who were forced to make bricks without straw? How can you pay the rents without selling linen? And how can you sell the linen if you have no market? Or if we have no rain to grow the flax? And do the rack-renters take account of any of this?"

The pastor looked directly at the newly married Garritys, his face set, with the hardness of a tombstone. His glowering at the land-holders shocked everyone. No one had ever seen him wear such an expression.

When they thought of the Reverend Innis they thought of his gleeful smile, how his small white teeth would suddenly show through his dark beard, giving his horseshoe face the aspect of a dark St. Nicholas. When he was not smiling, he always wore a pleasant expression. Almost as a matter of doctrine, the Reverend Innis was either in good humor or kept his own counsel; he never showed anger or even displeasure; he never—he gave the impression—submitted himself to these feelings.

"But what, then, has made us subject to these plagues?" the Reverend Innis asked. "Why the drought of last year? Why the bad markets for our linens?"

He paused—and his pauses were famous. When the Reverend Innis paused, he seemed to be putting the carbon of his thoughts under the pressure that produces diamonds. And his next words were often gems indeed; sayings so hard and pure that his parishioners could hardly see them at first for their radiance. Only when he turned them this way and that did his congregation begin to see all their lovely, sparkling lights.

"There were two phases to the migration! Abraham set out; and the Israelites carried Joseph's bones away!"

This sounded as if it made sense, but no one could be sure at first.

"Are we not living with an alien people?" he asked. "Are we not subject to the locusts that have come upon them; to the blood that they have spilled flowing in our rivers?

"Do we not know the hardness of their hearts? We have turned this country from a wasteland into one that would provide for all of our needs, and some of theirs as well, if we were not subject to their manipulations and wickedness. We cannot sell abroad the many goods that we are capable of producing; we may only sell to England at ruinous prices. This stifles our industry, for which we have, in former times, been rightly famous.

"And how are we rewarded? Are we not rewarded in the same manner as the Israelites, with ever greater burdens, not only bricks but bricks without straw! Not only tireless industry but slavery to economic taskmasters?

"And so the Death Angel has come among us," the Reverend Innis said, "reaping its grim harvest."

At that moment he looked so distraught that his two shaking fists might have suddenly turned against himself and raked his cheeks. His whole body was quivering with the tension of the occasion and the breaking thunder of his voice.

"And yet I have not cried out against this tyranny. And why? I have not protected you good folk from the Death Angel. I have not had the faith to speak. To spread the blood of the Lamb over the lintel of our house. And why?"

He paused once more, looking exhausted. He had his head twisted down to one side as if he might lay it on the lectern.

Finally, he looked straight down and spoke in such abject humility that Abram was embarrassed not only for him but for himself. The boy felt uncomfortably foolish, just as he did when found out in a bragging lie.

"But I had no faith. I lacked the smallest seed."

The Reverend Innis looked openly at his wife, Kate, in the box pew across the aisle from the Garritys. A pretty woman with wheat-colored hair, Kate Innis looked like the direct descendant of a Norse invader, with her high pillowy cheeks and full lips. When the Reverend Innis spoke again, he appealed for her understanding especially, as well as the congregation's.

"I asked for a sign. Moses was given signs. His rod turning into a serpent, his leprous hand made new in his bosom, the river water he poured out turning into blood. In the same way, I asked for a sign to confirm that we should complete the migration. That just as Abraham went into a far country, which brought his descendants unto Egypt where they were called a second time unto the true Promised Land, so we came from Scotland to this Ulster plantation and are now being called out of slavery unto our true country. The New World."

At this talk of signs, Abram had begun to feel a stirring and a lifting up that was as dreamlike, in its way, as Captain Lier looking to him for courage; but this seemed like the end of the dream, an old childhood dream that he was suddenly remembering. He had dreamed of angels—a satiny gray pool, a ladder, and the angels guiding him upward. He had forgotten this, and the memory rushed back so strongly that he felt himself rising again up that ladder, growing lighter, growing happier, growing exuberant.

"I asked for a sign," the Reverend Innis said. "And, O ye people, the Lord gave me a sign. 'This shall be your sign,' the Lord said to me. '*This shall be your sign.*' He told me to walk before my people. To go before you, now, and into this New World."

With these words, he wrenched himself toward the curling pulpit stairs and almost sprang down them, and then he walked all the way back up the center aisle and all the way down to the pulpit again. And he was no longer limping!

A commotion began to break out in the church. People grabbed their neighbors by the shoulder. Husbands and wives whispered together. Children were hushed and explained to. When they heard the news, they jumped up onto the pews or clambered up into their parents' arms to see better. Some men had three or four children clinging to them.

The Reverend Innis walked back and forth, up and down the aisle twice, moving nimbly and decisively over the mud-tracked stones and mortar, his feet swinging and hopping a bit, as if he were skating.

At the end of his second pass up the aisle, he stood before the pulpit and squatted down on his haunches and then stood back up again. Slowly. He had his hands on his hips, and his head turned to one side, like a Cossack dancing his squatting, leg-kicking dance. For a Scots-Presbyterian, and a Scots-Presbyterian in church, he was capering before the altar. (That's how it was talked of afterward.) His white-toothed smile was never more gleeful.

By this time, Abram was standing on the seat of the pew. He looked over at his family. His father was still seated, holding on to Zack, as if trying to keep the boy from rising into Abram's flying sky.

"The Lord has turned my mourning into dancing!" the Reverend Innis proclaimed. "Bless ye the name of the Lord!"

"Bless His name!" shouted someone in the congregation.

Abram jumped into the air, only realizing what he had done in mid-flight. He caught his fall by grabbing onto the back of the next pew. When he discovered he was not seriously hurt, he started spilling over with nervous laughter. Before he disgraced himself further, he scrambled into the aisle and ran out of the church.

He ran into the green and sun-filled late Irish morning, and, as soon as he cleared the wooden bridge at the end of the village, he felt the breeze at his back, pushing him on.

He ran down the main street of his whitewashed village, along the road to Omagh, through Carrick glen, and over the lane across the hills up to his home in its high meadow. As he ran, breathing hard, his blood racing, he felt the strange passion that had come to him spurring him on; and the harder he ran, the more pleasure he felt, as his feet fairly skimmed over the earth. He did not understand this feeling, but he never wanted it to stop, and he ran, and ran, and ran.

———

There, in the midst of the road to Larne, Abram recalled these things. How could he be untrue to them, to the hand of Providence? So he headed once more toward the ships.

CHAPTER 4

The Jaws of Hell

*B*y the time he arrived in Larne, with its narrow stone streets and rows of wooden storefronts, Abram had his plan. He would tour through the town close by the wharves, spot the dingiest, most dilapidated tavern—a place that his deepest instincts would tell him to avoid—and then let villainy take its course. He thought that Billy and Gillian would not be looking for him there, because they figured he'd be spending his gold at an expensive place.

First, though, he went into a shop and bought a needle and thread and a cotton handkerchief. Then he walked down to the wharves and sat, looking over a beach of dingy sand and the sluggish waters of low tide. Out some from the docks, the harbor reflected the evening sky and registered the big-headed clouds sailing in toward shore as darker patches on the moody waters. Three ships at anchor looked as if they might be capable of the passage to the New World. Their masts, draped with what looked to Abram like spider webbing, stood as tall as the oak he had climbed. The ships themselves, though, looked much smaller than the village church. How did they accommodate as many people?

He found a place amid a clutch of cargo to be loaded—a nest of barrels, hay bales, livestock cages, and chests—to take off his trousers. He turned them inside out, and after tearing the handkerchief in half and threading the tediously small eye of the needle, sewed three sides of one handkerchief piece into his trousers. He took out his money, reserving Billy's thirty shillings and locket for another use, and nested his pounds and change in the other half of the handkerchief; then he stuffed this muffling money bag into the newly made pocket and sewed it closed. Shaking the trousers, he found the coins made no sound. When he put his trousers back on, he jumped up and down several times to make sure the money would travel with him silently.

Some of Larne's taverns, like its other shops, had wooden fronts, with plate-glass windows and fluted pilasters propping up their bannered signs. Others looked like overgrown farmhouses, whitewashed, plaster-finished buildings crossed by dark Tudor finishings and marked out front with wooden signs hanging from grillwork fittings. The Quinn Brothers, Gunn's, Casey's.

Abram continued his tour until he came upon a tavern, not much bigger than a peat stack, that had been charred by fire. Its black door, with the sooty fingers of a recent fire thrown out around it, looked like the ash-encased opening of a kiln. The place had a new heavy thatch roof that came down low over its brow and a single boarded-up window. The sort of place Billy and Gillian might frequent themselves—might they be inside, after all? A slate board outside declared it Bailey's. Abram took a breath and prepared himself to walk into hell.

The last of the day's light still lingered outside, but across the threshold Abram entered into night. The smoke of clay pipes thickened the air. Two oil lamps burned behind the tavern keeper at the bar, which itself took up most of the available room, with only a horseshoe of space remaining. Half a dozen men sat at the outer ring of tables and three at the bar, pretty well crowding the place. No one took any notice of Abram. The tavern keeper probably thought he had come in to fetch a pail of beer for his family—a family whose credit had been exhausted at other taverns, since he had never seen the lad before.

Once his eyes adjusted to the dim light, Abram found that the customers looked as he had imagined and feared, reliably cut-throat. They had unkempt hair and ragged beards, beaten expressions and quick eyes, eager with want.

Abram plucked up his courage, stepped over to the bar, and climbed up on it. He half-stood, with his head just under the ceiling's wattles, and started singing in a loud voice—a voice that banged off the four walls and ricocheted through the sudden attention he commanded.

The cat's a puppy,
The dog's a pig,
Come here my lovely
And dance a jig.
We're off for glory
We're bound for fame.
The sea's unholy,
The land's a bane.
With you beside me,
I'll make my way.
Come here my lovely,
Let's clip and play.

Abram knew dozens of verses to this drinking ditty, and he kept singing, louder and louder, as the silence of his audience rolled back his way, threatening to smother him. By the end, he was almost screaming, as he remembered Billy and Gillian, the blows against his ear, and realized fully that he had thrown himself into the jaws of hell.

When he could sing no more from sheer terror, he said, "I'll be going to sea, and a man going to sea deserves a drink." He took five of Billy's thirty shillings, bent over, and slapped them down on the bar. "Rum for me and the lads who have come to see me on my way." He stretched out his arm, opened his palm, and swept it in a wide arc, from one side of the bar to the other.

A short, broad-chested man dressed in ancient discards of gentlemen's clothing sprang to his feet. When he did, the other patrons eased back in their chairs, as if content to follow his lead.

The man's limp declared itself as he came forward. His crippling differed from the Reverend Innis's old dragging step; this fellow used what appeared to be his shorter and less flexible leg like a walking staff, driving himself onward. He had the manner of a little general—in command, and letting others know it.

The little general offered his hand to Abram—to help him down and as a sign of friendship, but with a certain impatience that made

Abram feel that he might grip the hand only to find himself flying.

Once the man had helped him down, he put his arm around the boy and announced to the tavern, "Drink up, lads. Our brother wants to go to sea, and I, for one, believe he'll be on the boundless main sooner than Lord Chesterfield's monkey."

The tavern laughed, and then, as quickly as the little general's gaze swept over the room, quieted. The barman started handing round the flagons of rum Abram's shillings had purchased, and the men took them back to their seats, holding on to them with a secret satisfaction, as if this rum were more spirited than most. Knowing looks sheared off the corners of everyone's glance.

"Clear a place, Dribbler," the little general said to the slight man who had been sitting with him. The man hopped out of his seat and took another on the opposite side of the table. The little general almost pushed Abram down into the vacated chair, and then pulled it close beside his.

"So you've signed on with a ship's company and come to celebrate with your advance pay," he said. "I always drink mine up before going out on a voyage—I've yet to spy a floating tavern."

Abram confessed that he did not know what ship he would depart in. "I mean to immigrate," he said. "I can do more for my family working there than eating up their stores at home."

"Sure you can, lad," the little general said. "Only the rats and worms are well fed in this country. The poor die every day to see to it!" He brought his face very close to Abram's cheek. "You're right to go, sure you are." He had a youthful hairline and a strong jaw, fine, deep brown eyes, and a half-moon scar like an indented fingernail underneath his left cheekbone. A handsome man, actually. But his breath smelled strongly of rum, garlic, leeks, and cabbage, a dizzying combination.

"But what arrangements for the journey have you made?" the little general asked.

At this question the slight-built Dribbler leaned in close to them.

Instantly incensed, the little general put a hand over Dribbler's nose and mouth and pushed him back. "You are a strumpet's bucket, Dribbler!" he shouted. He stood up and continued the tongue-lashing. "I'm having a conversation with the lad, here. He doesn't want you knowing his business. He hasn't asked you into it. I won't have you taking advantage of the lad."

The little general looked to Abram to confirm all this, and having

looked, without Abram changing expression, the little general nodded.

When he sat back down, Dribbler moved his chair around the
side of the circular table close to his leader's. Abram watched for
another explosion, but none came.

Dribbler had a flat head and thin, dead black hair lying across
it, and weak eyes, but he had very fine teeth. After the excitement,
his mouth hung open and his babyish teeth glistened with saliva.
He was panting like a dog that wants to go with his master.

"A quick lad like you has a plan," the little general said, bringing
Abram's attention back to the issue.

"I'll be taking ship as an indentured servant. But only for a half
term. I have some money and a valuable or two."

The little general and Dribbler looked at each other. "You'll be
wanting a broker, then," the little general said.

"A broker," Dribbler echoed.

Abram asked what a broker might be.

"You can go and be a slave for life or a gentleman in a gnat's
eyelash. It depends on the arrangement the broker makes for you."

"You know about these things?" Abram asked.

"I've served as a broker—it's one of my enterprises," the little
general said.

"His clients are all a happy lot," Dribbler said, and giggled
strangely.

"They be satisfied, I can tell you that," the little general said
forcefully.

"I want to land in New York," Abram said. "The Reverend Innis
took most of our village there. I'd like to find my way to them, if I
could."

"I remember the party," the little general said, perhaps too
quickly. "I remember the Reverend Innis. Nearly the whole village
went."

"Innis was a great tall man, wasn't he?" Dribbler asked. "A great
tall man with red hair. He led them people off playing his bagpipes.
The wharves were full of the talk of it for days."

Abram let this pass. His request to land in New York might be
honored if he did not cause his broker any additional difficulty.

"But how much money . . . what have you got to trade for your
passage, beside your labor?" the little general asked.

Abram took out Billy the Tinker's gold locket and the rest of his
thirty shillings.

"Is that gold?" the little general asked as he snatched it up.

"Eighteen carat," Abram lied.

"And twenty-five shillings," Dribbler said, his teeth glistening all the more.

"Not very much for a broker to work with," the little general said. "But it might be possible for me to do something. A passage with a certain length of service. Not half, mind you. But we might be able to arrange for a deduction from the usual seven years."

"That would be good," Abram said.

"We should drink to the young man's health," Dribbler said.

"So we should," the little general said. "So we should. But let's have some of the better stock. It's fitting we drink the better stock for a lad off on such a long voyage. *Dribbler*," he said, and jerked his head toward the bar.

The ratlike man went to the bar, whispered there with the tavern keeper, and returned with a glazed earthenware pitcher.

"Bailey keeps this back for special occasions," the little general said. "He brings it out for a leave-taking when I have a little brokering work to do." The man's eyes narrowed.

He poured out Abram's drink, shoved it in front of him, hesitated, and then remembered to pour out a drink for himself. "To a new land. A new life!"

Abram took a long draught of the rum and coughed against the burning in his throat. He wondered how much of the noxious mixture he would have to imbibe before it accomplished its purpose.

He kept drinking, and the spirits made his head feel heavy and his stomach churn. He thought he might be sick and ruin everything, when something else began to happen: the top of his scalp became warm—it seemed to be catching fire—and the scene before him, this miniature hell called Bailey's, started dropping away from that burning like a caving floor.

He took a breath. He took another.

He saw the smiles breaking across the faces of the little general and Dribbler, and he felt his eyelids flutter, as if secretly waving good-bye.

Then his vision seemed to roll up like a burning leaf and . . . *ffft*, he went out.

PART II

—

Reading the Sea

CHAPTER 5

The Devil's Toothmarks

Spirits funneled out from the emptiness and turned round on him. Globular shadows, spotted white with chancres, danced closer, threatening him with their fists.

Where was he?

The place's mouth opened suddenly and the concavity above him had a moist sheen. He felt himself falling. He looked down to see more spirits rushing up to meet him. They meant to tear right through him. He felt them close, closer, *within*. They bolted suddenly out of his throat, and as this localized feeling gathered him out of delirium, he opened his eyes and saw his vomit on the blanket where he lay.

In the next instant the back of a leviathan bucked him upward and squashed his face back down into the mess. He heard a pounding, like someone driving posts into the ground with a sledgehammer.

He tried to enjoy the rise and fall of what he knew at last to be the ship beneath him—*he had succeeded!*—but the rise soared too high, and the fall came too quickly, and the pounding smashed his equilibrium and terrorized him.

He rolled over and looked around, and what he saw increased his panic; he had exchanged his dream for a living nightmare. Those globular shadows had multiplied into a swarm of people who covered every inch of the lamplit forecastle like bees in their hive. Three lumps crowded next to him in the lower bed of a double-decker bunk.

The bunks lined both walls, and from what he could see, each contained at least as many people as his. An equal complement clogged the aisle between, right back to where even more people fanned out into the semi-circular clearing at the opposite end of the hold.

He guessed the stairway to the upper deck must be there, but he couldn't see through the weaving bodies. The immigrants were as tightly packed as if they were being shipped in one of the iron-hooped hogsheads that people sat on in the aisles.

After wiping his face on his sleeve, he noticed that the place smelled like a compost heap dumped into the bottom of a privy. And for good reason. Slop jars littered the aisle. Burlap sacks of onions and potatoes, clustered in piles against which the immigrants' farm implements rested, further crowded the forecastle. The place hummed with a constant sound, desultory and yet desperate. It felt hot and drafty at the same time. And there was no escape.

Abram found himself waiting for someone to speak with him, but the hum came from people within families: mothers correcting their children; husbands and wives bickering. A freckle-faced boy, about his age or a little younger, lay next to him, then a broad-backed, big-hipped woman, and from what he could see over her rounded form, a golden-haired little girl.

They were at the very front tip of the forecastle, and Abram's side of the bunk stood virtually flush with the inside of the ship's bow. Only the outward curve of the prow itself allowed him a narrow escape.

Weakened by the ordeal, he slowly stood and looked over at the line of men. The one that had wavy hair, a reddish complexion, a bump of a nose, and pencil-point eyes cloaked by sagging lids, said, "Look who has come back from the dead, then."

Unexpectedly, these simple words and his kind expression drew Abram's thoughts away from his loneliness and seasickness.

The ship must have gone through a huge wave just then, as the hammering seemed to strike directly at the wall beside his head. Abram could feel the ship torque sideways as it shuddered through the crest. The fall of the bow, and his wobbly knees, sent him crashing to the floor. The man who had spoken helped him up.

Abram looked up into his face. One of the man's incisors was missing and his fiery complexion strangely resembled a hobgoblin's, but he had a reassuring smile and a kind manner.

"They tell us this is the way of it," the man said. "You and me won't be crossing more than once, will we?"

The man introduced himself as Mr. Leach. Others told Abram later that this man had come forward to claim him when he had been tossed down the gangway into their midst.

Mr. Leach explained to Abram that he was on *The Huntington*, a packet bound for Boston harbor. The man also explained the immigrant's schedule. Half slept while the other half kept to the aisle and the rear of the ship—the only way so many could be accommodated in this space. The crew brought their rations once a day. Mr. Leach would be claiming Abram's for him, if he liked, as part of his family—here the man pointed to the woman and the boy and girl sharing Abram's bunk.

They were only a day and a half at sea. It took Abram a few days and as many sea biscuits as he was allowed before his seasickness abated. He spent the time lying idly or standing dazedly on his feet, his nausea washing back against the rhythm of the waves. But when his head finally cleared, he wanted to go up on deck. Although this was permitted during the calm watches, when the sailors had little to do but pace the ship close by their posts, few of the passengers went up for long. The sea had inflicted such terror that they preferred not to look at it.

Abram first went up on a clear, breezy day, and the sheer expanse of the skies and the buffeting wind made him feel as if he would be blown away over the dark-stained waves, and he nearly retreated below. Just then a shift in the wind caused the second mate to sing out for the seamen to reef the topgallant sails.

The boy watched white-shirted, blue-trousered men clamber into the rigging like monkeys, elbows out, knees flexed. They went up as high as any oak tree grew, and Abram thought about being at the top of a giant oak that swayed sideways in the wind and rocked underneath at the same time. He wondered what the sea rushing past must look like to the sailors striding the crossbeams above. For a boy who loved to climb, this seemed as if it must be heaven. After that, he spent much of his waking shift on deck.

One day, standing by the rail at the foremast rigging in unusually calm weather, Abram noticed that the officer of the watch, the second mate, who was sitting close by the helmsman, had his chin resting on its pillowy double and his eyes closed. He had observed that the mates and the crewmen slept as often as possible on their watches. One of the sailors with whom he had struck up a friendship told him that their half-watch schedule never allowed them more than four hours of sleep. During high weather they often fell out every two hours. On this day, following a violent thunderstorm the previous night, the launch boat between the main and mizzen masts was full of sleeping sailors, and the men forward were slumbering amid the hogsheads stored at the bow. A sailor learned to sleep with anchor chains for his pillow.

Weaving through these slumberers, Abram crossed to the starboard side. He took hold of the rigging, and felt the stiff cords of the large hemp rope. He hoisted himself up onto the rail, then swung to the outside of the rigging, where its angle made climbing easier. He hesitated, looking at the rolling, white-foamed waters behind him. A moment later he began to climb. He wanted to get up high as fast as he could. The helmsman might see him and alert the mate, but he would have no better chance than today.

Each loop of the rigging provided a larger step than he felt comfortable with at first. From the crossbeam of the foresail, he spied a small, partially enclosed platform above the topgallant—the crow's nest. Thinking it would both shield him from view and provide a safe handhold, he made for it. The ship's pitch and yaw took every bit of his strength to master as he climbed. How did the sailors get up here when the seas ran high?

When at last he reached his perch and dared to look out for the first time, girded now with the waist-high, hoop-shaped enclosure, he felt as if he had launched himself into free air. The wind streamed past, and with each lifting swell he wanted to soar higher into it, to grow wings and lift up into the sky like a gull. To move through the streaming air as naturally as a fish swims in its kill, and then leap, perhaps, into the air of paradise. Indeed the ship beneath him had become a mere plank, a fallen tree in the midst of the limitless sea. He felt such a rush of excitement that he wanted to call out, to sing back to the wind.

The sea lay out below him, a waving, sparkling blue—God's bright ensign. The few clouds seemed within hand's reach. He looked ahead and scanned the fine, incised line at the horizon. He looked aft and saw how far the ship's bubbly white wake stretched out behind, the only tracks marking their headway.

Abram climbed back down that day without being detected, and said nothing about his adventure; and on every possible occasion after that he climbed once again into the crow's nest. The crew started to notice, but as he had appeared on deck more than any other passenger, he had become a favorite; and they had enough to bother about, their looks said, without worrying whether he dropped into the sea.

He liked to go aloft well before dawn and watch the sun rise, staying in the nest until he became sleepy again, about mid-morning. The sea began to teach him things about itself. At first he had seen it as a bleak landscape, without direction or portent. Then he discovered that he had already begun to read the sea before knowing it, in the way that he could read the riffles and pools of the Battenkill at home. On one of his secretive watches it came to him, suddenly, that it would rain the day after next, and that the seas would grow mountainous and the day so dark that it would seem the sun was keeping its own company on the other side of the world. Right then, his eyes and ears opened to the sea's language. What made the sea seem a blank was just that it shouted with such power and magnitude. Abram also began to detect subtle variations in the sea's smell. On the day he realized a storm was coming, the sea's brininess carried a taste of iron and sulfuric traces that made him sniff. The waves changed from bobbing pyramids with faceted sides to roiling swells as the storm started to gather its power.

From the crow's nest he liked watching the ship carve out its brimming way, especially before dawn when the sea had a bluish phosphorescent hue. Mostly, though, he kept his eyes on the horizon. He liked the idea that he would see what lay ahead first. He took as much pleasure in this as in the soaring sensation.

Before dawn, his keenness to look ahead, to see over the earth's curve into the future, fixed his attention at the dark western horizon, even as the sun crept up behind him and its first rays struck the back of his neck.

One morning, as he looked toward the indigo line in the distance, he witnessed a lightening of the darkness. For a moment a small fan of light appeared, embossed, it seemed, with a thrice-crossed mast or a bare, stiff-limbed tree. The sight startled him, as if he had been fearing the boogeyman's face would peer into his bedroom window and it had, except that his fear carried with it a mysterious awe that changed its character—as if the face belonged to someone who knew him. He thought of the oak tree that had saved him from Billy and Gillian. This thrice-crossed tree before him bruised the light around it with yellow and ocher shadows, making the darkness itself an ornament.

Abram looked behind him to make sure he had his directions right. The sun was still coming up there, like a limpid, bleeding egg yolk, the sea rupturing its bottom edge. He looked back to the western horizon, and the lightened place remained. He could not see the branching tree anymore, though.

In the next few minutes the whole sky filled with a clear, turquoise light. He kept looking at the place he had seen the tree, wondering if he had been shown something, deliberately.

———

Sixteen days at sea, Abram awoke in his bunk to Mrs. Leach's screaming. The big woman lay on her back with her hands straight up as if reaching for the rings of heaven. "The devil's coming to take me!" she screamed. "Dear sweet Lord!"

The woman's eyes were wide open but blind. Her skin looked red. He thought the devil might indeed have come for her and left his angry mark. Peculiarly, her little girl, Ellen, who always slept by her side, did not awaken. Curled into a ball, she had her arms crossed over her chest like an animal protecting itself. The Leach's son, Daniel, looked back at Abram from the opposite side of the bunk, his expression embarrassed. His mother shouldn't be making herself such a nuisance, the look said.

Mr. Leach cleared his son out of the way with one arm and shook his wife's shoulders. His hands came off her in the next moment as if he had grabbed a beehive. Quickly he rolled up her dress sleeves, hiked up her skirt, and turned her head to look behind her ears and at the nape of her neck. He put his hand to his mouth as if thinking, and then quickly took it away and began rubbing his hands together, as if he wanted to wash them.

"No," he muttered. "*No.*"

He looked at Abram and Daniel. "Come out of there," he said.

Daniel started to ask a question, and his father hushed him with a look so violent it made Abram feel guilty. Mr. Leach had the boys stand in the aisle on either side of him, the three together screening off the bunk from view.

Mr. Leach started whispering to them, looking neither right nor left. "Your mother . . . Mrs. Leach . . . is terrible sick, lads. It's the pox. The smallpox. Others are likely to get it. They already have, probably. But I do not want Mother and Ellen cast away, and they might be, you understand, if anybody knows about this. We'll say she was having nightmares, and we'll get them on their feet, if we can. If we can hide their state 'fore the blisters come, they'll be safe. Once the pox are on them, there'll be no advantage in tossing them to the waves. So keep quiet about it now and help me keep them quiet."

———

Mrs. Leach and her daughter never rose from their bed. Delirious with fever, arching their backs as if their spines would bend double, the two thrashed about and continued to call on God.

Others knew within the first day, but no one moved against the sick ones.

Despite their crowded berths, the other immigrants found a way to segregate the family into a small, cleared space. Mr. Leach, Daniel, and Abram were not allowed to go through the crowd up to the deck. They were totally isolated by the family's disease. Until, that is, others came down with it. The forecastle became a bedlam, with half of the immigrants succumbing to the plague.

Abram watched the blisters grow in uniform crops on Mrs. Leach and her daughter, first on their arms, then their legs, their faces, and was left to imagine where else. Each sore grew to about the size of a ha'penny. They were concave, with hard, round edges. These crusted up first, and then the whole blister hardened over and became a runny, raisin-colored scab.

Mr. Leach kept watch beside his wife and child. He talked in a low voice, trying to comfort them. His own agitation showed, though, as he began to confuse his speaking to them with his praying. In the same low voice with which he tried to comfort them, Abram heard him pray, "Please, dear suffering Lord, by thy wounds, and in remembrance of thy bloody drops of sweat in Gethsemane, take them or leave them to me, but do this thing quickly."

The little girl, Ellen, died first. Her father picked her dead body up in his arms, her long, golden hair trailing down to touch the floor. He had to hand his own daughter to the crewman who would throw her into the sea.

One night, soon after, when Mrs. Leach's breath became raspy and then choking, Mr. Leach drew Daniel and Abram close by the bedside. "You boys are going to live through this," he said. "You're strong. Strong young lads. But the pox is stronger, if you come down with it on your own. I'll variolate you then, and you'll live through it. You want to live, don't you?" He looked them both in the eye.

Abram felt so distracted and confined by this point that he was willing to try anything that would allow him to go back on deck. He wanted to be released from the double nightmare into which the pox had pulled them all. He did not know what Mr. Leach intended to do, but he volunteered, "Me first."

The man pulled a hand-knife from his pocket, and what he did made Abram sick immediately and for long afterwards. First, he had Abram pull up the sleeve of his shirt, bunching it tight at his shoulder, exposing his upper arm. Then Mr. Leach took up the back of his wife's hand and scraped out one of the pus-filled blisters with a circular motion that built-up the pus on the edge of the blade. He held Abram's arm tight just above the elbow, desperately tight, and then he took the disease-ridden blade and made a three-inch shallow cut in Abram's upper arm. He did this twice more. Abram felt no more than wincing pain from the cuts; but his head buzzed so much with confusion that his whole body felt almost numb.

"If you haven't already," Mr. Leach said, "you'll be getting the pox now. But not too severely. You'll probably live. And once it's left you, it doesn't come again. That's why I haven't been worried for myself."

At that, Mr. Leach raised the sleeve of his own arm, and Abram saw the crater-like pits decorating it.

"The demon does leave its tooth-marks," Mr. Leach said.

Daniel screamed with terror as Mr. Leach performed the same procedure on him.

The fever came upon Abram rapidly, and whether he imagined it in his delirium or heard it, he remembered the sound of Mrs. Leach's body being thrown overboard, the momentary splash, and then the quiet that kept lengthening out and never stopped. In clearer moments, he watched the pox spread over his body and tried to feel, without touching the blisters, as he had been warned, whether they had patterned his face. Sometimes the blisters broke out all at once with the shock of a dozen pinpricks; and he waited anxiously, tossing on his bunk, for the needles to start flying at him.

Abram's case proved mild. He battled the disease off within a week and was up and around by the time Daniel's brush with death came. He listened to the boy's labored breath, which sounded like someone trying to breathe under water, and fought his impulses to scream and run. Eventually Daniel recovered, too, awaking out of his sleep one day to say he was hungry.

Thirty-eight of the two hundred seventeen immigrants died in the epidemic, as well as three crew members, the man who had come down to collect little Ellen's body among them.

Once the epidemic started, the captain confined its victims to their quarters. Abram spent two and a half weeks shut up in the wooden-ringed hell. He started picking the scabs off as soon as his fears of the disease spreading abated, exposing crinkled circles of white, unpigmented skin. The disease marked his upper arms and thighs, leaving a moon-cratered map there, but spared his face.

He awoke early one morning, before dawn, as he knew by the sleepiness of the immigrants waiting in the aisle. Their heads nodded, then jerked away, warding off sleep until their shift in the bunks. The amber light of the lamps shone more dimly as the wicks guttered. Mr. Leach slept with Abram and Daniel now, and he lay at his son's side, his mouth open, not snoring, but humming mournfully with each breath, his dreams a requiem for the dead.

Abram decided he needed to escape. He hoped the crew knew little of the epidemic's victims and that his unmarked face would let him pass. His fellow immigrants might be more wary of him, so he walked down the aisle through them, his head ducked down, his hands in his pockets, and then pulled hard and fast at the rope bannister that led up through the hatch.

The cold of the still-dark morning on deck felt good, and the air incredibly light compared with the stew he'd had to breathe for so long below. Never had he been so glad just to breathe. The seas were running fast, although the stars were out, and the wind steady and brisk without the buffeting that came with a storm. The moon shone on the waters as it set, casting a road of light slightly starboard of their course. Two of the crew, huddled together under the foremast, looked up at him as he came on deck. Their eyes registered his presence and then closed on their own thoughts again.

He was up into the rigging before anyone else noticed, and he climbed into the crow's nest with a feeling of having come home. He realized, as he looked out over the moonlit waters, the fast seas, that he was going to live. He had never considered dying, exactly, and yet that thought had been as much in his blood as the pox. A rush of happiness and relief streamed through him as the wind streamed past his face, blowing back his lengthening dark hair, and a restfulness came upon him that he had not known for many days. Eventually, he sat down in the basket-shaped nest, and the swinging of the ship rocked him to sleep, although he had promised himself, sternly, that he would only rest.

The captain's raging voice woke him at mid-morning, the tirade carrying up to him as clearly as the watch bell.

"Look to your own liver, Mr. Vandenburg! The crew does not like dog watches? Be done with that. Be done or I'll let you watch the seas from a fishy angle. You'll no more be conspiring with these dogs. Jack likes Captain Jack well enough when the mate's not lapping up their piffle. Let the dogs go back to their vomit and you to your proper business, Mr. Vandenburg."

The captain and his first mate stood on the quarterdeck by the stairway to the poop. The captain kept threatening his stout first mate, his face too close to the taller man's, his voice growing more terrible, feeding on itself.

"If you are thinking it's unseemly for the captain to be disputing with his mate on deck, so it is. So it is. But a mate who finds it fitting to conspire with Jack fits himself for a lashing at sea, the noose at home, and a cramped, wooden room, with plenty of time to dispute with the worms. Do we agree on this, then, Mr. Vandenburg?

"Disputes aboard ship are a scandal and a pestilence. This ship has been subject to one, and it shall not be to the other, sir. Or I shall be judgment and wrath together. A scourge like unto God's own hand. For I am the Lord your God on this ship, Mr. Vandenburg. No one says me nay, here, not even the wind in our teeth. I relish it more than any man alive and bless its vengeance."

Abram thought the captain must be finished, but his anger renewed itself.

"Consider your last end, Mr. Vandenburg, and know that I hold it in my hand. I am the beginning and end of things for you, and if you forget this, pray that your end will come quickly. A thief in the night and a burning sun in the forenoon am I. You shall remember this. You shall not forget it."

Abram grew even more astonished as the speech kept wearing on. Each time he thought it ended, its violence provoked the captain to further excesses.

"Tell me what you have learned, then. *Tell me!*" The captain grabbed the bigger man's throat in his hand. He kept shouting at the first mate to explain himself, to justify his action, and at the same time held him in a grip so fierce the man could not breathe, much less speak. Even from the crow's nest's great height, Abram could see the mate's face purpling.

"You have not been with me long, and you shall not be with me longer unless you abide by my will. For my will moves this ship. Not the waves, not the wind. My will. It sets the sails, turns the helm, and keeps our course."

Here the mate collapsed at the captain's feet. The captain did not release his hold, but bent over the man, choking him still. Caught in the grip of a servitude as awful as the one at his neck, the mate kept looking at the captain and trying to heed his words even as the captain choked the life out of him.

"You go on your knees to me. You have it in mind to repent? There is no repentance on this ship, Mr. Vandenburg. There is no mercy. There is the will to live, which is my will and nothing else. That's the only salvation on this ship." With that, the captain threw the man away from him so that he tumbled backward and his head smacked against the binnacle.

The thump sent a tingling wave down Abram's spine that reminded him of that day in the shed with his father. "No!" Abram cried, not at the captain exactly, or the scene below him, but at the shiver itself and the memory of what it had cost him.

His cry attracted the captain's attention, though. "Fore mast," the captain called. "Who's that in the nest? Go above and escort the devil down here."

Abram saw the men go to the rigging, and decided in an instant that his life depended on obeying the captain's will before the captain could express it further. He did what few boys in his situation would have done, moving toward this dragon of a captain rather than away from him. He met the men at the lowest crossbeam, the yards of the foresail, and their transfixed looks, wild-eyed, made him feel he should be even more frightened than he was.

Down on the quarterdeck, Abram walked over to the captain as if to his death.

"Who do you be?" the captain asked.

Abram had exhausted his courage and could not speak.

The captain looked at him with an impatience that was still debating whether to turn nasty.

"He belongs to you," the first mate croaked out.

The captain turned to him.

"You bought up his indentures off that crimp in Larne," the first mate said, his voice steadying but hesitant and light. "He should make you considerable profit."

The captain looked at Abram, pushing out his broad lips with their curled-out edges. He wore a blue swallow-tailed coat, a pearly white vest, and gray leggings. Each garment looked as weathered as a tired old sail. Thinning brown hair arched to the side over his head, and gray patched his sideburns. He had devouring eyes. Eyes that held you and drew you into them, giving the impression of a man who only trusted that he knew a thing when he could consume it, in one fashion or another. He even took his breath with a greedy appetite. He bent over slightly when he addressed Abram and stared straight into his face.

"You climbed up into the nest," the captain said.

Abram could not tell from his tone whether this was a question, an indictment, or a simple statement of fact.

"You climbed up there on your own," he repeated. "Do you want to go to sea?" The captain shifted his eyes around at his men, exposing a line of gray teeth.

The crew grinned, wanting to be in on the joke, wanting to be past the incident with the mate.

"You must want to go to sea," he pressed.

"I like riding up there, sir," Abram said. "I like seeing what's before us."

The captain stood back up to his full height. "The boy likes the 'vantage of the nest," he announced to those on deck. He turned his attention back to Abram, his devouring eyes intent in a way the boy did not understand. "Tell me, then. How will you feel about it when ice sheathes the rigging and a night on the yards is like camping in a tree of fire?"

Abram could not be sure how he had come to this bargaining over a life at sea. Yet even with the captain's cruelty fresh in his mind, the fear of it in his stomach, he felt drawn to the idea. "I like seeing before me," Abram said. "I mean to make a fortune for my family."

The captain threw his head back. "The boy means to bargain!" he shouted. He waved his fists in the air, almost as if he were shadowboxing with the Almighty. "The boy means to bargain with me!" He looked back down and grabbed Abram by the shoulders. His eyes shone in a way that both excited Abram and made him suspicious. "You are as reckless as Captain Jack himself. By the devil's tail, I own you, boy. You can't be bargaining with your master."

But something in Captain Jack's eyes encouraged him to do just that. "I want a life that will allow me to make my way. You would be better to have your profit off me on the mainland than keep me for a poor servant. It is not in my nature to serve."

Captain Jack whirled round to his first mate, looked to his men, and smiled as if he were about to eat Christmas dinner.

"It's not in your nature to serve? It's not in anyone's nature, my lad. But those of us who can, make those of those who can't instruments of our will. You see that?" Captain Jack bent down to him and said very low, his voice becoming whispery. "I own you, boy. I can do with you what—" and here he exhaled through the last two words—"I *l-i-k-e*."

At that, he threw back his head and laughed, a laugh that seemed the male counterpart of Gillian's banshee wail. Then he clapped his arm around Abram's shoulder and put a hand to the side of his face, stroking it with his rough fingertips. "My boy, my boy," he said, muttering low.

He stepped back abruptly and brought himself to attention. "You don't know my full name, do you?" he asked. He paused for a moment, as if debating whether to give away the information. "And I don't know yours. But I own you, don't I?" He laughed that wild laugh again, but cut it off suddenly, so that the effect was like someone smashing a rum bottle on a table. "Captain Jack Hawks," he said.

"Abram White."

"Abram White?"

"Abram White, sir."

"Who means to make his fortune." Captain Jack's look settled, became almost fatherly. "As to that, we shall see. For now you are my cabin boy and take watches that won't blow you to the devil. You'll go above like a true Jack 'fore we land."

The captain put his arm around Abram again and urged him up

the stairs to the poop, leading him back to his cabin. The first mate looked at the boy as if he were marching off to the gallows, but Abram felt chosen in a way that made him think he might fare better with Captain Jack Hawks.

CHAPTER 6

Captain Jack

A bram took to life at sea, although his duties could be tedious and his master's nature, as he had seen in their first encounter, unpredictable and cruel. He was immediately put to work scrubbing the decks, assisting the cook, and keeping watches in mild weather. When the weather confined him to quarters, on "scrubbing in days," he picked oakum—making caulking material for the ship's seams out of old lines.

Captain Jack added his own personal services to the boy's other duties. He required Abram to sleep beside his bed, which seemed a luxury at first—a berth in the captain's private cabin with leather upholstered chairs and a windowed view astern. One troubling night, however, the boy came to understand why the captain wanted him there.

Awakened from a deep sleep in the dead hours, Abram saw Captain Jack sitting straight up in bed, ranting at him. "Look there! He's . . . his footsteps. Drain this. Drink . . . Put them to death . . . to death

. . . they may not tempt . . . Skewer the swine!"

When Abram's head cleared, he realized that the captain, despite his screaming, remained asleep, or caught in some ghostly realm between waking and sleeping. His spewing flecked his lips with spittle.

"Strike!" he cried. "By's blood! Healed by his . . . Striped . . . His eyes . . . Those wolf's eyes. Cut them . . . like the rake of a bear. The cat-o'. His steps. His steps. He's . . . the cat-o'. He's . . . for the wicked, my wicked . . ." He scrambled to stand, as if he would charge up on deck in his nightshirt.

Quickly, Abram put his hands to the man's barrel chest and pushed him back down. The captain rolled about fitfully on his bed, taking heaving breaths, and struggled as if trying to twist free from tightly wrapped bonds.

For all the violence of the man's words and writhing, he kept to his bed. His cursing slowed, until, at the last oath, his hand shot straight up, tipped by an accusing index finger. His arm remained in the quiet air for several moments, a comically stiff reminder of the murderous passion that had seized him.

Abram had been terrified in the beginning. In the fit's snoring aftermath, though, as he watched over his defenseless captain, it seemed an embarrassing secret they now shared.

Despite Captain Jack's tormented and tormenting nature, his bouts with nightmares, he could be charming. The same energy that drove his hand into a man's throat, and set him howling in the dead of night, also lifted his better spirits to Himalayan heights of good humor and grace. He would sit in his cabin with Abram and tell stories of his adventures. The time his ship had been boarded off the coast of Madagascar by a privateer whose captain turned out to be a former shipmate and gave him a holiday among the native girls of Kanaloa. The time he had set an Atlantic crossing record. All the way back to his own escape to the sea from a school ruled over by his minister-uncle in the south of England, near Brighton.

He had a way of putting one arm around Abram and the other to his chest, as if he meant, at once, to comfort the boy and steady his resolve. He would even stroke the curly hair lengthening down Abram's neck as he talked with him, which made the boy both squeamish and nostalgic for his mother's touch. When the captain spoke to Abram, his eyes said that he knew his cabin boy, understood him better than anyone. They shared, his look said, a secret knowledge and native understanding not given to others.

He seemed to pity the boy's youth, allowing him times of sheer play, encouraging Abram's habit of stealing extra helpings of molasses duff from the cook—a running joke that even the mush-faced cook, a half-crippled man with tufts of hair in his ears, came to enjoy.

On that first voyage, though, Abram aroused Captain Jack's ire when he caught the boy saying his nightly prayers. He was on his knees, facing the captain's bed, his forehead pressing into the cool wooden frame, when a numbing blow lifted into his tailbone, flattening his nose against the bed with the force of a counter punch. Another kick came immediately against the ribs in his back, just above his kidney. He lost his breath. The attack had come against him so suddenly that he hardly knew how to roll out of the way.

"You'll not be praying to our Lord of Fond Wishes in this privy chamber!" Captain Jack shouted. "You'll not be squealing like a wee pig to the Holy Butcher in here!"

Abram looked up at the glowering man.

"You do your praying up in the rigging if you want to, up where the angels take care of you. They do, don't they? Or what's the good of these nightly orisons?"

Abram's anger quickened his thinking. "So the devil said to the Lord," he shot back.

The captain looked as if he would kick him again. "I am the devil!" he shouted. "I'll be the devil to you, Saint Abram, if I catch you serving up your troubles to the Great Silence. You cannot serve God and . . . " Then he did kick Abram, looping his boot around the boy's hindquarter and smacking his buttock, the point of his toe bruising Abram's tailbone.

Abram remained where he was. Smarting from the blows and feeling belligerent himself, he did not quit his place.

Captain Jack fired the hatch back as he left, rattling its wooden blinds, sending a swirl of air past Abram's head.

The boy, once he had steadied himself, remembered the place where he had left off in his prayers: just at the point before the Lord's Prayer where he made his own petitions. He always asked God to bless his family. He remembered again, and more poignantly, why he had come to this pass: to save them. He wondered whether the hunger had taken another member of his family—his smallest brother, Zack, or Dorsey, or his mother. He had not come to serve the devil. He remembered the biblical Joseph, his years of tarrying in prison. He remembered Daniel in the lion's den. "O

- 81 -

Lord," he prayed, "preserve my mother and father, my sister, my brothers. Grant me time."

———

Soon after this incident, on a fair day, when they were sailing before the wind, the light diamond-sharp and the fast seas dazzling, Captain Jack ordered Abram aloft into the crow's nest. "Keep your eye thirty degrees to the northeast," he ordered.

From watching the captain work his navigational charts, Abram knew they were close to land. He had the feel of the hemp lines in his hands before he moved from the deck, he was so eager. He looked back at Captain Jack, though, and the appreciative nod in the man's gaze made Abram think he detected an apology, or at least the wish to improve the mood between them. He would be the first to see land on his first voyage.

He climbed aloft. He felt like shouting down to those below him when he reached his singular perch, but he knew such exuberance to be bad form. His release had to await the sighting.

After most of a four-hour watch, he noticed a doubling of the horizon's band, a thickening. This thickening grew into a quicksilver band at the horizon thirty-five degrees to the north. Or he thought it did. He could not be sure, at first, whether this band had not appeared from his eyes' own fatigue. Or whether it might have been produced by a school of sporting whales. The band grew, though, to a mercurial pool. He saw the pool had its own equatorial division, the start of trees on a bank, he guessed, and then he shouted out. "Land! Land 'ho, Captain! Land!"

The crew rushed to the rails, and soon the passengers were coming up on deck as well. Abram noticed people below him he had not seen since his days in their stygian forecastle.

———

The harbor pilot came out to them the next day, and they entered Boston harbor, after so long a voyage, in what seemed moments. Abram said good-bye to Mr. Leach and his son after they stood together and looked back toward the wide sea, the graveyard of Mrs. Leach and her daughter.

The square-faced man wanted assurances that Abram was being treated well by the captain. He offered to bargain for the boy's indentures, although Abram knew the man had no way of buying out his own.

"Captain Jack is another man in his quarters," Abram said, and saw how his light tone carried Mr. Leach toward a hopeful, albeit false, impression.

"We'll be making a home, should you be wanting one," Mr. Leach said. "Contact the agent. I'll get word to him where we'll be."

Abram watched Mr. Leach and his son walk down the gangplank, the boy's head cradled by his father's surrounding arm. He wanted to go with them so badly that he turned on his heel and marched to the captain's cabin, where he imprisoned himself until there could be no hope of finding them on the wharf. They had been at sea for more than three months, and yet, as the moments dragged by, Abram would have put the ship back out beyond the reach of land immediately if it had been within his power. He shut his ears against the shore's voices and resented its appeals. He tried to convince himself that he wanted nothing more than the sea. But, at eleven years of age, still a child, the tears and their humiliation came nonetheless. He would be far into manhood before he let himself understand why.

———

Captain Jack's nightmares, Abram soon learned, out on the sea again, were but a phase of a lunatic cycle. One nightmare followed another, until the captain could no longer sleep at all, either from fear or agitation. His temper grew short; he squinted up at the sun as if he intended to give God himself the evil eye. He would attack his private stores of rum to ease his rest, until his nightly drinking became an ongoing binge, with sips taken from his flask at any provocation.

He could not stop himself until he committed some violence. His seizure of the mate on Abram's first voyage had been such a cure. And, as before, when the cycle ended, Captain Jack rode his high spirits.

He took Abram more and more into his confidence, explaining his reasoning for steering north in bad weather—they could run downwind on the backside of the storm instead of beating their way back on course—when he spoke not a word to his chief mate or any of the crew.

Best of all, Captain Jack gave Abram unlimited access to his library. Large, heavy books in leather bindings lined the captain's cabin walls in ingeniously fitted, glass-enclosed cases with tight wooden cross-hatching that protected the panes in a squall. Most sailors contented themselves with the periodicals and newspapers that passed from ship to ship, bringing months and years-old news. But Captain Jack Hawks, as he explained to Abram, had made what he called a "study." In the course of this mental journey, he had collected enough books to keep a man in touch with his civilization—to put him at its heart—when at its farthest remove. Yet the captain himself had given up reading.

"I'm beyond books now," he would say. "I read the bones of men against the page of the sea. I read the stars' cold fire and steel writing its way through a man's bowels to the only period that counts." Then he would take a breath, and his face would fall. "But what hope those books inspired, lad! What hope . . ." and then his one cheek would hitch up and his eyes swivel over and down toward his cramping jaw, a nervous tic that made him look possessed.

Abram loved to read. He had learned very little more than how to read in the Glenwhirry grammar school, and he'd had no time to indulge this pleasure on the farm. The captain, not realizing his generosity, told Abram that as long as he did not neglect any of his duties, he could spend his time reading. So, when Abram was not running messages to the first officer or the helmsman or the quartermaster, not serving the meals, cleaning the captain's silver, dusting his shelves or sweeping his floor, when he was not on his sleeping watch but only at the ready, he read.

He read as he ate in his early adolescence—he could never get his fill. He grew some six inches in the next two years, and he read enough to leap up intellectually from a grammar school student to a shockingly well-educated man—although, like all autodidacts, his education suffered from spottiness.

He read books on astronomy and mathematics by Pythagoras and Aristotle and Galileo, and these came alive for him as he learned to navigate. He worked at the poems of Homer and Virgil and Ovid, and found they stayed in his memory. He did not care for the historians—history resisted him. He started works by Thucydides and Plutarch and the Venerable Bede, but they seemed flat compared to the poets. He felt lifted up by the philosophical and theological writings of Plato and Boethius, Augustine, John Foxe and Richard Hooker; he went back again and again to the literary works of Hesiod and Gower and Shakespeare and Spenser; and he discovered a curious new object, called the novel, about a shipwrecked sailor named Robinson Crusoe. He put in time working at grammars for

Latin and Greek and French, as well as manuals on seamanship and navigation.

Abram would sit with the mathematical and engineering volumes, drawing with a piece of chalk on a slate, like a schoolboy doing his homework, except that he never feared being graded. He simply puzzled things out for the sake of the thing he was puzzling. Had he fully savored the pleasure of knowing the book's contents? This question served as his only standard.

From the beginning, Captain Jack noticed the extravagant use Abram was making of his library. He watched the boy, with compass and ruler, plotting imaginary courses. Within a month on their first voyage, the captain tried him to see if he could take their position and extrapolate their progress on the ship's chart. Not only was Abram able to do this, but he showed the captain, soon after the first lesson, that his own calculations were a little in error, saving them from adding unnecessary days to their voyage.

After that incident, Captain Jack gave Abram a silver key to the desk in his cabin where he kept the ship's maps and charts. Abram would lay out one of the great rolls of parchment on the desk's wood and ivory inlaid surface and plot imaginary courses, reckoning the number of days from Nova Scotia to Abu Addis. He continued to keep his calculations on his black slate and he hoped, as he wiped his white marks off at day's end, that someday he would command more than his dreams.

The boy was already serving a more important end than he knew, since the black moods into which Captain Jack fell affected the captain's judgment severely at times, and the captain's ships, once Abram began doing their navigational charts, kept better time.

The captain understood how valuable the lad was proving much better than Abram himself, of course. Abram became the man's pet, almost his adopted son.

———

His third voyage, in his thirteenth year, to the northern French coast at Le Havre, put Abram close enough to home to send his savings to his family, which still included some of the spoils of his war with Billy the Tinker and most of his pawnbroking. He told them in his letter that he would always be their son—and their rescuer, he implied—if they would let him.

A letter from his mother arrived for him in New York six months later. Standing in the stylish brick customshouse, under a tall,

Christmas tree-shaped chandelier, he opened the vellum envelope. "*Mon cher*," the letter began, and he knew the rest would gratify his hopes. His mother was unusually candid. She addressed everything on his mind, avoiding nothing.

"You have shown your maman a more excellent way, taking her pewter idol and giving her a life more full, especially in God. I know you have acted out of love. As you say in your very beautiful letter, you did not run away, you ran ahead. So, our hearts follow after you. We long to see you again and know we will. You are here with us in the life your cadeaux are making possible. You are here in your maman's heart, from which you have never departed. No, not, mon fil, for a moment."

He learned from the letter that the money he had sent his family had enabled them to put in a flax crop and feed themselves, and he knew, from his newly acquired knowledge of trade, that the linen markets were improving. They would be realizing their profits on his mother's linen in the same season that brought this letter to hand. They would be all right now, he knew. They would live.

His father signed the letter as well, and, while he wrote nothing else, he did pen in "II Timothy 1:3–4, 14." Back in the captain's cabin, Abram looked up the verses:

"I thank God, whom I serve from my forefathers with pure conscience, that without ceasing I have remembrance of thee in my prayers night and day: Greatly desiring to see thee, being mindful of thy tears, that I may be filled with joy.

"That good thing which was committed unto thee keep by the Holy Ghost which dwelleth in us."

Each time he read it, the letter made him so happy and emotional he could hardly swallow, and when he read the verses and traced his father's hand, tears stung his eyes. He still carried the burden of what had passed between them, and he wanted to resign its weight, to give it back to what he still felt must be his father's greater strength.

His mother's first letter accepted him as the family's champion, and the years would confirm this role more and more. He sent them money each time he received his wages, and each time he wondered whether he would ever fulfill his ultimate pledge of taking them to the New World. After all, was he in the New World?

———

Abram stayed with Captain Jack because the man still owned his services. After their first voyage, the captain had extended the terms of Abram's indentures to a decade, accusing him of insubordinate behavior—climbing up into the crow's nest. The captain had witnesses, and Abram had not been at the proceedings to plead his case. Captain Jack informed him of the matter when he "caught him" stealing the molasses duff he had previously encouraged him to steal.

Abram grew into a man at sea as a virtual slave, but one treated, with a few violent exceptions, as an adopted son. He entered the life of a merchant seaman by the humblest route imaginable, by the "hawse holes," as seamen said in that time; but he had the opportunities of a gentleman who came in by the "cabin windows." At the same time, as an indentured servant, he had less personal freedom than the forward-most hand. This isolated him. The crewmen respected this lad who followed his crow's nest climbing with exhibitions of courage and even daring on every occasion. They saw the captain's regard for the boy, though, and few made any attempt to include Abram in their life off ship.

The attentions the captain paid him and the higher wages that irascible man arranged for his cabin boy-carpenter-cook-topman-boatswain mate-second-mate-first mate made Abram sensible of his advantages. So Captain Jack held sway over him, in several senses. Yet with that first kick against his tailbone, when the captain caught him at his prayers, his owner had lost any hope of winning Abram's heart.

Abram began praying as if prayer were a competition. He remembered, re-creating patchy sections with the patience of a master navigator, everything he had been taught in the Glenwhirry Presbyterian church, even making a practice of reciting The Shorter Form of the Westminster Catechism every day. While keeping his watches, he often meditated on the psalms, singing them to himself in the plainsong settings he knew so well.

This had an effect that he never would have anticipated: his prayers brought with them not only comfort but good judgment and, more than that, an ability to live alone, within himself, in the midst of his present circumstances, in peace. Without this, he would never have survived such isolation. He would have, at least, surrendered his ideals and taken up the drinking and libertine ways of his mates.

Abram was beginning to know and map out reaches of spiritual experience as far-flung as his travels. The shouting of the sea had told him much, but little in comparison to the silence in which he now lived.

CHAPTER 7

Backing Into Our Chains

Ten years after their first voyage, Captain Jack and Abram had circumnavigated the globe half a dozen times, having traded everything from ale to zinc, in every port of call known to civilized man or barbarian. They never did ship many passengers again; the smallpox epidemic aboard *The Huntington* had put Captain Jack off that enterprise, it seemed.

Abram had grown into a thin, athletic figure of a man, his lines as sharp and taut as crisp sails. His dark hair curled thickly past his shoulders, tied off into a tail at his neck. His piercing blue eyes had become, if anything, sharper.

Captain Jack's own lines had belled out everywhere, in such a way that he seemed to be sinking into his casklike stomach; jowls drew his long, gum-revealing lips down toward a double chin; and at rest, easing back in his chair, he had acquired a froggy contentment, with his devouring eyes fixed and goggling. Only a few wisps of his brown hair still blew over his pate, and his peninsular sideburns had turned as white as cotton bunting. Despite being costumed by age, he acted with an undying and even youthful will. On his feet, he displayed his old bantam quickness, although when he flew at one of his men now, he could not stop himself, either physically or emotionally; he had lost his ability to feint.

Abram now served as first mate, commanding half the watches and relaying the captain's wishes for the other half. He still took care of his master's private needs, although mostly through cooks and cabin boys. The captain's nightmares had grown worse, and Abram stayed near enough to subdue the old man personally when necessary. Abram even arranged for the violent episodes that brought an end to the captain's black moods. Sometimes it was enough to get him up in a threatening wind and have him command the ship from the deck. Sometimes Abram steered Captain Jack in the direction of traders who had been trying to diddle them. At other times, of course, the captain's bloody-mindedness took its own satisfactions, and the cat-o'-nine-tails stripped many a sailor's back unjustly, and often soured the ship's crew.

After their decade of travels together, in Abram's twenty-first year, Captain Jack and Abram were on the last leg of the famous triangular West Indies trade route. Their new ship, *The Mercy*, carried a cargo of rum, sugar, and the spices of the Caribbean, cinnamon, nutmeg, and chicory, as she made her way home to New York. Then, in the Bermuda latitude, *The Mercy* ran into a tropical storm.

Theirs had already been a disastrous voyage, with two crewmen lost—one to a storm off the North African coast that washed him off the bowsprit and one to a mysterious fever. Captain Jack had driven them through more weather than Abram had ever seen in one voyage, without compensating for their hardships through extra leave. The storms had taken away nearly all their Sundays, the sailors' only day off, which they devoted to doing their laundry and sewing, bathing when possible, smoking a pipe or two, and trading stories. This endless cycle of work actually seemed to improve the captain's mood; he had no need for a bout of violence, since the crew's travails kept hoisting his spirits.

The captain refused to visit any extra ports, even when their supplies ran so low that three of the nine crewmen before the mast suffered too much from scurvy to go aloft. No one bothered any more about the rings of blood their gums left with each bite of bread.

So when the hurricane struck, near the longed-for end of the voyage, the crew met its tearing winds with their determination already shredded. They had little left other than survival instinct.

From his station on deck Abram saw the storm coming and knew that the men, however much they hated Captain Jack, needed the old man's spirit to rally them. The captain's own fearlessness, his words of rebellion against the onslaught and the devil—or God—as its author, would serve to spur the crew on and give them hope. Otherwise, they might not survive.

Abram went down the hatchway and into the captain's book-lined cabin, where he found the aging man entering notes furiously in his journal, as though he would have his quill scratch the words through, not merely into, the paper. Even here in *The Mercy's* stern, the ship was already bucking so much that Abram had to hold on to the bedpost.

"Captain," Abram said. It was one of those times when—as Abram could tell from the man's studied inattention—the thing that must be said might turn into a pretext for deviltry.

"Mr. White," the captain said, and kept scribbling.

"We are in for a good blow. I'll need both watches to fall out, and the weather will keep them at it. You might speak to them."

"I may speak to them whenever I please, and not speak whenever it displeases me," the captain said, letting a little stuffy instruction into his voice, a warning.

Abram's experience led him to jump to his conclusion. "They may not hold up," he said.

The captain, whose writing desk set him in profile to the hatchway, looked to the side across his writing, directly at Abram. His eyes had grown wide, and he was still and composed in a way that held back all his power. The driving waves thundered against the ship, but the man's forcefulness almost drove away their threat.

"The hands are frightened, then?" he asked, and his eyes grew wider, his look more forthright.

"They were home in their minds," Abram said. "This comes as a cruelty."

The captain smiled. "They're terrified?"

Abram did not answer.

"Do you think they will throw themselves into the sea? Crave death? Run to the hag's bosom and fall into her rattling arms?"

Abram turned to go back on deck.

"Mr. White!" the captain called. "Mr. White!"

Abram turned back.

"They are almost dead already, ain't that so? Still, they will do their duty and carry me and this sugar and rum home to New York." The captain paused, and his next words came out disgruntled and what followed officious. "They will not die. That would be most discourteous." With that, he went back to his writing.

Abram knew Captain Jack was aware of his presence and that he would start his harangue again if he did not immediately exit. He risked another torturing speech, though, thinking he still might persuade the man. "I might say a word to them," Abram said.

Captain Jack turned abruptly in his chair, started to rise, but then turned the chair around, foursquare to Abram, and crossed his leg, a sovereign on a pitching throne. "What would you tell them, Mr. White? Would you tell them God will save them if they'd only believe? Will you stretch out your hand and utter, 'Peace, be still'?"

"Your blasphemy is your own," Abram said.

"The fear in their hearts is your God, Abram. You worship the thing that makes this worthy crew want to bolt up their shriveled lights and lungs. Speak to them if you like. Your encouragement will blow away as fast as your daily prayers."

Abram put his hand to the door's wooden latch.

"Come down in two bells for further orders," the captain said.

———

When Abram stepped back on deck, six bells had just been rung. It was three o'clock in the afternoon, yet the clouded sky held a baneful yellow tint, as if the whole world had grown bilious. The seas had begun washing over the forward deck. The waves struck the bow with a booming sound like a battering ram against a fortress door. The wind ripped past Abram's head, and he shaded his face and eyes from the buckshot wind and spray.

"All hands, reef topsails, ahoy!" Abram called, summoning the second watch to assist the first.

As soon as the men climbed aloft to reef the sails, a sound like thunder splitting the sky directed all hands' attention to the jib. It had blown to ribbons.

"Foremast, stow the jib, strike the bolt!" Abram commanded.

A rent opened next in the mainsail, which soon ripped from head to foot. "Lay up on that main yard and furl the sail before it blows to tatters!" Abram shouted.

The men gathered up the remains of the sail, their hands working like fish hooks to stay aloft. Then the fore topsail, which had already been double-reefed, cutting its exposed surface by half, split in two athwartship along the reef line.

"Down yard, haul out reef-tackles, lay out upon the yard for reefing," Abram commanded. The men did as ordered, resetting the sail close-reefed so that about a quarter of its full surface still took the wind. They needed some sail to drive and steady *The Mercy* through the heavy seas.

Then Abram heard an awful creak and swinging and looked up to see that the main royal had blown loose from its gaskets, flapping away from the quartering wind, causing the mast to whip about like a riding crop. Either the mast would soon splinter or the vessel capsize, rolling over at the top of a crest and corkscrewing its way to Davy Jones. The royal had to be brought in, or at least cut adrift.

Abram looked at the light hands of the starboard watch, the ones capable of climbing that high. They avoided his eyes, dreading the order to go aloft.

Abram told the man at the wheel, "Ease her back if she starts to yaw. Hold her in the road."

Abram himself then jumped aloft, climbing toward the highest point on the ship, the tip of the main mast where the royal waved in the wind like a flag of surrender. The ship rolled and pitched as he made his way; the mast whipped back and forth. The wind was blowing like scissors and thumbscrews. Every time the seas washed over the deck, Abram felt the shuddering vibrations in the mast.

Finally he reached the top yard. Using one of the double topsail ties as a lifeline, he tied it around his waist. He felt more secure then, although any moment the wind might take the entire mast—and him with it—into the sea. With his knife, he cut through the ties still holding the royal to its earrings, working out to leeward along the yard.

The careening sensation of a fall took over, and he had to wait until he awoke from the dizziness—that was the way it felt—to find himself still on the yard.

Then he did fall, or the wind simply brushed him off the yard end. The lifeline held him, but he was swinging to and fro, twisting round at the same time, and he only put his hands out in time to feel the blow of the mast against his elbow before his head slammed into it. Stunned and choking on the blood pouring from his mouth, he realized his jaw had been broken.

He caught hold of the mast and edged back out along the yard to finish the cutting away. The knife went through the last tie, and the sail was gone. He saw it winging in the air, diving toward the waters like a wounded stork.

He prepared to send the yard down—a long and difficult job. He had to hold on for minutes together against the ferocity of the wind that seemed to blow harder now, as if angered that he had accomplished half his purpose. The ship yawed more and more as it ploughed the mountainous waves, and the mast's circular pitching started to sicken him. He felt the nausea he had known only once before, when he awoke in the forecastle on his maiden voyage. He finished unbracing the yard, signaling for it to be lowered away.

As he started his descent, the men waved their arms and out-cheered the storm's thunder. Several reached up and lowered him the last length to the deck in their arms. Little thanks was given aboard ship and none ever asked. But The Mercy's crew owed Abram their lives.

On deck, Abram quickly got his bearings once again and went back to his station by the helmsman. His jaw had broken inward, a hairline fracture straight under his eye; the shooting pain racked his face, but he could still shout orders as the crew completed preparations to ride out the storm. He sent everyone aloft again to make the booms fast.

The storm was now at its height, blowing even harder than when Abram was aloft. One disaster after another struck the ship's gear. First, the mizzen topsail, already close-reefed, split from head to foot in its bunting. The fore topsail went next, in one rent, from clew to earring. One of the chain bobstays parted. The spritsail yard sprung in the slings. The martingale slued off to leeward. One of the main topgallant shrouds parted. And to crown it all, the anchor on the lee bow had worked loose and was thumping against the side of the ship.

Abram finally ordered all the sails furled, except for the spanker and the close-reefed main topsail. At the end, the spanker had to come down as well.

He issued orders as fast as he could, and still the crew was hard-pressed to put one thing to rights before the next demanded their attention. They took courage, though, from the first mate's bravery, and sprang to their tasks.

Abram shouted his encouragement as they worked, although the men could hardly hear even closely shouted orders above the storm.

The crew had just been sent down to dinner, when the main topsail itself showed signs of giving way. Abram ordered everyone back on deck to set the fore and main storm sails. They had just completed this when the main topsail shredded. The starboard watch stowed the remains and went below for its dinner, the larboard to follow.

The Mercy, under two storm sails, rode the hurricane out through that night and for the next eight days. The wind and the capsizing seas seemed to feed on themselves, like the captain's anger. Each man found himself questioning his sanity, locked in the solitary confinement of his own fear.

Through all this, Captain Jack remained in his cabin, communicating with the crew only through Abram and his second mate, Mr. Nordstrom. Captain Jack relished the situation, especially Nordstrom's growing unease, which he questioned Abram about daily.

Roger Nordstrom, who had worked his way up from a common seaman, was a towering fellow, more than six and a half feet, with clear eyes, friendly, boyish features, and a thatch of blond hair that often fell from its side part across his forehead. The Scandinavian ancestors who gave him the blond hair had also bestowed a brooding nature, and he would sit at his desk in the mates' cabin, across from Abram's bed, looking intently at his book or journal by the light of a small oil lamp.

The storm exacerbated his brooding, and he only broke out of its binding silence with sudden explosions of talk. His arms swung out wide, nearly as wide as the cabin, when he expressed his dismay at their circumstances and the captain's manner of prizing their oppression. "What way will he take after the storm, Abram? You know him. We need to make a port. By my knuckles, we will make port, won't we?"

While Abram's thoughts ran along similar lines, he would only say, "There's no use to your questions, Mr. Nordstrom."

Abram saw that the second mate put his questions to the cook, the carpenter, the steward, the boatswain's mate, and even the head of the larboard watch, a strong, redheaded fellow named Shickley.

Abram knew the captain would learn of this. Captain Jack could decipher the muttering of ship planks.

On the ninth day, while Abram kept his watch, *The Mercy* began to move along more easily. The seas were still high, but the foredeck stayed clear, the bow nosing up and over the highest swells. The sails that could be had already been repaired by the crew. Abram ordered another top mainsail set, ran the spanker on the mizzen mast, and kept the storm sail up on the foremast.

Suddenly a wave washed over the foredeck, the ship torqued sideways, and bobbed up in the next trough without a will to go forward. The next wave stood the ship on its stern and started it going backwards, "backing into its chains." In moments she would go down, even in these diminished seas.

As the next swell came on, the ship turned away and stopped abruptly, like a horse shying at a jump. Abram was catapulted into the air and thrown forward onto his hands and knees. The seas swamped the decks, washing him back to the poop's stairway. If he did not act quickly, they were finished.

He looked to Shickley, stationed by the foremast. He looked to the helmsman, a dough-faced sailor named Lincoln whose agate eyes were stony with fear. The man was gripping the tapered prongs of the wheel as if they were God's thumbs.

Then he looked out over the next few crests that might finish them, and he became aware of a dawning light at the western horizon, a glow that flashed there and struck him as if he had witnessed a great event from a tremendous distance. He heard a voice. How could he hear anyone in the storm? He looked around him, and back at Lincoln, who still stared straight ahead. Then he heard the voice say: "Behold also the ships, which though they be so great, and are driven of fierce winds, yet are they turned about with a very small helm."

Instantly, he knew what was wrong. The wheel-rope had parted. He should have known once the ship started to shy.

Abram put on a relieving tackle to windward and held the tiller up until Shickley and the helmsman could rove a new rope. The entire crew—Nordstrom, all the hands, even the cook, steward, and the other servants—appeared on deck. They had felt the ship backing into her chains, an experience akin to feeling the ship run aground, to feeling your own heart stop. Standing quietly on the bucking deck, spray flying at their heads, they watched the repairs being made, knowing that Abram had saved them for a second time.

They were his mute but thankful witnesses.

Even Captain Jack came up from below, shouting, "Look to the tiller." On deck he saw that Abram had already responded to the emergency, and with one accusing glance at the onlookers, he returned to his cabin.

Roger Nordstrom's questions gained force and currency as soon as they sailed out of the storm's shadow. The hurricane had spun them farther and farther east until they were left not too far off the coast of Spain. Prudence suggested they turn east, pick up provisions, make repairs, and then set sail for home once more. When Captain Jack set their course north, northwest, striking out directly for New York, the crew's bitterness produced a whispering silence on the ship.

The atmosphere worsened rapidly as the wind died and the seas flattened. *The Mercy* sat under a blue, pleasant sky, a few wispy clouds overhead, the seas sparkling, if sluggish, and the crew behaving in an agitated manner, yelling at one another about trifles.

Abram wished he would hear that other voice, that peaceful reciter, telling him how to escape this dilemma. The crew was sure to suffer, for unless their bitterness could be dispelled, the captain's violence would come against them. Among the hard things they had met up with—the storm's power, the unceasing demand of their own hunger—they had not encountered anything so strong as Captain Jack's will. The storm was only uncaring, their hunger natural; Captain Jack's will united earthly passion with a supernatural craving. It fed on every resistance an opponent might use to stop it. That was its infernal logic.

Abram thought about the coming second storm, and he thought about the voice and the light he had seen in the sky. Whatever would come, he would survive it. He had a new hope, in fact, that he would accomplish his original purpose of bringing his family to the New World. He still did not know how, of course. Even more astonishing, he began to suspect that God wanted other things of him as well— journeys beyond his childhood quest. Why else show him such mercies? The idea did not necessarily appeal to him, though. In many ways he felt that too much had been required of him already. The quiet voice that had spoken to him proved greater than the hurricane, and those natural forces were beyond his imaginings; if the fear of the Lord was the beginning of wisdom, he was certainly afraid.

————

When Shickley appeared at the mates' cabin door the first Sunday of their new course, Nordstrom pushing him through, Abram feared the worst.

The two men sat down across from Abram on Nordstrom's bunk, Nordstrom half bent over, hunching under the curving wall. Shickley had his pride, and a way of looking straight ahead, his eyes unseeing; he had a trick of placing himself before his superiors, simultaneously keeping their authority distant and his own thoughts concealed, all without giving offense. His close-cropped coppery hair and lightly freckled face gave him a youthful and yet experienced look—every inch a candidate for advancement. He was strong, hard-working, and he generally had good judgment. Abram liked him far more than he did Nordstrom.

"When we get a breath," Nordstrom said, "we ought to turn toward the Azores. The cargo'll not spoil."

Abram tilted his head and shrugged.

"You know we ought to," Nordstrom pressed. "Prudence demands it."

"Whether the captain agrees or not," Shickley said.

Nordstrom was a man to bluff, but not Shickley. If the mutiny had gone far enough for him to speak, it had come too far already.

"Mr. Nordstrom, Mr. Shickley, you are talking sedition. Those are the last such words I will hear. I'll have you in irons for the rest of the voyage if you persist."

Shickley took the force of Abram's words. He lowered his head, expelled a long and exhausted breath.

Nordstrom burst out, "You have been right about the captain, Abram. He feeds on death. How can you be at your prayers and cooperate with a man who means to be the end of us? A man who claims to be the devil himself? What duties do you owe to your God? If you say you love God but love not your neighbor, you are a liar, so the Scriptures say."

Regretting he had ever voiced his thoughts to Nordstrom, Abram let this recitation pass and said with a terrible evenness, "I'd have you in irons now, Nordstrom, if not for Mr. Shickley. He's twice the sailor you are and worthy of something better than your leadership." Abram watched them react to this. Shickley's eyes focused at last on him.

"Tell the hands," Abram said directly to Shickley, "that we live and die with the captain. We have no better option."

Nordstrom opened his arms wide, exploding silently with frustration, and barreled out of the cabin, banging against the walls as he went.

Shickley still sat, taking his own counsel. Abram watched the decision turning in his stomach. It rested uneasy, but it seemed to stay down. He gave a quick look up at his first mate. "You'll pray for a wind, won't you? Surely God favors prudence."

"And those that wait, Mr. Shickley," Abram said as they rose. "And those that wait."

Before he went out, Shickley said, "The men are ready to follow you. You've saved their lives more than once; they'll not go against you. But they would rather you were making the orders yourself."

Abram could not help but take satisfaction from this final speech. What he actually believed, though, was that the men would hold off as long as Shickley's patience held. Only three men on board were capable of taking *The Mercy* anywhere: the captain, Abram, and Shickley. Nordstrom had enough knowledge, but he blustered too much for the men to trust that knowledge. And Shickley, because he had never been counted a gentleman, would doubt his own abilities. He would rightly be slow to trust men who had turned away from legitimate authority, even if they were turning to him, for he had the gift of humility.

––––––––

Two days later a favorable wind did spring up, blowing north, northeast. They put out every bit of canvas they had been able to keep or repair—the royals, the skysails, and the spanker on the mizzen. They looked like a lovely white-feathered bird in full flight. The air freshened, became cooler, and they made their way rapidly, running before the wind. Still, their supplies were nearly exhausted, and if they ran into any trouble, they would have nothing but rainwater for days before they reached land.

Captain Jack's mood blackened as their circumstances improved. He kept his conferences with Abram unusually brief, and he received reports of *The Mercy's* progress with distaste and resentment. He reacted testily to any request, however simple, and he contended with Abram's most casual remark.

"We ought to make 37 degrees longitude tomorrow," Abram would say.

"Ought," the captain would croak. "There's no *ought* at sea, Mr. White. Can we make it? That's your duty, not the world's sufferance, its pleasure, or the collective will of your Master Navigator. If he's up there, he's been doodling with us since the day we began this accursed voyage."

"Will there be anything else?" Abram would ask.

"How *could* there be anything else?" Captain Jack would say in a fighting rage.

They were in for a violent episode, Abram knew, and he guessed that this time it would be directed against someone close to the captain. Nothing less than a rupture of an intimacy would do; he had reached that point in the cycle. Abram feared Nordstrom would suffer before journey's end, and the second mate would at least partially deserve it, even if the captain mistook the real reason. When the three took their meals together, Captain Jack often glared at Nordstrom and mimicked his wolfish table manners. He continued this caricaturing pantomime until the second mate noticed—a technique that maximized Nordstrom's shame.

———

The Sunday following the conspirators' meeting with Abram in his cabin, *The Mercy* was making good progress; the sky had clouded for the last few days, but the wind was still fresh. The men sat on deck, washing themselves with sea water, sewing up the holes in their duck trousers, and trying not to think of how slim rations had become. They smoked a pipe or two to keep down the hunger and make the day pleasant.

The captain skulked in his own quarters even more than usual on Sundays. That day, however, he came up on deck and stood in the middle of the ship by the mainsail. Everyone turned to him.

"Mr. Nordstrom, Hand Shickley," the captain called out, "accompany Mr. White over here."

As the three men converged from different parts of the ship to the mainsail, Captain Jack ordered all hands to step aft and gather on the quarterdeck.

"Mr. Nordstrom, Shickley, seize Mr. White," the captain said, his look daring them to disobey. "Seize him up!"

The two conspirators rocked on their feet, their hands half-gesturing, agitated.

"Seize him up!" the captain shouted.

Abram moved over toward the shrouds, and the two men stripped off his blue coat and white blowzy shirt. They tied his wrists to the shrouds and began to bind his feet, whispering, "The Captain's insane. He's mad."

"Stop!" the captain shouted. "I want his feet free."

The captain then took up one of the extra coiled lines and whipped a length of it through his hands, the rope flying out of its coil like a striking cobra. He went over to Abram and began trussing him up as he might have a prisoner. When irons were unavailable, prisoners at sea were tied around their neck, down along their spine, around their ankles, using double-hitches, slipknots, and Spanish quatros, in a way that made the binding tighter the more they struggled, bending their backs.

The rough, braided rope bit into Abram's skin. He heard the captain's greedy breath, the snorting through his nose. Captain Jack had only looked at him once before the incident began—a look that made Abram feel dead already, as if he were a slaughtered animal. He was being cinched up as if his bones contained only a frustrating strength, not nerve, not blood.

The captain moved to the pilothouse and came back. Abram heard the whiffle of the cat-o'-nine-tails being swung through the air.

"Mr. Nordstrom and Shickley and the busy old women with whom they've been gossiping have been planning on an expedition to the Azores," the captain said. "You have questioned my judgment. Appealed to a higher power. Prudence. Mercy. The Lord Great God in heaven. Jesus himself."

The captain whipped the air.

"I must say you have more religion than any crew I have ever commanded. The more you contemplated mutiny, the more religious you became."

The captain swung the whip in a great circle again.

Wuhvvvuhvuh.

"We stand on *The Mercy*, under this great sky, in the midst of the Atlantic seas, alone, gentlemen. You and I. Alone. I am in command. No one will stop my hand from any action. If the lightning comes, it will only come during a storm. Not today, not now under these porridge skies."

Wuhvvvuhvuh.

"Mr. White is the finest among you. Indeed, he is worth more than your sum. I have treated him, as you have observed, as if we

- 101 -

were of a certain familial relation. I have taught him. I have advanced him. I suppose I have more fellow feeling toward him than any other person."

The captain whipped the deck, cracking the air.

"But make no mistake—he belongs to me. He is, in fact, my servant—my slave. As are you all, or so I regard you, as long as I suffer you on this ship."

The captain's voice suddenly raised back into a shout from his murderously even tone. "I can do with you what I like! I can do with you what I like because it is my good pleasure!

"No one will say me nay. Not Hand Shickley, or Mr. Nordstrom, or even the good Abram White. Not, I hasten to say, the God of the good Abram White."

Abram could not see this, but he imagined the captain looking at the sky and shadowboxing with God as he had done at their first encounter. "O thou most holy far away!" The captain shouted, "See me and strike if you have a will to do it, or I will strike this thy servant until he bleeds the redemption from his heart. Hold my hand or I will flay his flesh until the height of your creation is the clay from which you made us! Great Absconder, O thou Deafness, sign! Speak! Gesture! Most unspeakable Nought!"

With that the whip shrieked through the air and striped Abram's back. His flinch sent an additional bolt of pain up his tensed spine into the base of his head.

He found himself breathing again after the pain. He heard the captain step beside him, and caught a pennant of eye and cheek looking him over. Then he felt the captain step back to striking distance again.

"Are we alone, Abram White? Are we alone? You have heard the blasphemy, and still we are alone. Perhaps if you called. The prayer of a righteous man availeth much. Call then. If you can summon up the Hidden One, I'll dive to hell a happy man!

"Call!" the captain commanded, and struck Abram's back. "Ring his stony ears, Abram." The whip struck again.

Abram could not help his struggling against the pain. The cinch began choking him as he struggled against it.

"Call!" Captain Jack shouted, and struck him again.

At first Abram had been terrorized; now he became angry. He wanted to defend his God from another slaying in the hearts of the crew—and perhaps in his own heart as well.

The captain struck once more, and Abram gave a strangled cry.

He shook his head, until the noose-like cinch choked off his rebellion.

The captain stepped close to him and held the cinch around his neck. Abram could feel the man's knuckles against his skin. "You are great for praying," the captain said. "Why won't you pray now?"

Abram knew that he must not speak; his silence would be his salvation. The helm of which the voice had spoken—that was a figure for a man's tongue. Controlling his tongue would save him. Silence would cause the captain's words to circle round on him and drop away. Abram tried to subdue his rage.

"Shickley, Nordstrom," the captain said, "cut Mr. White's hands down."

For a moment the ship seemed to return to its rocking progress, the men to breathe, the horror to pass. When Abram's hands were loose, though, the captain did not let go his hold on the noose. Drawing even closer to Abram, he kept one hand on the noose's cinch, the other on the rope down his back, and leveraging his hands apart, began choking him even more horribly.

Abram had only been conscious of the pain subsiding in his back for an instant when he found himself fainting. Gouts of black spattered his vision.

"Why won't you pray?" the captain asked, and his voice began to have a sentimental pleading in it. He let up enough on his choking grip to enable Abram to speak if he wished. "Why won't you pray?"

Abram said nothing. He concentrated on taking deep breaths to withstand what would follow.

"One prayer," Captain Jack said. He was so close now that his body pressed into Abram's back. They stepped free of the mainsail and began revolving slowly around the quarterdeck as the captain whispered like a lover into his ear. Abram caught sight of the crew's blanched expressions. "Why won't you pray, Abram? Why won't you?" the captain kept repeating.

"One prayer, Abram," he whispered, his grip starting to tighten again. "One prayer."

Then he tightened the noose so suddenly and fast that Abram knew beyond doubt what dying this way would be like. "I am going to kill you," Captain Jack said. "I have to kill you now if you won't pray. One prayer." His voice suddenly became loud, bellowing. "One prayer. One prayer to me!"

Then he tightened the noose to its killing limit.

Abram spun around and grabbed. He felt the man's Adam's apple in the ball of his right hand. He wanted to crush it and plunge his fingers through into the man's wet throat.

The captain jerked away and screamed for Abram to be seized.

Abram was flung on his back. He looked up to see the startled face and hulking figure of Roger Nordstrom, who looked like a man recovering from a deep, interior shock.

Abram was getting himself up when the captain, his own breathing still raw, pointed toward him and said, "Behold the man and his admirable quiet. But the voice that says, 'I will live' is greater, isn't it?" Captain Jack took a staggering step. "I don't need to kill you. I've done far worse. Haven't I?" He turned away and started to weave back to the hatchway and his cabin. "I've made my bloody point."

CHAPTER 8

The Circle of Nature

Abram was laid up for two days, and then returned to his duties. The welts and stripes opened up as he worked, and his shirt stuck to his weeping back. He could only shuffle forward, his spine sending lightning into his kidneys, and the memory of his humiliation rippled through his grimaces as he instructed the crew. Yet he abided by shipboard protocol that stipulated bed rest only for the dying, and the crew did what it could to ease his situation. Their behavior went beyond what they may have previously considered their best. Except for the second mate, Nordstrom, they loved Abram to a man.

Nordstrom never finished the voyage. When *The Mercy* spied a British Navy frigate off to starboard, the captain ordered that they run after her. Since this presented the chance of additional provisions, the crew fell to with alacrity. No one was ever sure of the exact terms of negotiation, but after Captain Jack emerged from his talk with the frigate's captain, Nordstrom had become one of His Ma-

jesty's seamen, a conscript, and *The Mercy* gained enough fresh water, bread, and hardtack for the remaining days until they made
port. In case they had missed the point about their virtual slavery,
the captain had underlined it: he had sold Nordstrom.

As the second mate shouldered his duffel over the gangway, he
looked at Abram one last time. He wore the same expression Abram
had seen when Nordstrom had thrown him away from the captain—
that hollow-eyed look of stunned regret at his own betraying nature.

Captain Jack, who had resumed his command without com-
ment, did not avoid Abram's eye when he conveyed his orders. He
looked at him steadily, staring through him, in fact, challenging
Abram to bring up the incident.

Abram went on as before; there was nothing else for him to do.

When *The Mercy* reached New York, Captain Jack rushed to report the "failed mutiny" to the governor, who extended Abram's
term of indenture another three years. And still Abram went on.

————

In another four months, back at sea on another trade run,
Abram's rage had reached such an intensity that hatred came off
him in waves, as heat undulates in distorting drafts off a desert floor.
Mocking him, the captain held up his hands to Abram one day as
if warming them before a fire. His pantomime was well understood
by both.

Abram's thoughts ran back to his first meeting with Captain
Jack, when he had watched another first mate being choked within
an inch of his life. Abram had thought he would fare better.

Besides his anger, other emotions bound him up and suffocated
him spiritually as effectively as the Spanish quatros had physically.
He remembered that he should love his enemies. What point did
his protest against the captain have—his Christian principles—if he
could not enact what those principles dictated?

The strangest thing was that he had *loved* Captain Jack. He had
enjoyed his maniacally high spirits, appreciated his special concern
for Abram's education, and vicariously savored the satisfactions the
man took in the sheer exertion of his will. Perhaps Abram was indeed just the same, and the captain had proved his point. When
Abram had these thoughts, he felt the noose tightening and his back
screaming as it bent backward.

He found himself plotting to murder the captain. Idly, at first.
They would land at St. John's in the Caribbean, and he would obtain

nectine, a slow poison that he would put in the captain's rum. Or he would simply encourage his drinking and instruct the cabin boy to withdraw when the nightmares came. Captain Jack might very well do himself some highly useful violence. Or he would persuade the crew that the captain had gone mad and would bind him in the hold. The man's spleen would rupture before they saw land and had to explain their actions. Which brought Abram right to the rebellion he had once so virtuously resisted, and the satisfaction he took in these thoughts, as pleasurable to him as his imaginings of a woman, made him shudder with grief for his failed humanity. The apostle wrote that all mankind's righteousness was as filthy rags. His skin felt as if it had been stitched together out of those bloodied cast-offs.

He realized why the cross drew the world's attention. A life willingly sacrificed, a life sacrificed for the undeserving, the sacrifice itself *chosen*, that was a miracle. That lay outside the circle of nature that looped around his limbs and trussed him up.

Daily he recited The Shorter Form of the Westminster Catechism, prayed almost continuously on his watches; but cutting through his every prayer, shearing away his peace, slashed his one wish: murder.

One night, dead in the middle of the Atlantic, running ahead of a stiff breeze that flattened Abram's blue serge coat and trousers against his back and legs as he stood on the quarterdeck, he felt a thumping vibration in his feet. He went aft to the helm and heard what he surmised must be the thumpings of the captain throwing a fit in his cabin. Abram felt a rush of excitement go through him as he saw his chance. His mind quieted. The thousand misgivings that should have restrained him dropped away. He would go down and assist the captain in his ricocheting delirium. With the ship pitching, the captain's head striking the wall at a chance angle might well break his neck cleanly. Even the shipping line knew of Captain Jack's black moods and rages. Who would doubt the story?

The cabin boy, a brown-headed lad so stout and dumb that he put up with his master better than most, appeared at the top of the hatch on the poop. "The captain's calling on the devil!" he screamed. "He's mortal strange!"

Abram told the helmsman to sing out if the wind shifted and went below. He found Captain Jack in a heap of bed sheets so wet the seas might have rushed in. The cabin, its strewn charts and instruments, overturned chairs and tables, looked as if it had been washed around as well. Captain Jack was arching his back and cursing with a great vehemence. Abram would have to drag him from the bed to accomplish his desperate plan.

Abram grabbed the man's wrists and looked into his face, thinking how best to end the nightmare. The heat burning in the man's wrists gave him a shock. Then the three pustules just below the captain's sparse hairline gave him another. He remembered Mr. Leach. He remembered the girl Ellen and Mrs. Leach—that splash and lengthening silence of the woman's burial he had heard in the midst of his own delirium. And it seemed to him the silence had finally answered itself: Captain Jack had smallpox.

"Fetch me a few reefing tethers," Abram called out to the cabin boy.

He pulled the captain as gently as possible from his bed, resting him on the floor; he changed the bedding while the captain moaned and thrashed at his ankles, and then put the man back in bed. When the cabin boy returned with the tethers, Abram sent him for a bucket of fresh water and a sop. Then Abram cut off the captain's clothes, using a short dagger, and fought a linen nightshirt over his head, as the captain, in his delirium, struck out with his open hands against Abram and the headboard and clawed the air above him. This dressing demanded such violence, and pitted the nurse so much against the delirious belligerence of his patient—who at one point stuck a finger in Abram's eye, and at another stung his jaw with a clenched fist—that Abram felt the temptation rising again to snap his neck.

When the captain had finally been changed to make him as comfortable as possible, Abram tethered his wrists and ankles to the bedposts. He tied him up—as he had dreamed of doing; if an eye for an eye, then a stripe for a stripe. Yet his business was not to strike the man, but to wipe his brow and limbs with the sop and see him through the night. The memory of his own variolated case of the pox had uncocked the trigger of his anger. He knew what the captain would suffer. Nothing but wounds that had registered deeper than thought could have stopped Abram's homicidal intention. The disease had saved him.

He wondered at how the man had avoided contracting the disease in his many years at sea; perhaps the captain's own blood had run with stronger toxins than the pox. If cruelty and hatred warded off disease, old Captain Jack should live forever, growing stronger into his own perverted immortality.

Abram looked at the sweating figure, the barrel chest pumping and gasping like a blacksmith's bellows, and saw a victim. And if the man ever regained consciousness, surely he must finally know himself a victim of his own lies. Where was his will now? His preening, strutting, combative, domineering, sadistic will? The food of worms. The food of worms as much as cowardice and sloth and betrayal and stupidity. And what of courage and valor and honor and glory and integrity? These too were the food of worms. Chum for the schools of fish that followed after burials at sea.

Captain Jack still might recover, but Abram knew that his own hatred had changed forever. He had taken the captain almost on his own terms, as a force greater than nature, supernatural in his own way. He had admired the man that much. A secret collusion with the captain's views, he now recognized, had taken root in his admiration and held his soul the way a root system holds the ball of earth in which it grows. His rage had come from loving the man who had turned out to be his torturer.

Abram watched the captain as the night wore on, picking up his hand now and again to check his fever, until the hand gave him the shock of heated iron. Abram doubted the captain would survive more than a day or two.

In the morning, the first light traveling over the sea fell across the pox-wounded head. The captain had turned his face severely to one side, straining away from his agony. The pox covered his whole body as densely as a colony of ants does its food. If the pustules ever encrusted—if the captain stayed out of his grave that long—he would look like the slimy roe of a gutted monster: death's caviar.

The second day, the captain opened his eyes. Abram, who had kept a nearly continual vigil, awaited one last heaving breath and the fixed-eye stare of a corpse. Instead, he looked over at Abram and began working his legs against the restraints, edging the bedding down enough to view his upper arms and his mounding stomach.

Abram watched the man take in how the pox had taken over his flesh. When the captain glanced back up at him, Abram knew that his perverted spiritual father, his nemesis, his friend, understood everything.

Captain Jack tried to speak. The words came out like the "ghost's language," as the sailors called it, of the shifting winds in a storm, the appeals sailors often swore they made as they swung past in the dark of a squall. He cleared his throat. He spoke again, and the words came out cracked and dissolving—old brick under carriage wheels—but Abram could understand them now.

"What fitting burial can a slave give to his master?" he asked.

"No one can have a duty toward me. Slip me away to the waters, and for once in your life, Saint Abram, get properly rummed. That's what you can do for me—honor me in profaning your code. Profane life! Profane death!"

"I'll see you have the proper obsequies," Abram said.

"Proper?" Captain Jack asked. "I disdain what's proper, and I intend to—" but here he broke off, choking on the waters that had already started to fill his lungs.

Abram cut to the heart of the matter, as he had learned to do long ago. "Why don't you repent?" he asked, wondering himself at the novelty of the idea.

"Repent?" Captain Jack asked, and closed his eyes. When he opened them again, he had seen more than he wanted. "My chance to repent came long ago," Captain Jack said. "My uncle who raised me, the clergyman in Bristol, he took me to the privy behind the manse and made me his . . . every Sunday evening, just after evensong. Our own ceremony. Afterwards, he always gave me the opportunity to repent. Right before he caned me. It was wicked what I had done. And I always had the opportunity to repent. But I denied him that final satisfaction."

Abram could think of nothing to say, nothing but how the logic of a whole life can lie hidden in silence.

"If you think I regret this, Mr. White, you are very much mistaken." He coughed again and struggled at length for breath to continue. "That man of God taught me in what God truly consists: a will to have one's satisfactions and enjoy them. I spurned his repentance because I had truly become his disciple. And I have kept that faith my life long. I will go to my grave a believer."

Abram could not speak. He was horrified but not pitying. Captain Jack did seem this devil's disciple, and while he understood accepting a torturer's terms, even loving them, he had turned away from that course with Captain Jack by the mercy of the disease. He had to think that other mercies might have given Captain Jack the same opportunity in the space of his life. He hoped so. He expected that much of his God.

The captain pulled on his restraints and raised his head a little on the pillow. He looked at Abram long and hard, his devouring eyes swallowing the younger man's thoughts as much as they ever had. "But I want you to know, Abram White, that you have not betrayed your God," he said.

"Listen to me now. I haven't much more to give you, but I will give you this." The captain coughed and choked on his coughing.

"There's an old story," the captain said, "about a knight of faith. Challenged as to his bravery, he rides out to meet a demon whose one sword blow will surely kill him.

"Along the way, he's entertained by a lord and his fair lady. For three days, early in the morning, the lord goes hunting. Each morning the lady slips into the knight's bedchamber and does her best to seduce him. The knight, although greatly moved, resists.

"The last day, knowing he faces death, he accepts a belt from her, a magical favor that she promises will spare his life in the terrible encounter to come. For the sake of his life, he accepts. Then he lies about this to the lord, his one fault."

The last part of the story came out in half-coughing fits. "He meets the demon in a ruined chapel. The rules of the combat allow the demon to strike the first blow, an unhindered chop at the knight's stooping neck. But the demon's great blade only nicks the fellow. His demonic persecutor turns out to be the hospitable lord in another magical disguise, who knows by this that the knight has only failed in taking a little regard for his own life."

Captain Jack stopped speaking for a moment. Abram hardly cared about the point of the story; it seemed to be costing the captain his last breath.

"You are not Jesus Christ, Abram," the captain said finally. "You would have killed me, but only when you knew your own death was close at hand. A nick. A nought.

"And in these last hours I have been at your mercy, and you have only kept watch, soothed my brow, rendered service. If your faith is a fondness in the world that I know, it is a fondness I am glad to have seen lived out. At least for this once.

"You choose the proper obsequies. But remember, and make no mistake, I hated your God—if not his servant—until the last.

"Into your hands I commend my spirit," Captain Jack said. "Oh, Murderer of the Innocent, Consoler of the Comfortable, and Deceiver of the Abandoned." And here he opened his restrained hands in one last mocking blessing, and then collapsed back into a stupefied sleep, from which he never awoke.

Abram buried him at sea the next day, reading out Judas's epitaph in the Scripture: "It had been good for that man had he not been born." He imagined the Lord had loved Judas, and he imagined the Scripture writer meant what he said. Thus Abram said good-bye to his captain without false sentiment, which was the only form of tribute the man would have appreciated.

————

Abram took command of *The Mercy* and brought it home to port, where he proved to the owners of the Vanderhorst Shipping Line, from the captain's own logs, that he had assumed many of the duties of command long before Captain Jack Hawks's death. Seeing this, the line gave him a chance to captain their next venture on *The Mercy*.

PART III

Bliss and Marriage

CHAPTER 9

Elysia

As much as the White's family history began in Ireland, it can also be traced to another home, another place, and in the vision of earthly happiness summed up by its name, Elysia. This estate of some two hundred thousand of Long Island's best acres had been deeded to Richard Nicolls in 1664 by King Charles II in gratitude for the patriarch's loyalty to the crown during the annexation of New Amsterdam. Thereafter, Richard Nicolls had served as governor of the province that was now New York, and his family prospered.

On Long Island's north coast, the Nicolls home, a huge, dark-stained saltbox, topped a promontory overlooking a private funnel-shaped harbor leading out to the Sound. Backed by a hill, the home looked both rustic and highly civilized, as if it were the throne of native kings. Elm trees, vase-shaped, with high trunks and soaring limbs, fanned out from the house like a courtly retinue. The stone-and-mortar steward's residence, several barns, craft buildings, a smokehouse, and fenced pens for horses and livestock could be glimpsed through the closely planted trees.

The churning sea at its doorstep freshened Elysia's air and kept its weathers clement. The surrounding pine woods and rolling fields were naturally hospitable, inviting the estate's one hundred farming tenants to rest in its shaded dells and plant its meadows.

Early in the fall of 1752, the patriarch's great-grandson Robert Nicolls had been Elysia's master for thirty years. He lived there as a widower for the second time, with his three youthful daughters, Felicity, Sarah, and Olivia. One night at the beginning of September, he asked his daughters to quit their usual after-dinner card playing and tête-a-têtes, as he would leave his reading, so that they could talk in the front sitting room.

The three sisters sat side by side on the plum upholstered settee, their hands in their laps, their slippered feet together. They were excited by this unusual gathering and looked like a trio waiting to sing. They wore silk frocks with round collars, cuffs, and hemlines trimmed with lace, and each had a dainty handkerchief hidden up one of those trimmed sleeves.

The eldest, Felicity, a handsome woman at eighteen, sat in the middle. Her dark hair was drawn back on the sides and hung down the back of her elegant neck in a rolled-in, flattened pleat. Her head was large and noble, pinched in just below eye-level, and her eyes were flat discs. She had a nose with a slightly pointed tip, not unbecoming, and a three-cornered smile.

Her youngest sister, Olivia, a fourteen-year-old known in the family as Livy, sat to her right. Livy had a long mane of blond hair—which, as now, she was still allowed to wear down from time to time—and a fresh and eager countenance. Still growing, her chest was as narrow as a boy's, but elsewhere she had a roundness about her, in her shoulders and upper arms and her unhappily broadening hips.

The middle sister, Sarah, at sixteen clearly a dark-haired beauty, sat to Felicity's left. She was deceptively tall and shapely. Her dark hair, gathered back in a loose bun, was rich with an underlying reddishness like polished mahogany. Her lips were full and bow-shaped, and her dark eyes looked as if she knew more than she should.

Bandy-legged and paunchy, Nicolls stood before his daughters with his back to the marble-framed, delft-tiled hearth. Slightly stoop-shouldered, he had an unusually large head, bald, except for a fringe of white hair, and oddly shaped; it narrowed at the level of his large, flaring ears, so that it appeared almost double-orbed. When he blinked, as he did often and noticeably, his eyes seemed to open from the center as if loosened and closed by a drawstring. When the drawstring allowed a peek into them, his small eyes were clear and blue and highly intelligent.

Nicolls crossed one buckled shoe over the other, patted his waistcoat at the watch pockets, and turned his head away. Then he clasped his fingers together, as if he were about to join his trio of offspring in the strains of their repressed song.

His eyes finally unloosened, and he said, "This past month, when I was in town, I met a gentleman at Mrs. Goldsbrow's. I think you must have read about him in those copies of the *Gazette* I supplied. I met that Captain Abram White who set the Atlantic-crossing record not long ago. The one who did so well by the Vanderhorst line. Not a better man to fend off privateers, they say. One story has him saving his cargo in the midst of shipwreck—toting the hogsheads and crates onto some forlorn beach off Fiji—then finding another vessel to get home in. A man of amazing resource."

The young women made hardly any outward movement, except for their feet arching in their slippers.

"He is a new thing, I think. I mean to say, he is a gentleman unlike others. An American gentleman, one might say. By birth common, he is far from a common man. It is not only these mercantile exploits we have read about—I suppose many have done as much in the service of gain. But he has spent much of his time devoted to his own improvement, through reading and study. At Mrs. Goldsbrow's he talked of my Roman compatriots as if he were a Cambridge man."

Nicolls paused as if to take questions. His daughters waited, but with bright eyes now, to see where this biographical sketch would lead.

"As I say, then, a most remarkable man. In his manner he is nice enough without being too fine. He knows not only courtesy, but when to disregard it. He is so little anxious for the approval of others that they give it in a twinkling. I would say . . . yes, I would . . . I would say that I hold him in high regard, and I would have you come to regard him favorably as well."

"We have not met this gentleman," Felicity said.

"The very issue. I have asked Cain Smith and his new wife— what do they call her? Tuppy? yes, Tuppy—to bring the good Captain White out here for a month's shooting. They are to arrive this next week."

Cain Smith had been one of Felicity's suitors before Robert Nicolls rejected his proposal of marriage. Nicolls liked Cain well enough as a friend of the family—he was distantly related to the prominent Delancey's, but knew him too well to agree to become his father-in-law. The two had managed the exchange so discreetly that her father believed Felicity had not suffered. But Smith's rapid marriage to Priscilla Pamela Beekman, a young woman of equal social station, had caused his eldest daughter more than a little heartache.

Olivia finally broke the uncomfortable silence. "You have gathered us together to announce just another smoke 'n oil? A shooting party?" she asked.

Robert Nicolls cleared his throat and his enormous head shook once, sharply. "This party, Livy, may be of greater interest than you suppose. I hope it will be, at least, to Felicity. I would like your opinion of this gentleman especially, my judicious daughter. And I would have you 'look to like' as the bard puts it. I think this man very eligible."

Her sisters on either side of her instantly turned their heads to see how she would reply.

"From what I have read, Father," Felicity said, "he seems at an age where he must already have his family."

"No, not as yet," Nicolls said. "His accomplishments are many, but they have not marked him with anything more than the lines of true character. You will not be disappointed, I think, in the way he presents himself." Nicolls gave a gritty-toothed smile and wagged his head, as he did when delighted, like a dog worrying a bone for pleasure.

"I will certainly do as you wish," Felicity said, and then thought to add, "as I always do."

"Very true, most true," Nicolls said. "For these things it would have been enough simply to speak with you. But I have called your sisters together with you for a particular reason. The first nights of our party, next Wednesday and for a few days following, I would like for your younger sisters to find other recreations during supper." Nicolls raised his hand to stop them from speaking. "I want this gentleman to see the party in a certain perspective. The two couples together, your older sister and this gentleman, Cain and his Tuppy—it seems provident to me to introduce a decided order."

"Oh, Father!" Olivia exclaimed. "Curiosity will consume us away! It will blacken our toes! You will not insist on this, will you?"

Robert Nicolls only smiled.

After another moment, Sarah spoke up. "Then you will be unescorted, Father. Surely I can do you that service. We might soften the tone of this for Livy as well. What if she took a glass of sherry before dinner with us?"

Nicolls looked at his daughter Sarah and true regret entered his voice as he said, "Not this once. You know what pleasure your company is to me, but in this matter we must both think of your sister's good."

"I was thinking of my sister's good," Sarah said, with emphasis.

"This is too severe," Olivia interrupted. "It is tantamount to incarceration, it is—"

But Sarah stopped her with a hand at her elbow. "Livy, what fashion of talk is that?" She turned her face up to the old gentleman. "We will think of Felicity's good in your terms, then, Father. You know how we long to see her happily married."

At the word, both her father and his eldest daughter stiffened as if Sarah had whistled a rock past a looking glass.

"Is he very handsome?" Olivia asked.

"That is not a question to be put to a gentleman," Nicolls said. "But, yes, he is."

———

Oh, the fate of being a middle daughter! During the next several days, Sarah Nicolls found herself dismayed and distracted by the part she always played in their domestic life. She had a terrible surplus of useless energy. She could find no place to settle in the house. She went out walking in the soft autumn weather for hours at a time, and when she returned, she could only put a book before her as a warrant for her own distracted daydreams.

Although Sarah had recognized her duty in quelling Livy's protests, she felt the injustice of her father's odd request at least as keenly, for Sarah at sixteen was well into her own marriageable years. Even at fourteen, it was true, Livy might have been given away, but Livy knew that her two sisters must be wed first. To be shunted back to the nursery now in this rude fashion made Sarah angry. If she did not love her older sister Felicity so well, which she did and truly, she might have found herself besieging her father with her own protests. That was what she wanted to do.

Each time Sarah became petulant, she would remember her love for her sister. This would calm her enough that she could pray, and her spiritual meditations would then give her peace for some hours.

The next time the least anticipation of the future presented itself, however, upon rising the next morning, for instance, or even getting up from the dinner table, she felt troubled. Felicity was discretion itself, but the whole household, all the house servants and field hands, were talking about "Felicity's intended." They had her sister already married to a man Sarah would not be allowed to meet.

Sarah Nicolls was not simply a spoiled girl seeking her own selfish way. Her agitation came from something far more serious; and her ability to calm herself reflected something far better than ordinary self-control. Her name provides a starting point for understanding her nature.

Sarah's mother, Nancy Nicolls, came from a prominent Puritan family, the Singletons. Not surprisingly, then, Nancy Singleton Nicolls wanted biblical names for her children. Robert Nicolls, a lover of all things Greek and Roman, wanted classical ones. They compromised with the eldest, Felicity, endowing her with their sense of what happiness or beatitude might mean.

When Nancy Nicolls became pregnant the second time, she claimed that she had been told in a dream by her dead younger sister to call the baby Sarah. In other things, Nancy's will molded itself to fit her husband's; but in the matter of her second child's name, because of this dream, she remained adamant, and she became almost frantic, muttering to herself constantly, before Nicolls allowed that if the child proved to be a girl, she would be called Sarah.

Significantly, with Olivia, Nicolls had his way, without protest.

Devoted to her father as Sarah was, the child proved, in temperament, sensibility, and the turnings of her mind, a Singleton. She was so much like her mother's family, her father's paternity might almost have been doubted.

The Singletons were people of fine sensibilities and high intelligence, but they had no capacity to live and let live. This was not mere perversity on their part. They simply could not screen their darkest fears and suspicions from their minds. In this broken world, friendships end, human love fails, illness and old age presage that one great inevitable, death. Most people live, however, as if this were not true, or only part of the truth, and a part needing little attention. But the Singletons, in their temperamental extremism, seemed to live always in an unremitting knowledge of these things, making it very difficult for them to get along in this world.

The male Singletons either became ministers or went insane; and several managed to accommodate both vocations in the same life. The women bore children as fast as possible with a crazed determination, as if this enterprise had to be accomplished before they, too, succumbed to madness.

Yet the Singletons' extremism also drove them to search after God, and God seemed to have a special fondness for finding these lost sheep. Some of the famous Puritan journals with their talk of "the comforts," moments of spiritual ecstasy, came from the pens of Singletons.

Puritans like the Singletons were enthusiasts, in the root sense of feeling they were filled with the Spirit of God. Many among them saw visions. Observing the life around them with a keen eye for ironic detail, they saw divine energies waving through the fields of their lives. The Singletons rose and fell with those waves. Their prophetic spirit blew where it would—and more frequently than not.

Sarah Nicolls' own religious education came directly from her Singleton mother. By her eighth birthday, Sarah could rattle off scores of Scripture verses from memory, prompted by key spiritual nouns. She knew twenty-seven verses on the subject of God's wrath, fourteen on the Lord's grace—admittedly a Puritan proportion— and she knew most of the psalms by heart. She was virtually a prodigy in theology, and could discuss passages from Michael Wigglesworth's *The Day of Doom* and Cotton Mather's *The Wonders of the Invisible World*, though she preferred Bunyan to these divines.

As a child, Sarah liked to make believe she was hoisting Pilgrim's great Burden of Sin, symbolized by her pillow, up the Stairs of Life, almost breaking herself in two once when she exaggerated the pillow's weight too dramatically and came down the front stairs backwards in a somersaulting heap. Fortunately, the sinful pillow cushioned her head on the way down.

Robert Nicolls did influence her mother's teachings in one important respect. He insisted that the family attend the local Church of England chapel, although he rarely went himself. Thus the ceremonial drama of morning prayer and the monthly Eucharist and evensong paired the words of Puritan divines with Anglican images of heaven. Sarah liked the quiet, liquid light that filled the chapel at evensong, and the candles that burned high up on the walls in their sconces, and the ornate wooden reredos behind the altar with its carved figures depicting God with His arms outspread presiding over a heaven that was a wonder of hierarchical order—the relative importance of the angels, apostles, martyrs, and saints expressed by a declining scale.

When Sarah prayed there, kneeling on one of the cushions embroidered with the family's initials, she often had the peculiar and overpowering sense that she had come to stay. Once her mother could not shake her out of a prayerful revery and had to carry her out of the chapel as if she were in a dead sleep. Afterwards, Sarah told her mother not to make Eli's mistake. She had not been asleep any more than the prophet-in-training, Samuel. This frightened her mother so much that she never bothered to ask what the Lord might have said.

Sarah had loved her mother intensely, in a different way than she cared for her father. Nancy Singleton had been fourteen at the time of her marriage to Robert Nicolls, who had already turned forty. She was a thin yet buxom girl, a soft wave rippling through her light brown hair and a hypnotic stillness resting in her deep eyes. She had attracted Nicolls' attention at a party given by her parents, where she recited a passage from Virgil: Dido's lament at the loss of Aeneas.

At the end of her performance, she took up her skirts to curtsy, revealing her slender ankles, and her New England Trojan lost all thought of founding another Rome. She was virtually sold to the middle-aged squire, who had lost his first wife some years earlier in childbirth—the child of that union stillborn. The Singletons were not so nice about their daughters' feelings in such matters, and Nancy became his second wife within a fortnight.

Nancy had little idea what to do as a wife, but Nicolls proved friendly, attentive, and required nothing of her except children. Being a Singleton, she was happy to oblige him as quickly as nature allowed.

Nancy cared for her own daughters as if they were dolls and then playmates. Sarah remembered that sometimes her mother would come into the nursery and get in bed with her and say, comfortingly, "You look cold, child. Would you have me rest beside you?" They would drift off to sleep together, later to be awakened by the family nurse, Martha. If it was a cold day, her mother would ask that tea with plenty of milk and sugar be brought to them. Her mother, her sister Felicity, and Sarah would stay in their nightgowns and have tea and toast, sitting on their beds with the covers over their feet, while Livy was taken out to be nursed by a servant.

Nancy Nicolls taught her daughters a world of information about the Scriptures, theology, and music because she treated her girls as if they were wonders, and they became almost that out of gratitude. She was naturally studious herself, always finding new subjects to investigate, and her example underlined her lessons.

When Robert Nicolls started employing tutors for his daughters, Nancy insisted on being instructed, too. Even a child of grammar school age like Sarah could see that her mother understood being someone's pupil far better than being the mistress of her own household. Nancy Singleton Nicolls was happy with her older husband, but something in her begged to remain in the nursery. Sarah remembered the many times her father had to retrieve his wife from among them or from the kitchen and escort her to her rightful place at his table. Her mother also spoke to them often of missing her brothers and sisters, and her prayers always included petitions for the safety of her family, the Singletons, "wherever," she would say, "in your sovereign will, you have disposed them to be." Thinking back, Sarah remembered her mother as an angel with hypnotic eyes, but somehow, at the same time, lonely and frightened and a bit lost.

In later life, Sarah's own fears reached back to those she had felt in her mother, and, most particularly, her own experience of her mother's death, which was the defining spiritual crisis of her childhood.

At eleven years of age, Sarah knelt by her bed one night, saying her prayers, when she suddenly felt as if someone was outside who meant to do them harm. Sometimes her father would be called out to deal with a drunken tenant or Indian sachem, who would shout at her father when he went out to them. But that night, despite her uneasiness, everything was quiet and still.

She thought of talking to Felicity, and then, feeling even more afraid, she thought of knocking on her mother's door and asking her to sit by her a while. Thinking of her mother, Sarah felt the fear gather, concentrate, and fly like a weapon toward its target.

Then she saw something in her imagination that she did not understand. The handle of the hand pump at the well was moving without anyone working it, moving by itself, and then out of it came an explosion of blood. She felt as if the blood were spattering onto her own face. Blinded by it, she started to scream and held up her overlapping hands against the spewing stream. She wanted to run away, but felt paralyzed. By that time, she suspected that Felicity must be standing beside her, asking her what was wrong, but still she could not move.

Then she felt herself being lifted up, and she opened her eyes to see her mother, who was holding her under her arms and telling her to get into bed. "You went to sleep at your prayers again, Sarah," she said. "Such terrible dreams you have, my darling. But they are phantasms. Nothing more. Sleep now." She would remember seeing her mother's face over her, the rippling waves of her hair past her cheeks, the sureness in her hypnotic look.

The fear did not leave absolutely, though. Nor did Sarah sleep. She lay in her bed until morning, possessed by the after-images of her vision. Sitting up, she saw that Felicity was awake in her bed, and she had one thought, to which she involuntarily gave voice: "Mother is dead."

"Don't be foolish," Felicity scolded in her older-sister tones, and rushed out of the room to tell their mother of her sister's frightful behavior. But seconds later Sarah looked up to see her father with his hands on Felicity's shoulders as he guided her back into the room. Then he awakened Livy, who was nine years old at the time, and sat them down together on Sarah's bed and told them that their mother had died very suddenly in the night.

Her father said, "Sarah—?" but never finished asking what must have been his question. He swept them into a collective embrace, and the three girls cried together and clung to him.

The surgeon reported that Nancy Nicolls' eyes looked like eggs frying in blood: her brain must have hemorrhaged.

What Sarah had experienced that night was lost for a time in their grief, but it would not be the last time she *knew* things. She was fey. She had what the Scots called "second sight."

So her agitation upon the occasion of the young sea captain's visit was a compound of her youthfulness and her Singleton temperament. For the Singletons were temperamentally unfitted to know anything but horror or God.

———

Sarah kept to her room, as promised, on the night of Captain White's arrival, except for one peek at the company from the short stairs just above the landing. She saw nothing of their father's guest except the top of his dark-haired head, with its blade-sharp side-part, and the triangular tip of his nose. Sarah also heard his voice;

it sounded youthful and yet contained, at the low end of the tenor range, with a trace of Irish lilt.

Livy wanted the two exiles to read aloud to each other, but Sarah told her to go to bed and then went to her own room, where she nurtured her daydreams, awaiting Felicity. The night before, Felicity had promised to tell her everything about the dinner.

Sarah sat on her poster bed, braced herself with pillows, took up a book, and then listened to the house. She could not hear the party's voices, only the sharp ring of a serving spoon being dropped in the kitchen and the occasional footfall of a servant. Underneath the quiet of the house, though, she heard the streamlike coursing of their lives toward a greater end.

Sarah was drowsy when Felicity finally came to her room. Her older sister did not look eager or excited or even downcast; she looked maddeningly composed. Her flat, dark eyes looked only pleasant, as pleasant as a hazy summer day—but one without a sun in the sky. She seemed, in her manner, to be drifting along in that hazy day. She picked up the silver potpourri box on Sarah's dressing table and sniffed it.

"Felicity," Sarah said, sharply, "you must come sit on the bed and keep your promise. What of the good Captain White?"

Felicity came closer and half-sat on the side of the bed, more dreamy than ever.

"Are you in love with him?" Sarah asked.

Felicity turned and looked at her impassively, as if she had heard nothing but her name being called. "Captain White is an interesting man," she said.

"Is he handsome, as father said?"

"Quite."

"He appeals?"

"I would think he would appeal to any woman."

Sarah knew that what she was asking had been deflected, but she was not sure in what direction. "Do you think he is a suitable match? Felicity, please, you must discover your thoughts to me. I have been waiting—we all have—this past *week*."

"I have never considered marrying a man like Abram. That is . . . you see, Abram, he asked me privately to use his Christian name. Yet he was not being forward. That is the puzzle he presents. He can be uncommonly informal, but without giving offense, as he has no pretensions. He is more quiet in manner than not. But he will laugh,

- 125 -

too. I have never met anyone like him before. As father says, he is a new thing."

"But what is your will in the matter? Your desire? When you look upon him, what are your affections?"

Felicity gave one of her broad, three-cornered smiles. "Sarah, your sentiments are always so much present to you. You know them immediately. I am always discovering mine. Sometimes at a very late hour." She paused, then went on to another matter. "This party includes Cain and his Tuppy—"

"That would confuse your thoughts," Sarah interrupted.

"It did," said Felicity. "I am a little astounded that Father invited them here so readily. And in this circumstance."

"I thought you agreed in his rejection of Cain's marriage offer?"

"My better judgment agreed. My sentiments can wander as far from my judgment as yours."

"This Tuppy must be a great disappointment," Sarah said, rattling away. "She looked monstrous from what I glimpsed from the stairs. Cain must have made this match almost in revenge—a violence to which father will be insensible. But Cain will have to live with the woman."

"Tuppy is charming. I hope we shall become friends."

Sarah hardly let a beat go by. "Then your judgment betrays you, because you cannot be at ease in the company of someone who reminds you of a sorrow."

Felicity kicked off her slippers and moved up beside her sister against the pillows. "My wise younger sister, what a contradiction you are. If you saw into yourself half as well as you see others, you would be a woman for the ages to remember."

"I think I see myself," Sarah said. "My passions deny what I see, though, and at times blind me altogether. Do you not feel these things?"

"What I feel seems to come from a distance, and I fear its arrival as one fears horrid storms. As I said, you are present in your emotions, and they to you—immediately. I have to pity you this. It must be—how shall I say this—almost a crucifying thing."

"It is life," Sarah said.

"Not as most choose to live it," Felicity said.

"I do not see that it is something I have chosen."

"I suppose we do not choose our natures."

They sat and reflected for a moment.

"What of Captain White, then?" asked Sarah impatiently.

"I have only one comfort in this," Felicity said, "and that is to do what father wishes. I would never be able to make such a decision."

"You would have married Cain if father had agreed?"

"I know who Cain is. I know his family. I even know why Father thought him an unsuitable match, and I would have known that just as well if Father had agreed. I would have gone to my wedding knowing why Cain should not be absolutely trusted, and I would have been prepared for the degree of betrayal that belongs to what Cain is. With Captain White, I am utterly at a loss. He may be an angel of light or a devil."

"He cannot be a devil, surely."

"What kind of life would we have? I am not sure I relish having a husband who is always away at sea."

"There can be no question of that, can there?" Sarah asked.

"What do you mean?"

"He is a celebrated man now. He cannot still be thinking of going to sea?"

"These things are just my concern. And not simply these things in themselves. It seems to me an even greater difficulty that I have no way of anticipating the answers to such questions."

"Father would not be thinking of a marriage to someone in trade."

"Sarah, sea captains are known as capitalists. They invest in their ventures, along with others, then reap the profits."

Sarah thought for a moment. "Explain your greatest concern again to me."

Felicity put her hand to her mouth, considering. "I do not know him. I do not understand him. And I do not know how I shall. He is a very good dinner companion. Most amiable. I think the way he presents himself true, but I am not sure I would ever know deception if I saw it in such a man."

"You should see him in unguarded moments, then."

Felicity turned on Sarah and said, almost as if scolding her, "We will be having tea. We will be dining. I will not be seeing him in unguarded moments."

Sarah took this and smiled to herself. "I can be your eyes."

"How so?"

"I will go out to the fields with the party in the morning."

"Father would never allow that."

"Boyd will let me join the beaters. I'll dress as a trousered retriever and watch how your Abram shoots. You can tell a lot by watching someone when he thinks he's not being seen."

"Sarah," Felicity said, softly rebuking her.

"You would value my opinion of him, wouldn't you?"

"They will shoot you, Sarah."

"Felicity, we ride to hounds. And I've heard other guests talk of shooting parties. I know what they do. The beaters and the dogs round the game back toward the shooters. The beaters are always well out of range, and the shooters do not fire at anything the beaters haven't put up. If I do not fly, I will not be shot at."

"How much can you possibly learn in this way? This is an excursion for your own pleasure."

Sarah gave Felicity the searing look of a woman scorned.

"You might learn something," Felicity said. "I do admit I would feel better about this gentleman, if gentleman he is, if you thought him worthy. You do see more than I at times. You will be careful?"

"I have no plans to take wing."

"Have you ever worn trousers before?"

"Never tell Father, but when I was a girl I used to sneak into the servants' quarters and costume myself. Trousers should be quite nice on a cold morning."

CHAPTER 10

A Smoke 'n Oil

The next morning, chief steward Boyd lent Sarah the costume she required, a boy's trousers and a tweed cap, his thick-skinned face screwing up in his indulgently sour way. "You keep out of range, Miss," he said. "If someone wings you, I'll be wringing that neck of yours."

Promising to take care, Sarah hurried to the workers' lodging, a long, bare log cabin the field hands used during planting and harvest. From there she watched the shooting party assemble behind the main house.

After they had tightened together in the predawn darkness for instructions, the party started its walk out to the fields. The dogs led, a brace of club spaniels who picked their way with high steps over the wet ground, their noses already rooting back and forth. Cain, her father, and Captain White followed. Then came the beaters, a gang of Boyd's fellow Irishmen in tweed caps like the one she wore, talking among themselves and tramping along.

When they were a distance away, Sarah left the lodging and straggled behind. The wind was fresh and cool on her face, and the lightening sky, with its pearly sheathing clouds, beckoned her onward over the shadowy ground. The birds were singing heartily in the surrounding pines and birches, and occasionally Sarah caught a throatier voice from the fields beyond.

She had walked out through the woods to the eastern meadows and cornfields many times before; yet the shooting prospects made her more attentive to the land. There were more hated ironwood trees than she could have imagined, and the recent cycles of hot and wet weather had made the sandy topsoil powdery. She started to understand why men preferred to take their walks with firearms.

Her father potched his land with cornfields, not so much for the ears, since the raccoons harvested more than his servants, but so that the pheasant and grouse would use the scorched-out stands for cover at this time of year. The birds could be anywhere, along the tree-lined streams that screened one field from another, or along the borders of the low-lying marshes with their thickets of staghorn sumac. The marshes always seemed to Sarah such disturbing places—sinister yet wonderful, too; both Bunyan's Slough of Despond and Moses' bulrushes.

The light was at their feet now, and the trees outlining the fields and the meadow grasses were shaggy with the reddish tinges of sunrise.

The party came over a rise and saw below them her father's favorite cornfield. It was bounded by a steeper, tree-covered hill on the opposite side and bracketed by a streambed on the right and marshlands at the left. The birds would be here, if anywhere. Sarah had often put one up on her walks this way. The powerful whoosh of the birds' sudden leap into the air always startled and thrilled her.

The party up ahead stopped, and the beaters slowed and grew quiet. She heard her father talking and strained to make out what he was saying.

"This is as good a place as I know for pheasant and grouse. I wish you good luck and good day, Abram. When you are ready, your beaters will see you home."

Captain White said something in reply, something about the dogs.

Her father's voice was much easier to discern. "Well, sir," he said, "I was planning on taking the dogs and the mongrel with me."

He looked over at Cain and wagged his head at his joke. "You shall have a good troupe of beaters. They know to split up and circle back toward you, some by the marsh, some by the stream. They will do so for the rest of the day. The birds should run where you can flush them. If your beaters put one up, it may still fly low enough for you to get off a shot. That's clear, then?"

Sarah wondered if the captain would be embarrassed that her father had been so full in his explanations. But his, "Yes, thank you, sir," carried nothing but gratitude.

"Begin your perambulations toward those birches on the far side," her father went on, "and you will probably have to kick one or two out from under your feet as Cain did last time. But go slowly. No one will think you rude on this occasion for using an element of surprise."

Her father and Cain and their contingent had no more than moved away toward their own hunting area, when the captain put up a bird. A fully plumed male pheasant, with a white ring around his neck and scarlet wattles, exploded out of the high grass in front of him. Its flapping leap sent out vibrating waves like a whipsawing board, drawing everyone's attention back to the hill above the field.

Captain White put his fowling piece to his shoulder before he had reset his weight, and the heavy gun lifted to where he sighted the bird for the briefest instant and then kept carrying higher. When he fired, the kick staggered him backwards, and he had to drop the gun and catch himself from sprawling on his rump.

As the pheasant winged over the trees, while the cloud of gunpowder still hung in the air, Sarah started to laugh with the others. Then she cut her laughter short as she realized its pitch might give her away.

Captain White stood and picked up his fowling piece. He looked at it for a moment to see if he had done it any damage, moving around on his feet, still rocking from the experience. When he looked up, framed by pure sky, Sarah saw him clearly for the first time. His face was lean and strong, and his wide, embarrassed smile brought out the lines that angled inward at the cleft of his chin, setting a triangle inside his square jaw. His eyes were clear and surprisingly steady. He swatted at his backside. Then his chin popped up as he called to her father, "I'm more used to my blunderbuss than your fowling piece, Squire. I should have brought that mob weapon for your riot of game."

Nicolls wagged his head and called back, "You'll do fine, Captain, once you get your sea legs."

The captain gestured in response, something between a friendly farewell and a salute, then walked eagerly forward, his expression intent and unconcerned.

Sarah looked back at her father once before the old gentleman disappeared into the bracketing woods; he was talking excitedly to the tall Cain Smith. She could not hear his words, but she knew her father was praising Captain White. He must have liked the man's composure, as did she.

Sarah went into the trees on the right and circled to the end of the field, taking care to keep Captain White in view while concealing herself. Occasionally, she would walk out into the field, just as a beater would, since she felt she would not be discovered and she could better observe the man. But when the captain came her way, she scrambled back into the protection of the encircling trees.

Not long after his first shot, Captain White put up a grouse, and his shot knocked the bird down. He missed on his third try, but then he became deadly accurate, knocking down at least a dozen birds in a row.

As the day wore on toward noon, Sarah became freer in her beater duties. She actually went and picked up a kill—holding it over her head and shaking it for Captain White to see—and then returned to the birch trees.

Before putting the bird away in the game bag, she held the creature for a moment in her hands. She saw game in the kitchen almost daily at this time of year, but the grouse looked much different here. She felt the warmth of its small body, the intricate foldings of its feathers, and the terrible, supple slackness in its neck. The grouse had been shot in the chest, where it was bleeding. She tried to close one of its eyes. The tacky ball rolled against her thumb and remained open. After another moment, she put it away, thinking she might lose her appetite that night.

By the end of the morning, Sarah had circled all the way around the right side of the field and was now near the marsh on the left side. Captain White stood at the center of the cornfield, almost lost in the rows. Now brave and unconcerned, Sarah walked in toward him. Suddenly, a magnificent pheasant flew up from beneath her feet.

When the shot came this time, Sarah not only heard the gun's report, but felt the vibration of its thunder in her eardrums.

She looked up and saw the pheasant beat its wings two more times, and then it glided, clearly wounded, into a thicket close to where she stood in the marshlands. Abram hollered for someone to go after it. Sarah looked around. Dennis and Tim were at the other side of the field; Shawn back by the game bag.

Abram yelled once more. "Why are you dawdling there? I want to know what's happened to the creature. Be off with you." He was fifty yards away through cornstalks, but Sarah knew he was yelling at her.

She ran toward the marsh, thinking she would retrieve the bird and retreat to the trees once more. She bounded onto the lower marshy ground, slipping toward the sumac. The ground was a bit drier than she had supposed, the going easier, but as she neared the staghorn sumac, her right foot disappeared into a hole, and she pitched forward. The muck on her face and hands felt slimy and smelled like salted eel. Still she pushed forward, getting herself up and into the midst of the thicket.

She saw a low, huddled form, too colorful to be a stone, in the midst of the antlerlike branches. She knelt down and reached out to it, and received a darting pain in the palm of her hand and sharp pecks against her forearms. Then the pheasant scuttled forward away from her.

She moved to her right and circled in behind the bird. Wounded, unable to fly, it stayed still. When she snatched it again, it stirred vigorously in her hands, its wings trying to throw off her grip, its head circling round. It eyed her furiously.

She sat down with the magnificent creature, trying to calm it by stroking its long, iridescent purple and green throat. As she stroked the bird, its head popped out of her half-closed fist. The pheasant rustled in her hands, its long bourbon and amber tail poking up into her neck.

Distantly, she heard Captain White halloing at her, but she ignored his calls. She had to find out how badly the pheasant was hurt. One of the bird's white-capped wings kept swinging out from its body like a loose-hinged door. When she reset it, she felt the break in the bone, and her fingers became sticky with the creature's blood. She realized that it would have to be killed or painstakingly nursed back to health.

The pheasant had grown quiet in her hands. Then suddenly, without warning, the bird clawed down into her thighs, and she heard a sound like a mass of kindling exploding in a bonfire. The sky was being torn off above her head. Sumac branches rained down on her, and the pheasant kicked and kicked and twisted to leap forward and away. She found herself screaming for the vengeance that had fallen upon them to stop. She kept screaming until she could hear herself clearly and knew that the sky had grown quiet again.

She started to stand up, but she felt dazed and unwell as she realized that Captain White had fired at her. Was she shot? Would she feel blood on her fingertips again from her own wounds?

Then she heard someone running toward her, and she was the wounded pheasant waiting in terror for another calamity.

She felt him standing above her, blocking out the sun, and when she turned toward him, she saw him bending over her slightly, gaping in shock and confusion.

"Are you hurt?" he asked, finding his voice.

Sarah did not answer at first. She was so purely angry that her curious circumstances seemed not to matter. She realized, though, that her hair had spilled out from beneath her cap over her shoulders.

"You will not kill this bird, sir!" she said finally.

He straightened, put his hands on his hips, and looked over the thicket as if the world itself must answer for this turn of events.

He looked back down at her. "I would like to be assured that you are not hurt," he said.

She thought to throw him off. "I amn't hurt. But my da, the steward Mr. Collins, will be wanting a word with you, sure."

He received this too placidly. "Your da? Miss Nicolls, your father spent all last evening praising your virtues. He cannot help but speak of you. Now tell me you are well, and forgive me for being so impetuous. Please."

He put out his hand to her and helped her up. "I only thought to rouse the beater to action. The shot's pattern must be greater than I imagined. I—"

She had kept hold of the pheasant as he kept explaining. Now, disturbed by the man's ruffled presence, the pheasant pecked Sarah hard at her ear.

She gave a short scream and grabbed the bird's head in her fist with such violence that she came close to wringing its neck.

"Now you are hurt," Captain White said, and the wound seemed finally to deliver him from his own guilt. He licked his thumb and index finger and rubbed the blood away at her earlobe, then took the bird from her hands and held it securely. An unexpected peace settled down on them.

She was standing in a marsh in a sumac thicket with a man who had nearly shot her. She looked up at him, at his face that was glowing with the morning's exertion, at his Irish blue eyes with their black pupils, at his long neck with its pointed Adam's apple. Mysteriously, she felt cared for. Had her mother drawn near in spirit?

She took out the handkerchief she always carried up her sleeve and wiped her brow. She felt a tug on it, and then he had taken it from her and was rubbing the last of the blood off her earlobe. She leaned closer to him, pleased by his ministrations despite the soreness of the wound.

"What shall I do with this noble bird, then?" he asked.

"I would have it taken back to the house," she said. "I'll nurse it there myself."

"As you like," he said. "And we shall return to the house as well. Your father's lands are too generous. This shooting became more slaughter than sport by mid-morning."

They began to make their way out of the thicket and through the marsh. The captain stopped to retrieve his gun, which had fallen on the sloppy ground.

As they were about to climb out of the marsh, Sarah reached out and caught his elbow. "Perhaps you had better let the creature go," she said. "I would prefer fewer explanations." She blushed; a scarlet rash, almost as vivid as the bird's wattles, burned up the side of her neck.

"We will give him to your da, Mr. Collins," he said. "He knows, doesn't he?"

"He lent me the breeches," she said.

They continued walking. "Why is it—why did you come out today?" the captain asked.

"Father has us more cooped up than chickens. I did not want to sit in the parlor and listen to the shooting. Women ride to hounds. I do not see why we should not be allowed to hunt birds as well."

"Can you handle firearms?"

"I could blow Tim's hat off with a musket," she said, and pointed at the trio of beaters whose heads were bobbing through the cornfields toward them.

They took a few more steps. "Yet you would prefer the birds not be killed," he said, and hefted the pheasant once more in evidence.

She flushed. "You catch me in a contradiction. But then it is a

- 135 -

woman's nature to be contradictory." She looked at him with a kind of sly triumph in her expression.

"Are you really a woman, then?" he asked. "These clothes, your actions—you have utterly confounded me."

He said this in such a lighthearted way that it did not please her very much. She looked away, refusing to catch his glance.

"I think you came out to watch me," he said. "As a spy for your sister? Not your father. He's a shrewd man, but not a man of guile."

"It is common of you to be so forward."

"Oh, I take this adventure as a great compliment. And now here's one for you. When I came upon the thicket, all my concern was for the pheasant, and then I found a far more radiant creature."

"You should not be saying such things to me," she said.

They stood together for a moment, listening to the beaters making their way toward them, rustling the stalks ever closer.

"Very true," the captain said, at last. But he put his hands at her shoulders and stared her full in the face, his look growing violently troubled. Then he threw his head back and let out a half-whistling breath with his eyes closed. "You should not have come out today," he said. "How am I to be a gentleman when Venus comes to me in breeches?"

———

Sarah's adventure became known immediately, since Abram felt obliged to acquaint her father personally with the story, preferring truth to rumor. The two met at the back of the house when Nicolls and Cain returned from the fields.

"I fired to get the beater's attention, sir," Abram said. "When the shot nicked the tops of the branches, I found the spread of the pattern to be greater than I imagined."

"Don't be troubled, good Captain," said his host. "I've done much the same thing—killed my best spaniel once when it wouldn't heed my whistle."

Abram had hoped to steer clear of any mention of killing, but he thought Nicolls genuine in his forgiveness.

The older man looked thoughtful for another moment, the drawstring of his eyes strangling tight. "It seems I've reined in my miss beyond endurance. We shall be a larger party tonight. I would rather the two young ones plague us at dinner than in this fashion."

"I found her a delightful girl, sir," Abram said in a reassuring voice.

"She is that," Nicolls said. "Delightful, and, as you see, a bit savage."

———

Felicity came to Sarah's room just as she finished cleaning up and donning a satiny blue dress with a tight bodice, spreading skirts, and lace-trimmed decolletage. She looked ten years older than she had in trousers.

"I said you would be shot," Felicity scolded.

"There was no question of that. It is a thing, though, to have a fowler's shot tear through the air above one's head. It sounded like the Last Judgment."

"It could have been yours, my foolish sister."

Sarah grabbed on to one of her bedposts and hung on it. "I saw a good deal of your Captain White," she said.

"Oh, I can hardly think of that now."

"You must. I learned a great many things about him."

Felicity raised her eyes to her sister sheepishly, wanting to know.

"He may be impatient at times, but in all other respects I think him quite admirable. He does not worry about the world's regard. He hardly thinks of himself, it would seem. This frees all his powers. He is so intent on his aims that he cannot help but accomplish them. They are his only concern."

"But how can you know this?"

Sarah explained about Abram's first shot knocking him backward, and then how quickly he adapted to the shooting.

"Still, good sister, I do not like his firing over your head, even if he thought you were only one of his beaters."

Felicity's dark eyes kept growing hazier, even as she was becoming more and more dreamy and slow in her movements and gestures.

"What is troubling you?" Sarah asked in exasperation.

"It is harder than I supposed with Cain and his Tuppy here," Felicity said. "I have been with her in the parlor this morning, and I do like her. She has a warm vitality and eagerness. She makes me think of Cain, though."

Sarah rolled her eyes, becoming impatient.

"And Captain White," Felicity said as if in explanation, "I believe what you say, but this confuses me more than ever. How can one live with a man who thinks of nothing but his desire? Prudence demands consideration of others, even of their worst thoughts. We do not live for ourselves."

"At times, sister, I think you would live as if already dead, with God and posterity's judgment rendered. We must have security, yes, but not so much as to forestall life itself. You want a husband not an epitaph."

Felicity looked displeased at this, but Sarah refused to soften her words.

———

After supper, the company gathered in the front sitting room. A fire was crackling in the hearth, serving as a convivial reminder to Sarah of the captain's crackling shot. The casement windows to the right brought in the enchanting night. The harpsichord, a white lacquered instrument with women in diaphanous robes dancing along its side, stood close by the windows, ready for the entertainment Sarah anticipated her father would request. Under the glow of the oil lamps, the wide planks of the pine floor shone around the rich crimson carpet.

"Another round?" Nicolls asked as they took their seats. "More punch? What a company this is," he said, directing the fuzzy-haired servant, Crump, to the punch cart. Nicolls moved his lips, tasting the satisfaction he took in the gathering. He preferred to stand as they talked, gesturing with his punch glass without spilling it, performing a kind of unconscious party trick.

"We should call ourselves Folderol & Company," Cain Smith said. "We're a theatrical sort of troupe, you see, devoted to our own entertainment."

Everyone nodded at him, granting his wit.

Cain and his wife sat together on the short settee to their host's left. Steeple-tall and lean, Cain's most remarkable feature was his head, whose magnificent bone structure testified to the pure appeal of anatomy. His sparse brown hair allowed for high temples, from where flange-like bones ran down to his brow, putting his unlined forehead and its sides at perfect right angles. That prominent brow and his strong nose created huge cavities for his gray eyes, and the cut of his jawline provided a curving complement to all that facial architecture.

His wife, Tuppy, was a surprise: a big woman, nearly as tall as her husband, broad-shouldered, square-hipped. She looked like the giant's wife in a fairy tale, not heavy but on a different scale than most women. She had thick hair the color of maple syrup and a pleasant, broad, rabbity face. The depressed grooves bracketing her soft nose even made it look even more like a rabbit's.

Sarah and her two sisters sat on the long settee opposite the fire. Abram White was on the right, with the harpsichord and the windows behind him.

"It seems that Cain and Captain White know each other," Sarah said. "How is that?"

"I told you," Felicity said, "they met when Cain booked passage on Captain White's vessel."

"I wanted the fastest crossing," Cain said, "as I was rushing to the court to appeal a landholding case for the Livingstons against the Schuylers, who were each, to tell the truth, intent on swindle. Abram kept running into privateers and killing them, which cost us a good deal of time, I must say. He's a wonder with a blunderbuss, Sarah. You are fortunate to have escaped."

Sarah blushed deeply at this.

"How did Cain meet Tuppy?" Livy asked, liberated from her childhood shyness by her older sister's frank inquiry.

"In a most indelicate way," the cheery Tuppy said. "My mother and I were being harassed by drunken villains in the Broad Street near Fraunces Tavern, and my gentleman came to our aid."

"Were the villains your clients?" Nicolls asked, teasing Cain. "Had you put them up to the job?"

"Well, they did me a great service, sir, though 'fore that I had only seen them whistling away their time in Mr. Fraunces' public house. They were criminals with a most discriminating taste, I should say, since they were assaulting a lady I had long wanted to meet." The couple looked at one another and grasped each other's hands.

"Captain White," Felicity said, "you approve of this friend who lawyers both for society and its dregs?"

"I think society and its dregs be closer relations than you imagine, miss," said Abram. "I would refer you to Mr. Smith's journey to the court. That proposition involved, as I think he said, 'swindle.'"

The girls looked to their father to see how he would weather this.

"Indeed it did, sir," Cain said, rescuing them all. "What you want a lawyer for generally ain't a pretty business, whoever does the wanting."

"Since we are relating histories," Nicolls said, "shall I tell you of my meeting with the good Captain White at Mrs. Goldbrow's gala?"

"My sisters and I think you have been very bad for delaying the recitation till now," Sarah said.

"Ecod, I have," said Nicolls, flourishing his glass. "To it, then. Cain was introducing Captain White all round, describing him as 'our Ulysses.' Old Vortmann was in his cups. A man should like his punch without wanting to swim in it, I always say. Take that as you will, Vortmann had done some navigating. He was blind already and going deaf. When he could not catch the good captain's name, or the name escaped his sodden recognition, he kept asking, 'Who is it then? Who?' Who, who, you understand, like the drunken old owl that he was."

The party laughed together.

"Abram came up and said, 'Nobody, sir. Nobody you will remember in the morning at least.' "

Cain broke out laughing; Tuppy and Felicity smiled to themselves.

"What are you laughing at?" Livy asked.

"Now take a moment, Livy. Nobody? Our Ulysses? You see, the good Captain White was capping old Vortmann and punning on Homer's poem at the same time. It was then I knew I had to talk with this man. I rapidly gained some inkling of the depth of his learning, the quickness of his mind. And I should say, if he will suffer not to shoot any more of my daughters, we may become closer still."

As everyone had been served a second time, Nicolls raised his glass, "To the good Captain Abram White."

"Here, here," Cain said.

They all took sips of their punch.

"Shall Nobody address you, then?" Abram asked the company. Humming approval went up. "I would resign this anonymous commission. As Abram I thank my hosts for a hospitality that Ulysses never knew until he reached his home." More humming approval as they sipped the captain's toast.

Sarah thought how Elysia might well become Abram's home, and yet his toast hardly sounded like campaigning.

"If my daughters will now oblige us, we should have some entertainment, I think," said Nicolls. "The Three Graces at the harpsichord!"

Cain, Tuppy, and Abram applauded in encouragement.

"Livy is a prodigy," Cain said.

"I have heard you all play exceedingly well," said Tuppy.

"If I did not fear missing her too much, I would send Livy to be trained in England," Nicolls said. "It sometimes seems to me she lacks the sense of decorum that someone of genius might impart to her there. But then she is very young."

Each of the sisters took her turn at the harpsichord. Felicity played a quadrille very competently. Playing seemed a thing that came easily enough to her, not something she had really worked at.

Livy then set into an ostentatiously technical piece by a little-known Italian composer. She had small, fat hands with dimples over the knuckles. The smallness made the spans of which her hands proved capable seem a wonder, ringing out so many arpeggios and diving runs that she seemed to swing at the keys as if she would knock the instrument's teeth out.

After many protests that her playing could only be an inglorious conclusion, Sarah sat down at the keyboard, choosing a quadrille, as Felicity had.

Sarah played slowly, haltingly, bent down rather close to the keyboard. Though her hands and wrists hovered in the correct position, she had not the accuracy of Felicity nor anything like the speed and sureness of Livy. Yet as she played, she forgot about the individual notes, as did her audience, and felt the movement of the piece so deeply that she seemed to dance in its embrace, like the sprightly dancers she was conjuring up. Then the music became the good Captain White, and she reached out her hand to his at each turn, felt the touch of his strong, rough grasp in return, and the secure sweep of his arm around her as they promenaded together.

At the end, the applause filtered slowly into her revery, and she regretted letting it go.

The company looked sated and tired, but they were as reluctant to abandon their entertainment as Sarah had been the quadrille.

Tuppy directed the conversation back to Abram. "One mystery remains," she said. "How did the good Captain White, our friend Abram, I should say, how did you enter upon your seafaring life?"

Abram hesitated. He looked at Sarah. "I ran away to sea," he said.

"Ecod!" said Tuppy. "We do have a man of adventure among us."

"Captain White must have had good reason," Felicity said, considerately.

"To judge by the way it has turned out," Nicolls said wryly.

"Pray, good Captain," Tuppy said, "tell us the tale."

"My darling," Cain said, "Abram has never vouchsafed that information to anyone. You must allow men their mysteries."

Abram kept looking at Sarah, and his voice was full of nostalgia and quiet reminiscence as he said, "My family in Ireland was starving. I thought I would come to this land as an indentured servant and send back my wages. I did a little better. But I still want to bring my family to this land."

Sarah saw Abram looking at her, as though he would have her react to this.

He should be looking at Felicity, she thought.

———

Alone in her room, Sarah prepared for sleep as if the journey called for the exercise of foresight and caution and, above all, thoroughness. Washing her face and hands did not satisfy her. She was already in her nightgown when she began washing, but she went on to stroke her neck down to the ring of bone beneath her throat and behind at the nape. She ended up soaking the gown's frilly collar past wearing.

Still not satisfied, she took her porcelain basin over by the fire, took off her sleeping chemise and underwear, and finished her wash.

Sarah found another nightgown in her wardrobe and picked through one of its drawers for a lace-trimmed sleeping cap—underlying strands of her hair were wet and she did not want to catch cold. She sat by the fire and combed out her hair for a second time that night, and then donned the sleeping cap, looping its long ties into a floppy bow under her chin.

Once in bed, she lay supine, her legs straight, her arms at her sides. The covers felt heavy but cool. She had forgotten her prayers, though, so she got out of bed again and knelt down by its side. She went through the Lord's Prayer and then the general confession from *The Book of Common Prayer*.

"Almighty and most merciful Father," she prayed. "We have erred, and strayed from thy ways like lost sheep. We have followed too much the devices and desires of our own hearts. We have offended against thy holy laws. We have left undone those things which we ought to have done; and we have done those things which we ought not to have done; and there is no health in us. But thou, O Lord, have mercy upon us miserable offenders. Spare thou those,

O God, who confess their faults. Restore thou those who are penitent. . . ."

The phrase "things done and left undone" had acquired several new meanings—what would she do or leave undone? She had one petition: that she would not ruin Felicity's life. But her wanting to protect her sister might guide her in several directions. If Captain White was drawn to her, then the intended match with Felicity must be called off. He would have to go away.

Sarah stood and crawled back into bed. She lay, as before, legs together, arms at her sides, but sleep did not come. She did not imagine that rolling over to her side would get her comfortable, and she did not know what would. Her thoughts became as uncomfortably still as her body.

Suddenly, she raised up and swiped the sleeping cap off her head, without even untying it, and threw it to the side. Her thick, lustrous hair spilled down over her shoulders in great, loose, twining strands. She was breathing hard.

She lay back down. After a moment she smelled something: a scorching scent. By the time she looked, her sleeping bonnet was too far gone to be rescued from the fire. It was hung up on the end of one of the logs, burning from the dancing ties and its lace fringes toward the crown, becoming a fiery diadem.

She felt cold, but she started to sweat, and then she broke out into sudden, booming laughter, feeling the sky tear away again above her head. She wanted to rush up into it and fly like the angels with the good Captain White.

CHAPTER 11

—

Things Done

Sarah was not the only one who was having trouble sleeping.

After the evening gathering ended, Abram had gone to his corner room on the second floor, which had windows facing the sea along the outer wall and a fireplace at the far end. When he looked in the wardrobe to see how the servants had arranged his clothing, he found his few changes close together in the cavernous interior like lonely travelers in an empty customs office.

He put out the lamp and, by the light of the well-laid fire, changed into his nightshirt, his shadow a dancing taper against the far wall. He lay down in the four-poster bed hoping for a sublime forgetfulness. He was tired after the day's shooting and the evening's entertainment, but he found his mind skipping off the surface of sleep.

After what seemed hours of struggle, his lower back tightening up more and more, he got up and sat by the fire. The blaze on the hearth had burned down to a skeletal heap of glowing embers, but he could still feel the heat against his shins. The rest of the room was cool. Drafts flowed up his spine under his nightshirt.

He tried to redirect his thoughts to Felicity, and told himself that they might well be a very happy couple. She would be a handsome woman in her own parlor. She favored her father, yes, but in an entirely womanly fashion.

His thoughts swiveled back to Sarah, however, as if oiled. He kept thinking about her creamy skin, the pink coral of her lips. Her decolletage, and the way her dress tucked in to her small waist before cupping over her hips. The lovely shadows under her cheekbones in the lamplight. The knowledge harbored in her eyes. She was the kind of young woman whose looks he would never tire of; in fact, as he recalled to his embarrassment, he had hardly been able to keep from staring at her.

He had seen pretty girls before, he reminded himself. Nor did Sarah's adventurous side entirely surprise him. As a sailor, he had encountered women who did their spying in their own behalf. When Sarah played the harpsichord, though, Abram had felt emotions he had never known before. Under her fingertips, the music became charged with the excitement of the dancers as they paired off; he could feel the clumsy relief of their hands touching for the first time, and the lightness of his imagined partner, his hand at the small of her back, as he guided her round in a circle. Sarah caught the flirtatious character of the dance, its constant allusion to more powerful emotions kept at a distance. The quadrille never lost its maddening poise, and neither, her playing seemed to suggest, would she.

Abram could not keep himself from hoping that he had inspired those hidden sensibilities, even as he sensed that life held ranges of emotion unknown to him but vital within this girl. He had been so overcome by all of this that he had blurted out his grand ambition in life—confessed it to her. This mere girl had him acting like a boy rather than a man who had attained four and thirty years.

The one time he was being offered the eldest daughter, by a noble and wealthy father, he had been instantly taken with her younger sister. He wanted to get away, to go back to his rooms in New York. He would be tasting the ashes of this experience for a long time to come, he thought, and he might as well start forgetting it immediately. He tried to redirect his thoughts toward his enjoyment of the shooting, forgetting about Felicity and the whole business. Still, he kept hearing Sarah's music, and when he pictured her, his bones burned within him with a glowing, emberlike fire.

As always, he looked toward the sea for his deliverance. Turning away from the hearth, he got up and walked to the window, looking out at the indigo patch of ocean beyond the cliff's edge. The two elms at either side of the lawn shook in the easterly wind that had come up, but the faraway sea looked still and quiet and inviting.

In the star-strewn sky he could see the Pleiades, Orion, Cassiopeia—all the winking and pulsing and glittering host by which he navigated. He thought of taking a reckoning, doing the calculations in his head. Then a star with a bluish-green tint caught his attention. It shone with a constant light; seemed almost to stare back at him. Distracted by the events of the evening, he was perplexed for a moment, and then he recognized this searching light as Venus.

He had called her Venus in breeches. What reckoning indeed must he make from that sighting?

He did not know if he could possibly sleep. And if he did go away, would he ever retrieve his thoughts from this girl and the possibilities for happiness she had awakened?

———

In the early evening, several days later, Abram watched Robert Nicolls and Sarah strolling up the fence-lined road. Abram was in the apple orchard behind the house, pleasing himself and the cook by picking a few choice baking apples. He could see the two without being seen, although he had not come out with any intention of spying.

Father and daughter walked very slowly, and Nicolls flicked his gaitered calf out with every step like a show horse. The old gentleman had his arm around his daughter and his lips to her ear, as if counseling with her seriously. Then they stopped, threw their heads back, clapped their hands, and their whooping laughter carried all the way up the hill to Abram.

Were they talking about him? he wondered. If that were the case, Nicolls seemed to be taking no great offense, even after days of pointed looks in which Abram followed up his confession with silent entreaties.

Something in their manner did trouble him, however: the way the two fell into step with each other, and the way that Sarah tilted her head to her father's whispers, repositioning a loose strand of hair behind her ear, reminded him of a married couple. Abram began to wonder about favorites and what Nicolls' feelings of loss might be should Sarah marry.

Abram also wondered how he would advance the idea. It was not until that moment that he knew he would try, and his heart almost leapt into his throat at the thought. He could no longer deny that he wanted Sarah. He wanted her with a desire that was as strong as it was sudden. He remembered waking up at sea for the first time. Now, as then, he felt as if he had been reborn in another world; everything was so changed he hardly knew himself, and yet he could not doubt the transformation; the swelling of his emotions, like the swelling sea, tipped and turned and buoyed up his every thought. He had to have her.

Nicolls had invited him to Elysia to meet Felicity, to consider marrying Felicity, and he would be obliged, at some point, to speak to that issue. He might use the occasion to shift Nicolls' line of sight. Aristocrats such as Robert Nicolls could afford to indulge their natural tenderheartedness toward their daughters. Nicolls would try, Abram thought, to honor both Felicity's and Sarah's feelings, if he could.

How would he prepare the way for his feelings toward Sarah to be welcomed? He tossed an apple up and let it fall to the level of his knees before snatching it, overhand, out of the air. A trick, indeed.

––––––––

The next day, while the two men were drinking sherry alone in Nicolls' study, Abram thought he would test the waters, and soon found himself beyond the sight of land.

"You have rightly spoken of your daughters as the three graces, sir," Abram said, "for they are music, poetry, and art personified. But if I had to, I would award the palm to Sarah. She is a delight."

Nicolls' eyes opened and closed as if he had mistakenly peered into the sun. He swished the golden sherry around in his glass, staring at the soothing liquor. "You enjoyed her imposture the other day, did you?" he asked. "It's a wonder I didn't recognize my own daughter among the servants." His tone and his sideways glance left Abram guessing as to how much Nicolls had heard and how much he had known all along.

"You spoke with her about this, sir?"

Nicolls hesitated before replying. He cupped his hands and chewed his almost white lips, as though preparing to deliver a speech. "Sarah has spirit," he said. "But in excess. I'm not sure it would do for anyone to pursue a girl who knows no more than to tramp out into the fields."

"Has she spoken of me to you?" Abram asked.

"Your first meeting required it, I thought."

"But subsequently?"

"You may have noticed how I enjoy conversing with my daughters. Especially Sarah."

"Has she spoken of me with approval?"

"She thinks you eligible enough."

"But has she spoken as if she might one day . . . regard me with affection?"

"You have only just met, sir," Nicolls said. He closed his eyes against his agitation. "The affections of a young girl are various," he said. "They spring up like mayflowers and wither as quickly. Surely you realize this."

"I'm afraid, Squire," Abram said, "that my affections tend the same way."

"Your affections then are brief and insubstantial? The dew of the morning? I thought I saw some beard on your cheeks, Captain White." The apertures of Nicolls' round eyes unloosed, and his suddenly baggy eyes gave him a baleful look, indeed.

But Abram would not back down. Having come this far, he wanted to press the conversation to its conclusion. "I could never be fair to Felicity now," he said.

Nicolls looked at him as if he were a schoolboy in need of instruction. "It has always been the tradition of this family, good Captain," he said, "for the eldest daughter to marry first. A tradition many people respect."

He waited for the appropriate reply, but Abram said nothing.

"Felicity should be a handsome woman in her own home," Nicolls said.

"Those were my thoughts."

"And there have been many who wished to provide her with such a home, including your friend, Cain Smith. But I thought I saw a particular virtue in you." Nicolls tapped the side of his nose with his forefinger, signaling Abram, it seemed, to consider his reply carefully.

Abram offered a flanking maneuver. "I have found," he said, "that men value a thing according to their preferences. Why a sailor wants a ferret is something he may explain to you at length, and in the end you know nothing but that he wants it."

Nicolls wiped his face with his hand. "Forgive me," he said, "if I find the comparison of my daughter to an amusing rodent unseemly." He waited, then snorted out a laugh. "Perhaps I should reconsider the wisdom of wanting an independent son-in-law. Friends will say my liberalism has undone me."

Abram felt he knew enough of the man's character to say, "You would not have embarked on this course if you cared overly much for men's opinions."

"Ah, but I do care for Felicity's opinion, and I must," Nicolls said, close again, quite suddenly, to anger. "So does Sarah. She would not damage her sister for the love of the fairest Adonis." The old gentleman crossed his arms and legs and looked at Abram as if he could hardly pretend to be that. Blotchy gray shadows marbled his face.

"Felicity has impressed me as a young woman of uncommon good sense," Abram said, straining to keep his composure. He waited for the compliment to do its disqualifying work.

Nicolls rubbed his forehead, taking Abram's point, it seemed, that good sense had to argue against forcing such a match. They said nothing more for a time.

When Nicolls finally broke their uncomfortable silence, he went off in another direction, becoming unexpectedly mysterious. "Sarah has been a comfort to me," he said. "But I am not sure she would be to you . . . or anyone else."

Easing back in his chair, the old gentleman swung his buckled shoe out and back, and his next words were addressed to the ceiling in an almost prayerful voice. "You must remember what I am about to say, and you must not come back upon me later asking why I let you have her."

Then he gave Abram a look that held his attention. "What I know about my missy is much greater than you can know, but I have said all I will in giving you this warning. Her Singleton grandmother spent her last days mad as a tinker's bell. She spent her time gluing scraps of paper together. We could not let her approach a library for fear of what she would do to the books." He stopped, wagged his head, gave that gritty-toothed smile. "The spirit you see in Sarah now may become another spirit," he said. "It may not. But I have warned you."

Abram wanted to believe the old gentleman was jesting, but Nicolls was leaning back, sucking in the air and puffing it out as if blowing away a host of demons.

"You give me permission to court her then?" Abram asked.

"Is that all you have heard?"

"I have been so very much hoping I would."

"A madness indeed, isn't it, that would make us so deaf, dumb, and blind."

"How's that, sir?"

"Love."

Abram waited before making his declaration. "I think I do love her, sir."

"You had better love her. She may well give you ample opportunity to prove it."

Abram made no reply to this, but stood up to leave.

"Let's be clear then," Nicolls said. "I am giving you permission to win her. If her affections truly tend in the same way, come back to me. I am not fully resolved on this matter."

"You will speak with Felicity?" Abram asked, embarrassed.

"I doubt the matter will overly trouble her."

———

Hearing through Cain and Tuppy that Nicolls had talked with Felicity, Abram asked the three sisters to take a walk the next afternoon. They went out along a lane lined with maple trees, their autumn dress resplendent in the sun, scattering a confetti of cherry, lemon, and burnt-orange at their feet. He counted on Felicity and Livy walking conveniently ahead, and they obliged—almost from the first fencepost.

Sarah and Abram strolled side by side, talking of the cook's buttermilk pie at their midday meal and other failing topics. Abram complimented her father's shooting. He asked after the pheasant.

Boyd had rigged up an ingenious pen, she said. The chickens seemed to be delighted to have a new neighbor.

They walked for a while with the silence growing, the pressure inside their chests expanding.

"Why have we come out today?" Sarah asked suddenly. She did not wait for an answer. "You are silly to be interested in me," she said matter-of-factly. "Felicity would make you a better match." She tried to look relieved to have introduced the topic on both their minds, but her neck started to color.

Abram had not counted on her leading the way. He thought he should try to surprise her in turn. "I know what you were feeling when you played the harpsichord for me," he said.

"I was not playing solely for you."

"You were dancing with me. In your mind, you were taking my hand at every turn."

She stepped quickly ahead of him, her combativeness at the ready, like a stone thrown with underspin accelerating on its second hop. "Are all your decisions guided by such fancies? I am not sure it would be prudent for anyone to marry a gentleman like that."

He did not understand how she could admit to what he had said and turn his remark against him at the same time. He began to doubt that this outing supplied the right setting for their conversation. Stopping in the middle of the lane, he faced her, reached out, and took both of her hands in his.

She gave him a wild look, her eyes darting around. But she was smiling, or trying to—one side of her upper lip caught on her pretty teeth. She clasped his hands tightly, as though she did not want to get away from him so much as escape the choices before them. Her spirit was indeed higher than he could ever have imagined, and he wondered whether to go on.

He thought he would try just once more. "Do you know," he said, "how two ships communicate with each other in the dark? They take a lantern and put a leather hood over it. Then the officer stands at the rail with the lantern in its hood and covers and uncovers it. The light flashes out over the waters to the other ship in a sequence that the officers on board recognize as a code. They write the sequence of flashes down, and then they decipher the message."

"What do they do at midday?" she asked, tilting her head.

He ignored her remark. "The night we met," he said, "before I went to bed, I read the stars. Most evenings, I will look up, wherever I am, and find my position by the heavens." He knew what he would say to her now, what he would confess and withhold, and he was already wondering how she would react. "Two nights ago, I could see Venus." He let go of one of her hands and pointed low to the northwestern sky. "About there. Can you follow my line?"

She drew closer and turned her back to look along his arm. Then she turned round again and moved to him and held his waist. He could see little of her but her upturned face, and he felt as if her body were folding itself into his own. "I had called you 'Venus in breeches' that day, remember? And it seemed to me that Venus was spelling out your name."

He looked down with the thought that he might kiss her, but before his courage succeeded, she had skipped away from him, down the lane.

Then she turned back toward him. "She may have," she said. "And I hope you received her message gladly. But what do you want from me, Abram White? What do you intend?"

He did not want to throw the question across the distance between them, nor had he anticipated them arriving so quickly at statements of intentions; but there seemed no avoiding the distance or the question as a bridge. He called it out to her: "For us to marry."

"Why did you discuss this matter first with my father?"

He crossed the distance between them and stood close to her. "I did not want to arouse the hope of what might prove impossible. This way, only I can be disappointed."

"Would you be?" she asked.

Underneath her flirtatious ways, he saw, she had real questions. "Who knows why it is, Sarah Nicolls, that a gentleman walks into a room, pleased with his own life, and walks out again in desperate need of the young woman who has played the harpsichord for him. But that did happen to me. And I think something like this happened for you as well."

"Which is why I must know your feelings. How can I trust you when you have me at such a disadvantage? An older man. A sea captain. And, I'm glad to say, a good shot."

They laughed, and the laughter carried them together.

They were eager and clumsy. Sarah's hands rushed to his face and back around him. He found her so lovely that he hardly knew what to do—the riches of her hair and skin and scent confused him and made him hesitate, like a man before a meal of bewildering variety.

From the first she kissed him as if she had no intention of stopping. And they might not have stopped, there in the midst of that fair day, with a light breeze carrying the forest's mossy scent and the ground growing soft under their feet, if Abram had not looked up and seen Felicity and Livy heading back toward them down the lane.

CHAPTER 12

―――

Dreams of a Lifetime

A bram had received Sarah's first kisses as her pledge to marry. He was almost certain she had thought of their embracing, at the time, as her answer as well. Yet, somehow, their engagement remained an open question, even as the very nature of their understanding seemed to change from day to day.

Abram's decisiveness was met by an alluring reticence in Sarah. She dallied. She dallied with great charm, with a gift for surprise that gave the waiting its own fascination, with impulsive sprints ahead before shocking retreats, and with an ill-concealed relish at how her stalling unsettled the good captain. Even in the fields of love she played the deceptive beater.

Every seasonable afternoon Sarah and he walked out together, chaperoned by Felicity or Livy or both—at least to the first dusty gold stand of withered corn at the back of the third field from the house. There, a wooded hillock rose up; its path, crossed and trenched by seasonal streams, could be muddy after a night's rain, which provided an excuse for the chaperoning sister to turn back. Abram and Sarah would promise to catch up. They only wanted to rest a while in the shade, to enjoy the cool, pine-scented enclosure the trees made against the heat-filled hazy afternoons, before they, too, would return. Dallying there, the moments they requested stretched into the hours when they conveniently lost track of time. It occurred to Abram at times that he was too old to be tramping about in the woods for the sake of stolen kisses, yet he did not care.

It came to him, as well, that if he was really going to marry this girl, he would be obliged, his life long, to talk to her. This, after years of self-possession and the silence of his life at sea, he was not well-prepared to do. He even came to see that the very thing that made him trustworthy in the eyes of men might prove an unhelpful mystery to Sarah. He had no conversation. Even when he had gone out in society, he needed little. When asked, he could quickly state his views on politics and commerce, and these were thought to be sound. This satisfied the gentlemen. And the ladies required little more from him than that he wear a kind expression and pose one or two questions. They entertained themselves talking at him, gaining him the reputation of being an admirable listener.

With Sarah, however, this did not suffice. She needed him to take her into the quiet, the place within him where he knew what he wanted and what he must do.

He began to tell her about his life, thinking that if she knew the details she could infer the sense they made. As he had never spoken of his life at length before, he was as surprised as she at the words he found, and what these words revealed to him counted for almost as much as what they told her.

He also wanted her to understand important discoveries he had made, especially the reading of the sea. He asked her father's permission to take her riding, alone this once, out to the eastern-most point of the long beach, where they could see the Sound on their left and the waters of Stony Brook Harbor on their right. If they were fortunate enough to run into a little weather, the wind picking up and the clouds scudding lower, he might show her how differently changing conditions affected two bodies of water and the confusion to be expected from their coming together.

As it happened, on the day they rode out, a pearly gray ceiling of clouds covered the sky, with more ominous black-weighted banks drifting underneath. The wind kept shifting directions, and the day felt close and fresh by turns.

Sarah, dressed in her riding skirt and soft leather boots, rode a tall chestnut mare, very pretty but with a broad girth from overfeeding; Abram had been given a black stallion. She challenged him to a race, and, not much of a horseman, he couldn't coax the speed out of the stallion that she could from her overweight mare. When she circled back to him, he cautioned her that they shouldn't wear the horses out. Her triumphant look made him laugh at his own humbug. "All right," he said, "you will command all our chariots."

When they reached the beach's terminus, they dismounted and stood together, looking toward the sea. Abram stood behind Sarah and put his arms around her, his upper arms covering her shoulders, his fingers knitted together low on her stomach. He had never taken this liberty with her before, embracing her from behind, and he held her cautiously. What continually shocked Abram was that Sarah, a sixteen-year-old who had never been courted before, never seemed shocked at any of his liberties, as though she had anticipated or imagined them long in advance.

The whitecaps on the Sound side appeared, already, like fanged serpents in comparison with the gentle rollers in the harbor. Unknitting his fingers to gesture with one hand or the other, but always hugging her to him with a forearm, Abram talked about the sea, why the waves out in the Sound looked as if they were streaming in toward them faster than usual because of the offshore winds, and how the differences between the two bodies of water were caused by more than the simple sheltering effect of the beach.

"The water itself," Abram said, "knows whether it belongs to the Sound or the harbor. Seas are not great depressions in the earth filled by the rain. They are like countries. The waters know their country, and each has its own character. But it is not a character you are allowed to befriend. An ocean is too great for friendship. It can only be known, or partly known. The sea hides much of what it knows within itself."

"Like you," she said.

"No, no. No," he said, and laughed. "I am discovering that women are great poets, for they are always thinking that anything you say means something else."

"You could tell me what you do mean," she said.

"Well, I am trying to tell you something of what I know so that you can know me."

"I would like to know," she said, "why you have never married."

"I can't tell you, Sarah, what I don't know myself. I suppose, though, because I have not been in a position to marry."

"You are a ship's captain."

"By the grace of God," he said. "And I have had other obligations." He let go of her and stepped before her. If he was going to make a long speech, he needed pacing room.

Then he told her about the incident on *The Mercy* when he had heard the voice and seen the light flash out, realizing as he did so that they had never spoken of religious matters before. But he was finding that he trusted her.

"I am considered a brave and sometimes even a great man," he said, "but if I have done anything great, it has not been my greatness that has accomplished it. I have been the recipient of great mercies.

"And I have not done the thing I set out to do. I have supported my family, but as I told you the first night we dined together, I have always meant to bring them to this land.

"Then, I believe, God would have me do something more, beyond this promise I made so long ago—a promise I made more to myself, I suppose in the end, than to my family. Their letters sometimes contemplate immigration. They are still in difficulties, if none so severe as when I left home. Truly, I am not sure what their will in the matter would finally be.

"So, dear Sarah, what I am trying to say is that I do not see myself as others see me. I am only a man with many intentions, some only partially conceived."

At the end of his account, she said, without malice, "You are a fraud."

"I never asked for such divine favors," he said, perhaps too quickly.

"But you must acknowledge them."

"Tell me how."

"In gratitude for God's favors, you must do something with the privileges you have been given. You must at least ascertain your family's true circumstances. They and others will listen to you, if you are about to do something charitable for them."

Her discernment startled Abram. She not only knew about God's graces, she knew about people as well. Her insight clarified her identity in a new way, made who she was more present to him, and yet introduced further mysteries.

"Do you consider yourself pious?" he asked, wanting to know her beliefs.

"I am not pious," she said. "And I have no particular virtue. But

I can *see* certain things. And I do believe. Most earnestly."

She went over and sat on the top of a sand dune. The way she moved, with such gravity and precision, reminded Abram of a judge taking his seat in a court, or the clerk of a church's governing session taking his seat among the elders. She reached down and cropped some blades of dune grass growing at her feet.

"On the day of my mother's death," she said, "I became hysterical and ill. She died toward morning, they say. That's when I recovered."

He thought of what her father had told him, recalled the old man's warnings. But this experience, the way she spoke of it, gave him hope. "Have you had other such experiences?" he asked.

"A number," she said. She wasn't looking at him now; she seemed, almost, ashamed. "It does not have anything to do with me," she said. "These times come upon me, and they are less a mercy than a hardship. Yet they do remind me of my Creator."

The wild hope sprang up within that she could tell him what to do about his ultimate destiny. "What must I do, then?" he asked. "Beyond my family, what must I do?"

"That is not for me to say," she said.

"But can you 'see' what I might do?" he asked, his tone lighter.

"I hope to be there with you to see it," she said.

———

On the afternoon of the day before Abram's stay was to end, the two once again walked out together unaccompanied, this time to gather watercress for the cook. When they had found the patch, Abram picked two handfuls and lay them in a clump to one side. After wetting the cheesecloth liner of their basket in the spring that fed the patch, Abram enfolded the tender plants in the cloth, packed the basket, and handed it to Sarah. The air about them had grown pungent with the cress's biting green scent.

Sarah was wearing a rough gabardine hunting dress and a close-fitting red jacket that made Abram very conscious of her breathing. He had to keep himself from smothering that rise and fall in his embrace. Late golden light slanted through the trees and outlined her left side with a fiery glow, eclipsing the rest of her into a shadowy silhouette.

With his lover's heart, Abram believed the fire of her spirit burned more intensely than any sunburst, although that spirit had its shadowy side, too. He was very much in love. And what was strange was that this feeling of his had detached itself from her dark hair, the petite rounded toes of her riding boots, her quietly knowing expressions—from anything he could specify—and had buried itself wholly and completely just in *her*. He loved *her*. So much of his life, in so short a time, was now so concentrated on *her* that he felt as if he already lived with her—he did in his thoughts at least. She was his double, and he would never know rest again until he lost himself in their ecstasy. He was as mad as all lovers are, and he hoped for mercy.

After he handed her the basket, he said, "I will be going away day after tomorrow. I would like to speak of our understanding."

"You will have to speak first," she said, "of what you mean."

"You know I want you to marry me."

"I think I know very little about you," she said.

"Sarah," he said, almost barking at her, "we speak of these things one day, and on the next you act as if what we have said has been of no consequence."

She put down the basket and approached him. Standing at his side, she placed her hands, one on top of the other, on his left shoulder and drew so close to him that he could feel her breath on his cheek. "Have you ever asked me, then, to marry you?"

"You know I have."

"You have spoken to my father."

He turned to her, caught her up in his arms, and held her so tightly that he noticed with satisfaction her sharp intake of breath. "Sarah Nicolls," he said, "I am asking you for the honor of your hand in marriage. I vow I will love you dearly and provide for your every need."

Quickly, she slipped her hand behind his head, kissed him on the mouth, and then, just as quickly, danced away. "Now the question has been posed," she said, throwing this back over her shoulder.

"And so it must be answered."

She turned full to him, like a soldier, who, by keeping his hands straight at his sides, wishes to appear unafraid, confident, and earnest. "Come back to me in the spring, or whenever your next voyage sees you back to New York."

"No!"

She did not flinch. "Then what do you propose?"

He found, suddenly, to his horror, that he had not worked out his plans in explicit detail, and he knew enough of her anxious spirit by this time to understand that this alone might arouse distrust in Sarah. He did have one idea, and he tried to carry the issue by being brusque about it.

"I am too old for long social observances," he said, "and your sister is not wed yet. It would be better if we conspired to visit the minister of the nearest chapel privately."

She waited a moment before speaking. "I did not want to marry at all before my sister," she said, and knowing the modulations of her voice, how it dropped even lower when she spoke with genuine feeling, he knew this to be almost a fixed idea. "This will not be pleasant for her."

"Then you will?" he asked, hopeful now.

"Where would we live?"

"I was going to ask your father if we might return here for a time. My rooms in the city would not be comfortable for more than a short stay."

He watched her take a breath and saw her shoulders fall as the tension left her. She came back to him and held him, her body resting easily against his. He sensed her great relief; he could not be sure exactly why, whether from having reached the end of their jousting, having made up her mind, or something else.

"Don't tell me when," she said abruptly, as if pulling the thought from the air. She looked into his face and shook her head as she repeated, "Don't tell me."

"But I want you to be ready."

"I will have my things packed. They will be made ready within the next few days. The servants will tell you when all the preparations are complete. The Smiths can return to town without you, and you can stay on here. You can, can't you? And then, when everything is ready—conspire with father all you like—come and take me."

He had to wonder at whatever it was in him that caused him to love her. The ways in which she differed from anyone he had ever met, her strangeness—almost exotic, wild—stole into what was lonely in him. He sensed how removed she was from others, from everyone; like him, she had been given a solitary life. The idea of sharing their isolation drew him to her powerfully. Bound together, hand and foot, they would be two prisoners whose jailor, solitude, could not know that he had granted his captives' deepest wish—to be together.

CHAPTER 13

A Pennywhistle for Your Thoughts

That evening, after dinner, Abram acquainted Robert Nicolls with the elopement plans they had contrived. The old gentleman stood in the midst of his library fingering *The Metamorphoses* by Ovid, his index finger marking his place, as if he did not want to lose his mooring in that imaginary world.

"I suppose a small, private ceremony would be fitting," he said, "with Felicity as yet a maid. But I would not deny Sarah her occasion to celebrate."

"Sir, I believe she prefers this arrangement. She has asked not even to know the time."

Nicolls at last put his book down on his desk. "I'm not sure I take your meaning."

"The day, the hour—the exact opportunity is to be a surprise."

"You are to 'come upon her unawares'?" Nicolls asked. "You must know the penalties in the stories of antiquity for that! Every groom suffers a metamorphosis, but not into a stag, a tree, a brook. It's usually enough to become a husband!" He wagged his head so vigorously that his large ears seemed about to flap. "What do you make of such a wish, sir?"

Abram took a step back, shying like the predicted stag. "Her spirits are very high."

"They are indeed, good Captain. They are indeed. She also knows herself better than I would have guessed."

Abram found himself mystified once again.

"Or she may have struck upon this scheme without fully understanding its genius. What do you suppose? How well do you know this woman you propose to marry?"

"I'm afraid your reasoning seems the thing I must discover. And I confess, I do not comprehend your argument."

"Sarah would avoid leave-takings altogether in this life. She has never fully recovered from her mother's death. So she proposes to be spirited away. As Zeus did Leda! As Apollo did Daphne! You are the god and she the shepherdess on the mountainside. An ingenious solution!" Nicolls' sphincterish eyes enlarged and shone with a silverish dazzle on Abram.

Abram did not understand, and he thought better of making any reply.

"And yet, you are a sea captain. And there will be many partings in Sarah's life. That is what she must scarcely have thought of! That has been all my concern." He turned away, looking suddenly injured and bitter.

"I have not my fortune yet," Abram said. "That's very true. I thought, if it suits you, that Sarah and I might make our home with you in these next years. Until I come home from the sea."

Nicolls turned around and looked as if he had won an unexpected prize. "Yes, I think that would answer very well," he said. "She would not be too much alone then." His voice rushed on as he thought aloud. "Sarah has been a comfort to me, and your company a pleasure. This home supplies more than the needed room. We should be a very happy joint venture—as you commercial men say." The old gentleman was becoming more and more excited, rocking onto the balls of his feet. "Yes. A most admirable solution. Just what I would have proposed."

Then Nicolls came over to him and did something extraordinary: he grabbed Abram by the back of his neck and kept his hand atop the knob of his spine. He looked up into Abram's face and repeated, "Zeus and Leda! Apollo and Daphne! Or shall it be Artemis and Actaeon? This very night I have been reading about that unwitting intruder, changed into a stag and hunted down by his own dogs. O good Captain! What a chase she may set you on!" By the end, his eyes were tearing.

Abram backed away uncomfortably, wondering why the old gentleman's happiness should make him so suspicious. He mumbled something about this being agreed and that he would let Nicolls know the date and time as soon as these were arranged.

———

As it happened, Abram had to cancel the original date on which he intended to whisk Sarah off. Her clothes had already been packed, and he had the ceremony scheduled, when she informed him that her wedding dress would not be ready for another week; so, whatever he intended, she said, they could not leave before then. He took his revenge by rescheduling the event for a week after the dress would arrive.

Since the local chapel had only a circuit minister, they would travel to the nearest village with a Church of England minister, nearly a day's ride distant. At noon on the eve of the wedding, Nicolls rode off, telling his three girls that he had business to attend to in New York. Sarah pouted furiously at dinner and went to bed early, which suited Abram's intentions so well he wondered whether she had guessed what was afoot.

She could take an eternity dressing, he had found, and the more important the occasion, the more she dawdled. He was not going to wait, pacing about, while she readied herself for their supposedly clandestine departure. His plan called for quick action.

He had sent to the city for a coach-and-four. They were stabled not far away, and the driver had been given instructions to come to the house about midnight. He was to pull up at a dead walk, with as little clop and jangle as possible.

When the coach arrived, an hour late, it sounded to Abram like a calliope. But the stomping rumble, the rolling clatter and creakings, the whinnying and snorting came to a halt at last.

Its arrival triggered Abram's simple plan. Dressed in his captain's uniform, his best boots shined, his snail-shaped hat in hand, his ruby stick-pin at his lapel, he made his way quickly up the stairs to Sarah's room. He met Felicity and Livy in the hallway, who, having been informed of that night's events, were dressed and ready to see their sister off. He gave them each a kiss on the cheek; he did not know why—for luck, he supposed, and courage.

He entered Sarah's room and found her in her four-poster bed, buried underneath several layers of bedclothes, asleep. An oil lamp still burned low by her bedside. He came closer and, just for a moment, stopped, amazed at her restfulness at such a time, fascinated by her cool, pale cheek against the pillow.

He pulled back the covers, and she stirred but did not wake. Curled on her side, she was wearing a white nightdress with a high lace-trimmed collar. The nightdress emphasized the child that remained in her, and yet what he could see of her shrouded figure was more womanish than he had expected or dared hoped. So much so that he forgot for the moment what he had come for and found himself staring dumbly at her, with all of a man's hopeless fascination in the woman he loves. It struck him then that from now on he would be permitted to touch her without restrictions. Why it had not occurred to him before that he must marry, he could not think.

His thoughts cast forward to their wedding night, tomorrow, a lover's eternity. He touched her forehead to wake her, smoothing her hair back from her brow, as if comforting someone with a fever.

She shook her head, her eyelids tightened, and then she tried to sit up suddenly, crying out, "No!"

Then he saw her fearful eyes focus on him, and she looked about at where she was. Her expression grew timid and curious.

"It is time," he said.

"Is it?" she asked.

"We are to be married at dawn."

She looked about her again, more quickly, uneasily, as if expecting others to appear.

Abram knew he would have to move decisively now. Slipping one hand under her shoulders and another under her thighs, he started to pick her up in his arms. She mistook his intention and tried to kiss him, their mouths bumping clumsily as he stood up. He could tell from the way she broke off the kiss that she wanted to get down. Heaving her up into the air and catching her more securely a second time—denying her request—he swung out the door and started down the stairs.

Conscious of Sarah's startled look, he kept his eyes on the passageway before him. He nodded to Felicity and Livy as he passed them on the landing. They stood frozen, amazed at his action, hardly calling out their good-byes. The fuzzy-haired Crump opened the front door, and they swept outside.

The coach's height made for difficulties, but he managed by turning sideways, putting Sarah's feet over its threshold, and catapulting her in. He took a breath and scrambled in after her, hoping he had not done her any damage.

She was sitting back in one corner of the cab, her arms out to each side, bracing herself still against her landing.

"You will be dressing as we travel," he said, trying to dispel the moment by being as matter-of-fact as possible. He opened up a trunk that Felicity had directed the coachman to place on the forward bench. His winter coat had been placed there as well, and he put this on now, his studied movements offering a practical lesson in the art of dressing in a cab.

Opening the hatch of the cab, he called out, "Driver! Move on!" The coach lurched forward, and they caught their balance.

"Hurry, Sarah," he said. "The night air—" Making an exaggerated effort out of turning to one side, he added, "I'll close my eyes. Think of yourself as being alone. But hurry, please, Sarah. You mustn't take a chill."

"I will not hurry," she said, her voice brassy with anger. "You must not have any proper idea of how a woman dresses! You will have to help me."

He was surprised at her anger. He wanted to say something about their elopement—they were doing this together, after all. "Your sisters told me I might have to help," he said, weakly.

"What improper imaginations they must have had," she said with accusing embarrassment.

"They said you would be very much covered by the time you required my assistance."

"But my hair!"

"I like it brushed back over your shoulders. You look lovely that way. I prefer it."

"This is my wedding," she said. "I shall do what I can—and my hair must be put up." She started sorting through the trunk, glancing at him now and again, anger and embarrassment chasing across her face.

She took out her beaver coat and pulled it over her shoulders. Then she placed a series of undergarments on the upholstered, crimson bench. Half-standing in the bouncing coach, facing him, but with her head turned severely away, she began to dress.

Her wedding dress, when she put it on, made it seem day in the coach long before the sun came up. She sat sideways on the seat across from him and asked, rather gruffly, for his help with the fastenings at the back of her dress. Even in the chilly cab he felt the heat of her body against his fingers as he hooked the loops. By the time he finished with the last, he was impatient with desire for her.

She did look, there in the bouncing cab, combing out her hair, like a goddess who had been stumbled upon in an off moment. He watched her, remembering Nicolls' reference to the penalties mere mortals suffered for intruding on the gods. But the long strokes of the brush seemed to be working out her annoyance. As she continued to brush her hair, she took admiring glances at the pearl-studded fretwork over the bodice and down the arms of her gown and its sheer fall to her white-slippered toes. Her pride made him love her all the more.

He wanted to tell her. He wanted her to know how close he was to tears. He wanted so much for them to be happy in this moment, and he wanted to say the words, the right words, whatever they might be.

He crossed over and sat beside her and put his arm around her. She leaned away from him, pulling the brush through her long hair so that her hands kept traveling away from his. He kissed her behind her ear and at the nape of her neck. She pushed him away and continued brushing.

He put his hand on her shoulder, left it there a moment on the silken embroidery, and then jostled her shoulder in a friendly way. When she did not respond, he did it again.

She flashed around and punched him in the chest with the wooden brush. She landed the next blow against his head, and he grabbed her forearms and tried to smother her assault in his embrace.

He had her arms locked up in his, and as a way of saying he was not hurt and had taken no offense, he tried to kiss her.

She bit his cheek so hard that the pain exploded behind his right eye and reached upward toward his temple and into his scalp.

He cried out and dove to the other side of the coach. His face suddenly felt wet and rubbery and then began to sting, and he put his fingers to his cheek and felt the blood.

With the oily blood on his fingertips, he had to resist the impulse to strike her—a desire almost as powerful and immediate as a reflex. He had to breathe hard and long to calm his anger.

Looking up at her, he saw that she was barricaded in one corner of the opposite seat, staring at him, her lips quivering and her jaw clenched as if her teeth would soon chatter.

He waited as the fury left him. This took a while, and the moment kept rounding back toward violence like a barbed hook. As he dabbed at the wound with his handkerchief, he used the pain's diminishing as the hourglass of his anger.

When he had grown calm and needed, himself, to be comforted—to be reassured that they were not on their way to disaster—he crossed over to her side of the cab, placed himself beside her, and held her. He kept trying to think of what he should say. At least she did not resist him this time.

He started kissing her once more, and this time he did not stop when she showed only fear, and he did not stop when she responded listlessly; he did not stop, indeed, until she was returning all the niceties of his affections. Her fingers smoothed his hair back and played with the curls around his ears. She kissed the vivid ring of teeth marks on his cheek, her apology in her soft lips. At last she seemed to want him as much as he did her.

"Artemis," Abram muttered.

"Who? Antonia? Who is that? Do you know me, husband?"

"I am learning to, Sarah," he said.

She pulled her head back and looked at him. "The bridegroom's cheek is turning purple," she said. "The minister will think you have lately returned from the cannibals." She laughed a hard, dismissive laugh and kissed him again before he could say anything in reply.

———

By the time the coach stopped and they saw the sunrise and the white, clapboard chapel rising behind the cozy graveyard, with its headstones knocked at all angles, they were both at the height of impatience.

Robert Nicolls greeted them in the foyer, and his round eyes looked like whirlpools when he saw the purple tattoo on Abram's cheek. But he said nothing, as the couple had obviously worked out their differences. Together they walked down the aisle toward the waiting minister.

When the white-wigged minister wrapped his stole around their joined hands, Abram could not help but note what feeling Sarah conveyed in the subtle manipulations of her clasp—how she rubbed his hands as if they were an Aladdin's lamp.

"By the power invested in me, I declare you man and wife," the minister said. "May the Lord bless you and cause His face to shine upon you. May He rise up to meet you in the morning and rest with you at night. May He cause your union to bear fruit and the days of your offspring to be long and happy. Amen."

The minister opened his rheumy eyes. "You may kiss . . . ah, well, you have commenced, haven't you," he said.

Abram and Sarah were already embracing as if the world could hardly expect any more discretion from them.

Robert Nicolls witnessed this event with the inevitable twinges of fatherly jealousy. But he approved the foolishness of his son-in-law, satisfied at last that he was not too cold a man to control his Sarah.

Before he saw them off, Nicolls put his head amongst theirs in a joint embrace, and when they rolled away, he took out a little threepenny whistle and played an Irish jig, dancing to his own music about the graveyard.

CHAPTER 14

———

Snooping

They went, after a night's stay at an inn, to Abram's rooms in New York. He lived in a red brick building, with black shuttered windows, a white lintel at the roofline, and a cupola topped with a dolphin weather vane. His rooms on the northwest corner looked out over a broad tree-lined avenue bordered by similar buildings on the other side. Rising over the opposite houses and the trees, the newly hoisted masts of ships that lay in the yards along the East River spanned out against the sky, so huge they appeared much closer than they were, so imposing that they dwarfed landlocked life with the possibilities of the sea.

In the mornings, Sarah liked to stand at the parlor window and look out at the rising masts and wonder about the life they would be leading. She had these mornings to herself, as Abram went out early each day to stretch his legs, see his friends at the shipyards, and gossip about activity in the harbor.

Abram's man, Hodges, prepared her breakfast. He proved to be the first really unpleasant surprise in their marriage. A tall creature with a bristling wave of brown hair and pop-eyes, Hodges resembled his master in only one respect, his high waist; but he imitated him in all things to the point of impersonation. He was one of those servants who nodded to his master's statements as if approving. He added touches to his standard black and white livery—a subtly snail-shaped hat when he went out, a duplicate ruby stickpin—that aped Abram's dress. He insinuated his right to agree to every order, and his laugh always echoed Abram's: the same explosive laugh, the same abrupt cut-off, a hiccup too late.

The first morning as Sarah ate, Hodges stood to her left and behind her, near the pantry door, watching. She sensed his gaze traveling over her shoulder. Her knife kept sliding off her plate, staining the white tablecloth with marmalade. Then she failed to hook the nub of the lid under the teapot's rim when she looked inside to see if there was enough for a last cup. The lid fell into her cup as she poured.

Hodges tidied up the teapot mess. He went on to arrange her knife and fork on her plate with an agonizing deliberation before he cleared the table.

Sarah soon insisted that Hodges set out her breakfast and then leave the house to run his errands. She wanted to send him away completely and told Abram so. Her husband said this was impossible. Hodges had come aboard Captain Jack's ship in a "trade" when the Royal Navy had commandeered one of their best crewmen. Afraid of heights, Hodges was virtually useless as a seaman. Captain Jack would have beaten him to death if Abram had not insisted on making the man his own personal servant. Sarah, discerning that Abram enjoyed being kind to weaknesses he could never permit himself, dropped the matter.

Still, she waited until Hodges left the house before venturing from her bedroom in the morning. She would come out in her robe and slippers and stand at the window, drinking her tea, looking toward the looming masts and their long, crisscrossing shadows in the early morning sun. This was her time to think, to take stock. She felt happy yet uneasy, and not merely because of Hodges.

When Abram had gotten up out of their bed the first morning of their married life, she had watched his efficient and energetic dressing with dismay. She wanted to say, "Come back to bed." As he shot his arms and legs through his shirt and trousers so fast the ruffling cloth snapped, and buttoned his buttons with a magician's dexterity, she felt more and more neglected. He had been so passionate the night before. Now he seemed content to leave, resuming his old life without her. She realized how little she knew him.

These feelings did not diminish as the days progressed. The force of his life as it resided in his habits—his morning walks, the way he could be quiet for hours on end, and his constant toil through one task after another, maddeningly unhurried and efficient—set him apart from her across seas of experience. She felt islanded at times, and strangely alone.

Abram seemed unaware that she was troubled, and perhaps, she thought, she should be less troubled by these things. She knew that some of her feelings were entirely of her own creation, even though these were the ones she understood hardly at all.

Many of her morning reflections, once she had accustomed herself to Abram's sunrise departures, began in the lingering warmth, the cocoon, of the previous night's embraces. Abram had an inventive and patient nature as a lover, and in the daytime she liked to savor the memories of those intimacies.

One morning, as she slipped about the bare wood floors of Abram's rooms in her stocking feet, she found herself opening up the cabinets, the bureaus, his wardrobe. All of these had locks, but he had shown her the pantry drawer where he kept the ring of keys.

His clothes in the wardrobe delighted her. By running her finger underneath the lapel of his dinner jacket, she could almost feel the density of his chest, its pliable strength. The way the coat parted when she undid its buttons—the two sides swinging open—made her want to grab him.

That he should have lived alone for so long, so successfully, troubled her. She was glad, in a way, that he would not depend too much upon her, yet she could not be entirely happy at the thought.

Since her mother's death, she had not felt as at ease in anyone's company. Or her own. She had found herself turning around and looking for someone, as if she were being followed by a friend who never caught up. Abram had finally been there, and he had married her. But she did not trust his love for her yet.

She slipped out of the bedroom into the parlor. A writing desk, with a locked drawer, stood close by her window there. When Sarah unlocked the drawer, she found a velvet pouch the color of dark-green moss. Within the pouch lay a compass, what looked like two rulers hinged together, a small spy glass, and a brown leather-bound book. A cradle of rolled parchments lay behind this pouch, and when Sarah took these out she found them to be the nautical charts Abram used to plot his journeys.

She could tell which wanderings had been pleasurable for him. Small, coded notations by the various ports of call held abbreviated comments written in backwards letters that she deciphered by studying them in her hand mirror. Abram had gone to great difficulty to conceal the strange names that bounced back to her, some of them obviously only the names of exotic dishes and beverages, but some of them what might be the names of mountains, rivers . . . or other women. What was she to make of a name like Kokolioko? Caspersia? Tanoowau? Or Zuni? And remembrances like "her arms reach out to me," "she lies at her Lord's feet," and "never forget."

She picked up the leather-bound volume and scanned its weathered gray pages. The first third of the book had almost nothing in it but dates and a long series of geographical positions, numbers for longitudes, latitudes, and times. Then little by little a few comments entered in; notations like the ones on the charts, at first, and then more expanded thoughts.

Sarah went to the back of the book to examine the most recent entries. They dated from the last social season when Abram had been dining at the tables of society.

> Mrs. Fitch thinks that she will get a son-in-law for her daughter by charming the man herself. Does she not see that any man will be more curious about her girl's figure (plump) than anxious that her mother be a pleasant dinner companion?

At least, Sarah thought ruefully, I did not have that problem. She read on.

> I am not sure why I have begun to mix in society. I wonder what vanity in me it appeals to. What colors the air at these dinners is that I am obviously after a wife from a suitable family. I am not sure this is the case. Sometimes those around me tell me I am in want of someone to look after me. When I say I have my man, Hodges, they arch their eyebrows and cock their heads like conspirators waiting for an intended accomplice to get the point. The flesh is weak enough without encouragement!

Sarah had wondered about his experiences with other women. Now she began to be afraid of reading further.

> Sat by a Miss Evelyn Teasdale at dinner this evening. Miss

Teasdale's hair is like a shower of gold. She has fair skin, blushes very much so that the heightened color of her cheeks makes the gold of her hair burn all the more brightly. She is neat and precise in all her movements and responded to my every remark with courteous and thoughtful replies and met my witticisms with delicate laughter. The one mar on her beauty is the roughened texture of her complexion, which, despite a heavy layer of powder, shows the writing of youthful pustules that maturity has erased only imperfectly. Still, she has a compact and promising figure, and when she first sat down beside me I envied the chair she sat on its privilege of holding her.

By the end of dinner, after doing my best to entertain Miss Teasdale, even telling several sea stories to her and the rest of the company like a windy mariner in a tavern, I had exhausted my sociable energies, and looking into Miss Teasdale's eyes I found no rest there, only the same willingness to continue on with her courteous and thoughtful replies and her delicate laughter.

These are the occasions when I ask myself what a seaman like myself is doing looking into the eyes of young ladies.

In the end I feel more isolated than ever, but now discomfited by this isolation, and I wish that I had never entered into this business—whatever it may be.

In truth, Sarah thought, what did he think this Miss Teasdale's "promising" figure was promising him?

A noise in the street below startled her, and she stirred guiltily. She should not be reading this, she knew. Yet her curiosity took her further into the privacy of her husband's thoughts.

The Haverstocks, the Smiths, the Furloughs, the Livingstons, the Delanceys, these people invite me to share their tables with them and think of me as a daring character and a useful friend. But am I a gentleman? My rank and this new land allow them to associate with me, but I think they prefer to consider me something of an aristocratic pirate rather than acknowledge too directly my humble origins—they would have turned aside when I was but a common seamen or boatswain's mate.

Sarah liked this more serious entry better, but the next considered Miss Teasdale once more. She should stop reading now—yet she knew she wouldn't.

I saw Miss Teasdale again tonight. She made me think of a time very long ago when I refused to go with my shipmates to spend our pay on sporting women.

What I do not find in Miss Teasdale's eyes makes me remember what I knew I would never find, in another way, with tavern ladies. Perhaps my supreme contentment in my solitude has been, at least partially, the excuse of the seaman who decides, after he has lost a race to the topmast, that the prize wasn't worth the winning.

How is it that I know what I do not find in Miss Teasdale's eyes? I cannot name it. But what I do know now is that my searchings are being carried by a deep current I cannot resist. I might yet deflect myself from where it intends to carry me, but it would be useless now to turn against it.

In those days of chaste dissatisfaction, I used to sit in my boatswain's cabin, where every complaint of the vessel—every creak and shuddering—echoed my own groaning. I felt trapped in those quarters as I never had aboard ship before and never have since—as if I were being taken to a land where I would always be in want of some commodity that I needed but could not name. What I cannot name is what I do not find in Miss Teasdale's eyes.

Sarah's jealousy was passing and being replaced by sympathy. Abram was not so distant a creature. His needs were much like her own. The next entry might bring him closer still.

Now I feel twenty-three again, and my rooms here in town are like that boatswain's cabin, a place where I listen to the wind making the trees on the avenue clatter and moan. I gaze up through this window toward a night sky that feels as menacingly dark as the waters before a storm, and wonder if indeed I am not, like Poseidon, confined by my own watery nature.

I would breathe in the air driving a high, running sea! But where is that spirit and what is her name? I am horribly alone, because the shadow of the woman I am looking for, her ghost, bedevils me, and I feel as if I am chasing the air. By my hand, can she truly exist? If I ever do find her, I must be willing to sacrifice everything for her love.

Sarah felt the ground beneath her tip and swing around as if she had dismounted from a bucking horse. She was trembling, she discovered, and she had an airy feeling in her knees.

Somehow Abram had found her. He had found her despite himself and the years when he could not have admitted he was looking.

And she had found him—the right one, indeed, running after him into the fields. What she had sensed in him immediately, but had been unable to name, herself, until now, was his interior depth, his ample soul—what she was tempted to call his spiritual greatness. It was as if he had taken the seas themselves and all that they proclaimed into his soul. She had married him, perhaps, without being sure that she could love him as she wanted to love someone, with an ambition greater in its scope than the broad seas. She could admit this now. But it no longer mattered. She wanted to serve him, to give him children—to have his children. This seemed to her the necessary complement to all that inward power—an outward domain. She wanted to fill up the earth, or at least their own world, with children.

She bundled the charts back into the drawer's depth, retrieved the instruments into the pouch, and lay the book beside them, her hand momentarily unwilling to let it go, her fingers feeling the soft and slightly spongy calfskin. Then she tied the bow on the velvet pouch and closed up the writing desk.

She stood for another moment by the window, just to one side, making sure not to expose herself to view from the street. While the autumn day might prove chilly, the sun was bright and threw a radiant warmth against her skin.

The carpenters in the shipyard were hoisting materials up onto the top spar of a newly erected mast, and they were hammering at what Sarah could tell would become a basket-shaped crow's nest, connecting the surrounding staves to the platform base. She remembered Abram's story about crawling up into the crow's nest on his first voyage. Reading his diary had given her just such a vantage point.

———

Those weeks in Abram's rooms would remain in Sarah's memory as an ideal time, a time of living for each other. She grew more accustomed to his habits, understanding that his early rising, his methodical tasks, were part of his way of fitting himself into the world—of making himself comfortable with the energies that drove him.

It helped that he was quick to notice how she liked things. When he saw that she hid her washbasin away after using it each morning, he began to do the same with his. When she made a centerpiece for the dining room table, finding the odd, robin's egg blue china bowl and filling it with dried, speckled corn, he began buying silver and glass centerpieces—a new one every week, until she told him to stop.

Abram also made it possible for her slow rising to be as much a part of the household routine as his cockcrow walks by insisting that Hodges keep following her casual breakfast order. Abram never left her at Hodges' mercy; what she wanted became the household's law, despite the valet's obvious jealousy.

Most remarkably, when the walls of the rooms grew strangely rigid against the outward pressure of their interiors, and when the same expanding emptiness crowded Sarah's thoughts and she began to feel desperate, Abram knew what to do. Or, he learned what to do. He would come and sit beside her and put his hand on her knee; then he would rub the narrowing muscle above her knee, until, persuaded by the gentle attentions of his thumb and forefinger, she felt some of the pressure go, her shoulders drop, her neck muscles untwist. He would relax then as well—except that when he did, he became aware of the chronic pain in his lower back. He'd give her a kiss and ask her to return the favor, to rub his back. As she did so, Sarah would think of the first thing to say, or he would, and soon they would be telling each other stories. They were learning to draw together when the accidents of life threatened their union.

Sometimes, deep in the night, Sarah would wake up—just open her eyes and be awake. Abram was beside her. And she was happy.

CHAPTER 15

The Idyll

*A*bram arrived home from his walk early one morning and found Sarah in the bedroom, seated at her vanity, pushing the ends of her eyebrows up with her fingertips, deciding whether she wanted to pluck them and lift the ends with her paint. Abram's cheeks were red, and he sniffled after coming into the warm house out of the cold morning air.

"Look to your packing, fairest," he said, "we are going on a journey."

Sarah turned around, startled by the possibilities of what those words might mean coming from Abram.

He walked over to his wardrobe, giving her his instructions as he searched through his own clothing. "I have Vanderhorst's yacht. I thought we would sail to the Palisades across the Hudson. There's a promontory there I'd like to show you. We can spend the night at my favorite inn."

"I can be ready tomorrow," Sarah said, her voice countering his commands with her own matter-of-factness. "It sounds a very pleasant idea."

"The tide will only be with us for the next several hours," he said, his voice rushing outward like that tide. "You need only dress for a little weather and a walk. I will ask Hodges to help you pack a trunk." He saw the look she was giving him. "One trunk, *one*. That should be sufficient for your night things and a change for the morrow."

"You take such license, Abram," she said, her mouth twisting.

He walked over to her at the vanity. "Were there other engagements?" he asked, tentative, serious, open.

She felt suddenly foolish. She was finding the habit of being coy hard to shake. "I will manage the trunk," she said. She looked up into his face. "Madam will be ready in a trice."

Abram bent over and kissed her, a lingering one that reminded her of the walks they had taken together during their brief courtship and their first embraces. When Abram left, she wanted to follow him out of the room, and she rushed through her packing.

While she was looking through her wardrobe, deciding what to wear and what to pack, she uncovered the trousers she had worn out into the fields. She had kept them as a memento of that time. Thinking to surprise and, she hoped, delight Abram by appearing once again as his hunting servant, she donned the breeches. She tucked them down into a pair of riding boots, and covered the breeches and the tops of the boots with a riding skirt. Even if she did not have the opportunity—or courage—to take off the skirt later, she would at least be warm. She had often envied men the insulation of their trousers.

Abram had hired a carriage to transport them and their luggage to the Great Dock, where they boarded a thirty-foot, five-ton yacht called *The Idyll*. The day was one of those last fair days in early November when, although the trees have shed their leaves, the light still dances, weightless and bright. It spangled the light chop in the harbor with glittering sunbeams. The sky had an aqua cast, and the deeper waters reflected a rich, lapis blue.

The light breeze felt chilly in the harbor and then much colder once they started crossing the Hudson. The wind turned increasingly against them, and Abram shouted out his orders to the three-man crew in a forceful voice. "Coming abeam! Let her luff there. Now set your forward stay, Mr. Hallet. Now! Mr. Hallet." The ship gathered its energies, lifted, and started to drive, and Abram's mastery of the ship, the crew, and, it almost seemed, the elements of wind and water, lifted Sarah's heart and set it sailing as well.

From a distance the Palisades, the cliffs on the other side of the river, looked like no more than a step up into the land; but as they drew nearer and then sailed under them, Sarah could not imagine how they would climb to the top of these stone-faced giants.

Birds wheeled out of the stumpy evergreens that grew in the crags of this perpendicular aerie, and Sarah found herself looking almost straight up at them, her hand shading her eyes, her neck canted back as far as it would go. Among the sea gulls, the terns, and the hawks, three eagles glided. She watched a brown-headed eagle swoop down and pick such a large fish out of the river that the bird's recovering flight had a long swag to it. Its wings beat murderously against the too-light air, their tips throwing up spray as the eagle strained to rise. And then, after the low arc of the swag, the eagle, having gained sufficient speed, banked up at a surprising angle and flew back to its nest on an unswerving course. The creature's performance thrilled Sarah so much that her own heart seemed to pump heavily through its own weightedness. She sat down on a stern post, with a hand to her chest, feeling its methodical thump— its own glide—return.

The crew dropped anchor at a site where the cliffs were so sheer and so close that Sarah could no longer see the evergreens on top. She thought of what she might say to Abram. How did he think she was to climb these? She was not that boyish. She did not even know how a man like Abram could accomplish such a thing.

But as she was wondering how to excuse herself, he left the wheel and came over to her. "There's an access around the corner of that cliff. It's no more than a vigorous walk to the top," he said, and kissed her on the cheek.

They rowed toward the cliffs in a skiff—Abram, Sarah, and Abram's man, Hodges—leaving the crew aboard the yacht. Organizing and sailing across the river had taken them the better part of the morning, and by now it was well past midday. Sarah wondered whether they could climb up the cliffs and back down before dark. She still did not see any corner they might round, only a sheer rock wall, flush with the river. She wondered whether the birds ever started rock slides.

They did round the predicted corner, though, where the cliffs parted—to Sarah, almost miraculously—and the river backwashed inland. The uniform color of the stone made this breach invisible from any distance greater than a stone's throw.

Sarah wondered how Abram had found this place—how he knew about it. "Have you taken your other women here?" she asked mischievously.

"I have never known another woman I thought would appreciate it," he said, looking at her out of the corner of his eye.

When Abram had landed the skiff back in the small inlet, he and Hodges helped Sarah out of the boat. Even here the land rose so steeply that the moment her foot hit the ground, she had to start climbing. She leaned into the mountain to keep her balance and stretched out her hands. They were surrounded by pine forest. Light, falling through the trees, dappled the ground ahead of them, but Sarah could little afford to appreciate her surroundings; she had to make sure of her footing on the carpet of pine needles. Abram walked ahead without a word, and there was nothing for her to do but follow.

Soon she could stand up a little more and view her surroundings. The trees thinned out and the light poured through onto fern-covered glades. She could not only smell the scent of the pine needles and the decaying leaves, but the moisture of the river backwashed into the air as well.

Finally, they emerged into grassy, level fields, turned, and began to loop their way back through the trees to the edge of the promontory. But not, Sarah hoped, too quickly. She was walking directly behind Abram now, and she wanted to reach out, tug at his long coat, and hold him back a little. Could he know, as well as the pace of his steps suggested, where he was going?

Then, suddenly—and here Abram had to slow her walk with the gate of his arm—they stepped out onto a large slab of gray rock that ended in the air. Five more steps, past the last switchy maple saplings, and they reached the middle of the slab. The rock they stood on was slightly concave, a basin held up to the ambrosial skies. When Sarah lifted her gaze from her feet, she took in her first glimpse of the land on the other side of the river. A nubby blanket of evergreens edged the water. Then the ground seemed to rise, to curl up, as it went back toward the horizon, where it met them, at last, at eye level. Another two steps and the city was there. Dominated by white church spires, it looked like an encampment of huddled figures guarded over by lean, tapering sentries. She took another step and the wharves were there, the dry docks and the ships in harbor. They looked like the miniatures whose masts were hoisted in bottles.

Sarah had never seen a view like this before. It gave her an odd feeling and provoked strange and unexpected thoughts. It made her wonder how God could care about people, people you couldn't even see from this height and distance, although you knew they must be there, walking in the streets, as concerned with their affairs as ever. She wondered at her own silent prayer for children, the insistent passion of it. *For as the heavens are higher than the earth*, she remembered from Isaiah, *so are my ways higher than your ways, and my thoughts than your thoughts.*

She took another step, trying to see their yacht below, but as she did she felt as if she were being drawn downward. She stepped back quickly, took a deep breath through her nose, and cleared her head.

———

Abram told Hodges he might smoke his pipe if he liked, and suggested that perhaps he could set out the picnic they had brought at the edge of that last meadow. As he often had since Abram's marriage, Hodges resisted his master's polite order. A man of sudden starts and stops, like a cat in its inexplicable, ears-up dashes, he now adopted a feline laziness and determination to hang about watching them, until Abram glared back, and he sprung away.

His man departed, Abram approached Sarah. He held her, smoothed loose strands of her long hair that the wind had played with, and kissed her with his hands cupped at the base of her neck. Then, partially letting her go, he kept her close to him with one arm around her shoulder as they both looked out toward the city. "Are you glad we came?" he asked.

"Most glad," she said, and thought in the next instant how unexpectedly the idea of God's distance had intruded into their day.

Then he kissed her again, this time as he usually did only at night. His arms pulled her to him, ever more closely, until her fingers began to claw at the back of his upper arms. She began to wonder if he thought to make love to her there. She was confused in her will when he stopped and more confused because he had.

"Let's have the tea," he said.

Remembering her inspiration back at their rooms, she told him that he should walk ahead. She would join him in a moment; she needed time to compose herself.

"I don't want to leave you alone in this place," he said.

"Only go out of sight," she said, and gave him a playful push.

When he had tromped away, looking back quizzically at her several times as he went, Sarah whipped off her riding skirt, folded it, and placed it at the base of three maple saplings that were growing together. Then she circled to the left, back down toward the route they had taken to the promontory.

She moved as quietly as one of the nearby Manhattans. Peering through the trees, she caught sight of Abram. He stood halfway between the rock slab and the meadow, his hands on his hips, rocking impatiently on his heels and toes, looking up at the trees. She waited behind an elm tree, hiding. Soon he began to call out to her as she expected he would. She remembered him calling out to the beater to come out of the thicket. He turned and walked back toward the rock slab, a greater urgency in his calls now—he was already worried.

She went to about the place where he had been and climbed up into the first high branch of a tree. She had to jump, pull herself up, and dig at the thick-barked trunk of the tree with her boots to scramble up. She hoped that after he had searched in vain he would take this same line back to the meadow.

Hodges, having heard his master's calls, came straight toward her and spied her in the tree. "Madame," he said, almost, but not quite, daring to scold her.

Embarrassed but determined, she glared at him and motioned him to go away.

He obeyed her, but turned his head away slowly, with the definite implication of shaking it at the nonsense his master's new bride had introduced into his life.

If Abram spotted her as easily as Hodges, this wouldn't even be much of a game, but she counted on her husband's far greater distraction at her loss.

At last he came by. Right by. He paused directly under the tree where she was hiding. Most conveniently.

She jumped onto his back, toppling them both, and they landed side by side on the prickly blanket of pine needles. Before she could move, he had raised himself up on his knees to look down at her. It was then that he saw the breeches. His angry, confused look exploded into amusement and shimmering light.

He grabbed the cuffs of her trousers and held on to them like the driver of a coach-and-four with the reins in his hands. "Where have these come from, then?" he asked, and gave them a yank for emphasis.

She raised one eyebrow at him.

"My wife has changed into a woodland nymph, I see, hanging about with the fairies and the sprites in the trees."

She still did not say anything.

"I wonder how far she has changed," he said. "If I take off these boots will I find cloven hoofs? Or the fishy feet of a naiad?" And here he pulled on the trousers so hard that the long blouse she had tucked into them tumbled free.

He seemed to be a little shocked at what he had done, as was she, but Sarah recovered quickly. Sitting up, she looked around, as did he. Hodges could not be seen. They laughed and held each other and lay down together once again. The pine needles and cones made an inconveniently hard and sticky bed. Even so, Sarah would remember the coolness of the breeze and the warmth of Abram, like mulled wine with its sugars singeing the tongue.

Sarah had wondered once or twice about the whereabouts of Hodges, and then she thought no more of him for a long time. As they gave each other one last kiss, she heard a rustling in the trees some distance away and a flatted whistling coming from the same direction.

With her blouse tucked back in, Sarah remembered her skirt, and she ran back to retrieve it. Abram called after her, "Sarah!" She turned and pantomimed fitting the skirt about her as a reply. Before she turned away, she could see Hodges coming up behind Abram, holding a teapot in both hands as if to present his master with an offended party's evidence.

When she returned to the edge of the meadow, her skirt once again concealing her breeches, Hodges was packing up the china and silver he had set out for their afternoon tea. Abram held out a piece of lemon cake for her. She put out her hands to take it, but then he raised it to her lips, and she came closer and ate the cake out of his hands, conscious of the crumbs flaking her mouth and spilling on the ground. She cast a sidelong glance at Hodges to see how he was taking this, and she saw him half-turn, as he was bending over to put a plate into the basket, and draw his arm into his stomach as if bracing himself.

When she had almost finished the piece of cake, with her mouth still full, she leaned forward and kissed Abram, mostly to smear his lips with the icing, as hers were. He laughed and asked Hodges for a napkin. Evidently in their fall or tussling her cheek had become streaked with dirt, and now Abram licked the thumb of his clean hand, smoothed the dirt away, and dabbed at the place with the cloth. He had a matter-of-fact way of doing this, caring for her skin; he was never timid about touching her, but he never handled her callously either.

Abram reached down and retrieved a cup of tea they had kept out for her, and although the tea was cold by this time, she would have liked another cup to quench her thirst. They would have one when they were back on board, Abram said; they had to get back to the yacht now. The sun would soon start to set, and they still had to sail along the Palisades to the inn where they were to stay that night.

The steep slope through the woods carried their jostling feet down to their rowboat in a quarter of the time it had taken them to climb up.

Abram and Hodges poled them out of the narrows between the cliffs, refitted the oars through the rings, and put their backs into the last two hundred yards to the yacht. The wind had freshened and become gusty. Out on the river, whitecaps schooled up at the rip lines of the gusts. Since the sun had been warm when they started up the cliff, she had left her cloth coat in the rowboat; now she wrapped it around her and huddled down on the bench in the stern. The freshness of the wind and the moist chill off the waters put something like the scent of mint in the air. The sun, low in the sky above the spire-topped city, cast straight shafts of light from its quarter position so that it looked like a starry cross with a circle at its center.

Sarah turned back to the Palisades, expecting to see birds reefing against the breeze, but not one of the many she had seen earlier that day was in sight. The world seemed remarkably clear, glassy, limpid. She watched the two men rowing side by side, the captain and his servant; the captain seemed the happier in his work by far. And she—against expectations, but with a certainty that these feelings had been building in her all day—she realized suddenly how happy she was, how much she loved her husband, and tears sprang to her eyes.

Abram saw the tears falling and questioned her with his look. She shouted through a gust that it was the wind, smiled, and shaded her eyes against the accused but innocent breeze. She was only six-teen, yet it seemed to her that she had been waiting to be in love in just this way for the longest time. What gave her feelings their teary poignancy was that she realized she had wished this without any real hope it would come to pass. She had not been hopeful, she knew suddenly, since her mother had died.

Boarding the yacht provided a useful distraction. She helped pull up the side ladder, against the crew's objections, and then she was ready to go aft and sip her tea like the captain's wife. But she wanted Abram to herself at this moment; she wanted to tease him, to pester him, to sit on his lap. She turned to him and asked if he could have Hodges bring the tea to their cabin—that's where she was going. She wondered why she could not say, *And I want you to join me there.* She made this appeal silently, however, reaching up and smoothing down a lock of his hair at the back of his neck.

"I want to see us under way," he said. "I'll tell Hodges."

Then she did not want to leave his side, but she had committed herself, so she went down to their cabin.

Soon after she heard the ringing draw of the anchor chain, they were under way, sailing upriver toward the inn, and Hodges brought her tea. She sat on the bed, which was not much more than an extended shelf built into the side of the oak wall. The entire cabin was made of oak, and she felt as if she had been stored inside a cask. She discovered, lying down, that her toes just reached the bottom edge of the small shelf; she might manage to sleep on it well enough, but how did someone as tall as Abram ever get comfortable? And what if they had been sleeping together here tonight? She thought of the inn for the first time with a sense of urgency. Then she sat up and sipped her tea.

She was impatient for Abram to come down to her. Would he know this? Sarah sometimes felt she understood what Abram was feeling about her better then Abram himself understood his own feelings about her. Of course, she had been so overpowered by her own emotion not an hour ago that she had hidden her tears in the wind.

Then, he came through the hatchway and closed it behind him. He embraced her and held her to his chest. What stunned her at moments like this was the privilege, the bounty, of their life together. Not to have someone, and then, after a few improbable dramatic events, to have someone, a husband, in your life who would step right to you and hold you seemed beyond reckoning. Why not before? Why now? How could people live in the world without this after once knowing it?

He kissed her and then asked, "What did you make of the day?"

She wanted to say so much more than simply compliment his arrangements. Perhaps she would find a way through the pleasantries to what she wanted to say. "I am very glad of it," she said.

"Did you see the eagle swoop down and take his fish?"

"Oh, yes. I didn't know you had."

"It nearly took him back down into its watery element."

"But was it an omen of our day?" she asked, and wondered if he understood what she was angling toward.

A light came into his eyes, and he swooped down his head and bit her—very pleasantly—on the neck. "The vastness of the woman," he said. "The sea of life she is."

"Only the eagle's prey," she said. She pushed him off a little, afraid he would mark her. And then she added, vexed at herself and him for feeling the need to prompt his compliments, but doing so nevertheless. "Am I?"

He stepped back and took her hands. "What I meant to say when I came down here, I suppose, was that I love you so very much. Sometimes the habit of witty conversation betrays us. Turns us . . . me . . . from what I mean to say. I feel honored to have you as my wife—that is what I meant to say. And I do love you."

When she discovered herself needing to break through barriers, he was often on the other side, she found, in true courtesy giving her a hand across. Now was the time when she, too, should find what it was in her heart to say.

"I am surprised that I found you," she said. "I didn't quite know that I had, even when we married. You are the person I want—have always wanted. The one I thought of when I looked ahead to this— the time when life truly begins. I love you, Abram."

She stood up, clung to him, and kissed him in a way that was meant to let him know how much she loved him.

"We will be anchoring again soon," he said.

"I know," she said. "I know." She could not quite let go, however.

Just then calls from the deck indicated the crew's sighting of the inn. Abram pinched the bridge of his nose, as if by sympathetic magic this might pinch off the racing of his blood.

"I have to get back on deck," he said. "The yacht needs mooring."

She was thinking about how much she enjoyed moving him in this way, and she found his loss of control delightful. She, in turn, had to acknowledge that she could not be as restrained about her need for his presence as she might have liked to pretend, and when he turned to go up on deck, she found herself taking a quick stride to catch up.

On deck a stiff breeze met them, and the evening star, a silvery sliver of glass, stood alone, low in the northern sky. Abram shouted instructions to the crew. He wanted the yacht to come about just before they let go the chains. They stood about a mile off their destination.

Abram went to the stern and took the wheel, and Sarah followed after. She stood on his right and took his arm, high up, where her hand began to warm between his upper arm and his side. The boat bounced heavily through the choppy waves, and the jib and mainsail bellied out in the determined breeze. Abram tried to say something to her but the breeze blew away the words.

He bent down to her and half-shouted into her ear, "I love you!"

She kissed his ear quickly in reply and wrapped her arms around his waist. She clung to his side as he piloted the yacht with one hand and held her against him with the other.

She remembered the line from Shakespeare, " 'Twere now to die, 'twere now to be most happy," and tears started to her eyes once more.

———

The yacht came about and glided into the calmer waters of a cove, where an inn rested, now at high tide, nearly at the water's edge on a claw-footed peninsula. The inn itself, a structure of long, dark-stained planks dominated by a four-square chimney, with leaded casement windows, seemed to take into itself the gathering shadows, promising rest and sweet dreams.

Abram rowed Sarah into shore. He had asked Hodges to remain on board with the crew. The oars seemed to sweep down and through the silence they shared, this immense and ever-deepening sea of experience. Half-thoughts came to Sarah's mind, which almost issued into speech, but then nosed back under the smooth and serene surface of those waters. The sky had grown nearly dark, and the early stars were out. The cranking of the oars and their splash sounded, in that moment, as perfectly suspended as the stars, like a lullaby.

A slight old woman, the proprietress, met them at the door of the inn. She kept her hands cupped together and bowed a little, but not in a servile manner, in welcoming them. Dressed in a long black dress with a full skirt and satiny patina, complemented by a pearl necklace, she seemed the lady of the house having a few guests in for the evening. She said little, but she had the strange air—her head cocked to one side and slightly thrust forward—of listening at all times to a lively conversation. And when she did speak, it was as if she were interjecting remarks in this unheard conversation, which seemed of a wittily conspiratorial nature. Her name was Mrs. Mildred Young.

Mrs. Young did not tell them when or if dinner would be served, but after they had put away their things and washed up, Abram led Sarah downstairs again. Mrs. Young met them at the landing and walked them into the dining room, where places had been set for them at a long, round-ended cherrywood table.

She brought them a fish chowder as a first course. She did not leave the room after serving them, however, but took a chair next to Sarah and turned it round so that when she spoke her words traveled over Sarah's left shoulder and insinuated themselves into her ear like whispers.

"There's a bit of eel in it," she said, meaning the chowder. "It will be good for him." She reached out and gave Sarah's elbow a quick squeeze.

Sarah gave the woman a look, but then Mrs. Young bit her lower lip and looked so uncannily like a guilty child that Sarah was almost ready to find her cheekiness endearing. She looked to Abram, whom Mrs. Young had placed at the head of the table.

"Mildred is a saucy one," he said. "Don't bother about what she's saying."

The woman glanced at Abram and then turned back to Sarah, the glance indicating she knew the man about whom she was about to speak. "He pretended to be the solitary sort," she said. "I knew he would come in here with a pretty young girl someday." Then she turned back to Abram. "Too pretty for you, maybe," she said.

Sarah sipped several spoonfuls of her chowder.

"But he is a good man, your sea captain," Mrs. Young said, her tone as quickly secretive as mice scampering into a pantry. "I bet he is," and underneath this last statement a gossipy query extended in every direction.

Sarah might not have decided to like the woman if she had not, as she did right then, shown that her curiosity sprang from a sisterly sympathy. Mrs. Young reached out and touched her dark hair. Then she poured Sarah a glass of cider out of an earthen pitcher and held it out to her. She would do anything for her young guest, the gesture seemed to say.

Sarah looked up from under her brows and said, in a breathy and breathless voice, "He is *wicked*," and they both squealed like little girls. Abram looked at them as if he wished for another man in the room.

Abram and Sarah hardly saw her after that, as she busied herself in serving. She brought them johnnycakes and fiddleheads, a platter of haddock, oysters in a vinegar dressing, roasted pork, and finally, plum pudding.

When Sarah had first sat down to dinner, she had felt very hungry indeed, famished, and yet she found that after one or two bites of each dish she lost her appetite—she could do no more than salute the parade of dishes as they passed by.

Her true intention, her appetite, her desire, went to the cause of this feasting, the source of this celebration, which was their love, and this must be nourishing her, she concluded, in a hidden and mysterious way. She remembered the scripture about "having bread of which you know not." She wondered whether she might think of such a thing—perhaps this was blasphemous. She wanted to feel that what she and Abram shared was holy, and yet it had such humor and gaiety and even buffoonery about it.

She looked across the table to Abram, who was eating as methodically and purposefully as a plough horse, *feeding*, it seemed to her, and she wondered at the arabesques of thoughts dancing in her head. She laughed to herself, considering just how foolish this man chewing his food might think her if he knew what a religion she was inclined to make of their passion.

Later, when they went upstairs to their room, Mildred Young stood at the landing with a hurricane lamp in her hand and watched them with that conspiratorial air of hers. Sarah gave her a little wave good-night. As they made their way up the second flight of the bent-armed staircase, she looked back again and saw that the old woman was still watching—and Sarah blew her a kiss. Mrs. Young blew one back. What the old woman would have given, Sarah knew, to share the least part of their life.

In their bedroom, Abram stood by the bed, struggling to take off his boots. She watched him hopping around on one foot, like a long-legged heron trying to leap up into flight out of a bog.

She crossed to him. "If you will permit me, sir, I will be your valet."

Abram looked at her as if uncertain he wanted to play, but not wanting to offend her.

"Let me help you," she said, more simply.

He began to slip off his coat, and she held it so that he could clear his long arms. Then she undid the nailhead-sized buttons of his outer blouse, at first quickly to demonstrate her dexterity, and then, looking up into his eyes, with the greatest care. When she had him stripped down to the rough wool shirt he wore beneath his blouse, and his pants and boots, she made him sit down on the bed and started working at his boots, with some difficulty.

"Hodges would never treat me in such a rude manner, Miss."

"There are many limits to Hodges' attentions," she said knowingly. She was having trouble with the boots.

"Let me, Sarah," Abram said.

"No."

"Yes. I don't care for you doing this."

This made her more determined, and she pulled so hard that she rocked backwards when the boot came off. She knew she looked less than feminine, which was undoubtedly why Abram found the attention a mixed blessing. She got the other boot off in much less time.

Abram stood up, and he clasped her with both hands at her rib cage and lifted her into the air, holding her, with his tremendous strength, straight out from him so that she could not snatch at any more buttons, and deposited her on the bed. He bent down and took her right boot in his hands and pulled it off with the kind of strength that makes the difficult easy. Then he cupped her stockinged heel in his hands and rubbed her calf, until her toes started to tingle in response.

"Does Hodges do this for you?" she asked.

"Stop it," he said. "Stop playing now." He gazed up at her, with nothing guarded, shaded, or hesitant; his soul had welled up and filled his expression as tears well up and fill the eyes—he was as *present* to her as he could possibly be.

In his look there was so much of *him* that he appeared mysterious; she almost did not recognize him. If he had not been rubbing her leg, she might have forgotten who it was kneeling before her. He looked . . . transfigured—that was the only way she could understand it. Transfigured by his love for her. It was as if every time she had seen something of who he truly was—in his sideways, mischievous glance, in his long but nimble-fingered hold on a teacup, in the way his face would fall and the color drain out when he was exasperated—every glint that had ever flashed from the light of his soul now poured through him.

She felt strangely calm, and yet excited, and the idea came to her that she would conceive his child that night.

CHAPTER 16

Happy at Home

Abram and Sarah returned to the Nicolls home the week before Thanksgiving in a post chaise pulled by a chestnut stallion. Livy ran out to meet them as they came up the stone-fence lined road, shouting her greetings through the carriage window above the clatter of the horse and coach.

"You've come home!" she called. "You're home!"

Felicity was there when they stepped down, smiling, but the haziness of her expression reserved her true feelings. She stepped forward and kissed Sarah on the cheek, and Livy bounced up and hugged both of them together, asking, "How long was your journey?"

Felicity remarked that the house had been too quiet.

The four walked in a group into the house, where they met Robert Nicolls in the front hallway. He kissed his daughter and shook his son-in-law's hand. "We are together as a household at last," the old gentleman said.

No one knew how to respond to this. They looked at each other: the sea captain son-in-law to his aristocratic father-in-law, the middle married daughter to her as-yet-unmarried elder sister, the soon-departing husband to his young bride, the youngest daughter to the adults-who-would-know-what-to-do. They all smiled and tried to laugh, but when this failed to produce an ease in conversation, Nicolls said he would see to some refreshment and Abram went out to the chaise to see about their trunks. Felicity followed her father, Sarah went after Abram, and Livy was left in the hall, feeling that she was still somehow awaiting the couple's arrival.

———

Two rifts in the new household developed quickly, the first between sisters and the second between father and son-in-law.

Felicity's increasing reserve became painfully apparent to everyone. She kept glancing downward until her bowed head became almost a fixed attitude. She had always been given to wringing her hands, and this habit added to her penitent image.

The day before Thanksgiving, when Felicity and Sarah were alone in the parlor working at their needlepoint, Sarah approached her sister about her downcast and troubled manner. "I have been wondering," Sarah said, "whether Abram and I have been wise in returning here."

"Please, dear sister," Felicity said, looking more troubled than ever, "do not think that." She looked as if she would go on but could not find the words.

"You find no pleasure in our company. In my company."

"Forgive me if I . . . if your marriage makes me think of myself," Felicity said. "I would rather be happy for you in the way that Livy is. And I try to be."

"With very little success," Sarah said, but in a kind and quiet voice that eased into this painful truth.

"I hope it will not be long," Felicity said, "before I know the same happiness you do." She started to cry, the tears falling although she still smiled, that paradox of rain on a sunny day—the devil, as old stories have it, whipping his wife.

"You might have," Sarah said, hinting at her darker suspicions. "You might have wed our captain yourself."

Her older sister flinched as if Sarah had threatened to slap her.

"Look at me and tell me it is not so," Sarah said, starting to feel desperate herself now.

Felicity raised her chin and tried to speak as if from the lectern of her greater wisdom. "Abram needs someone who will venture along with him. He needs your spirit."

"Do you wish you had that spirit?"

"*No.* I wish only to say . . . you were right. Abram is a fine man, indeed. But you are the one who is right for him."

"This is how you must be counseling yourself, isn't it? This is what you would like to believe . . . the words you are using to drive away your sense of loss."

Sarah saw how much her sister was suffering. Her hands, gripping the frame of her needlepoint, were shaking. The tremor almost passed into Sarah's heart as well, but then her possessiveness returned. "Have you fallen in love with him, then?"

Felicity stood up quickly, gathering her needlepoint as if someone were about to snatch it away, and left the room. Her cries started to escape her in the echoing hall before she raced her bursting sadness up the stairs and hid herself away in her room.

While not unaware of Felicity's unhappiness and Sarah's consternation, Nicolls and Abram were dealing with concerns of their own. The two men continued to be friendly, but both were at a loss as to how to treat each other. It was one thing for Nicolls to take Abram up. But how far had he been raised? And Abram had grown tired of superiors and relished being done with them. Father and son, they were not, and did not want to be. Friends? But how to be friends and be in love, from different angles, with the same woman?

For a while they kept to the lines of social acquaintance, speaking whenever they encountered each other in the house, nodding, offering a remark on the other's health or the weather. They soon whipped through every possible remark about the constantly cloudy weather—a storm without rain or any clearing.

Robert Nicolls began touring his lands almost daily, talking with his tenants about their harvests. Or he shut himself up in his library, even taking some of his meals there.

The old gentleman tried to compensate for his frequent absences with overly generous gestures. At Thanksgiving he asked the good captain, as he persisted calling him, to sit at the head of their table. This made no one happy—not his daughters, not Abram, not the old gentleman himself. Sensing this, Abram declined. Nicolls insisted. They barely avoided ruining the meal. Livy rescued them by saying, "I would have the chair with the arms—I never have yet," and seized the place herself. Nicolls carved at her left hand, making a grand joke of all this for the servants.

Nicolls also gave up his bedchamber to Sarah and Abram. No one intended the arrangement to be permanent. It was understood that when Abram went to sea again, Sarah would return to her old room and Nicolls to his. Why Abram had stood there nodding when he first listened to these plans, however, he soon questioned.

———

Sarah began to see troubling changes in Abram. When they took up residence in her father's bedroom, she noticed how nervous this made Abram. Not that he was not good-spirited about it; he was too good-spirited. When the servants brought their trunks in, he remarked on the painted flower panels of the wardrobes and their cherry inlays. He liked the fleur-de-lys wallpaper. What could be better, he said, than the view of the sea from these windows and a perspective of the woods from those at the head of the room. She wished he would be quiet. His step gave his true feelings away, for he moved indecisively about the room, prowling, trapped.

In bed that first night he lay flat on his back, his face pointed upward and his hands folded at his stomach, like someone in a coffin. In the days and weeks that followed, when they made love, he seemed to have lost his taste for holding her afterward. She felt he wanted to get up and scramble into his clothes.

During the day, he took long walks; often he was gone for hours on these scouting forays over the island. He began having Hodges carry out a lunch so he would not have to return at midday.

Although Abram invited Sarah to accompany him, she felt she was not really wanted on these walking tours. She tried once, bargaining in advance for a half-day trip. As they set off, she flirted with Abram, her hand laced over the crook of his arm, but she was not able to divert his attention from simply making headway, and soon she was trailing along miserably.

The early December weather was cold and raw now, with a threatening swirl of snowflakes in the air, but Abram went out in any weather. He and Hodges would sometimes take the launch out into the Sound and work at their fishing until they brought home more tomcod, halibut, mackerel, and smelt than the household could cook, salt, or smoke. Abram became a great oysterman and clammer and possessed no sense of restraint or dignity about his success, extolling the virtues of brute labor at the dinner table.

"Never a happy sailor but that he's doing," Abram would say.

Too true, Sarah thought.

One night, just before dropping off to sleep, when unbidden thoughts are as true as dreams, Abram joked about feeling stranded with Sarah on a desert island. He was her slave, he said, battling Dame Nature for their sustenance. She knew the life they were leading did make him feel stranded.

Sarah might have felt more than stranded herself, indeed abandoned, except for her growing conviction that she had conceived that night at the inn. It was almost as if she could be content because she had taken what she needed from Abram.

She felt a strange, light hunger in the mornings that became nausea as soon as she had taken her first nibbles at breakfast. More than once she had to excuse herself and rush out into the fresh air. Maggie, the cook, and her sisters had begun to tease her about her growing tummy and her poor appetite, accusing her of eating tea biscuits in bed. They became even more openly suspicious, almost blunt, when Sarah and Abram transformed her old room into a nursery, with a chest of drawers, a changing table, and a huge wicker cradle big enough for twin five-year-olds that Abram gave to Sarah as a promissory gift. Abram himself knew nothing of her maternal suspicions and acted too preoccupied, except for one or two brief instances, to inquire.

Sarah wanted to be certain, however, and passed off the nursery as a hopeful diversion. The truth was, she enjoyed making her questioners wait. She felt a little smug and even vengeful, especially as Felicity's melancholy jealousy continued. Sarah resented not being able to confide in her older sister as she had her whole life, but Felicity's barely hidden feelings for Abram made confidences impossible.

So, alone with her thoughts, she meditated on her condition. The thought that the pregnancy would alter the way she felt for most of a year, the idea that it would replace the cycle of pain, blood, and loss with a burgeoning growth and weight, pleased her. She did not mind that she would be, as her husband might have imagined it, at full sail. She found herself cupping her right hand under her navel, anticipating the first belling. A child, her child. Her symptoms filled her mind with a pregnancy of speculation nearly as absolute, in its own way, as the physical condition. She could think of nothing else most of the time, and her happiness outstripped her worry about Abram's increasing distance; he could be no nearer to her, after all, than dwelling within her in the presence of the child. Even when he returned to sea, part of him would be in her arms and at her side.

———

Christmas lightened everyone's spirits, and the New Year's celebration, her father's favorite holiday with its frivolity and pagan resolutions, gave Sarah hope that the household's uneasiness might be rung out with the old year. She almost made her announcement several times.

Soon the weather closed in on them, though, the lowering skies, useless roads, and numbing winter cold wrapping them up in a tight package.

As much as Sarah resented being left behind by Abram, she liked his moodiness when he was shut up even less. The brooding and distant person he became removed the man she loved to a far greater distance than his excursions. She could not seem to reach him no matter how far she went, no matter how subservient or shrewish she became.

One Wednesday morning at cockcrow the skies remained dark, portending the kind of day that never seemed to dawn, with the persistent darkness of the night brooding over the puddles that must be gathering from the steady rain. Sarah, who had been awakened by her own restlessness, slipped back into bed and held Abram's warm back, wishing they could fly past this day together, wishing that it would stay so dark she could whisper to him to go back to sleep, that it wasn't time to get up yet. She touched the dark curls at the back of his neck. She enjoyed this part of their life, this closeness, this casual privilege of lying like two spoons together. For a moment she dared hope that they might outwit the isolating weather. She needed a plan—to devise something they could do together.

He turned over before she had thought of anything, though, and delivered a smacking summons to the day. Abram always awoke in the same manner, instantly alert, his eyes full and open and then narrowing with the secret knowledge of his life. Then he would turn and give her cheek a loud, smacking kiss.

He rolled away from her, whipped the covers back, exposing their pocket of warmth to the cold so that she grabbed at the bedclothes, and strode across the room to the windows to look out.

He let the curtain close a moment too soon. She knew, just from that, how disappointed he was. He stood sideways to her in his nightshirt next to his wardrobe. When it was cold, he always kept his big toes arched up, and he stood that way now, balancing awkwardly, as if on stilts. His lips curled in and his cheeks bunched as he shot his legs through his trousers and buckled up his belt with a vengeful speed, and she knew he was buckling himself up as well. This was what she had dreaded.

She thought of what she might say to stop the rest of the day from happening. Still, she could think of nothing. The moments before he had finished dressing, as he washed his face and hands, grew too long, and he forgot to put his basin away in the lower cabinet of the vanity before leaving the room.

At breakfast, the whole family looked glum. There was very little conversation, and no one ate much. The cook, Maggie, through her emissary, Crump—who served in his waistcoat and knee-breeches livery—could persuade no one to have another helping of molasses duff. Breakfast had its own decorum, however, which demanded that they remain seated through a second cup of tea.

Abram finally broke their silence in a tone of voice somewhere between making an announcement and giving an order. "It looks a day for picking oakum."

They turned to him for an explanation.

"When weather keeps the crew below decks, they make small repairs."

"Oakum?" Livy asked.

"Tarred hemp for caulking the seams and decks."

"We should ride this storm out dry enough," Nicolls said, his tone openly weary.

"But something must need doing. This silver could be polished."

Nicolls glanced at Abram, and then, as if unwilling to focus on anyone who might divine his thoughts, he raised his teacup, draining it quickly. He patted his mouth with his serviette and muttered about seeing to his accounts as he left the table.

Despite her father's reaction, Sarah's spirits lifted. Abram had found something to do—and something they could do together. She would work like a sea jack to avoid the day dragging on as it had started.

Abram had the servants lay out the silver, even the ewers and the oyster-shaped crumbers that they never used. He enlisted Hodges and Maggie and Darby, the scullery maid, and proposed to work right alongside them until they had polished every last spoon. Sarah sat down beside Abram and set to work on spoons and forks and knives whose filigree trapped a bluish-green corrosion that seemed as resistant to her polishing cloth as the metal itself.

She tried to be lighthearted and joke with the democratic company, but the servants were clearly taking their cues from Abram—even white-haired Maggie, to whose skirts Sarah had clung for protection as a child. Abram worked with a silent determination and thoroughness that was much more like grim enterprise than play. He worked much more quickly than Sarah, and he did a better job—a better job than any of the servants as well.

Still, when she had finished three place settings, Sarah thought he would be pleased. "What do you think of that, then?" she asked him. "Will you keep me in your service?"

Abram glanced over at her work. "I plan on keeping you, my dear, until the end of time. But you had better do those servings again if you mean them to be used by company."

She looked to see if he were joking, but he, the captain of this crew, had already and pointedly passed on to examining Hodges' work. She had been thinking that she would set her husband's place with one of these settings at their midday dinner, and she excused herself to avoid a show of temper.

Abram looked happier at dinner, which made Sarah angrier. He could talk of nothing but polishing the silver. Why could her husband not devote himself to cultivating his mind like her father? He had told her how he had educated himself as a boy, reading everything in his captain's library, but she had seen nothing of this side of him. Her father had told her that he expected to have many pleasurable conversations with Abram; instead, her father, the true head of the household, felt pressured into shutting himself up in his library, as he was today, taking his meal in there on a salver. Probably a salver that Abram had so recently polished. Then Salome carrying John the Baptist's bloody head came to mind, and Sarah thought frantically how she could change her mood. She could not be sure what she feared, apart from her own violent emotions, but more and more she sensed that some disaster awaited.

After dinner she decided she would take a long nap. Abram almost never napped after eating, a habit common to her family. She knew she was going to be angry at him for not lying down beside her, but she would also be angry at him if he did. She would find his presence, especially if he were happy, somehow insulting. So she went to her bed alone, with a barely suppressible desire to claw her down pillows open and let out an explosion of feathers.

When she woke from her nap, she had a peculiar taste in her mouth, a taste she remembered but could not place. Where was Abram? She could hear the rain still drilling down. The peculiar taste had something of the rain and something of the silver plate in it. It was oily and had a tang to it. She wondered whether a trace of the polishing cream had somehow worked its way into the corner of her mouth. Her eyes felt especially moist, as if her body were reacting sympathetically to the weepy skies. She could not place what it was—the taste.

She felt odd in other ways, too, awaking with the sense of emerging back into a world in which actions had been taken to influence her fate. She reminded herself that nothing very much could be wrong. Nothing had happened. Yet she did not believe this.

She should find Abram. Then she wondered whether this would be wise. It might be better if they escaped each other's company for a time. She thought of reading. She thought of changing her clothes. Noticing the high-standing writing desk that Abram had brought out here from the city, she thought of moving it across to the other side of the room. It rested close by his wardrobe, and she had felt from the beginning that this was too crowded an arrangement, like two self-important gentlemen in the same household.

But she did not move the writing desk. She did not move at all. She stayed still, half-sitting up on the bed, clutching the quilt around her.

What would she do? She thought of finding Maggie and asking her what help she might need in preparing supper. Maggie had mothered her by taking her into the life of the kitchen after Sarah's own mother died. She had not asked to help in a long time—only when, like this, she wanted to be comforted.

She put on her list slippers, wrapped her shawl around her shoulders, trapping its ends underneath her upper arms to keep it in place, and went down the stairs, through the hall, and into the kitchen. Maggie was there, cooking. So was Hodges. They stopped talking when they saw her.

Maggie's figure rested on thin, long ankles. Her massive hips tilted beneath her pleated dress as she stood at the kitchen's wooden counter. Her plentiful white hair was gathered into a knot on the top of her head, its wealth resting like the upturned brim of a full hat around her head. She had once suffered a stroke, from which she had largely recovered, except that her facial muscles remained slack, giving her eyes a naked, startled look. She spoke from her thin, mushy mouth as if another intelligence than the one animating her eyes controlled her words. Knowing that her voice conveyed the true sense of her mind, though, and used to her glaring look, Sarah rested easily in her presence.

"Give me something to do," Sarah said. "This weather makes me feel the want of employment."

Hodges stood up, tossed the yellowed leaves of an old town paper he had been holding into the fire, and left the room. He bowed a little to Sarah as he passed, but without looking at her.

"You want something to do, Miss," Maggie said. "Where might that husband of yours be?" Not waiting for an answer, she turned to the counter, picked up a pot of carrots and beets, and set them on the worktable along with a sharp knife.

"I think he must be in the sitting room, reading," Sarah said. She sat down and picked up the knife.

"So far away, then, is he?" Maggie, being incapable of giving a knowing look, had become even more adept at making insinuations with her voice. Her startled look seemed to amplify this troubling remark.

"I said he is just at hand," Sarah said.

"So you did."

"When he is so close, I feel at times that he may be furthest away," Sarah said, her voice asking for Maggie's help.

"He will be at sea soon," Maggie said.

"He has said nothing to me of such plans."

"That is what he does," Maggie said. "And must do. You cannot put a gull in a cage like a finch, dear."

"How can I wish for him to go to sea?"

"What have I always told you? A wife wishes for her husband's happiness or loses her own."

"But what shall I do? How shall I be occupied?"

Maggie turned back to her mixing bowl. "You should keep busy enough with your family."

"My former employments can be nothing to me now."

"Not your father and sisters," Maggie said, and her eyes were so filled with light and her tone so joyfully expectant that her flat look became almost merry.

Sarah looked up and held Maggie's eyes for a moment. "We have no family as yet." She paused, sliced another carrot. She looked to see that she had not lost Maggie's attention, and then said, voicing her own argument, "He should stay until that time."

"Can you tell him how long that may be?" Maggie asked.

"Not as yet."

"You are full of 'as yets.' He will be calling you 'as yet' his Arab bride."

"For us to be at peace would shorten the time."

"Listen to Eve's daughter," Maggie said, "complaining that her man cannot be happy in the cause of his misery."

Sarah was preparing a remark about hasty judgments, when her father's steward, Boyd, broke into the room from the back door. Water sluiced off his oilskin coat and splattered about as he removed it. He had been taking care of the livestock and, despite the wet, his wool trousers and thick-soled boots were redolent of the barn—the smell of oats, the animals, their dirt. When he took off his soft-brimmed hat, his monumental head, with its hooklike curls growing toward each other over his balding pate, rose up nearly into the rough-beamed ceiling, which made the kitchen seem smaller, closed-in, almost as if it had fallen round his shoulders like a mantle.

Boyd was king in Maggie's kitchen. He had no sooner come in than she set his tea to brewing and sliced him a piece of iced spice cake. Knowing he would want to have his own afternoon chat with Maggie, Sarah felt disappointed at having to leave with so much left unsaid. She asked if she might have a cup of tea herself—she would take it with her, she said. The tension increased as she waited.

Sarah was not having a day that inspired pleasantries. After receiving her tea in a cup patterned with gentlemen bowing before their ladies, she left the two servants to themselves and wandered up the stairs to the landing on the second floor, where the window facing inland had a window seat with a gingham-covered cushion. Although this embrasure welcomed her into its semi-secretive home, Sarah had never crouched in this place, not even as a child at play. Her mother had discouraged make-believe, Sarah remembered. So she had never taken her playful fancies out into the open, beyond the nursery or her own room.

She chose to sit here now partly because this place seemed at its most unwelcoming, almost a way of thrusting herself out into the weather, where the rain continued to fall, driving hard against the window when the wind swung around toward the bay. In the slate blue light of the failing day—this day that had had no dawn—she could see the upper branches of the copper beech tree and the dark rectangle of the barn beyond with its breadloaf roof.

She leaned her back against one side of the casing, held her teacup in both hands, and put her feet up on the cushion so that her toes touched the opposite side. The window seat was drafty, and her left arm felt tight with the cold. She stayed, though, concentrating on how warm the cup of tea made her palms feel. She felt guilty about feeling so sorry for herself, but she did not intend to stop, not yet. She did wonder how she would react if someone walked by—what she would say.

She tried to think about the good things of the past months—to count her blessings, as she had always been advised. But the way she and Abram had kissed before the rector of the chapel embarrassed her now. Her sneak attack on Abram from the trees at the Palisades seemed silly. Perhaps everything had been a mistake from the beginning. She could almost break the eggshell teacup in her hands, she felt such frustration. She wondered if her state of mind might be bad for the baby and got up from the window seat. Her shoulder felt so sore and tight from the cold that it reminded her of the time she had broken her collarbone.

Suppertime arrived at last, with its consoling promise of Yorkshire pudding. She thought her father might entertain them with tales from his reading: he liked to recount for them the plots of Roman comedies by Terence and Plautus. But Abram led off with another account of his silver-polishing triumph, asking them to admire, once more, the sparkling cutlery. Not only had everyone tired of hearing of silver, but this seemed to put her father off especially: he spoke not a word about his reading. They heard their spoons—so newly polished—scraping the bottoms of their china bowls when finishing their chowder.

At the end of the meal, Sarah looked at the bottom crust of the custard pie that she had been taught to leave on her dessert plate. In her sour mood the slim wedge looked like a mocking tongue. She turned the plate so that its tip pointed at Abram, and felt better.

"Shall we play whist?" Felicity asked as they gathered in the sitting room. "You have been reading all day, Father. Come and play. Sarah and Abram?"

"I should like to play," said Livy.

"I have always been lucky in high weather," Abram said.

Her father's step veered away from the table. "My book needs finishing, dear," he said, in a tone that meant he would be finishing it the rest of the evening.

"Forgive me," Sarah said, waving her book. "I vowed I'd attend the Reverend Wigglesworth on wagering and the vanity of human wishes."

The others each gave her their Sarah-has-her-moods looks and began playing three-handed, with Abram bidding two hands, which nettled Sarah since Abram knew more about the game than her two sisters. Felicity and Livy wanted his company, that was clear, and they would let him trounce them in order to get it.

Sarah took her book and put her feet up on the settee, rotating her shoulders slightly away from the players, turning her back on them in a way she judged too discreet to be called to account. It would have pleased her, though, if they had noticed. She would almost have found one of Felicity's short lectures soothing. The sugars and spices of supper had already dissolved and left the mysterious taste covering her tongue like the silver's former corrosion. There was something salty about it, she noticed now. It insinuated its character as if it might be medicinal or poisonous. She wished her preoccupation with the taste would go away.

The threesome's chatty game of whist fanned out into her thoughts, sweeping around and drawing her in to the place at the table she had refused. Abram won several hands with even more ease than Sarah had anticipated. Felicity and Livy managed the occasional victory that kept the game interesting.

"You play too well for us, Abram," Felicity said. "Only foolhardiness allows us the bids, and you make us pay so dearly every time for that!"

"If I listen to any more of that, you'll set me next time. You are winning a nice enough share."

"You must have done nothing on your ships but play cards," said Felicity. "That is why you have sailed everywhere and back—you navigated at a gaming table."

"I'll steer my course now," Abram said, picking up a fresh hand. "Three spades."

"Three spades?" Livy asked.

"You are determined to make me a prophet, aren't you?" Felicity asked. "You are going to run up the bid to show us what you can do."

"Your bid, Livy," Abram said.

"How do you always know what I am holding?" Livy asked. "He must be able to look through the backs of the cards."

"Your expression gives you away," Felicity said.

"It does not," Livy said. "I always look contrary to my true intentions."

"So you do," Abram said.

Livy let out a cry of exasperation. "Ooooohhh! You are an evil man, aren't you."

Sarah turned in time to see her younger sister throw her hand of cards at Abram, then scold herself in breathy mutterings for being so intemperate. Abram rose quickly and helped her gather up the cards that had fluttered to the floor.

Sarah could hardly pretend to read. Once again, as she had too many times since returning home, she found herself watching her sisters flattering her husband: Felicity, with her superior mind, Livy, with her uncontrolled physical overtures. Felicity's infatuation with Abram had as yet not diminished her social graces; embarrassed with Sarah, she managed to remain composed in Abram's presence. What did that say?

Sarah told herself to remain at a safe distance from the game; she was better off as the aloof wife, confident and generous in the wealth of her husband's love.

She found herself getting up from the settee and walking over to the table, nevertheless.

They asked her immediately if she wanted to play. "Please," Felicity said, "we will only keep proving your husband's superiority otherwise."

"I will deal again," Livy said, and snatched up the cards from in front of the other two.

But whose partner would she be?

Every combination multiplied the chances of conflict. She preferred to play with Felicity: they would have their chances against Abram and Livy. If Sarah played well, Felicity's mind might not appear so superior after all.

"Felicity and I would have the best chance," Sarah said.

"But Abram and you are the more natural pair," Felicity said, and there was a hint of instruction in her voice that Sarah did not like at all. "You must give Livy and me a chance to get ours back."

Her anger at Felicity's mothering persuaded Sarah, and she sat down opposite her husband.

Sarah looked over at her father, now drowsing in his chair, his copy of Plautus on his knee, his stomach, in his slouched position, bulging casklike under his breeches, his hands grasping the buckle of his belt—holding on to the reins in his dreaming—his withered calves crossed at the ankles. She wanted him to wake up suddenly, as he often did from his post-prandial slumbers, find himself embarrassed to be sleeping in their midst, and rock onto his feet to say his good-nights. That might give her an excuse to play a hand or two and do the same.

At first the cards Sarah and Abram drew happened to be consistently good ones. They won a hand. They won two. She could not remember what had been worrying her—she had never known, had she?

In the next few hands, however, Felicity and Livy started to set them. Abram and Sarah still drew good hands, but at those crucial junctures where one's partner must have the next trump or an ace of an off-suit for a high bid to succeed, Livy—yes, Livy—kept pulling these winning cards out of her hand, quietly, with a greater capacity for silent cunning than Sarah had ever sensed in her before. Livy placed them down on the table, fixing them there with her fat, peasantlike thumb.

"Let's moderate our bidding," Abram said.

"We should both do that," Sarah said.

But in the next hands, Felicity started fielding superior cards and finished their chances in the rubber.

As this happened, Abram began to look around him, as if looking for help from another quarter—or so Sarah thought. He resented her for spoiling the last part of his evening; he had been doing so well alone. Her sisters' attentions had been directed at him, whereas now they were quite clearly in gleeful league with each other, with Livy racing around the table to hug Felicity after every victorious hand. He must be angry with her, Sarah thought.

"Where is Hodges?" Abram asked, his voice now more tense than Sarah had ever heard it. "I want another glass of port. Hodges!"

The rooster-haired valet appeared, and Abram upbraided him for his slowness while he served his master.

As Felicity tallied their score—unnecessarily, Sarah thought—Sarah bit the side of her cheek, tension having set her jaw, and the taste of blood rose in her mouth, with its tangy and yet oily savor. The pain shot through her cheek. It patterned and drew her feelings into its net like the spider's web of a stone-struck mirror.

When the pain started to clear, she realized what had caused the mysterious taste in her mouth that day. She chewed on one side of her lower lip when upset—even in her sleep, according to her sisters. That side of her lip, as she ran her tongue over it now, felt dry and cracked. She must have been causing the lip to bleed, sipping its flow, right through the day. It frightened her that she could be aware of the taste without knowing its cause.

She looked up to see Abram scowling at her, as if he believed her wounded expression to be a childish reaction to their fortunes in whist. "That's a most unpleasant expression, Abram."

"I might say the same of yours. You need not look so crestfallen. It was only a game of chance."

"You need not instruct me in the presence of my sisters, thank you."

He did not reply immediately, but kept looking at the cards in his hands, rearranging them and tapping them on the table. He sorted them one final time and rapped them on the table. "The presence of your sisters, their manner, should instruct you," he said. "We were a very happy party earlier."

He was glaring at her. She had never seen the disciplining captain before now, and he frightened her.

"You pleaded with me to join you," she said, not giving up.

"I only wish I could remember why," he said. His anger made his face sharper. He looked capable of slicing her apart. "Your pouting, your angry looks, your discourteous tongue makes it impossible to recall."

She was going to say something about his needing to remember before he came to her bed, when she bit the side of her cheek yet again. The pain brought the collapse, the disintegration, the implosion that had threatened all day, and she ran out of the room, crying and humiliated.

By the time the throbbing in her cheek subsided, Sarah felt ready for Abram to come into their bedroom after her. She waited, sitting on the bed so long she wondered whether he had guessed at her thoughts about excluding him. Perhaps she had made him even angrier than she was—she had never seen him so upset before.

She got off the bed and began to pace. She felt as if she were newly arrived at the home of a stranger, without any knowledge of how she got there, without instructions as to what to do next. This frightened her. How could she feel like this in her own home? Where did she belong?

Her hands were ice. She felt her heart accelerating, and she sat back down on the bed. But her heart beat even faster. She stood up again. Her forehead beaded with perspiration, and wet drops ran into the hollow of her back as well. Trying to clear her mind, she considered what might be wrong with her. She had never felt like this before, though, and she was starting to panic.

She stumbled to Abram's desk, thinking whether she should call out. She was not sure what she would say. She reminded herself of the desk's history, how she had stood beside it in their city lodgings and looked out toward the masts rising from the shipyards. But tonight the continuing rain and its doubling darkness made her afraid of looking out. Her childhood fears of the windows as dark faces, peering in, came back to her. Only the solid walls around her were reassuring.

The paper's fleur-de-lys pattern drew her attention. She reached out, and as her fingertips touched the cold wall she felt a dull ache in her abdomen.

The baby. She could not afford to be in this state of mind with a baby coming. If she did not calm down—if another pain came—perhaps she would lose the baby. But another contraction did hit her, a much heavier one that buckled her knees, striking her down into a half crouch. She held her thighs and squeezed her eyes tight against the pain.

Then the pain finally let her up. She stood on her feet and wondered what to do. She could not lose the baby. She must think what to do—where to go. She had thought to find safety here, in these walls, but now she knew she needed to get out.

The pain came again. Tears streamed down her face. She looked and saw that her petticoats were stained with blood. *She was losing the baby.*

The thought terrorized her. Her vision mysteriously contracted, a white, gauzy ring obscuring everything at the periphery. Her thoughts were as scattered as buckshot and rushed away as fast. She felt, too, as if she had suddenly lost her hearing, and then realized that her ears were full of the throbbing of her own blood. She was going to vomit. She had to get outside—into the open air.

Whirling toward the door, she stumbled down the stairs and rushed through the hall, into the kitchen, and out into the storm.

The muddy ground soaked and caked her slippered feet and stockings and the hem of her dress. The added weight almost tripped her. She clutched her skirts. Her feet kept slipping over the uneven ground in the dark.

The fine, cold rain came down so hard it stung her skin. She went on, blindly, her long dark hair coming undone and falling around her eyes and clinging wet and cold to the back of her neck.

She went on, sensing everything was lost. Still, she had to get away. To put everything from her. What she wanted lay hidden in the expanding darkness around her.

―――――――

From the front parlor Abram had seen Sarah leave the house. He hesitated going after her, thinking the weather would cure her pique. He wanted her to have the full satisfaction of being doused. Losing at whist, Sarah's petulance, and their subsequent words had made him livid, and he was the kind of man who would feel his anger the next day like a hangover.

But when Sarah did not return immediately, he knew his duty, and he put on his oilskin and made his way out into the stinging rain.

He searched through the barns and stables and up the hill into a blackness that he found as chilling as the freezing rain. She had disappeared. He was considering organizing Hodges and Boyd into a search party when he heard her voice in the privy.

She was sobbing and wet and engulfed in the stench of the fumes that hung in the air. For reasons he could not guess at, she had removed her dress and sat over the open seat in her undergarments. Bent over from the waist, her long hair fell over her knees and nearly touched the muddy floor. She rocked from side to side.

"Sarah," he shouted. "What the devil . . . you must come back into the house. Stand up now!"

She did not move. He kept the door open with his body to catch the minimal light and the air. The wind and rain drove at him from behind, ruffling the sleeves and tail of the oilskin, swinging the door shut against him. He kicked back against it violently, and when it tried to close again he warded it off with his heel.

"We only had words. What are words? Stand up and let me help you!"

He waited. She kept rocking from side to side. Finally, not in response to any specific plea, she stood up. "I'll help you in," he said, knowing that the night had turned from petty anger and headed off into the blackness of the storm itself.

He took her up under the arms, lifted her to him, and pulled her out the door. When he picked her up, his arms under her back and knees, he pulled her as close to him as he could, putting the strength of his anxiety for her into the embrace.

Inside the house, Maggie undressed her and put her to bed,

- 212 -

where Sarah lay in an exhausted stupor. She could not bring herself to care about anything enough to raise her head.

For several days she lay in a listless state that was so mysterious and frightening it kept the household almost as quiet as she.

They soon had a midwife in who lived at a neighboring farm. But after she had examined Sarah, the woman told them that she had not miscarried. She was having her monthly course, that was all. Why the girl was in such a state, she could not say.

Even as Sarah began to feel better, enough to look at the day again at first light, to eat the meals that were brought to her bed, she knew that her burgeoning dream was gone. She had begun to think of herself as the mother of Abram's child, and now perhaps she never would be. She could not drive this constant thought and fear from her mind, and it did not help that Maggie shushed her for being foolish when she mentioned it. That made it all too clear that she was the child again.

CHAPTER 17

Bright Idea

*I*n the following days, Abram took Hodges and his own worries about Sarah off to the Mashkill River mud flats where he started clamming at dawn. His shovel turned over yards of the sand's smooth surface, its low tide wetpack marked only by the air-hole perforations of the clams. With each scoop of his shovel, a dozen or more steamers shriveled back into their shells. Crouched down on his knees, Hodges waddled after him, sorting through the sand, his reddening fingers stashing the rough, scored shells in his gunnysack.

Abram woke up feeling cold these days, and the chill of the mud flats, with its slicing wet air, gave him a chance to labor against the frightening chill that had driven Sarah from him when the nor'easter rounded against them both.

He thought of his vows, *for better for worse, in sickness and in health*, and considered what was required of him. He had married a beautiful young woman after uncommonly long years of bachelorhood, and her youth and his years alone affected him in unexpected ways. Sometimes, he saw her as little more than a girl, as full of surprises and willfulness as a child. He preferred thinking of her this way at times, since it gave him the leverage of distance. Occasionally he understood how close they had drawn; her power to release in him desires and cravings for simple human pleasures that he had presumed dead. His every longing to be released from his solitary life went out to her and knitted them together. For more than twenty years, no one had touched him with affection. Once when she put her hand to the back of his neck, he felt so grateful that tears came to his yes. But now the easiness of their honeymooning had come to an end.

When they lay in bed now and he reached out to touch her, he felt her body stiffen. Or she embraced him in a way that seemed false, which he had verified once by simply turning away from her. She never moved, never reached out to touch his back. The silence that lingered made him feel as if his bones were bleeding.

Sarah had regained her health, but she had not recovered. She sat by the windows in their room for much of the day, wearing dresses he had never seen before, formless pinafores the color of the wet sand surrounding him, dresses from her last growing-up years that were candidating for rags. How he wanted to strip them off and wipe away the smudge and blear that kept him from seeing her as she used to be—or her from seeing him as he must have once appeared.

What was he to do?

He looked toward where the stream running through the mud flats broadened out into the shallow bay, with its fringe of tall corn grass. A line of sea gulls bobbed in the bright blue water, waiting in folded-wing contentment for the mysterious promptings that set them flying. The sun was rising, and its light dazzled the waters.

An outer shoal protected the bay, and he could see the ocean's waves, at least a thousand yards from where he stood, crashing against it; their cannonading white plumes distantly counterpointed the wash at his feet.

The coldness in him started to melt under the sun's influence; he rested in the ease of work begun and the strength to do it. The scooping sound of his spade in the sand sliced back, parried, the fear cutting into him. The sands yielded their plenty almost too easily, as if God delighted in excess. How could so many things go wrong in a world like this?

Suddenly angry, he raised his shovel above his head and brought it down on a tightly packed handful of dislodged steamers. The one directly under the shovel's heel cracked and splintered, bits of the shell driving down into the embryolike animal with its milky sheathing and gummy blue caul.

There, he thought, enraged now, that would have been what she would have lost: nothing.

Abram lifted his eyes and saw Hodges looking at him as if he were mad.

At once he felt ashamed and shook his head. That other time his impulses had turned murderous came to mind, those final months with Captain Jack, and he wondered why his own efforts to put things right—to champion his family in Ireland, to give his young wife the home and family she wanted—why his best efforts made him want to kill people.

He tried to dismiss this. "Hodges," he said, "gather this lot up."

His man moved hesitantly toward him, like a sand crab whose legs can just as easily reverse their direction.

Abram looked out toward the breaking waves. He thought again of his family in Ireland. He thought of Sarah.

The next moment, the bobbing gulls sprang into the air as one, and Abram's voice echoed as they wheeled above him—the man who had thrown out his arms and shouted what might have been a hallelujah at the still-rising sun.

———

In late January, two feet of snow fell on Long Island. Melting during the day and refreezing at night, the snow turned into a treacherous cake of ice, moating the household. Still, Abram got out a raft of letters, and received the answers that he hoped for. As soon as he knew his prospects, he planned out what he would say to Sarah.

A February thaw came, with a moist and almost warm breeze from the south, which lifted the naked tree limbs as if they were being roused from their sleep. Abram asked Sarah to come out walking with him after breakfast on the third day of better weather.

The remaining ice lay in patches on the lee side of the evergreens as they made their way down to the beach. They skirted the cove and walked arm-in-arm along the strand to the west where the powerful sets of waves broke and gathered, festooning the misty scene with their white water sashes.

The thunder and wash of the waves seemed to shut Sarah into herself, and the blue-gray light of the misty day enveloped both of them in an absorbing inner quiet. Abram's arm around Sarah's shoulder tethered him, though, to her and his purpose, and each step he took brought him closer to the frontier of their conversation. Did he anticipate a battle? He thought of his news as glad tidings, but Sarah had so much a mind of her own that he feared what she would say. He almost laughed at the control she had over him. He guessed he was in love.

He squeezed her to him more closely and turned her away from the sea toward the dunes where they could huddle beneath the wind and hear each other. He kissed her and tasted the marmalade she'd had for breakfast,

They sat down side by side and leaned back against the curl of a dune. He put his right arm over her, his hand niched under her arm, and kissed her again. She slid underneath him and kissed him back, as if he had finally signaled the purpose of their trip. He saw that he had confused her, and himself, with an offer he didn't mean to make, and he gave her a smack on the lips, punctuating an end to that.

"What do you have to say to me?" she asked, her look narrowing, the discomfort of leaning back on her elbows showing.

Already he was at a disadvantage. He tried to find the enthusiasm that had prompted his mud flat hallelujah. "I know now how we shall get on," he said. "I have an idea. It's such a good idea, my lady, that I think it can only be partly my own. It seems an inspiration."

She waited for him to explain himself, her expression flat.

"I've told you of my family and how I went to sea to save them."

She sat up.

"And now I have taken on the obligation of our family—to provide for you and the children we shall soon have."

She turned her head away, her thoughts undoubtedly curving back around to her own obsessions, and he reached out and touched the profiled side of her cheek, which squared her back toward him.

"So how might I do both . . . at once?"

Her look opened.

"You are not a woman whose husband should be away at sea, Sarah White. Your father told me that before we married, and I have a better notion why now. But we cannot long remain here. You know the why of that yourself. You cannot be fully your own mistress in this place. We cannot—" and here Abram's words broke off, as he did not know how to describe his own uneasiness with her father and the way Sarah herself had reassumed the role of middle sister.

"So what will you do, husband?" Sarah asked, helping.

"I will use all I know in an enterprise that should secure us a living and a household. I'll sail to Ireland, recruit pilgrims, and settle them in the Hudson Valley. While I was clamming, I suddenly realized that with Cain Smith's Beekman relations, his Livingston clients, and his distant Delancey connection, we could put together a most ambitious speculation. Cain has set up the joint company. Once the pilgrims have been landed, I will receive a huge parcel in payment for my services. We will do well on the voyage itself, then on rents for collateral parcels, and finally on some speculative selling."

Sarah took a moment, considering. "That's an idea. I'm sure our marriage gave your partners some of their confidence." Then she reached out to him for the first time in weeks, her hand at his lapel.

He drew her closer. "I suppose my father was right," he said, nearly whispering. "There are Garritys everywhere. But this time their name will be White, and I'll do my renters justice."

"That's what you must do," she said, and squeezed him. "Yes, you must. After our child is born."

He held her out from him. "Our child?"

Her lashes flicked down and her eyes roved away. "Not yet. But by the spring, with these prospects, we should be happier, and then a little more time . . . it should not be long."

He understood that Sarah had outlined what she would assume to be a contract, if he did not contradict her.

"I am to sail within the next six weeks. The pilgrims must be landed in time to sow a late crop. They may starve otherwise. Their intended neighbors, the Livingstons, can help nurse them through one winter, but these are my people, my family. I cannot bring them to their deaths."

"There are too many arrangements for such an early departure," she said dismissively.

"They have been made."

She looked up at him. He could see the muscles in her jaw bunch. He thought she might slap him.

"This is our hope. You look as if I had betrayed you," he said.

She started to stand, and he reached up and sat her back down with a thump. Which prompted an explosion.

"You cannot be off before you have given me a child. That is our happiness, the thing itself and much more than the means. I have only lately felt capable again of thinking of this. You cannot *leave!*"

Her look held the fury of a woman, the anger of a child, and a desperation that crossed the two, balled them up, and sent them flying. If his ideas flashed across the skies, her anger ascended there.

He thought of taking her into his arms, but he remembered the time in the carriage when she had bitten his face. He tried to stare her down, and their eyes locked so hard he thought his might split open. Sweet blessed mercy, she made him angry!

He stood up. "It's done," he said, looking down on the part in her dark hair.

Then he walked off, the sand giving way beneath his feet, defying his efforts to be quick and dignified. This made him so angry he found himself pathetic. He turned back once, and, as he expected, she was not following.

———

Two days later, his father-in-law took ill. Robert Nicolls' labored breathing and climbing fever soon made it clear that his head cold was turning into pneumonia. He improved when he was able to sleep through the night, but the illness had found the susceptibility of his age, and it kept pulling him lower into its suffocating waters.

"Father is ill," Sarah said. "There can be no question of you going now."

Her argument failed to persuade him, and he went into the old gentleman's room one morning to tell him this—or to find out why. He found his father-in-law enthroned by half a dozen pillows, wearing a white nightgown with lace at the sleeves, his books scattered over the bedclothes.

The servants had let Abram know that Robert Nicolls, nearing what might be his death, was keeping up his correspondence, reading enough in snatches to recount fresh anecdotes from the lives of the noble Romans to visitors, and spending time with Boyd reviewing tenant leases and plans for the spring plantings. He was resisting death as if it were an opponent whose ultimate victory might be delayed by vigilance.

"Abram!" Nicolls said in greeting. "They have me—" his voice broke with spluttery coughing, "they have me incarcerated with pillows. Come in." His labored breathing and the strange burbling musicality of his voice, a swirl of water and clicking rocks, told Abram that the pneumonia had grown much worse.

Nicolls slumped back, instantly fatigued. Abram noticed that the once-inflated belly lay much flatter under the covers. His complexion looked boiled by the fever, red at his big ears and nose with their patterns of broken blood vessels, and purplish shadows bagged his eyes and striped his cheeks. His eyes hardly blinked, as if he were willing himself open to the world. His fingernails, especially the thumbs, had lost their pinkish transparency and were now a dull butterscotch. He had once gestured freely with those hands, but now they rested on the bedclothes, his wrists bobbing from time to time, like young birds attempting to fly.

After Abram greeted Nicolls with a willfully cheerful spirit, the silence grew for a long moment.

"I have just been going back through Marcus Aurelius," Nicolls said to both their relief.

Abram could see the thick leather volume at the old gentleman's right hand.

"My time for stoicism has come, don't you think?" Nicolls shook his head, a miniature of his good-natured wag, and in this instance, it seemed, a denial.

"I don't know him," Abram said.

"Never read him aboard ship? Marcus Aurelius makes for equanimity, a difficult virtue in my condition. The sea itself seems to have taught you its practice."

"We cannot be too much at peace with you ill," Abram said.

"Most especially Sarah," Nicolls said, helping him to the point. "I think others might imagine I should tweak your concern for her. I know your concern. I have always known it." His wrists pumped. "You know about her mother's death?" he asked.

"Yes."

"Not simply what I told you," Nicolls said. "How it came about? How Sarah took it?"

"Yes."

Nicolls coughed into his hands, grabbed a handkerchief off his bed table, and bent over until his forehead nearly touched the bedclothes. His throat cleared, he leaned back. His mouth hung half open as he took his breaths. He could not keep himself from sneaking a look at the handkerchief before he put it away. Abram had already noticed the blood spotting through.

"Excuse me." He fetched another handkerchief and wiped his

mouth. "You should know something else. To make the decision before you. Sarah's grandmother on the Singleton side . . . Puritans and mystics those people . . . Did I tell you this? Ecod, it bears repeating. That woman ended her life tearing the pages out of books," Nicolls said. "Any book that came to hand. She collected rags." He said this as if he could not have rendered a more harsh indictment or spoken more fully. His wrists pumped again, and then his hands went skittering over the bedclothes. "You have reason to be concerned."

Abram stepped to the side and back again. "How would you judge my intended enterprise? Sarah has told you of it?"

"A risky venture, I would say, except for the character of the man—" Nicolls succumbed to another coughing fit. "Except for your character. That makes it a practical surety. Which is why it might well be delayed. You should always find the capital you need. Speculation has become a fever—one with a greater tenacity than mine."

Abram walked from the foot of the bed over to the hearth and its white mantel with grooved lintels. Nicolls did not turn his eyes, but fingered his Marcus Aurelius, giving his son-in-law time to consider.

"I mean to make a fortune," Abram said, and laughed, remembering his cabin-boy pronouncement to Captain Jack.

"So you shall. Without my help. That we both prefer, although my daughter may not."

"I cannot be ruled by simple misgivings."

"Simple?" Nicolls coughed once more, and the sound seemed to explode Abram's "simple."

"Or threats of madness."

"You took my remarks as threats?" The slight irony in his voice drove against Abram's conviction, loosening the boards of the walls, causing the foundation to groan.

"You might be ruled," Nicolls said, "by the counsels of prudence and patience. I could suggest that to you."

"I cannot be ruled by my wife, or her family," Abram said, his position more clear than he had wished to make it—even to himself.

The air between them seemed as diseased as the old gentleman's lungs, and then, like a clearing cough, Nicolls' manners saved them. "No," he said. "No." He waited. "I wish you did not feel it a question of being ruled. A man so eminently suited to be his own captain might understand it as counsel. Perhaps I mistake your feeling for command. Is it something you are still earning?"

Abram's ears burned. He had to admit the justice of the remark, though. "I suppose it is. I have not kept my promises as yet."

"Promises!" Nicolls exclaimed, and erupted into laughter, then coughing, then a mixture of both from which he twisted round in bed, trying to fling them off. "Excuse me," he said, clearing his throat and almost scouring the inside of his lips and gums with his handkerchief. "By my lights. Marcus Aurelius advises quiet, not promises. At least to me, I'm afraid."

"I have not read him, as I said, and I don't think I shall."

Nicolls took this in, and then said, in a soft voice, "No. He would not suit you."

Abram wanted to reciprocate this kindness. He also wanted an accord, whatever that might mean. The old gentleman was clearly dying. He thought back to their first meetings and momentarily regretted their marital tie; without it they might have continued on as friends. "Truth, sir," he said, his voice very quiet, "do you think she will go mad? It is just that it's hard for me to credit. Why should she? I do love her."

Robert Nicolls raised up in bed and rubbed his temples and eyes with thumb and forefinger. He gave a stern wag of his head, crossed his arms, opened his mouth as if to speak, then, thinking better of it, dropped his eyes and rubbed his hands together. He waited. Finally, his hands opened, fingertips fluttering, like a blossom bursting open. "You are in greater difficulty than you know—I say this as your friend, not as Sarah's father. But the difficulty, I concede, might well dictate swift action as much as forbearance." He pinched his nose. "You are a religious man. What does your faith tell you? I have only the cold comfort of Marcus Aurelius." He stopped for a moment to grin. "Perhaps, like Solomon, you should ask first for wisdom. Marcus Aurelius and I have no objection to being her beneficiary."

Abram stepped to the bedside and took his father-in-law's hands in his. This was unlike them both, and their double-handclasp sent a shock through their expressions. Abram let go after one compulsive squeeze.

The truth was, he loved the man's daughter, but as far as friendship could go, his extended more naturally to this old man. Nicolls had picked those feelings out of the flames, and Abram was grateful. Unable to speak as yet, he watched his father-in-law take his labored breaths, which seemed even more aggravated by his own emotions.

"This enterprise," Abram said, finally, "seems to me the expression of all that I am. I can find nothing deeper. Nothing . . . else. Having her children must be the same for Sarah."

"The point, exactly."

"But one makes way for the other."

"Are these prayers?"

"In this, I can only pray to be stopped."

"I understand that well. And I agree with it." Nicolls paused, and then said, reflectively, "I have never understood it as Christianity, though. It may be. Do you think it is?"

Abram rolled in his lips and answered this question only with a quiet look, a shrug, a lifting of the eyebrows. They were in accord and agreed at last by virtue of what remained hidden from them both.

"Sail away, then, Irish lad," the old gentleman said. "Sail away."

Once her father approved of Abram's plans, Sarah's formal opposition was forgotten. She did let Abram know that he was more or less killing her. Instead, withdrawing from their common life, she anticipated his departure by resuming, even more than before, her life as the middle sister of the family. She made a point of asking Felicity at the table what they were to do the next day, meaning the three sisters. She spent time with Livy hanging about the horses, and chatted with her, in Abram's presence, about riding trips in the spring.

When Abram was alone with Sarah, he knew, by unmistakable signs, that she felt her wifely duties to be just that. This numbed him, and more and more, as his departure approached, when they got into bed he kissed her cheek and said good-night.

The day Abram left, Sarah rallied. The change that came over her began in the night. While Abram slept, she moved over to him and woke him with amorous entreaties.

Afterward, she slept little. Rising well before he did, she dressed by the light of one candle. The house slept on, buffeted by the wind and whistling in its dreams. Sarah could see nothing at the windows but the icicles hanging under the eaves. The night and the cold even muffled the roosters.

She went down to the kitchen and started breakfast. A few embers still burned in the stove, which helped her build a fire, and she had an iron pot boiling when Maggie arrived to cook the porridge, fry a rasher of bacon, and start the drop biscuits. Sarah lowered several duck eggs into the boiling water and watched their spotted shells bob among the bubbles until they were hard-boiled.

When Abram came into the kitchen, he looked at Sarah as if he suspected her of a last design to stop him from leaving. She gave him his breakfast promptly, though, and almost rushed him through his meal.

Abram planned to ride the length of the island with Hodges. Two days from now they would spend the night at The Christopher Inn at the western end of the island, from where they would be ferried to the port of New York.

After saying his good-byes to Robert Nicolls upstairs, bidding her sisters and the house servants adieu, Abram asked Sarah to put on a coat and come out with him to the barn. Hodges should be saddling their horses, he said. They would be riding inland to the Sachem Trail, so they might as well leave from out back.

She came out to where Abram stood on the flagstone path that led out to the barn and the pens. He put out his arm to her under his gull-gray riding cape, offered to enfold her in his wing. Before they cleared the hedgerows, Abram turned her round to face him. Her determined look said that she would miss him—but life held too many wonders to be sad for long. This worried him more than her pouting; her manner shifted on top of her emotions like plates from different sets of china, with spillage imminent.

"Are you sorry to see me go?" he asked her.

"I am already thinking of your return," she said, her low, rough voice marshalling the words to her own aid.

"A becoming sentiment," he said, not believing her.

She looked timid and angry at once, as if she still had hopes of dissuading him. Abram thought of himself as a man who gave orders, but he knew that he could no more order her to march to his drum than he could regiment, drill, and parade a flock of sea gulls. At the first taps she went fluttering, and then it was all leaps and grabs and useless snares.

"We will be apart for some months," Abram said, trying. "Please tell me why you have been so unhappy."

"You have given me no happiness."

This quickly exasperated him. "Think of our days in New York. How could you have been happier?"

"You have not given me what I want. A child. What I need when you are away."

"We will have children."

"So you say."

"Children come from . . . we cannot have children unless we are at peace with each other."

"Beware of them when they say to you, peace, peace, for there is no peace," Sarah said, a Singleton quoting her Bible.

He started to stalk away.

She stopped him. "I'm afraid that I will never . . . I do not know if I can have children."

"The midwife said nothing to me of this."

"It is not what the midwife said. It is a feeling I have. A *horrible* feeling." She looked at him, her eyes full and twitching with fear, and she was biting one side of her lip, keeping it curled under her sharp teeth. Her eyebrows were so pinched that her unlined forehead showed how it would mark in years to come, with a chevron of lines at her widow's peak.

The wind was coming inland, and it carried the distant pounding of the sea. He wondered for a moment whether Sarah had experienced something like his crow's nest revelations.

He thought he would give her a chance to say as much. "I cannot let a 'horrible feeling' guide me. Is it only that?"

"You did not care when I . . . when I was not pregnant. I have been so ill."

She had not seized her opportunity. His strength for this was failing. "I have done nothing but minister to your needs for weeks."

They looked at each other, almost coolly, as they receded back into themselves, the gap between them growing to a chasm, and for the first time he realized—as he experienced his own loneliness again—that who he was might be misery to her.

Abram had heard some men say that they found it a good policy in love to say the exact opposite of what they were feeling when angry. He tried this, and said, "I will miss you."

"Will you?" she asked, questioning, doubtful.

He embraced her, and he felt his strength, as he held her, gather into it the force of his desire that they be happy again. Where was the Sarah who had sailed with him to the Palisades? He did want to return to her.

She kissed him, her lips warming, her cheeks still cold. She broke off the kiss, and before he could think why, he felt her shaking and heard her first sob.

He wrapped his arms around her all the more tightly and spoke in a rush, with his cheek against her dark hair. "*Sarah*. I cannot know if this is best. I think it is. That is all a man can do. Think, reason, and choose. Whether the Lord has opened the way or the way is simply open . . . my heart . . . *you are my heart*." As he said this, he realized with a great lurch of that organ how true this was, and beads of perspiration broke out at his hairline. He gulped a breath and cried, "But leave me my soul, or I can be nothing to you."

"I will, I will," she said, and her words renewed the tremors of her tears.

"You are loving me to death," he said, explaining, desperate.

"No," she said. "No. The child I want is only something of you to touch . . . something of you to hold in your absence. It is you, I want. *You*."

They both wanted to believe this, with the strained hopefulness of the newly married. Their hold on each other grew so tight it became painful. Abram let go a little and kissed her, and she kissed him back so hard that his head started to swim and he nearly lost his balance. He felt sensations of warmth under his breastbone, and he realized, after a moment, that it was as if he were feeling her sensations, not his. He started to question his own sanity, and then understood: one flesh.

So they parted that day for the first time since their marriage, and as Abram rode away, looking back toward Sarah—whose waves and calls were lifting her onto her tiptoes—he understood how much his life had changed. The love he felt for her had become his guide, his rudder, the prow that kept him in the road and moving forward.

Part IV

—

Escapes in Broad Daylight

CHAPTER 18

The Return

With Cain Smith's financial backing, Abram secured a thirty-ton brig and ran the only cargoes that could be ferried straight back to England: hardwoods for furniture and provincial government documents. He dropped these and most of his crew in Bristol and then sailed for Larne with a trustworthy remnant.

Gathering mists and clinging showers rose up over the claw-footed coastline as they came in late one afternoon, the sea as black and silvered as a landed salmon. The pilot's launch that set out to meet them disappeared into the closing weather and popped out of what had become a dense white cloud. It had to be tethered to the side and the pilot hosted as they waited through the night.

Abram, alone in his wainscotted cabin, felt the tedium of a delayed landing in a way he never had. Hodges had stayed in New York, so he had no one close with a sympathetic ear. Abram had been all over the world, but he had not come home since running away at eleven years of age. He might have, but he had preferred to wait until he could gather his family up and fulfill his promise. It had taken him more than twenty years. He wondered at having memories that stretched that far back, for his father and mother, Dorsey and his brothers appeared in his mind as he had left them. But he had seen himself in the mirror and knew the truth. The years would have changed them as they had him.

Their letters said these last years, with his assistance, had been kinder. Still, there were many difficulties. At times, in recent years, even his father sounded tired of Ireland. Would his family want to immigrate? He had not written them directly about his venture. He would be obliged to go through with the enterprise whatever their feelings, so he had chosen to make his appeals in person.

He was back in Ireland, or almost, and he felt so agitated that he did not know whether to swim ashore or head the ship toward the North Sea. He longed for Sarah, and this surprised him to a degree since the memory of his family had always filled out his notion of home. Everything else in his life had seemed temporal or expedient for the moment. Now he realized that his family itself might belong to a particular time—that all things were of this nature. He turned against these thoughts as landing jangles and fidgets, trying to conjure the joy of keeping his pledge. But he stayed tense.

The pilot brought them in the next day under low rainy skies. His ship, which he had re-christened *The Camille* after his mother, dropped anchor a little way from the wharves. He remembered his first glimpse of ocean-going vessels tied up against these long, tar-blackened, stilt-supported piers—ships much like the two channel crossers there now.

When he had finished his business with the pilot in the customs house, he stepped out into the streets of Larne. It was not a place he knew well, having been there but once; only the central church with its gothic arches placed him. When the off-shore wind turned round and came down off the hills, he caught the scent of his homeland—its grasses and soil as individual as a signature—and he knew he was truly at home.

He started to hear his accent in the street, the roll in the r's in the bun seller's voice as the old, rag-clad woman greeted him with, "Sure, and it would be a fine day if not for the rain." He answered her in a brogue that had all the stops pulled, his tongue fluttering through his r's as if a butterfly were beating its way out of his mouth.

People nodded and spoke their greetings as he took his long strides over the cobblestone and brick streets; the same people wearing their city clothes, handsome long jackets, and ornamental aprons who had taken care not to notice him on his last visit here. He felt as if he were that same little boy masquerading as a man of position, and this gave him a secretive thrill. He blessed that little boy and wondered at his courage.

He had been drifting—the implementation of his plan was his to devise—but then he conceived a first purpose, inspired by his memories. He went up to a fish monger. This short-legged merchant had stopped his cart at the curb close to a central square and was braying out to all, "Fish, Lovely Fish, The Soul of the Deep, 'Seidon's Blessings and Bounty, Crabs a' Penny!" Abram asked him the way to his original point of departure, that hellish tavern Bailey's.

The unshaven, red-faced man, all long-lipped mouth and watery eyes, quit calling just long enough to give him a dumbfounded look and say, "Follow any brigand you may find, sir, or hard starboard at the following corner."

Abram put a copper in the man's hand and went his way.

Bailey's shocked him by still being there. It had a new roof, again—and its sign now hung over the street. The walls had grown so sooty that he could no longer distinguish the original fingers of fire about its door, although he thought he detected a leafy shadow. He hadn't remembered the place having a small window or that the glass was stained—a red flagon in an uplifted, toasting hand. The tavern looked a bit more inviting than twenty years ago.

Inside, its darkness blinded him for a moment, and by the time he could distinguish the horseshoe bar, the ring of tables, the barman stepped toward him, at the ready. Abram looked at the space between the top of the bar and the low ceiling and realized how short he must have been to stand up there. He asked for a pint as something to hold and took a seat at the table where the Little General and Dribbler had shanghaied him.

Then he saw someone he thought he recognized. Could it be? She was at the bar in a faded red dress, the top partly unbuttoned in a pathetic sort of way, as thin or thinner than she had been, slumped on a stool, her arm braced on the bar against sleep or drunkenness. It must be Gillian. She still had that *stretched* look, and her matted freckles had weathered the years and their scoring. Her thin hair was untied and trailed down to the floor. She looked like a banshee well on her way to becoming a weird sister, an old witch.

Abram took a sudden and full quaff of his pint, half-choked on its yeasty malt, and pulled around in his chair so that he could see her at an angle where he would be less seen. Had he come here for this or something like this? But why Gillian? Why not the Little General and Dribbler? Or even Dorgan the pawn broker.

In another moment, as she crossed her legs and tried to raise her head, he had decided he wanted to talk to her. She was nearly unconscious—why should he feel threatened?

He took his pint and sat on the stool next to her. She took no notice. He touched her balancing forearm.

Her eyes opened. "Who wants to be the spry boy this morning?" She took him in. "Ho there, Captain, you pulled into the right port." She threw her arm around him, suddenly alive. "You've been away at sea, have you? Nothing but the lady on your prow to keep you company, and she's a wooden type." She laughed the old, wild banshee laugh.

Abram was astonished that she could revive from her stupor so quickly.

She held his cheeks between her hands and brought her narrow face and faintly bluish lips close to his. "She'll take her shellacking, but a man wants comfort. A kiss from something more than the waves. You drop anchor, Captain. Spend some time with me."

He put his hand in the middle of her flat chest and pushed her away.

She threw herself back around his shoulders. "You're the strong one. Buy us a pint."

He should have gotten away from her then, if he was going to get away easily. Instead, he raised his index finger to the barman, who had been eyeing them as he towel-dried his tankards.

She moved to the edge of her stool, her bony knees pressing against his, and insinuated her cupped hand around his waist. "Where will we go then, Captain? Any lodgings in town? Michael here can have his boy run up a beer bucket. He knows the way to my place if you're too lately arrived."

She smirked and turned her eyes down. He saw the thousands of paper-cut lines that spread out in every direction from the bridge of her nose and turned into the striated cords of her long neck. Her hair was very dirty, and the roots writhed in uncombed twists that patched her hair with bald spots. Her breath made it difficult to bear her near him, not simply because of the drink but the smell of decaying teeth that came along with it. Still, this was his own banshee.

"Gillian," he said.

Her eyes briefly crossed, she looked at him so hard. "How is it you know my name?" She looked toward the barman. "I'm getting forgetful, Michael, though my bones remember every packet."

Abram called her name again.

Her voice was unsure. "If we knew each other in the back country, sir, I don't care to remember it. Because I don't. So I've been going by Sally, thank you."

"You remember Billy the Tinker, Gillian?"

Her eyes popped. "You wouldn't be Billy."

"And a trip to Larne with a wee lad in tow."

She took a moment. "He made off with our shillings, that one, never known how. Looked to disappear like a leprechaun, and Billy thought he'd fooled with God's own and told me to leave it." She said all this at once as if he had struck a reflex and the words kicked themselves out.

"What a dickey lad he was," Abram said.

"Or so we thought," Gillian said. "A reed of a child and no one at his back, and then he diddled us proper."

Abram waited for her to get the point.

"How is it . . . you know . . . no one would know these things but the bairn himself. You would be he, then, sir?"

He saw how frightened she was and anticipated the guilty reverence she must put on when caught in something. He did not want to see this. "The same. I've come back to repay you." He fumbled in his pockets, and she leaned away as if he might pull a knife. He put two sovereigns before her, along with the ring that had been in the box, an item he had always carried as a good-luck charm.

"Me ring," she said.

"Your own."

"I'll not be seeing Billy," she said, starting to smile.

He pushed out his lips to say that didn't matter.

"But oh, dickey lad," Gillian said suddenly, and she reached out and touched the ear that Billy had pummeled. "It didn't go bad on you, then?" she asked.

Her touch brought a transformation. Instantly he was no longer the captain, but that dickey lad she took him for, almost as if he found himself shrinking back to the frightened dimensions of his boyhood. He glanced away and saw the Little General and Dribbler in the corner. He turned, trying to refocus his eyes, and Dorgan walked through the door. The bar seemed to be pitching like a ship in a squall, and then an indescribable emotion shot through him.

"Dickey?" Gillian asked.

Everything he had been on the threshold of feeling—waiting for the landing, walking the streets, remembering his family—burst into his mind, and a star shower of grief and nostalgia and longing fell through the silence and solitude in which he had lived. He grabbed on to Gillian and wept.

After some moments, Michael the barman asked Gillian, "He started before he got here, then, did he?"

He felt the resonances of Gillian's voice as she said, "He's come home, you mullet. The dickey lad's come home."

The next day, after giving Gillian a decent meal, another five pounds, and useless advice, he took the coach to Ballymena. There he rented a private carriage with two shining black horses, their ears high, their manes cut short and braided. The cab was plump and round like a pumpkin and rocked more gently than most on its spring suspension. The carriage looked so fine with its gleaming cherrywood cabinetry, it almost appeared fragile. No one had ever taken it up to Glenwhirry.

People came out of the cottages and pubs as he drove by. He kept the baize green curtains over the windows, peeking from behind them just enough to see a glimpse of the round faces calling after him. His extravagance was creating the stir he wanted.

His appearance at his parents' home should take place without fanfare, though. He wanted to walk up through the meadow to the thatch-roofed buildings that soon rolled into view.

Standing in the lane, he could hardly believe he was in the right place. Everything looked so much smaller than he remembered. Then, too, there were window boxes filled with pansies, a wooden pen by the barn, and a plough horse grazing in the field north of the cottage. The buildings had been recently white-washed, and everything looked cozier, if diminutive.

He walked up the rutted cart path to the cottage, which rested with a quiet, unknowing steadfastness on the escarpment of the hill. The cottage seemed to be withdrawing further from him as his view of it jostled with his ascending steps. Then the smells of chickens, manure, and burning peat reached out to him. His steps slowed as he looked closely at the door to see if anyone would come out to greet him, and who that someone might be.

He thought of calling out. The quiet of the place unsettled him. He stopped for a moment and considered whether his unexpected appearance would cause his mother too great a fright. He might turn round and send up a message from the village. The years assailed him again. Why had he ever let so much time go by?

He went up to the low door and knocked. It opened. His mother ... grown diminutive herself ... his mother ... her hair silvered, the rose-colored shadows around her eyes ... his mother ... her face only a little heavier with the years ... his mother ... a neat woman with her hands clasped together in a white-aproned, dark-blue dress with a spreading pleated skirt ... his mother stood at last before him.

"*Maman*," he said.

Her eyes registered the shock. Her hands unclasped and went up as if she were beholding a vision. "Oh, oh, oh," she said, as if warming up for the scream that came next. "Abram!"

She reached for him and he took her up into his arms. "Oh, Abram, you've come home, you've come home," she said. "You have come home, *enfin, mon cher*. Oh, Abram, Abram, Abram." She was crying and wailing and kissing and pressing her head against his chest.

"*Maman*," he said. "*Maman*." Then he started to cry, so hard that he did not know whether he was crying for joy or something else. He felt how much he had missed her all at once, and he remembered never having anyone to tell his adventures to in all those long years—things too deep to put in letters that might never reach their destination. He remembered the silence of his years as Captain Jack's servant, its length, its hardness, its remorseless discipline. He thought that he was the one who might not survive such a bone-shattering joy, if this indeed was joy, and he held on to her for life: for the life that he had led and all the living that had vanished; for a life that had maintained the merest shred of a reason, a golden string that he had followed back to her. "*Maman*," he said, and this one word would have to be his amen to those twenty years.

She brought him into the house and sat him down on a wooden, spindle-backed bench across from the smoldering peat fire. Stroking his hair, she seemed to sense how distraught he had become.

"*Mon pauvre, petit*," she said. "*Mon petit si brave*. You have come home, and what a man you are now. My little one and now such a jewel."

"*Maman*," he said, absolutely the little boy again. "How I missed you. I should never have gone away."

She held him, rocking back and forth, muttering her comforts.

"No, no. I could not have done for you what your mistress has," she cooed. "The sea has made you into someone so magnificent. And now given you to your wife. *Ç'est ça*. As it should be." She kissed him on the forehead and his cheek. "But, oh what joy I have in seeing these things. I have lived to see them. I see them in every bit of you."

She was his mother, instantly, as if he had never left; someone more eloquent and knowing than he would ever be. It was coming to an end, that powerful emotion that had nearly slain him. He hugged her again, and her soft, plump body felt like the one thing he had truly missed in all those long years. They were together again. He felt his spirit returning, and his emotion reaffirmed how thoroughly his struggles had been devoted to her.

"Where is father?" he asked.

She looked down briefly and turned her head slightly away. "He's with Lorraine," she said.

At first the name struck him as if it might have belonged to a family friend, and then the memory of his baby sister who had died so long ago came back. Too late after all, the voice inside him said. "When?" he asked.

"One night this winter. I woke up one morning and—"

"As he slept?"

She nodded.

He waited for what he would have to feel now. He thought of the incident that had come between them. The trout. The accident in the barn. His feelings for his father were still partly tied to these things and the rivalry that had sent him to sea. But those troubles had little to do with what he would have liked to have known of his father: the man who had written to him so encouragingly through the years. He did not know that man as he wished to, and now he never would. So what he came to feel, at least immediately, was not so much grief as a deep regret.

"He was very proud," his mother said.

A criticism? No, he thought the next moment, not of him, *of me*. He had never been lashed with so many contradictory emotions.

"I wanted to talk with him," he said. "I wanted to know him."

"He came back to me," she said mysteriously. "With your help, a bit of prosperity, the man I married came back. No one knew him when he left. Not the man himself. But you brought him back. And so he is here for you now."

He did not understand how this could be so, but he left it for the moment.

"You live by yourself, then?"

She looked toward the window as if company might appear. "Dorsey and her husband are close by. They live in the Burns place. I wrote this?"

He nodded yes.

He stood up and paced to the opposite side of the room and back. Looking down at the fastidiously dressed woman, he noticed the amber pin holding her hair in its tight coil. He remembered her old, white draw-string cap, with wisps of her once-auburn hair spiraling around its indentions. The pin, her crisp, pleated dress suggested that she had finished her life's work and was enjoying her ease and her bit of prosperity. He wondered whether she would have any taste for adventure and a new life. At the same time, looking at her, his arms felt strung with an eager tension, his desire to lift her up and carry her away.

"*Maman*," he said, "I want to take you back. I want to take the whole family back with me. I have lands that the family and their neighbors here can work for nothing. I've come to take a whole ship of immigrants back to the New World."

She looked at him, her expression so placid he might have been talking about the weather.

"I want you to come and live with Sarah and me. Everyone else has had you for these twenty years. I want to make the rest of your life a joy, and you will make mine that if you consent."

As these words rushed out, he almost felt as if he should be getting down on one knee, and this embarrassed him.

She looked at him as if he were telling an ingenious fib, nodding the whole way, as mothers would do.

"*Maman*," he said. "Truly."

"Would you like tea?" she asked. She went to the slatted china cabinet, from which he had stolen her pewter serving tray, and retrieved a teapot. She measured out the tea from a tin on the sideboard. Then she went over to the hearth and pulled the kettle off its hook and poured hot water over the leaves.

"The New World," he said to her back. "The lands are in New York. They are part of a land grant given to a family named Livingston. I am a partner in this venture."

Without turning back to him, she suddenly asked, "What are the terms?"

"There are different lots," he said. "But I have one, among the best, that I own entire. I have designated part of that for Dorsey and Zack and Noah and their families. On the other lots, for our neighbors, all that is required for ten years is that the land be worked. But you are to be with me, and we may be living in Massachusetts."

"That's not possible. They cannot be giving land away."

"After ten years, there will be rents. Or the opportunity to buy the land fee simple. The land has gone unsettled for too long, the owners feel, and the only way to increase its value is to place settlers on it. They have nothing from it now. They will have nothing from it in ten years unless someone works it. Then they can sell other parcels nearby for a good price. People want to live with other people."

"But will they throw Dorsey and her brothers off the land then?"

"No. I own their land."

She looked at him, still doubtful.

"The owners needed someone to recruit their tenants. They did, that is, after my friend Cain Smith and I suggested this speculation. We should prosper. We should make a fortune."

His mother had always had the wisest head for business in the family, and he could tell that she saw the logic of it now. "Come have your tea," she said.

"How are they situated? Dorsey and my wee brothers?"

She did not look up, but stared at the table. "The leases are coming up for renewal again. You've come at the right time."

He wanted to give out a whoop, but her downcast manner stopped him. "*Maman?*" he asked.

She came over to him and took his hand and stroked it. She made no sound, but he could see tears welling up in her eyes. "So you've come home and kept your promises," she said, fighting back the tears and biting her lips. "I don't doubt what you say is true. Who could doubt a son who—" She paused, and the tears started running straight down her blanched cheeks. "Who could doubt your faithfulness. But I've grown used to certain things. Dorsey and I . . . I'm not sure I want to be without Dorsey."

He thought of the plans he was already putting into place for the move to Massachusetts, for his thoughts had run far ahead of what he had admitted to Sarah. He was already planning to invest his earnings from the immigration venture into a shipbuilding company. These plans might accommodate Dorsey and her family, but not easily; her husband was a farmer, not a ship builder. "Dorsey and Hugh can decide if they would like to come with us," he said.

"I want to stay with Dorsey. I don't mean . . . I am glad for what you have done," she said, and grabbed the hand she had been stroking.

He saw what his mother's long years with his sister meant. Dorsey and Hugh would much prefer, he was sure, to take their own lease from him and be independent. He was losing his mother again; not so absolutely this time, but still, she would be living away from him. The ocean could be crossed, but some distances could not.

Bitterness tempted him, but if only for the sake of his own achievement, his heart quickly turned toward reconciling hopes. "Are you ready for a new life, then? With Dorsey?"

"They are ready. And what I have comes from you, so I must be ready."

His mother had never lacked courage, and the warmth of his pride in her evaporated any jealous sentimentality. "It won't be as easy for you right away. I'll see that the Livingstons extend their help to you first."

She nodded, and he could see her relief, although it was hard for him to like it.

She stood up and embraced him. He was not carrying her, as he had planned; she was on her own two feet. But she was in his arms, and after so many years, that must mean he had succeeded.

———

The fiddles sounded uncannily like bagpipes, the bows of brothers Zack, Noah, and brother-in-law Hugh working back down on the low, droning E string, as they whipsawed through a country reel. The buckled shoes of the men on the wide-board floor provided a scuffling percussion, as the men's line met the ladies'. Husbands in brocaded waistcoats turned their smartly aproned wives round and handed them to uncles, and uncles passed them along to cousins, and on again to family friends so close they were treated as blood relations. The high-spirited music, the dancers' steps, talking, and laughter filled the lamplit room with a warm joy.

On the eve of their pilgrimage, the White family had rented out a nearby tavern, The Shadows, in Glenwhirry, for a proper reunion and leave-taking.

Abram stood watching, with his sister Dorsey close by his side. In the month that he had been home, when Abram wasn't out canvassing for pilgrims with Zack, his big-boned brother, Abram went to Dorsey's side. He slept at his mother's cottage, but he dropped by for tea and on any other pretense he could think of at Dorsey's. He felt the same easiness in her company that he had as a lad, and it flooded his soul with delight and comfort and rest.

Dorsey had married well, too. He had taken to her husband, Hugh, almost instantly. A bull of a man, his thatch of hair was heathered with gray and stood up like the heather on the moors in a wind. With a blunt nose, thick-skinned cheeks that crowded his eyes, and fingers like blunt, twisted carrots, he might have been the rudest peasant, but intelligence and native grace raised him up far higher than his six feet. He had a ready smile and a laugh that hurricaned out from the dead calm at the center of his soul.

"Your man can play," Abram said to his sister.

Dorsey looked down at her punch glass and smiled to herself. "He has the knack of it," she said. The curves of her brow swept smoothly down into the bridge of her nose which flared right at the tip. All the lines of her face had an almost vase-like quality of repose. Her almond eyes were warm and brown, and the dusky rose shadows of her mother's eyes were just touching her own.

She looked back up at the musicians and dancers, and Abram followed her line of sight, but he kept her in the corner of his eyes. Dorsey looked older, of course, tiny wrinkles already feathering her parchment skin, but so much the same as he remembered that he kept having to remind himself of the time that had passed.

"I've known gentlemen, but no one so gentle, I think," Abram said, complimenting her husband again.

"He's like Father," Dorsey said.

This surprised Abram. "Our father like that?" he asked. "Maybe before I can remember."

"After, as well. You never knew Father. But there he is, playing that fiddle, if you can see him."

He did not like this, and he did not believe it. "My memories are better than that," he said. "Who could take your man's hope from him?"

"You think he volunteered for the journey?" Dorsey asked.

All that might have gone on between husband and wife swept through the conversation and left the space between Abram and his sister suddenly bare.

"Hugh was ready enough, I suppose," Dorsey said, "but he's had the way prepared. He's lived with the story of the grand eldest brother and his promised return. There was romance enough in that even for a Boylan. But he's a man of the home ground like Father."

The grand eldest brother? Even Abram found his own story implausible. That he should be this man, with his family gathered about him ready to depart for the New World, gave him a discomfiting shock—as when his ship started backing into its chains. The scene reached beyond what was truly possible, or likely, as in a dream, and he had the same sense of surprise at its unfolding that quickens the heart in dreams. He remembered hearing Captain Lier in the Glenwhirry church, the first time the world proved this . . . open.

"Are you feeling well?" Dorsey asked.

"It's coming about, this. Such a long dream."

"Yes it is," Dorsey said in a steady voice. "For good reasons. Don't worry. It's not so much *you* that's done the persuading. The leases coming up. Mrs. Garrity putting the land on the open market and letting the Catholic clans bid—that's what's carrying the motion."

Abram took a sip of his punch and felt the tingle of the oranges and the rum way down in his throat. His brother-in-law was leading out in the next reel. He was crouching down, the bull with his horns lowered, and his playing retarded the theme so that the racing melody charged at them when Zack and Noah joined in.

Abram said, "A man of the home ground—" and then saw Dorsey cupping her ear and realized she could not hear him over the music.

He took her elbow and led her outside. They continued on down the cobblestone street; they kept silent until they had outpaced Glenwhirry's shops so that the nightshirted merchants and their bonneted wives in the second-story sleeping lofts that overhung the street would not be disturbed.

The night was misty and damp and still, and it drew close around them. They walked into a blind landscape, where only the road, their togetherness, and their memories guided them.

"So what is it, then, that you want to say?" Dorsey asked as she took his arm and hugged it.

"I wish I had been a man of the home ground. I've traveled so far, and yet so much of what I love is here."

"But we are going now. It's too late to think about that."

"No. I mean, I suppose I thought the grand eldest brother was leading, after all, a grand life, surrounded by such grand people."

"So we, your family, grew smaller?"

He felt a stab of pain at this, as he hadn't quite seen this consequence. "I could not imagine you. Not fully, not with such generosity of spirit as you have."

"Nor we you, Captain."

"What is this I'm feeling, Dorsey? When I embrace *Maman*, I feel like I'm holding all the time that we've lost, and I wish that I could gather it up that way. I wish I could just sweep it all up into my arms. It's a joy, and it's a sadness too, that I'm feeling."

"Then you know why Father stayed and could not leave."

"I'm not such a man, but I admire your Hugh. I admire . . . Father. Or I understand more of his heart."

"Here's an Irish trick for you then," Dorsey said. They had left Glenwhirry's shops far behind and were standing at one side of the sandy lane, in the midst of the night, beside an oak that had loomed out of the darkness at their left hand. The air was even heavier beyond the town and filled with the smell of the wet new grass and last year's rottings. Dorsey put her arm around Abram's neck, leaned up to put her cheek closer to his, and pointed off into the murky night. "Look at the night and remember your father's heart. This man of the home ground. A man about your age when his son left home. What do you see?"

Abram felt squeamish at this, but Dorsey did not let him go, so he waited, feeling more and more the younger brother. Then he remembered his father; he saw him clearer than he had in many years, as if he were standing out there in the night.

Suddenly, he felt himself being hoisted up and put on his father's shoulders and carried to see the vegetable garden up on the hill behind the house. That had been their daily ritual at a time he had thought forever lost to memory. He could not have been more than three or four. Once, he had pulled up some heads of lettuce to make sure their roots were growing, and his father, after quickly replanting them, sat with him on the ground, brought him close, and told him, "God watches what we cannot see."

Now Abram looped his arm around Dorsey and brought her closer. "*Maman* told me that Father was here for me."

"Have you seen your Irish ghost, then?"

"Much more. He's very near, isn't he?"

"Yes. It took a long time for me to sense him, as well. But now he brushes past me all the time."

"It's not so much a cloud of witnesses in the heavenlies," Abram said, "as it is a gang of intruders."

They laughed together. He remembered sharing this same rueful laughter just before he had left Dorsey standing in the garden, so long ago.

He hadn't asked the question until now, but it seemed the time. "How long after I left did you tell our parents?"

"Mother met me at the door. We watched you on the lane on the next rise. Father nearly broke up the barn, insisting that he go after you. Mother wouldn't let him. 'I gave him my salver,' she said. 'He has the best we can do for him. He has a chance. We should pray he doesn't turn round.' "

"Mother did that?"

"Papa almost . . . he found himself about to do some violence to Mother. That stopped him. Only that. He could not cross her will that way, and she made it clear he would have to."

"I looked for him on the road," Abram said.

"He looked for your return every day of his life. He had the most faith that you would come back."

Abram's body felt fathoms of pressure, as if he were diving into a warm China sea, his eardrums ready to explode. He remembered being knocked unconscious, swimming down like the cannibal trout into its hole. Had the pressures of those depths blinded him to their treasures, their pearls?

He turned Dorsey back toward the tavern. They did not speak. He felt his father keeping step with them; so much so that he would have talked to the air if Dorsey had not been there. What he wanted to say was, "You should have told me," and "I should have known."

Back inside, a zither and a bassoon had joined the fiddlers. The tune this quintet played speeded up with each pass over the bridge, and the dancers were now going round with such force that they were glancing over their shoulders to save themselves from embarrassing collisions. The women's pannier-spread skirts whirled out so that their white stockings and petticoats bottomed the pumpkin and plum confection of their skirts with a white froth. The cheerful, hand-clapping gentlemen on the sidelines looked on, while the ladies, who were looking to keep clear of the others, now glanced at the quintet as if to see where the maniacal tune might end.

Then, before they knew it, Dorsey's husband leaped into the air at the end of a final verse, and the crash of his boots signaled a long, humming, arpeggio-graced, final chord. The company clapped and clapped, while the ladies who had been dancing touched their high-collared throats, catching their breath.

Abram had thought to make a speech, and now seemed the time, since the tavern felt like a squeeze-box with a ripped lining—a wheezing place for sure.

He walked over to the bar and beat out a marshalling drumroll on the seat of a stool. He picked it up and hammered out another call to attention.

"Let the good people of Glenwhirry know," he called, "that I have come to see them to a land of milk and honey. They'll be traveling to their home, to their own Ulster, but not an Ulster like this, owned and leased and sublet and subleased and—" Abram paused, motioning for his family to join in, as they all said, "*subjugated!*"

Everyone recognized the speech that Abram had been giving—and Zack, too, as the enterprise's second agent—on street corners, in taverns, and, with certain modifications, in churches for the last month.

"No, not an Ulster like this," Abram continued, his voice sing-songy with the familiarity of the words, "but Ulster County, in the province of New York, where the land is free . . . for a space of ten years, and a new life awaits."

"To the new Ulster! The new Ulster! To the new Ulster!" the company cried out.

Zack stepped into the center of the room from his fiddling station and yelled, "To Captain Abram White! The man who kept his promise!"

The shout that followed sounded as if they were razing the walls with sledgehammers.

Abram gestured with his two hands spread wide, tamping down the noise with patting palms. "I want to thank my family and our neighbors for the confidence you have shown in this enterprise. Tonight is a time of rejoicing. It's also a time to consider what's ahead."

"I'll be telling you what's ahead," said a woman by the door. People turned. It was old Mrs. Garrity, the landowner.

Abram had heard that she disliked his activities. She was floating the lands on the open market, taking away the farmer's traditional right to secure the land first if he could, but she wanted as many bidders as possible. Abram had thought to talk with her but had conveniently forgotten. He could not believe she had come here.

"R-r-r-ruin and a-bomb-bination!" Mrs. Garrity yodeled. The comical slurring was not meant; she was very drunk. Men wiped their faces with their hands, so as not to look.

"You are off following this adventur-r-r-er," Mrs. Garrity announced, "who has for-r-gotten you these twenty years. Oh! and such a hear-r . . . such a hero he is! Loo-look at him now, will you." Mrs. Garrity's big-nosed face was circling round. She repeated her call to look at Abram, as if she were trying to instruct her own boiled eyes where to focus.

Abram thought how to handle this. She was making a scene, but he didn't think she could cause many second thoughts in her condition.

Mrs. Garrity had become a baggy thing, cheeks like money pouches and a chest that rested on her apron string. "I'll show you how to 'andle isss kind!" she screamed. With that, her eyes leveled, she ducked her head, and charged at Abram like an outraged chicken.

He saw her coming and caught her in a waltzing embrace. One look over at the fiddlers, and they started to play again. After two or three steps, as Abram held Mrs. Garrity's hand way out and steadied her with his other hand at the deeply cushioned small of her back, she ceased trying to rush forward and looked up at him as if he were the biggest cloud in the sky she had ever seen.

A few more rocking steps, and Abram handed Mrs. Garrity off to his mother and her friend, Mrs. McDougle, who took her outside and eventually handed her along to some of the boys, who took her home.

Abram stepped forward when he had his chance again. "Ruin and abomination!" he declared. There were titters. "Let's hope we have not heard from our Cassandra." Abram thought he might get a laugh from this, but did not.

He did not have everyone's attention back from the incident, and he stood still for a long moment while the company collected itself once again.

"You'll be working hard, it's true," he said, "and the first year might be leaner than any you've known—that's also true, and there's not a man here who can claim I ever said any different. But I give you my pledge, a promise as good as the one I made twenty years ago to come back and take my family to the New World: if your welfare and my profit ever come in conflict, I'll find another ship and see you back home with your ticket paid and clear. Now, is that fair enough for you?"

The shouting and hubbub said it was. They never would be needing such a pledge, many commented, so he could take his pledge, and God bless him, they were satisfied.

"Now Zack will be telling you of the particulars for our departure tomorrow, and something of the boarding procedure when we reach Larne."

Stout Zack came to stand beside Abram and said, "Be ready by first light tomorrow—if you sleep or no, be ready. We'll be forming our party in the street here. . . ."

Zack would be staying on in Ireland as Abram's agent, because this enterprise had taught them that many more such ventures might succeed, and Zack longed not so much for a new country as he did a means of escaping farming. So he would be a city man now and Abram's partner across the waters. Abram had liked his younger brother's idea well enough to guarantee Zack a living during the next few years.

Abram left the tavern again, alone this time, and wandered the misty lane. He remembered his exhilaration as he ran away from that miraculous church service in which the Reverend Innis had bent his knee so truly to the Lord. He had nothing of that wild, winging feeling now, although he could still remember it, remember the rush and sweep of it, remember it pushing him and leading him on, catching him up and sending his heart sailing.

He did not want to leave his homeland now, although all his life had conspired to see this moment—the end of his boyhood quest. Sarah was waiting for him, and he truly wanted to be back with her; he had learned how good it could be to live within one's family, and also that he had only one chance to experience this in full measure, and that was to create, with Sarah, his own. For he could not gather the past up; he could only make peace with its haunting presence and live with gratitude for its blessings.

Right then, he was glad of the mistiness and the dark, and his easy, heavy steps, and the knowledge that beyond his sight lay the high green fields of his native land. Strangely, at the moment of his success, he could not remember its old meanings. He realized how little belonged to him, how much had been given, and the terrifying mercy of the unknown.

CHAPTER 19

———

Legal Testaments

The last miles to Elysia, Abram and Hodges rode at a gallop, rushing by rocky outcroppings, down culverts, and rimming skillet-shaped ponds. The November afternoon felt cold and suspiciously humid. The bare-limbed trees had matted the woods with dark mustard and tea-colored leaves. The two men had been riding all day, but their close arrival had them jockeying with each other as they outdistanced even their own fatigue.

In the four months since Abram's ship entered New York's harbor, Abram had settled his mother and his kin in the shadow of a tree-nubbled Catskill mountain. They had put a crop in together, something Abram had not done since he was a boy. The growing season, they had learned, was short, so they had preserved as much as they could before the vegetables were fully matured.

Abram, Hugh, and Noah had built a barn and a cold-storage cellar, and Abram had bought five dairy cattle and driven them all the way from Sullivanville. They hayed the wild fields for fodder and made their first wheels of cheese. Abram discovered the local streams were filled with brook trout, and he caught and smoked hundreds.

Then, convinced that his family would not starve, he bid them, as his mother insisted, "*Adieu*, only *adieu*."

He had ridden down to New York City first, retrieved Hodges from his rooms, and now together they were nearing what Hodges called "that outlandish farm in the wilderness."

When Abram caught sight of the west meadow's stone fence, he spurred his horse. His black charger bolted forward into a flat glide, and Abram had that old boyish sense of sailing over the land with the wind at his back.

He was going home. He had triumphed. He was on his way to gaining a "competency," a fortune sufficient to see his family throughout his life—and completed his childhood quest in the bargain. This was the first time he had truly savored these things. Perhaps because he had Sarah to tell.

Sarah had her own news, he already knew. Abram had found a letter from her waiting for him when he arrived in New York with the Ulster immigrants, telling him that her father had died soon after his departure. She wished him home as soon as possible; legal matters—which Abram interpreted to mean the provisions of Robert Nicolls' will—needed attending.

Abram had put the matter in Cain Smith's hands until he returned to New York. A letter from Cain had reached him in Ulster County, congratulating him, cryptically, on "the most happily timed marriage since the invention of legal testaments." But Cain was down in Philadelphia when Abram returned to New York, and so he still did not know the terms of the inheritance.

When Abram reined in his horse before the house, pulling up abruptly so that his charger bucked and wheeled and shied, he waited a moment, but no one appeared. Hodges came up after him, bringing his sorrel mare to a skitterish stop, and as the clopping sounds of the mare's hoofs went out over the main house and through the elm trees, Abram thought that everyone must be away. Elysia seemed strangely still.

Then Sarah walked out alone from the house. Her hands clasped together, she moved with a happy, restrained dignity. The sight of her shocked him: for an instant, the scrim of their history fell, the gauzy screen of their conflicts, and he saw her candidly, as he had seen her that first time in the parlor; she was magnificent, darkly radiant, moonlight with its spiritual shadows. Who wouldn't love her?

Out of the corner of his eye, he saw the shutters move at the downstairs casement window. Felicity and Livy.

He had taken Sarah into his arms before he was sure he had gotten his feet under him in dismounting. Their first kiss turned the world inside out. He felt himself wheeling into a fall, and then her weight in his arms centered them.

She was small and trim and soft, and he breathed in her scent of clove and dew and bread. Her skin was cool at his touch and warming as he held her. He felt an ache go through him, and swallowed down hard on his choking emotions. Had he ever cried for happiness before? She was in his arms, and that gathering up that he had spoken of with Dorsey came to mind: his encircling arms seemed to have captured what was and would be—the past carrying into the future.

At least he hoped so. His doubts remained, he had to admit even then.

He picked her up in his arms, her full ruffled, striped skirt flapping like an unbattened sail. He kissed her briefly and headed into the house. Turning to look back, he nodded once in Hodges' direction, which meant that his man should take care of the horses and what needed doing. Hodges gave him the look of a father watching his son show off.

Abram paused long enough in the foyer to say hello to Felicity and Livy, and then carried Sarah up the stairs.

On the landing, she started to say, "We are using—" thought better of it and said, "At the end of the hall." Which meant that they would be sleeping again in Robert Nicolls' room.

"Your father—" he said.

She reached up with both hands and gave him a long kiss, shaking her head as she did so, telling him to leave the discussion of her father to another time.

They were through the door and on the bed.

"You are home, then," she whispered, "home from the sea and your travels?"

"If you haven't moved the bed, my Penelope."

"It cannot be moved," she said, completing the allusion to *The Odyssey*. "You must be the swineherd, not the hero, if you don't remember that."

"I remember *everything* about our bed."

Her answering smile told him more than words.

Much later, as they lay in bed watching the evening shadows gather, as they heard the branches of the elms clacking in the wind that buffeted the house, as they wished for more wood on the fire, watching it smolder—much later, they began to talk.

"Have I ever been so happy?" Abram asked. He put his fingers in Sarah's dark hair behind her ear and ran his thumb along her jaw. "When I saw you walk out from the house, I remembered seeing you at the harpsichord the first time. You have always had a light that draws me and makes everyone else drop away."

"Everything I feel comes from you, Abram," Sarah said. "Happiness or worry, its center lies in you."

"No more worry," Abram said. "We must be at peace now. I have acquired a competency. We will make our own home. There will be no more going to sea. Except, perhaps, in a yacht with you, jewel of Elysia."

Sarah propped herself up on her elbow and looked at him, her eyes wide open. "Did Cain Smith tell you of Papa's wishes?"

"Not the terms. I was speaking of my venture—what I have earned. The passages brought us a tidy sum, and the future landholdings and future rents should last our children's children."

"We must be charitable, then," she said. "You will want to use your portion to acknowledge God's graces." She pulled herself much closer to him. "Otherwise we will not know what to do with the vastness of it!"

She rolled quickly onto her back, opened her arms wide, and shook her small fists in glee, punching the air, and then crossed her arms over her chest.

Then she moved quickly back to him and touched his shoulder. "We will have a child now, I am sure of it. Many children. I want as many as we can have, and they will all be splendidly talented and well-educated and live at Elysia in peace and comfort."

Abram thought of the plans he had made to buy the Hopkins shipbuilding company in Newburyport, Massachusetts. "Yes, we will have our family now, I'm sure." He hesitated, thinking of what he did not want to say as yet. "I never doubted this time would come. Was it so hard for you to believe?"

"It was the hardest thing I have ever had in my life, next to Mother's and Father's passing," she said, instantly serious. "The last two things together—" She looked up at him. "The months you were on these shores without returning here were cruel."

Abram rubbed his eyes and then pulled at the covers. "I am sorry about your father," he said. "He was the most impressive man of his generation I ever knew. Our relations obscured this sentiment, but I am not simply speaking well of him now that he has passed. He had more natural kindness than many saints."

He waited to see if Sarah would respond to this. She kept silent, and the silence still swarmed with her unspoken accusations.

"I had to see that my family would not starve this winter," Abram said. "I did not want our triumph to become grief."

He saw Sarah wince at the word "grief."

"The law's demands are rarely as exacting as those of nature. I could do nothing here that I cannot make up for now."

"Nothing can compensate for absence at certain times."

Hadn't the completion of his childhood quest taught him just this? "No," he said. The next thing to say was very hard, and he said it with as much tenderness as the words allowed. "But many things cannot be remedied in this life." He watched how she took this. "Sarah?"

"You are home," Sarah said, wearying. "And you have been given Elysia thrice over. I hope you are grateful for that."

"Thrice over?"

"Once when we were wed, again upon your return, and by virtue of Papa's will."

"As I said, I do not know its terms."

Sarah hesitated, as if she were about to break a taboo. She grabbed Abram's hand and fingered his ring, invoking, it seemed, the protection of their bond. "Father divided our land into thirds. An equal portion for each daughter. But it does not go to us, or to our husbands, but to our children—the next generation. We have it in trust for them.

"You have been appointed the trustee for our portion, and Felicity's and Livy's until they marry. An additional percentage accrues to us for each year you manage the lands by yourself. If Felicity and Livy do not marry, we are to keep them suitably during their lives, and then their portion as well comes to our children.

"So you see, we are truly secure. You are the lord of this house."

She was telling him that he was wealthy beyond his imaginings, news he had been avoiding, he saw now, for months. "What if I do not choose to manage this estate?"

She lay back down on her pillow and closed her eyes. "Why would you ask such a question?"

"Were there any provisions?"

"You would have to talk to Cain about that. I certainly do not remember any such provisions."

"Your father would have known that I might want to establish us elsewhere."

"But where? This is *Elysia.*"

"What did the will say?"

"I think there was some mention of you selling your holdings. But then cousin Meredith would come to take charge. We cannot leave my sisters to him. He is an awful man. You cannot really be thinking of these things."

"I have crossed an ocean, Sarah. How could I not have had my own thoughts?"

She got out of bed and slipped her dress back on and went to the hearth, where she threw log after log on the andirons. The thump of each log landed heavily against Abram's peace of mind. She used a bellows to revive the coals beneath, stoking the fire into a blaze. She continued adding on logs and positioning them, the fire tools ringing out her displeasure.

Finally, there was so much wood in the shallow hearth that the fire couldn't draw properly, and the room grew smoky. She took the hooking tool and snatched a log or two out, and the smoke started to diminish. Its cindery smell hung in the air and scratched at the back of their throats, making them cough.

When she had at last finished with her incendiary fit, Abram said, "I have not said what I will do."

She wheeled round on him. "What *you* will do? The inheritance is mine and my children's. Why should this be a matter of what you will do?"

In fairness, he did not know the answer to this question, only its brute irrelevance. "Your father left the choice to me."

"How can you speak of 'us' when it pleases you and 'me' when it concerns matters of import? *I* have the greater moral claim, even if the law fails to recognize it."

That was true.

"Your love should see more clearly than the blind law."

That was true as well. "Come back to bed, Sarah. We will talk of these things. I want to explain my thinking."

She put her hands on her hips and stared at him. Then she

started working her hair back into a twist, walking over to her dressing table, from which she retrieved her bonnet and jammed it on. Long strands of her hair trailed at the sides of her cheeks, and she could only flick these behind her ears.

"Sleep with your thoughts and find how warm they keep you," she said.

"*Sarah.*"

"I am sure they are waiting supper on us," she said. "Be down promptly. I will not think of excuses for you." With that, she left their room.

He would remember the way she said this, her mouth at a mean angle, her forehead purpling, her upper arms tightening against her sides. When he had been mid-crossing, he was reminded, in the middle of a ravaging Atlantic storm beating them off course, it had been her anger at the delay that he feared.

Abram and Sarah settled into the uneasiest of truces at Elysia. Sarah took charge of the household, marshalling the servants, demonstrating the ease with which she could slip into the role of the estate's mistress. Abram felt that she presumed at times with Felicity and that her orders boxed the servants ears more than necessary, but he had to admit, grudgingly, that authority suited her. She was more generous when in charge than when dependent.

Toward Abram, though, Sarah maintained the attitude of an aristocrat coaching a country cousin in the ways of society. He quickly grew to hate her little nods and facial stiffenings that indicated whether he should say grace at meals or put his arm around a farmer as he explained the quit rents. (Yes to the one, never to the other.) But to say something would have meant that he had to say it all, and Abram waited on his own thoughts and the decision to which they would lead.

Hodges was not so restrained. "She's candidating for queen, that one is," he kept commenting. "I'd give her the job, Captain," and made a fist with one hand and socked it into the other.

The Smiths, the Haverstocks, the Livingstons, the Proctors, the Delanceys, and other members of society that Abram had met during his days of bachelorhood in the city wrote him letters of condolence, managing to work in subtle congratulations on what they took to be his new station. He sent them equivocal replies and kept corresponding with Hopkins & Company, the firm whose shipbuilding business he planned to buy. The company and Abram had all but signed the papers, although he could still back out.

He found himself managing the estate's lands, and he had to admit that he liked this much more than his former make-work walks and clam digging. When he would deal with one of the renters or go out to meet the local Indian sachem about a hunting-rights dispute, Sarah's beaming appreciation became almost comical; he expected her to press her hands together and go into a swooning sigh. Of course, if he would let her know that he was taking on the management of Elysia and giving up his own plans, the anxiety that was exaggerating all her reactions would go away and the fine qualities of her husbandry remain. He would probably even start caring for her again.

So Abram was in crisis. He would look out the downstairs study window, Nicolls' old library that Abram felt was the best captain's cabin he had ever had, and look past the elms toward the cliff and the bay. He'd take his old ship's compass from his tall writing desk that he had moved into the study and draw circle after circle, connecting these with ruled lines—charting a course, he supposed, but on blank paper, without a map. What sextant lay to hand? What clock?

He started reciting the Westminster Catechism again. He filled his mind with it, almost humming it after a while. What is the end of man? To know God and to love Him forever. But what did this most basic question mean in his situation? A verse his mother had emphasized to him kept coming to mind: "For unto whomsoever much is given, of him shall be much required." He had been given much indeed. What was required?

And why shipbuilding? He could arrange to ferry many more pilgrims across the waters, it was true. Would that be at least a partial recompense for all the mercies that had been shown him?

Somehow, becoming a country gentleman seemed like quitting. To Sarah, though, he knew, this was life.

———

Abram waited through the winter, keeping his own counsel. He found things to dicker about with Hopkins & Company. Sarah became calmer, started to presume he had acquiesced. Still, nothing had been said, and this silence dampened everything else.

As the spring came on, Sarah started tending her father's grave, riding out to the graveyard one morning each week. On the second week in April, just before Easter, Abram asked if he might come along.

Sarah said, "I had hoped you would want to." There was something like love in her voice for the first time in months.

So they rode out one morning, both of them on his horse, Sarah holding on to his waist. The graveyard stood half a mile off in a copse of alders; the old gentleman's father, mother, and sister had been buried there long ago, followed by both his wives.

The spring season seemed to deny, at least for Abram, that their errand could be attached to mourning or grief. The apple trees were blossoming early, their white petals and scent floating on the wind. The green of the newly leafed hardwood trees shone in its vigor and made each tree pop out under a fitfully cloudy sky.

They found the slate gravestones in their copse of alders. Abram could tell the old gentleman's immediately; it was a dull and uniform blue, while the older ones were gray and streaked with salt deposits from the sea breezes. The alders formed a natural sanctuary, with a clean, bare interior but for one sapling.

Abram helped Sarah down, tied up the animal, and walked to the graves. Saying only that she would be back, Sarah left him there and walked out of the copse. When she returned, her arms were full of wildflowers—wild carrot, day lilies, branches of forsythia. She put these to one side and began to weed the still built-up mound of the grave.

Abram noticed the Latin motto on her father's gravestone: *Semper soles cognouit et tempora tempestata.* "He knew only the sun and fair weather." Abram wondered if this, although it expressed the man, did not present him as a little indifferent to the fate of the wives who lay beside him, with their abbreviated lives. Even here, Abram could not help but both admire Nicolls and judge him, exactly as he had in life.

After the hold of the place relented, after the graves came to seem as much facts as mysteries and Sarah had nearly finished her gardening, Abram raised her up and put his arm around her.

"Do you think," he asked, his voice gentle, "he would have thought you to be such a dutiful daughter?"

"Felicity would have been his choice."

"She might have been his guess," Abram said. "You would have been his choice."

He saw her bite her lip.

She took several steps away from him and hugged her shoulders. "I wish—" she began, stopped, and exhaled the wish's airy substance. "Father did not keep our Lord much company," she said with so much bitterness that she was plainly accusing God of the greater fault.

" 'Surely the God of the universe shall do right,' " Abram said, quoting the only Scripture he knew for the occasion, knowing it was hardly enough. Her bitterness told him how much sorrow she was always holding back.

"I would see him once more," she said, "in the old way, at home. That is all my desire."

"Even so, Sarah," he said, and took a breath, "I wish your desire were a little to your husband."

She looked up at him and her look grew withering. "That's the curse of women," she said.

She took a moment, and he awaited her worst.

"You weren't here," she said finally.

"I am now, and I shall be."

She only looked down.

"It's been months," he said, "and we have not talked about what truly stands between us."

Her next look questioned him, as if she could not imagine what he meant, and simultaneously dared him to speak of it.

"I have hinted of this before," he said. "But I want to reveal to you the fullness of the matter now."

Then slowly, in detail, he unfolded his plan to buy the Hopkins shipyard. He felt the new prospects of their life together opening up as he did, and he felt Sarah moving along with him, if hesitantly, her skirts catching at objectionable hedgerows as she twisted where she stood.

But with her first words, she rushed back home. "Our life is at Elysia. My sisters are dependent upon us."

"They have the wealth of the world. My reports say your cousin Meredith is no monster. And Felicity will be marrying sooner than she can know."

"You have arranged this?"

"The birds and flowers and her seventy thousand acres are arranging it. The roads will be glutted with the traffic this summer. You should see her suitors' correspondence."

"She will need your help in choosing."

"Felicity?"

"She is less wise in this than you imagine. You must prevent an unsuitable match."

Hodges' line about Sarah candidating for queen came to mind, and its remedy. "Be that as it may, this is a temporary concern."

"Why should we give up our home for an unknown enterprise? We have lived here for several generations already."

He wanted to change the direction of the compass. "Why do you imagine your father ever invited me here, Sarah?"

"I can only wonder at that, too."

"Please. Why do you think he found me an attractive gentleman?"

"He favored your learning. Your reading."

"He favored my enterprise. He understood that I knew myself, and that who I am has been given to me by God alone."

"These are flattering thoughts."

"True thoughts."

"His thinking can be most clearly read in his last wishes."

"Yes, they can. He allowed me the choice, because he knew I would want to make it."

"What of my wishes? My choice?"

"He judged me fit to take your will into account."

"Has my will ever counted in your plans?" she asked, challenging.

"No," he said. He glared at her and was almost glad that she glared right back. "But you have counted," he said. "My will hears your voice more readily than my own hunger. It anticipates your wishes more quickly than thirst."

"You presume, Abram."

"I think I must," he said. "This is what I have found being a husband to be—presuming in the service of love, because nothing but audacity is equal to the challenge." He watched her. She almost concealed her reaction. "And now I want to know whether you will come with me willingly to Newburyport?"

She stepped away from him. "How you walk on my father's grave," she said.

"We will be together now. Do you hate me so much that you refuse to receive what you say you have always wanted? A home? A family? That would be without reason."

"We have greater opportunities for both now, here, in this place."

This carried them back to the beginning of the argument, and he refused to speak.

She looked down at the grave. "I will miss you, Father. You gave me to this *pirate*." She gave Abram a look he hoped not to remember. Then she turned on her heel and walked briskly toward the horse, mounted the animal, and galloped off.

All things considered, Abram was glad for the walk back. He did not want to be on that horse.

———

Abram awoke in the feed barn, curled up in the bed of hay he had gathered round him the night before. The hogsheads and shipping crates stacked in a lopsided ziggurat to the right of the barn door rose up over his right shoulder, the temple of this day and its sacrifices. He waited a moment before beginning all that would follow. The late spring morning was only cool, not chilly, promising a warm day. His back would feel anviled by the night once he moved; but in his first waking moments, the day and its stillness, broken only by swallows under the eaves and their chirping hatchlings, conspired to lull him back to sleep.

He stood, felt how his vertebrae had been flattened, and walked out of the barn, past the house, and down on the front lawn to where he could see the cove. The Sound lay over the tops of the cliff's scrub pines, robin's egg blue and soft in the morning light. Instinctively, he set his feet for the pitch of a deck, then caught himself. No decks this time, and looking to windward would probably mean trying to look in several directions at once—that's how Abram's married life kept coming at him.

He supposed Sarah and he were not a very good match. Or too good. Too alike. They were leaving because Abram had finally decided he could not play the part of country gentleman for long.

At first he had told himself that shipbuilding and transporting pilgrims were the life-work God had given him, the service the Lord demanded for His mercies. He still felt he must acknowledge the love God had shown him, but his current plans fell short of answering that need. They groped toward what was required, if that. And yet a life at Elysia seemed a turning away, for reasons he could not really specify. What he could specify was all in the natural order. He was used to enterprise and command, and while life at Elysia had elements of these, it was too comfortable, too slow. It wasn't for him.

This explanation hardly suited his wife, and even carried poorly with his society friends and business partners, who had presumed he would relinquish his proposed venture. He had even had trouble securing the additional financing he needed; Cain Smith backed away and nearly out of the venture, until Abram tapped a Van Rensselaer source and Cain saw he could not be stopped.

Abram needed the additional financing because he had tried to accommodate Sarah. He relinquished control of Elysia to Meredith Nicolls only conditionally. He did not sell Sarah's share, as proposed in the will, but entered into a secondary agreement with Meredith that let him run the place for renewable five-year terms, with favorable cancellation provisions should Abram and Sarah choose to return. In this way, Sarah's children would retain almost their full inheritance.

Meredith was not a man to quibble about being presented the control of a fortune. A quiet, almost wordless gentleman in his fifties, his dark-graying hair swept up like meringue above a pudding-and-pie face. Cousin Meredith was an "awful man" only in the odd vacancy that haunted his appearance when excited. After staring at the legal papers with his red-rimmed eyes, his look strangely emptying as his excitement grew, he signed.

Sarah had reacted in several ways to Abram's final decision. When he told her, alone in their room one night as she brushed out her hair, her hand only hesitated for the briefest instant. "As I expected," she said, with a perturbed diffidence.

The next day, though, and for many thereafter, she lived as if in a dream. Her steps slowed. She hardly spoke. In fact, she hardly gestured. She sat by herself much of the time, her expression vacant. Yet her stillness, the way she sat with her hands in her lap and her feet close together, conveyed her wish to escape. She looked down, but kept her chin slightly raised, as if her spirit yearned to swing through this world into a different plane.

Then, when the arrangements were upon them, Sarah's spirits suddenly improved. She recovered her energies enough to direct the house-moving enterprise. But she did this without her former ease and generosity. She was acting like a new officer, Abram thought, carrying on her duties at all times as if being watched. But who would be watching?

Abram had promised her she could build her own home in Newburyport, and she took to sketching out the house she wanted. She improvised upon the Georgian plans she found in a pattern book:

two stories of brick elegance, topped by a golden cupola and a pheasant weathervane. Wisteria curled around the columned entrance, providing a blooming canopy.

But when Abram started assisting Hodges and the other servants in the packing, Sarah changed again, growing testy. When he began building the crates for their furniture, plate, and clothing, she became enraged. "Is this how it is to be? Are you destroying my life to become a carpenter?"

He had never supposed carpentry could be offensive. "Our Lord was a carpenter," he said and then wished he hadn't.

In the end, Sarah's unpredictable responses to the situation so frustrated and enraged Abram that he devoted himself to his barnyard carpentry morning and night. He put their belongings in the wooden crates he had built and hammered them shut as if sealing coffins against Judgment Day.

The more he worked at this manual labor, the angrier and more distant Sarah became. Her husbanding of her energies, her gathering of her courage, reached a taut stage in which she was hardly willing to speak, and she performed every simple action with a violent resignation. Her face had fallen into a set expression he had never seen before, an expression not too distant from Maggie's blankness, or the infernal counterpart to cousin Meredith's hollow-eyed excitement. It was as if Sarah regarded everyone around her as a ghost, or sensed ghostly presences veiled in their flesh. He had never seen anyone more frightened.

Every motion he made toward depicting how much better their life would be was received by Sarah as an attack. He could do nothing, she made it clear, but make things worse. *Why?*

As he stood looking out at the cove on this final morning, he had to admit he knew the answer to that question. He knew and had always known. He knew how *he* responded at having his ways of moving in the world balked. When his father had frustrated his will, he had run away. Faced with Sarah's wishes before his return to Ireland, he had chosen his own and left.

To want something, to feel you must *be* what you want, that passion had driven him back and forth across the oceans of the world. It had led him into Captain Jack's cabin to kill the man.

He had been delivered from his rage by smallpox.

What would deliver Sarah?

She might have a child in Newburyport. Grace and nature were going to have to cooperate in some fashion.

Perhaps he was secretly hoping for the divine hand to give him another unwarranted assist. To hear the eternal's voice. At that, he remembered Sarah saying, "You *presume*."

He looked out over the sea, and he thought of their trip to the Palisades, the good omen of the eagle taking its fish. The sky was empty of everything but the faintest sheathing of cloud. The usual sea gulls were gathered, dropping down on a blistery white spot on the ocean's surface. Bluefish had corralled a school of shad and were tearing into them so furiously that the gulls would lose their webbed toes if they weren't careful.

Abram looked up at the sky as if to tell God he did not consider this amusing.

At this dreadful prompt, Abram walked into the house and up to their bedroom to dress. He expected to find Sarah sleeping, but she had already left the room. He thought it strange that he had not seen her in the kitchen as he passed through. She could have stepped outside, of course, to look at the day as he had.

He put on his summer uniform, made of linen, and thought of the days on shipboard that were as hot as this day promised to be. He could go in his silk shirt, but at least at the beginning he wanted to be fitted out with all his colors flying, including a ribbon tied into a bow at his neck. The greater the sense of authority he conveyed, he thought, the better.

When he went downstairs to the kitchen, he found Maggie cooking breakfast, and he asked after Sarah. Maggie had not seen her, and this too was unusual. He called for Hodges and asked him to help search Sarah out.

They looked about the house and the barns and along the walks that went out from the house. Still, she was not to be found.

Felicity and Livy and even cousin Meredith were recruited, and they all began searching.

Abram walked out by the stream that led down to the cove. Her disappearance had angered him, and by the time he reached the beach, he was ready to order the tides to obey him.

She was not on the beach. He saw a ketch reaching out toward the Atlantic and wondered, half-jokingly, if she had arranged to get herself kidnapped. The blues were still feeding.

When he got back to the house, Felicity approached him on the flagstone walkway. She looked as if she wished to speak, but said nothing. She took his arm and led him back toward the house. She seemed possessed of that mysterious stillness he had met with at his arrival last winter.

Across the threshold, she said, "I found her." He wrenched around to question her, but she did not let go of his arm. She walked him from the hall into the parlor, and even there she kept holding on to his arm, not speaking, her unspoken horror communicating itself to him.

"I'm afraid she's horribly unwell, Abram," Felicity said at last. "I don't know what you are to do."

"Where is she?" he asked. "Tell me where she is. You must. Is someone attending her?"

"I wanted you to see her first."

"Where is she?"

Felicity put her hand over Abram's forearm and squeezed it. Then she turned and walked out of the parlor and up the stairs, with Abram following.

She went into Sarah's old bedroom—the room Sarah had turned into a nursery during their first months at Elysia, making the whole household suspicious. No one had gone in there since the end of Sarah's false pregnancy.

Inside the room, Abram smelled strong soaps and powders still competing with must, and behind these, he thought, the lavender scent Sarah had used at the time of their first meeting.

The room had nothing in it except a chest, a table, and the huge wicker cradle he had given Sarah in the first year of their marriage.

Abram cleared his throat, upset that Felicity still had not brought him to Sarah.

Felicity stepped closer to the wicker cradle, more a child's bed than an infant's, and opened her arm for Abram to step beside her.

Sarah's curled form in the child's bed caught Abram's eye like his own reflection in an unsuspected mirror: he saw her without knowing her. Her position, curled up with her feet tucked tight against her buttocks, appeared impossible and comical and yet there she was.

He prepared himself to be cold-hearted and ruthless at this play-acting. His order for her to get up nearly exploded from him. But then he stopped. He could see by the smoothness of her brow that she was asleep. No, not asleep, but withdrawn from the world, as she had been in the days following her false pregnancy; but this time she had traveled infinitely further away. She rolled her head toward them, opened her eyes, and did not see them, or saw only the ghosts she had been courting and was now reconciled to.

Hodges came into the room. And Maggie. This embarrassed and then panicked Abram. Cold water shot into his veins. Perspiration dampened his hairline. In his confusion, he thought Sarah might never leave that room.

He bent down and lifted her in his cradling arms. He noticed the host now gathered around him: Felicity, Livy, Hodges, Maggie, cousin Meredith. Their faces looked like the sailors who had witnessed Captain Jack strangling him.

They had to leave and now. Abram carried Sarah downstairs, out of the house and to the barn, where the carriage waited. Once more, as he had at their elopement, he put her into the carriage, this time with all the care he could manage despite his own despair.

In the shortest time possible, they departed for Newburyport. With Hodges driving on the box, and Sarah, still unmoved and unmoving, beside him, Abram watched the pine woods, cornfields, and marshes of Elysia fall behind them in their doleful wake.

PART V

All in All

CHAPTER 20

Angels of the Lord

That is why we have been so forward as to promote this occasion," said Abram, appealing with his shaking, long-fingered hands to the Reverend and Mrs. Jonathan Edwards, as well as to Sarah, in the parlor of his hosts' Stockbridge manse.

"We feel that no one but the author of *A Faithful Narrative* can understand the straits we find ourselves in. We believe that God has been so gracious to us as to secure our eternal destiny. The Spirit has manifested himself to us in ways no less surprising, I think, than your narrative recounts. Yet we do not know the charity proper to man and wife."

Abram kept his head turned toward the minister and his wife, but he shut his eyes as he said, "Our union needs an awakening— or quickening. We are living as brother and sister."

At this, Sarah, who had been listening calmly to Abram's narrative of their life, looked as if she might be choking.

After two years in Newburyport, Abram's White Star Ship Building Company was prospering, and the broad-shouldered elegance of Sarah's Georgian dream home stood on High Street surrounded by copper beech trees.

Sarah's spirits had rallied on the second day after their departure from Elysia. She had come out of her swoon, saying, irritably, "How long will it be?" as if redirecting a boring conversation.

She remained far from happy, though. The past two years had seen a constant knitting and unknitting in their marriage. Thus, finally, Abram had persuaded her that they should seek counsel from the most famous pastor of the Great Awakening, Jonathan Edwards. They had read his book *A Faithful Narrative of Surprising Conversions* and several other works, with Abram arguing that Edwards alone understood religious affections such as theirs—the foreknowledge, the voices—well enough to help.

Edwards sat in a Windsor chair, his spindly legs shifting as he heard Abram's recitation. He wore a white, softly ruffled wig and a fine, dark cleric's suit, with strips of thin, closely cropped fur marking the pockets. His high ministerial collar, made of fine linen, looked like a delicate serviette falling to his breastbone, except that it was divided down the middle, twin-tailed, like two markers trailing out of his encyclopedic understanding.

The man had a long, patrician nose and sensitive, pinched lips. He had a way of popping open his eyes as if affrighted, and a twitching, itchy manner. He smoked a clay pipe and seemed to be constantly flicking loose tobacco or the spidery hatchlings of his imagination off his clothes. But when his gaze rested and grew full, it seemed to travel through its object—once, under that gaze, Abram almost turned around to see who might be coming up from behind.

Although he had replied to Abram's written inquiry pleasantly enough, inviting the couple to visit, if indeed they were willing to brave possible Indian attack, the pastor had been awkward in his greetings and much distracted, muttering about his writing: he spoke in a disconnected way of beauty and the "being of the world" and "clear ideas." He certainly had no conversation, no social exchanges.

Like Edwards, his wife, who was also named Sarah, was finely dressed in a white-lace bonnet and a dark-green bombazine dress, with very fashionable and full spreading skirts. She wore a white and pink porcelain locket, with pure silver fittings, around her neck, and she had a way of smiling to herself at most times, as if debating whether to tell some giddy secret. This unnerved Abram even more than her husband's nervous tics.

The manse was not much more than a two-story shack, and the Edwards' furniture was so outsized for their present accommodations that their Windsor chairs, settees, inlaid tables, and kettle-bottomed cabinets looked more packed-in than arranged. Seven years before, in 1750, Edwards had been dismissed from his pastorate in the Northampton Church whose awakening had made him famous. His former life still huddled around him in his reduced circumstances, this virtual exile.

The manner of the Edwards impressed Abram as so peculiar that he wondered whether he and Sarah should have come. But now that Abram had told their story, made his confession, he saw that the divine was interested in a new way.

"You say you are a mariner? Your letter addressed this."

"I was a ship captain for ten years. I build ships now—the new schooners."

"The compass," Edwards said, reflectively, "the compass is a providential invention. I have been writing of this. As the devil has made gains in Europe, the Lord has opened up vast continents to His word through this invention—I mean, the compass for itself and as a metaphor, a way of signifying the reliability of modern shipping. You can be a part of this." The pastor's own clear idea was coming into focus now, and his enthusiasm increasing. "You can play a great part in it. Perhaps the Lord intends you to take a leading part in the great missionary enterprise that must extend from these shores. The Light that we harbor here must go forth."

"I have felt called to this, but obscurely," Abram said. "I do not see the way as yet."

Edwards turned to—or on—Abram's Sarah. Sarah Edwards, seeming to anticipate what he would say, leaned over to him and caught his hand, as it reached out to gesture, in a friendly clasp.

Edwards looked at his wife, gave an embarrassed smile, and settled himself before speaking. "Your husband has described you as someone with great spiritual gifts. Often, the wife is the more gifted." Edwards glanced once again at his own Sarah. "Are you resisting him in this calling?"

Abram waited for Sarah to declare herself; he had the sense, from her enthusiasm for this journey, that she would be able to discover her condition as she could not at home. Sarah had lived for the past two years in a dull way, impatient and yet uninvolved. Her former radiance returned only on special occasions: the day of their move into their new home, for example. Otherwise, she lived as if waiting for something; something she could no longer remember.

"Abram has no love for me," Sarah said finally, her conviction shaking in her low voice, a sudden tremor that shook their little company. "This call he speaks of is merely the costume of his own ambitions."

Sarah had been silent until this time, and her sudden speaking dumbfounded Edwards and his wife, and left Abram as tightly twisted round in his chair as a tourniquet.

"Abram saw me, a pretty young woman at the harpsichord," Sarah went on, a little out of breath, "and he wanted me. That is not love. That is appetite."

Sarah stood up, and she was breathing hard as her voice kept rising. "Love sacrifices. Abram has sacrificed nothing, except my happiness. He took me away from my home and family, and now he has brought me here to have his piracy sanctioned by God."

The older couple were looking at her as if they had never seen her like before. Abram thought of her father's warning, and his own utter lack of caution.

"He told you of Captain Hawks," Sarah said, continuing. "How Abram laments what he suffered at that man's hands! How he flatters himself with the notion that he learned wisdom as a result. But I tell you that I have become Abram's slave on the tyrannical ship of this marriage. I am being suffocated quite as much as Abram was in his master's throttling hands. Abram went into that man's cabin to kill the man. Nothing but the Lord's intervention stayed his hand.

"What am I to do? Run away? Take my husband's life? I have nowhere to go and no father to protect me. I hate this man, and I want nothing from him but to be taken home and allowed to grieve for the ill choice my father allowed me to make."

Sarah looked around her, as if verifying that she had nowhere to run, and then she sat down. She glared at everyone, and in the next moment broke into tears.

"Young woman," Jonathan Edwards said, his voice kind and searching for a way to reach her. "Young woman, you must know . . . think of this . . . appetite and Providence often agree. True virtue consists in seeing the will of God and acting for love of it alone, but simple appetite often agrees with the same behavior. Perhaps your husband's intention must be corrected, as everyone's must, but even in this light his choices may prove in conformity with the divine plan."

At this Sarah Edwards stood up, her fine, wide, dark-green bombazine skirts spreading, and her bonneted head leaned down to her husband's, and she kissed him on the cheek. She stepped over to Sarah and took the young woman's hands from her face. She grasped her hand and led her from the room.

The two men sat in silence as Abram thought what to say, while the furies Sarah had unleashed continued to rage. Finally, kneeling in his imagination to her vengeance, Abram asked, "Do you think she is speaking the truth?"

"Undoubtedly she is," Edwards said. "You are one of those men who will always be 'in the right'—in the wrong manner. You need to repent of this, as does the world. For this is just what Adam's fall means. There is none righteous. No not one. My church in Northampton sent me into exile here, as you may know, because, like you, I made it my terrifying practice to be in the right. And there was much wrong in it.

"Now they have called me to be president of this College of New Jersey, lately called Princeton. I will go there and be in the right again, until they find out the wrong in me. Perhaps God will be merciful, though, and make me His own before they decide to unmake me once again. Do you understand these things?"

Abram thought for a moment. He might not have been able to explain exactly why, but he considered the man's sentiments just. "I believe so," he said at last. "How is it that anyone can get along? Mrs. Edwards and you seem so much in agreement."

"We let each other pretend to be in the right until we know what the other knows; then we forgive. My Sarah has much the greater heart and has used it well in this practice. We have also been fortunate in that my good has been more nearly her good from the beginning. Her father did allow your Sarah a poor choice. He allowed you both into this mistake. But that is the entire abysmal matter of this world, and Christ takes exactly this and makes it our felicity. If we will let Him."

These words were what Abram had come to hear, but would he have come, he wondered, if he had known what they would be?

They waited, to see if they could go on in this line. Abram decided to change the subject. "It will be pleasant for you," Abram said, "to be back in society. These years on the frontier must have been exceedingly demanding."

Edwards looked up, took a breath, and a great wistfulness came over him. "These may have been my best years," he said. "My preaching to the Indian congregation may well have been my best. The writing I have done, certainly my best. Although the living, as you say, has been the hardest. Mostly because—and I tell this to you alone—I have come round to see the justice of Northampton's position. I was right in the issue, but wrong in my delay at addressing it and my manner in the engagement itself."

Again Abram sought a change of subject. "When do you leave for New Jersey?"

"We are due to leave within the next month. I am going to take one of the new smallpox inoculations as my first act as president, to set an example for the undergraduates. Many are still superstitious about these things."

Abram reminded Edwards again of the smallpox he had known aboard ship. "I was not inoculated," Abram said, "but variolated, a much ruder procedure than you will know."

"But how?" asked the pastor. "Would you show me? I have a scientific bent that must see a thing."

Abram stood, took off his long coat, and rolled up his sleeve to show the great man where he had been scarred.

———

Mrs. Edwards led Sarah out to the village green before the wooden church with its shingled spire. It was one of those days in late March in New England when the brooding gray skies have rested so long above the earth that they seem to defy the notion of spring. The clutch of Stockbridge's weather-darkened buildings looked as bleak as ashes.

Yet the green was brightening. The crocuses, with their wildly hopeful oranges and reds and whites and blues, were coming up in conspiratorial clusters. Snow frosted the Berkshire mountains surrounding the village, but the distantly ammonia-like scent of its melting touched the air.

Sarah felt better to be out in the open, and she was grateful for the older woman's arranging this escape. But Mrs. Edwards kept skipping or hopping as she walked along, and as she had hold of Sarah's elbow, the younger women felt almost rudely pulled into the air with her.

"Shall we go further?" Sarah asked.

Mrs. Edwards kept walking, skipping ahead even faster.

"Why are you doing that?" Sarah finally asked.

"Hopping?"

"Yes."

"Because I am so full of the wonderful comfort and grace of my Savior."

"This day? With me?"

Mrs. Edwards stopped. She put her hands on Sarah's shoulders for a moment. "Daughter of Thunder!" she exclaimed. "You are the tempest. You are the sea storm. You are such a holy indignation!"

This irritated and embarrassed the younger woman. She did not know how to take it, or if she would.

"You would rather die than not have things just as you wish," said Mrs. Edwards. "Mercy and misery, child, you are wonderful. You are the murderer you wish your husband had been, killing and slaughtering the life you have. Herod going after the innocents. Salome dancing for the Baptist's head. They were clumsy compared to you. You deserve our admiration and obedience." Here, the strange woman kissed Sarah on both cheeks and then hopped a little ways from her.

Sarah moved after her, despite herself. The woman infuriated her. Yet, in the midst of her anger, she wanted only to seize her, not to strike her. It came to Sarah that Mrs. Edwards had a discernment that was like Sarah's own. She did not know this from what the woman had said, although she understood the accusation being made well enough. Sarah knew because Mrs. Edwards was saying all these things as if revealing a secret that *delighted* her.

Still, as she caught up to the older woman, Sarah's concern was that the justice of her case be maintained. "You know I am in the right," she said.

"As you say."

"What I have said is the truth."

"Yes, I believe it to be. Your husband is an exceedingly selfish man. As is mine."

This stopped Sarah. The next thing she said came out of her own logic, one that leapt like the older woman's walk. "But you have had your children," Sarah said. "The youngest are still with you."

Somehow, Mrs. Edwards seemed to understand how the terms connected. "Yes," the older woman said. "*Eleven*. The Lord has been exceedingly merciful and kind to me."

Sarah wanted, with that, to rush at her and strike her because she was so obviously gloating, and Sarah thought that the woman must know how Sarah's own childless state affected her.

Which, in another moment, the older woman confirmed. She approached Sarah and laid both her hands on Sarah's stomach, palpating the area like a midwife. "So you have not had a child." The older woman continued to pat her.

"I do not care for these attentions," Sarah said. "If you need to . . . is this some sorcery?"

"Do you know the Scriptures in which Simeon and the prophetess Anna recognize their Savior as a babe?"

"The Spirit is speaking to you?"

Mrs. Edwards took Sarah's arm again and began to walk once more. Her voice became less giddy as she said, "You must leave your anger. You have justice on your side. But leave justice now for mercy, a much greater thing. Then shall come your fulfillment, as it does to each of us who wait for it."

Sarah began to weep. "I have been so alone. I did not know I could live for so long without comfort."

"Who is the Comforter?"

Sarah kept wanting to shake the older woman. "How is it that I can believe and be an atheist at once? For I know how to answer you, but not how to find this comfort."

"You must renounce your will—even a will that is true—for something truer, and far beyond your own imagining."

"How?"

Mrs. Edwards stopped walking. "Turn back to the green."

Sarah turned around, and she saw that a large party had gathered there. They wore a different cut of clothing, the women's unpleasingly stiff, with the collars buttoned up under the chin. The men wore beards and were not very fashionable: they had short topcoats and vests rather than waistcoats. The children were playing with hoops taller than they were, rolling them along with the aid of sticks. The women had stiff hats on as well, like men's hats, except small enough to rest just on the crown of their hair.

The company had brought food in baskets and were laying it out, as if for the sort of banquet that Abram and she had once shared in the Palisades. There must have been over one hundred in the company. She could not understand how she had not heard them gathering.

They took loaves of bread from their wicker baskets, and then she recognized them.

"Not a great nation," Sarah mumbled, astounded, "but a holy people. They will be here."

"Yes," Mrs. Edwards said. "They will if your obedience allows it. You will be many, traveling over the world, but never belonging—no, not even in your own homeland. You will be at once a child and an ancient, without memory, living in boundless hope, triumphing only in last things. The Lord's flaming coal shall touch your tongues. You shall hunger after this gift, and become a desperate people who cannot remember the names of their own children. You will then forget what you are longing for today, and so forget yourselves.

"Only to the Lord will you be truly known, and He shall reward you and chastise you and take you roughly to His side like the youth who says no and yet obeys. Then you will be His alone, a deeper wish and conception, and His love shall be all in all.

"The White family will be a great one," Sarah Edwards pronounced, "the Lord's own servants for generations to come."

"Why have I been shown these things?" Sarah asked.

"Because of how dear you are to the Lord's own heart. He wants you to enjoy His dwelling with you."

"My, my, my—" Sarah said, gasping.

"My soul magnifies the Lord," Sarah Edwards said.

"And my spirit rejoices in God my Savior," Sarah White replied, almost automatically, and with these words she came into possession of the older woman's giddy secret.

Then the two Sarahs were caught up into what must have been Paul's third heaven, for it seemed to the younger Sarah that the happiness of Elysia was nothing to this, and she was willing, at last, to leave its joys behind.

The two women stood together, embracing each other. They were bearers of the faith that in each generation has led Sarah to laugh at the angel's prophecy and be its fulfillment.

CHAPTER 21

———

Another Garden

The next day, Abram and Sarah traveled home, jouncing along together on the oxblood-upholstered bench seat in their coach. They watched the bare wooded countryside out either window, aware, as they had been on coming to see the Edwards, that they might stray into a raiding party fighting the Indian wars. These hostilities caused their anxiety, they told themselves; they explained their speaking so little—the hush in the creaking cab.

Neither knew anything of the other's true feelings—they had both been too stunned to speak by their different revelations—before Abram took Sarah's left hand, kissed it, and encompassed it with his other hand in a warm clasp. Sarah moved closer to him, letting her weight rest against his side, and worked her hand between his, massaging his hand with her thumb and forefinger; then she scratched his palm, scoring it with deft strokes—before her strong fingers laced once again through his. She put her hand on the crook of his arm and slid it up to give his biceps a squeeze. They looked at each other, and they knew they had traveled a long way, yet still had some distance to go.

————————

They had been at home in Newburyport for two days, the hush prevailing, when Sarah walked down the slope behind their house to the vegetable garden and its toolshed. It was early in the morning and chilly, the rime of the night's frost still on the grass; but the bright sun promised to warm the day and Sarah in her snug olive brown coat. She sat down on the bench in front of the shed and was watching one of the year's first returning robins pace about the turned-earth of the garden when Abram halloed after her from the oak trees at the back of the house.

He came toward her with long strides, letting the slope carry him even faster, as if he had some news or particular reason to join her. But after another greeting, he merely sat down next to her and stretched, enjoying the sunny morning along with her. Why wasn't he at the shipyard? Sarah wondered. He had left the house more than two hours ago.

"What brings you home?" she asked.

"Oh, the day, and you, my exceptional wife." He put his arm around her and gave her a hug.

He still remained bound up in his own peculiar silence, though: the silence she could never understand. Yet she had her own silence now, didn't she? Wondering at what she had seen or foreseen, pondering these things, like Mary, in her heart.

"I am not sure if I feel I have truly returned to this place," she said, not wanting to let the occasion to speak pass. "My thoughts are still so much with Mrs. Edwards."

"Before we left," Abram said, "Reverend Edwards told me . . . he said you and Mrs. Edwards would be the first in the chorus. He said he had never seen his wife so comforted and moved in her soul—that you two had grown together . . . into God . . . beyond anything he had ever known. What happened, Sarah? I have hesitated to ask, but I would consider it such kindness if you would tell me."

"I was shown something," she said.

"Yes?"

"But tell me first," Sarah said, stopping his questions, "were you shown anything?"

Abram put his hand over his mouth, and then scratched his cheek and its long sideburn. "I should say."

"Tell me," she said.

"The brokenness of the world," he said. Then added quickly, correcting himself, "No, the brokenness in me. Everything you have accused me of, that and more and failings still hidden in wisdom's grasp. But chiefly what I was shown is this: my pride. I loved you for myself, and persuaded myself that God had made me so wise, I need not love you for Him. But my selfish love has been destroying what it thought to bless. How poor I am in the unselfish love—the godly love—I should have for you. You, dear Sarah, who are so worthy of it."

Sarah felt suddenly on the verge of tears, but managed to say, "Worthy?"

"Another man sees you. A man who does not need you for his comfort or his vanity. A man who sees your tenderness, your kindness, your hope, your love—how alive you are. He sees, he glimpses, what God sees. How precious you are to him. How you belong to him. If I can remember what this other man within me sees, then I will become the husband you deserve. God help me be that man."

He took her into his arms, and she clung to him. She pressed her head against his chest and pulled him to her as if she would burrow into his heart. He held her tightly enough for her to believe that she had come that near. They enjoyed a moment together, an instant, an hour, a time—that time in the garden, as they would recall it—when time did not matter.

"But what of you?" Abram asked finally as they broke away.

Sarah smoothed her skirts out and then held his arm. "What of me? There has been too much of me. But I have finally learned, I think, that nothing but faithfulness matters. In it lie all God's promises."

"Did you *see* something of what has been promised?" Abram ducked his head around and searched for her to return his inquiring look.

"Nothing has been promised to us that is not promised to everyone."

"Did you see your children?"

Sarah was still reluctant to tell Abram her vision, not because she disbelieved it, but because she knew the frailty of her own faithfulness. "I saw our family on the green in a future day," she said. "Not our family so much as God's family, if we will be faithful. I do not know if I am capable of what the Lord may require of us. What I have seen terrifies as much as inspires."

"No one is worthy of such things," Abram said. "Such things come to be only by God's grace. So we will pray for a double portion of that grace: one for my pride and one for your frailty, and let God be all in all."

NOTES FROM THE AUTHOR

———

Perhaps a few details from my research would enhance the reader's enjoyment of *First Light*.

PART I

———

1. A caution to geographers: my Irish lad's journey to the sea winds over a deliberately imaginary map.
2. The great Scotch-Irish immigration to the New World began in the year of Abram's birth, 1718. Ministers such as James Mc-Gregor of Aghadowey—who employed the analogy of Moses and the children of Israel—did, in fact, lead such expeditions. Thomas Lechmere, the surveyor-general of the customs at Boston, expected twenty such expeditions in the spring of 1719, but how many actually made the journey remains in dispute.

    A new wave of Ulster Scots went out in 1728, the year Rev. Innis leads the Glenwhirry congregation away.

    Abram departs in 1729, the year Jonathan Swift published "A Modest Proposal," in which the writer has his mouthpiece propose cannibalism as a solution to the "Irish problem." Swift's irony works out to its absurd conclusion the cruel policies of the English mercantile system.
3. Billy and Gillian use "dickey" as an all-purpose slang expression. In that time the word would have implied that Abram looked in bad condition; that he was "shaky" or "weak." Like our word "bad," though, "dickey," as used in the text, can imply its opposite, especially in the sense of being cunning or shrewd.
4. Lord Dunbar is a stand-in for all the English absentee landlords

who controlled and benefitted from the "plantation" of the Scots into Ireland in the seventeenth century and thereafter. Likewise, the Garritys represent a class of middle men.

PART II

5. The storm sequence owes much to Henry Dana's *Two Years Before the Mast*. I have drawn many other nautical details from Richard Jeffrey Cleveland's *Voyages and Commercial Enterprises of the Sons of New England* (1857). Although Cleveland lived in and wrote about a time somewhat later than Abram White, he was a man much like my protagonist, and his factual account of his sea travels comes across as far more fabulous than anything invented here. Other nautical details are drawn from *Seamanship in the Age of Sail*.

PART III

6. Abram's being taken up by society corresponds with the high social mobility of the eighteenth century. Benjamin Franklin, in his *Autobiography*, mentions how the Governor of New York invites him to dinner after hearing that a young man with a significant library in tow has lately arrived in port. Good conversation counted for a lot back then.

7. My Nicolls family are said to be directly descended from Colonel Richard Nicolls. Actually, after introducing the "Duke's Laws" as Governor of New York, Colonel Richard Nicolls sailed back to England in 1667. Not too many years later, fighting by the side of the Duke of York at Sobbay against the Dutch in 1672, Richard Nicolls was killed by a cannonball. This "instrument of his death and his immortality" is enclosed in the upper corner of the marble monument that marks his tomb in the northeast corner of the chancel of the Ampthill church in England. Colonel Richard Nicolls was never married; he had no direct descendants. Therefore, my fictional Nicolls family cannot be and should not be associated with any other "Nicolls" or "Nicoll" family.

Historians may note that Matthias Nicoll accompanied Richard Nicolls on the original expedition to New York in 1664, and later founded a family prominent on Long Island for the next three centuries. It was long supposed that Matthias must be Colonel Nicolls' nephew, but no common progenitor has ever been found.

Matthias acquired property at Cow Neck and Plandome, now Manhasset, Queens County, Long Island. His son William, who married a Van Rensselaer, moved the family to Islip, which he named after his birthplace and that of his ancestors. He later purchased nearly half of Shelter Island, where the famous District Attorney of New York, De Lancey Nicoll (1854–1931) would be born.

8. Although no individual historical venture exactly resembles Abram's money-making scheme, land speculation became widespread during the mid-eighteenth century. Many landholders and consortiums imported immigrant parties from various parts of Europe, especially Germany. By this time, the great landholders of New York, the Beekmans, and others, understood that their land would prove worthless to them if left undeveloped. They were, in fact, willing to excuse rents for long periods or even give away land, in order to sell adjacent parcels whose value rose precipitously once an area had been settled. Abram's idea would have been eminently possible.

9. You can still go to Fraunces Tavern in downtown New York.

PART V

10. What we now call the French and Indian War made Stockbridge in the Berkshire Mountains a hazardous place to visit from 1754 to 1763.

11. When he died, Edwards was writing a grand summation of his work, synthesizing its historical and theological dimensions. His sermon, "The History of Redemption," represents the general direction of this work, and many of his remarks to Abram are influenced by it.

The notion that providence and appetite often agree is to be found throughout Edwards' writings.

Sarah Edwards' astounding religious experiences are recounted in Edwards' work, *Some Thoughts Concerning the Present Revival of Religion in New England.* She did, indeed, *hop* when under the influence of the Holy Spirit, and she would swoon away for hours together, enjoying, she claimed, the presence of God. (Once again, my inventions are far less "imagi-native" than the historical record.) Indeed, much of Edwards' work, including *A Treatise Concerning Religious Affections*, was heavily influenced by his wife's spiritual giftedness. He was constantly attempting to understand and describe the authentic "religious affections" she experienced, and at the same time es-tablish reasonable criteria by which these experiences could be distinguished from their fraudulent counterparts—mere enthu-siasm or hysteria. Edwards clearly understood that he was not as spiritually gifted as his wife.

12. Edwards died from the smallpox inoculation he tells Abram about. He was trying to set a good example for his undergrad-uate charges at The College of New Jersey (later Princeton Uni-versity).